# WHO'S AFRAID OF BANK $$?

THE NOVEL

E. Maverick Ringo, IV

First Edition, First Printing



*Book designed by Author*

*Cover Graphic by "Ricky"*

Library of Congress Control Number—LCCN: 2012950952

Manufactured in the United States of America

*An OceanBreeze Book*

ISBN-13: 978-0615698427
ISBN-10: 0615698425

## DEDICATION

To everyone with a goal including all my nieces and nephews, hoping your dreams come through.

---

## ACKNOWLEDGMENTS

Thanks to T for being there and for teaching me the way of conflict. And to Johnny, thanks for the conversations.

## DISCLAIMER

# PART 1: RIGGED

*"I had no desire to live, no prospect of earning a living, no way to pay the bills."*
Anonymous

# CHAPTER 1

Shortly after we received our first class assignment a fellow student blogged, "It was a freakish message, Homies."

But, "Was it," another student questioned.

At the next session of our business class we realized the message in fact wasn't freakish; the behavior wasn't out of the norm for them.

The class continued, and we continued to interact.

Close to the end of the class the second student, whose name I found out to be Siri, sent me a text on my Blackberry saying, "The system is rigged. It's up to us to fix it, Tagg."

In the summary of the so-called freakish message, the author had written, "Remember to keep them separated, and constantly change the date credits are posted to accounts; nature dictates we stay afloat."

The message, like so many from the same source, was sent in the form of an e-mail, and was directed for "Executive Staff Only." A watermark in the document as well as a rubberstamping across the smaller type categorized the communication as "Secret."

I read and re-read the e-mail for understanding. The last two lines of type were, "Your's Truly," followed by two spaces, and then there was the word, "Corporate."

# CHAPTER 2

And there were three suitcases in the back seats of Mom's Caravan as she drove faster than I can ever recall her going; Dad, sat beside her. He was to his usual quiet self.

It was a darkish, tropical-storm-type, windy South Florida day. Mom was wearing a Marlin's T-shirt, and when I think of where they were going, it made sense.

From our place of seating, the freeway view of Palm Beach, Broward County and Miami/Dade was nonetheless captivating as my baby sister Grace, and I sat in the seats before the last set.

"You always said she believes in the system," I said to Mom, knowing her patience was waning as we tried to carry on a discussion about events that were quickly changing our lives.

"*The great system*. I know, Soldier. At fourteen I can see how you could have such wildly different views," She replied. "What I can't put my head to is why she just doesn't cash her 'dogan' checks. Your Granny thinks she's God!"

I shook my head; I was in disagreement. And I saw Mom watching me from her rearview mirror.

"You ever wonder why I hate her," she said.

Why she hates her? I had to chew on the question momentarily. Why would Mom ask a stupid question like that? I was just a kid. When your mother says some birdbrain thing about her own parent, and you're just at the age of trying to figure out who you are, why you are here, and what the heck the adults in your life are doing with theirs, what are you to think?

An unsound kid might ask, "F'ed up?"

I questioned, "Insanity?" Sometimes I think that runs in our family.

Why's love so hard to find? I don't know.

I searched my head, and the only thing in there I felt would not create more tension was, "Mom?"

My younger sister Grace was like our mother, mostly having a

contentious relationship with our grandmother. Alongside, she had always been more frank, and some say, mean as compared to me. She provided quite a different response. She was actually smiling, and it was not even her regular smile; there was something sinister about her.

I remembered how Grandma felt that one person, any person, regardless of where they came from, "who their daddy is, was, or not," could help to make the world a better place.

"Grandma said we shouldn't put any more strain on the country right now," I said.

Mom butted in, "What she calls this economy?"

The two-step-backward, one step-forward-economy, was the answer, and I said that, to hear Grace finishing the last part with me.

"That's it! That's your Granny, you two," Mom responded speedily. "I hope she doesn't crack up before we get back."

****$$****

When Mom talked about our getting back, she wasn't referring to Grace or me. We were on our way to nowhere we needed to "get back" from. We were only a couple blocks from Grandma's white, brick middle-class abode at 1226 Jack Street in Miami. And as we departed the car, Mom pushed her head out the window and reminded us to study, but tried to retract those words as fast as she said them. She moved her attention from "you two" to "Grace," my nagging sister.

"Young Lady, you study," Mom shouted. Here she sounded like a correction officer before pointing at me, a less stern or concerned look to her face. "I know, Son—I know we won't have any problem with you."

A compliment I felt, but one I knew could be dangerous as Mom could turn on me as quickly as she did on Grace. That's just our blood.

As Mom and Dad waved good-byes to us, I looked towards the vehicle that was already moving and saw in my path Mr. Saul and his wife, Ms. Cynthia, Grandma's two "lovebird" neighbors.

In those days, Ms. Cynthia never seemed to stop talking about God, but this day they were watering their yard, and she responded with a Queen Elizabeth style waving at Grandma that lasted long enough for Grace and me to escape any conversation.

Hoping not to have another verse from the Book of Psalms or James, sometimes Proverbs pushed down our throats again by Ms. Cynthia, I was quick, darting on to Grandma's brown-green lawn, Grace, only inches followed. We quickly approached the half-opened door, and then through the corridor and the path to Grandma's "Library" where we didn't find her as she told us she would be.

Where is she, my first question came. I looked at Grace in surprise and she was as startled as I was. Grandma always waited there for us. Where was she now?

What we found was a cup of steaming tea on one of her tables, a note saying "go to Shines", and a croissant next to it. Piles of books were stacked on another table, and the bottle of ink of her favorite ballpoint pen was left opened.

Grandma Muley was not around but her wall-sized plasma Toshiba was. And it was blasting out what she liked as a hobby: the morning business news.

A reporter on CNCB was giving a summary of recent business mishaps with captions running at the bottom of the TV, and I couldn't stop but to look. People were protesting one moment; in another, something was spilling into the air.

"And this has been a period of continuous business disaster after disaster," the reporter claimed as I eyed Grace making her way towards the remote control.

"What's going on," I asked.

She did not answer. She grabbed the gadget and pressed the mute button. She didn't care I was there.

"What you doing," I re-phrased my question, but again Grace acted as if there was nothing of concern to her.

****$$****

I don't like inconsiderate people, and neither did Grandma. We never liked rude people. And I don't like nagging ones either. Those are probably the only rules I have when it comes to me with people. Grace can sometimes come across as being anyone of those…anytime. And that's her, out-front.

I didn't want to make a fuss this day as Grace loved to come up against me and Grandma about the simplest of things. At times she would do anything just to get us going. It so happened that with Mom I almost always took second place when it came to issues with Grace and me.

I studied the words that were coming fast at the bottom of the TV, a relatively new five-footer that made the pictures crisp; I concluded the usual: the words were not as compelling as the pictures, nor for that matter, the concerns in my head.

The TV showed a number of scenes that were repeats, I noted, including an oil spill from what I remembered were a few years earlier. There was something about Toyota and cars running wild without their accelerators being pressed. The announcer referred to this as "pedal misapplication." There was another piece about workers trapped in mines. A billionaire businessman came out of nowhere and faced a barrage of reporters' questions about hacking of people's phone, and then they got to how Congress was in the mess of a lifetime. The screen changed, and then it changed again, and with that, the reporter was questioning whether our country had lost its "moral compass." He questioned whether citizens would ever be able to enjoy the quality of life "we once had?"

That sounded like how Grandma would come to talk, and I always questioned her "good old days" kind of talking, but I didn't say a thing; I kept my eyes to the TV. Maybe it would reveal answers to some questions compressing my own brain. The reporter began to close the hour with a group of executives of banking institutions testifying in front of Congress. A Congressman called the executives greedy. The citizens protesting flashed back on. A Cheetos commercial brought in the new hour.

When it was over, Grace told me all that stuff was boring, a waste of God-given, good time, and we should have been focusing on something more critical. I told her I differed, period. My goal, one day, was to have a business like Grandma, but of course, make a thousand times, maybe ten thousand times what she was hauling in. That was my whole plan, and I must say, motive for enrolling in my two AP classes, one heavy in business, and the other computers. Those, I would come to admit was what helped me to understand this whole story: How Grandma fitted in. How she was considered. How she function. How she operated with us. The how. The why. The whole shebang as one "Buffalo" band calls it.

# CHAPTER 3

From the age of four or five I could remember Mom and Dad talking about how Grandma was "different." As the years leapt along, I would get to see what they were talking about. Grandma, known to outsiders as Madam Muley, Ms. Sandra, Sandy, Love, or even Ms. Muley, was many things to many people, and as complex as some thought of her, I got to love her. Yes, she was pretty. Two, she was smart. Skipping along, she loved to go shopping, and that was a really cool thing.

Did I say she was once the most productive person in the world? If I didn't, I'm guilty; I don't usually miss "bigging" her up on that one.

If I were given the opportunity to add one more character trait about Grandma, it would be that she was a respectable person who, not only helped others, but also respected the system. Kind of rare combination Dad once remarked when he spoke more than one consecutive word. For me, this woman was the real deal!

Once I was asked to write an essay: "who is the one person you would look up to in this country"—it was Grandma. In part, I wrote, "In spite of only being five-foot, two-inch, she is *a giant,* and I've known that way before I got to my teens. She never once missed voting in an election, we learned. She pays her bills before they come due, and she has been waving both the country's and Florida flags in front of her modest house for most of my life. Once I saw her helped tons of people get back on their feet after one of our devastating Florida hurricanes; that was also the year she started her business."

Since then, Grandma's life has changed. She weaned me from sucking my fingers. She won several local and statewide humanitarian awards. And she has fought many battles for what she deemed were right causes.

One little caveat—even though she, was in her mid-seventies, you wouldn't easily think she was that age. She mostly carried herself like someone decades younger. "Shave off ten or fifteen years from your perception if you really want to get to know her." That's what her neighbor across the street, Mr. Bruce once was overheard saying to another old fart with whom he was talking about Grandma' "bounciness."

"I bet you $20 bucks she does that Brazilian butt-shaping exercise," the other man said.

Shaving off some of her years had never been hard for me to do. I eavesdropped as the two men played judge and jury sorting out how Grandma ended up with what she had.

I had done enough research to know the truth. She earned it!

There was even a time, I knew of Grandma competing with Mom who claimed to be only fifty-two then, the only difference at that time to me was that Grandma sometimes was so stuck in her thinking, we felt opening a coconut to be an easier task than reaching her.

I prefer to count Grandma's acumens, though. I heard another man once telling her she was a "cutie pie," and I looked at her and saw why he had this opinion of her. Her pictures of her dating years were no less striking than then, a confident looking angel, showing a mixture of Elizabeth Taylor and Ingrid Bergman, in their twenties and thirties. In their own ways, these women were goddesses, and so had Grandma. I don't think she ever lost that.

As she went through the years, she developed a liking for a choice color: blue, and as we made our way around a crowded Macy's department store I saw and heard her admiring more and more blue dresses.

"Why blue," Grace murmured. She and I had pondered that one for years. For the twelve years of Grace's life and fourteen of mine, I don't believe we had ever not seen Grandma included that color in her mix.

"And I won't today. Not today," she said to us.

The three of us made our way through a wall of people, towards a cash register.

****$$****

We had a ton of bags in our hands and carts, passing a vendor pushing a cart with candies strapped around his waist. Grandma looked at the man and winked; I saw the man as weird having food that people eat, wrapped that way on his body, and that made me think strange. Strange.

"G, you remember how Gramps used to say she's the *"sweetest"* thing on Planet E?"

Even though we were walking, Grandma was still admiring her purchases. She, however, did not hesitate to respond, "Leave the dead at the grave yard. Let's pay and then…"

"Ice-cream!" Grace popped out before Grandma completed what she wanted to say.

Typically, I was more like Grandma and think about "practical" uses for money—A 401k, starting a business; how about some stocks? Some exciting IPO's were heading to the market. But Mom had told us her cell phone had broken and we happened to be passing not far from some.

I suggested, "Mom wants a new cell. She wants the new 4G."

"Four what?" Grandma inquired.

Grace pointed to an I-phone in a nearby showcase. "Old lady, you don't know nothing about nothing," she said.

"I-phone, Grandma," I clarified in a calm voice, hoping to keep our energies high.

Grandma never cared about any of the technology that Grace and I would fight for, including my Blackberry nor the new laptop I almost always carried with me to do my homework.

****$$****

I would like to tell you about my class-work and the way they had us do thing on the run those days, the content of things we were called to study at such an early age, and all that, but I don't think it's appropriate yet. Grace already called me, too egoistic. When I told her I was going to tell this story, she said, "think, breathe Granny, and what was happening with her. Don't screw it up, Tagg. Granny's first, and she always said first thing first. That's who the writing should be all about."

I've tried.

Instead of giving her attention to Grace and me, Grandma was now admiring a couple colorful see-thru "nighties" she had bought. That brought some new questions to my mind.

Grace had not gotten off the I-phone thing in all of this, however, and became a singer on the spot. "You-phone, me-phone, I-phone." She repeated her song three times, the second and third rounds with a nice music to it.

"You don't buy stuff for people who don't need," Grandma said, after a delay. The words came from a half-opened mouth as if she wasn't the kind of person who could release the latches of her jaws to let out as loudly and as freely as she wanted when and where she felt like doing so.

"Except she can't call us if we're sick," Grace said as a group of bundled up boys about my age passed by in the periphery. The boys glanced back for a second take at Grace's frame that was in better shape than most girls her age. They made some comments to each other, laughed loudly, and then carried on.

Nearby, a man passed by talking with someone on his phone, and I heard him telling the other how concerned he was about "the funny weather" we were having. I for one liked the warm days and breezy nights, and a hurricane threat here or there was generally like Christmas for Grace and me. After all, it didn't take much of a hurricane warning for our parents and even Grandma to fill up her house with all the things we never had on an ongoing basis. Time off from school was always icing on the cake for Grace.

Life in South Florida was a lot better than many places, in my book, yet I often questioned what snow must feel like. Grandma said when she was young in Michigan and Ohio, "it was no joke" despite her earning the distinction of intermediate level skier back then.

"She can't call to see how he's doing in school," Grace said with an annoying sound to her voice as she pointed at me.

I was thinking this could be an early Mother's Day gift from us.

"That's what happens when you waste your money on all the wrong things," Grandma responded before long.

Simultaneously, Grace and I were saying in our own ways that Mom needed the phone, but Grandma was as adamant telling us that she needed to keep her money in her pocket.

"Where it belongs," she added emphatically.

Grace gave me a high-five and repeated that Grandma needed the phone, but that only irritated Grandma so much that she dove for a pill in her purse. And as she came up, she labeled us as "lazies." She counseled us we needed to stop spending other people's money and instead learn how to earn money through what she called real and legitimate work. She said we needed to learn how to get ourselves on "the right side of the dollar bill."

A lady passing by looked at me pitifully as Grandma scolded us. The lady then stared at Grandma with a noticeable look of disgust, as if someone in her own life had told her she was "nothing" or maybe "a user," so she had a commitment to make it known, she heard what Grandma had done to us. More notable, the lady's admonishing look at Grandma seemed to give Grace some sort of authority, maybe confidence to say what she had on her mind.

"She can call you five years, whenever," Grace said.

Grandma released some stuck-in breath, and immediately I could feel she was softening up.

"Not for her, but because of you, my Soldiers," Grandma said in a broken up way, telling me she was uncomfortable with what she was doing. I didn't think she owed us anything. In fact, I knew that to be the case considering what she had already given us in our young lives.

"Go ahead; get it quick," Grandma said.

Grace and I began to head in the direction of the cell phones, but just then Grandma stopped us, and her index finger trumped her words.

"Under the usual condition, only so," she said

"Of course, Grandma. Of course, I replied and then Grace joined in, "We help you with books because the customers will be *flying* off the 'booking' wall."

"Good! You know the routine, Soldiers," Grandma replied. "Now, make haste. The ladies at Shines will be horrified if they don't get a piece of me today. I've been letting them down. Now, hurry!"

# CHAPTER 4

It was a busy, tumultuous week for our family and that included me. My AP business classes were taking a lot of my time, and I was behind with a long handwritten list of things to do.

I'm not known for complaining. No, not me. "A go-getter." Yes, that was one of my many nicknames back then. Yet I had to speak of all that had occurred that busy week.

The business class was faring up as the most important study in my whole life that far. It wasn't that I was ever bothered by the inconvenience of *when*, either, as such a class would help me to understand the core of things. With time, it would help me to understand even Corporate's e-mails, and not only that, but how behaviors propagate behaviors. The latter was another key lesson Grandma insisted we learn before we got to some point in life she referred to as "the point of no return."

Our teacher was Dr. S. Erskine, a tall, middle-age Ukrainian woman who had immigrated here when she was in her early twenties. She had made it that we only had to show up in the classroom a couple times over the term. Other than that our class consisted of watching videos of what she proudly coined "WikiCreeps:" "Videos of what goes on in the corporate world so [we] could get a handle on what to expect in our modern world of business." The next part of our job was to report back on what we thought.

She said what we were studying was what was happening in businesses, big and small, day after day, and it was our responsibility to understand the "iconology and symbolism" behind the images.

The key to the class was that we were to write back to the teacher within three hour of receiving any and all assignments to say what we saw and what we felt about it. This was done via, e-mails, blogs, tweets, and to a lesser degree, texting. Dr. Erskine referred to these as the speed of doing modern business, and told us if we did things her way, we would get seventy-five percent of our grade, a "C" guaranteed, a pass. Ten percent of our grade went to how well we wrote, and the other fifteen percent was for other things like interactions with fellow students via the Internet. "All good and dandy," the first string in a blog noted. But that was only so for some of them until we learned about the *when* part.

The catch about the class was that we usually had to stop doing whatever we were doing and respond to the assignment immediately or our best grade would be such a lowly alphabet we would wish we had chosen golf. At least that's the way Dr. Erskine explained how we were to think about her and her class.

So then, that was the *what* and the *when*. The where was wherever we found ourselves when the *what* and *when* proved urgent. And that happened to be the case, our day at the mall: my next video assignment, waiting in queue, in less than thirty-six hours was humming for attention.

We were in line when my laptop started its beeping, the signal I had to surrender whatever I was doing. I had to respond.

The particular assignment was for us to review and give feedback on a video of a Finance Congressional Committee posing questions to one of several bank executives on consumer issues.

Our executive, who was wearing a handsome red tie, said he was the CEO from some bank that had two dollar signs in its name. I couldn't recall the name of the bank initially, but I remembered the man as being tall and as outstanding as his tie. I further recall imaging my own father looking and carrying himself like the man in the video, when Dad was a younger, a more charming man.

When Dad was in his twenties and thirties he spent years in the corporate world too, getting his suits from Neiman, Nordstrom and the like; no different than the cool "Capitan" in the video. He was holding on to his suspenders as he bounced around an office carrying himself like he was the boss of everything—the bank, the firms they lent money to, anything, I meant everything that came in his world.

"Cool. Cool," I said as I looked.

Not far from the Cool Capitan another man said he was from East-West Bank, also a CEO I gathered, but this one looked kind of frightened and would never really command my respect of calling him by his job title again. He just came across as wimpy: He never looked up when he talked, and seemed to get an amazing amount of information incorrect. The others would be OK, in my mind.

As the video rolled, they all came parading on the screen before the Congress, and then things slowed down. There came a part where a Congressman confronted the CEO from the bank with the dollar signs in his bank's name. The Congressman referred to the CEO as "Corporate."

"We keep seeing you here on The Hill, Boss," the Congressman, having identified himself as a Senator Roper," continued. "What gets me and this body is no matter how many times you come here, you never give us answer to what we ask you."

Corporate looked directly as if into the forehead of Senator Roper. He moved his eyes to the left of the Senator's face, followed by the right, and then his eyes were steady as if beaming directly into the Congressman's.

"We're doing more than anybody in the industry at this time to create transparency," Corporate said. "What else do you expect?"

Senator Roper slapped his palm on to his chin. He knew he shouldn't have called the CEO "Boss." He checked in with other members in the room. "I guess he still doesn't understand why we asked him to come."

****$$****

A couple of my classmate chatted that Corporate was funny in part; one alarmed, "tricky."

The video proceeded. Corporate appeared agitated and was speechless to questions after questions, upsetting a Congresswoman who I wouldn't call fat, maybe overweight; I use "overweight" because Grandma said it's not "kosher" to refer to people with "derogatory" terms like fat. She liked kind ways of saying things, when that was possible.

The Congresswoman took control of the room.

"Something's not right here," the Congresswoman said. "Let's take a recess."

****$$****

"That was fast," I concluded and found myself letting out a loud sigh. I looked up. Grandma had made her way to the front of one of the many long lines, and she had her bankcard out as she usually would, ready to pay. Grace was playing with the I-phone, and the store clerk had lifted his eyes to us; it was Grandma's turn.

"Will that be debit or credit, Ma'am," the department store clerk asked giving keen emphasis to the last word.

"Me? Credit cards? Too many problems," Grandma said as I felt the weight and softness of her hand on my shoulder. I knew she hated credit cards because from the time I was ten she had Grace and me cut up every card she had except a single Visa and an American Express; she said they were evil.

Once she had that under control, she had us help her track what was happening with her bank account. For years, it was that if she forwarded money to her account before 9:00 am on a weekday, that money would consistently show up in her account balance four day later. If she used her debit card in a point-of-sale transaction, the charges showed immediately. Grace and I had the rhythm down to the "T," and Grandma liked us for that. She said we were helping her "win her battles."

"Not since this one was born. Aah ah," Grandma replied to the clerk.

The clerk parsed his lip and shook his head.

"You got a point, Miss. Not even the government has the power or integrity to get them in line anymore," he said.

I glanced behind us to see an antsy looking set of people in queue as Grandma spoke again.

"And, you won't see me with one until *they do,"* Grandma said.

The clerk lifted his hand to the crowd in line that looked more anxious than when I had studied them a few seconds earlier. His hand seemed to be saying he'll get to them soon, but his mouth did not change course or speed.

"More and more customers saying *that* these days," he said. "Limit's low, fees high."

"That's the price of their promissory note," Grandma concluded.

****$$****

In typical Grandma's fashion, it was another half-hour before we began to head out the store, which again for us was a task moving through the hustle and bustle of all sorts of people in shopping anxiety and conversations. People seemed to be chatting about everything, buying like the economy was actually good, and eating at all the places the smell of good food was blowing from, and there were lots of them.

I bumped and knocked on people trying to make it out, and as we approached the escalator, I heard a lady with a much younger Black man asked of him if he heard what had happened. I didn't turn my head. I didn't want to draw attention, but I kept my ears opened, nonetheless; I listened.

Momentarily, the two didn't say anything else, but once we got to the bottom of the escalator, they stopped us and asked Grandma for the time.

By this hour Grandma had come to the realization she was running out of time for us to catch the postman, Mr. Castro, her God-sent mailman who stopped at her house daily and waited sometimes ten, sometimes fifteen or more minutes to ensure Grandma's customer deliveries got on his truck and off to Brooklyn, South Africa, France, or wherever they were supposed to go as quickly as possible.

Grandma replied to the lady as if time was everything that now mattered. "Twelve after two." She did not look at the couple then.

The lady, who was about the same age and appearance of another I used to see on Cable named Kate Gosselin, seemed to have more time than us and looked Grace and me up and down, and up and down again, and my guess, she concluded we must have been tightly-wrapped young people. "Nice kids," she said.

"When their parents are kicking it in *paradise*, you know who gets them." Grandma responded abruptly.

The Black man with the lady told us that he was from Nassau. "In the Bahamas," he stressed in his Caribbean accent. He then looked at Grandma, "Rat race. Where to?"

At this point I knew we were rushing, but I didn't realize Grandma had completely shifted from her shopping mode to the other one:

her business thinking; and when she found herself in that one, we knew that meant "think getting things done, think money, think profitability."

I apparently interrupted all that when I extended my hand to the nice man. "I'm Grandma's Soldier, and who are you," I asked of the Black man.

Grandma pulled roughly at me. "C'mon son. Got to get to…"

At first the Black man took that with offence and then it looked like surprise, but as quickly he was composed again. He did all this so rapidly, however, I swear he learned this in the military. People out here are not that quick to adjust.

"Everybody's on overdrive these days," he said through a sunshine, Caribbean laugh. "Everybody's on a hot date."

It must have been some sort of cosmic or God thing going on, but a handsome and smartly dressed man about Grandma's age was passing right then and I found myself whispering a song Grandma had taught us the last time we had spent an extended period with her. It went like this:

"Some enchanted evening, you may see a stranger
You may see a stranger, across a crowded room
And somehow you know, you know even then
That somewhere you'll see her or him again & again."

Why? Why after all these years of Grandpa's passing, why was Grandma still not having fun? I began to rub my left and right index finger together suggesting Grandma's intimacy with the man. Grandma looked at me. She knew what I was doing. She never liked that kind of antics, you know. She called me, "Silly Boy. Silly Son."

I was even her silly soldier.

****$$****

In the concourse, the Black man and the older lady headed in their direction arguing about their encounter with us.

"Are you nuts," I heard her going at him.

He shook his head as if he was admitting he was.

"She could be your grandmother, too," the lady said to him.

Grandma, noticing that the two were still close enough to us, seemed to forget intermittently about her time commitments and shouted at the man. "Was it a date you said?"

The man shook his head slightly, but enough to show a *yes* to Grandma's question.

"How do you do that," Grandma continued.

Something else I'm supposed to include in this account of events happening that day, but I can't remember what it was, and I hate when that happens. I do know it's important to tell, but gash. The part I remember was that we headed in our direction; the mixed couple went in theirs. And I do remember Grace deciding it was her time to poke fun at Grandma.

"Granny's got a boy friend. Granny's got a man," she sang.

"Keep your bearings, Soldiers. We have a long road to travel. To clear," Grandma added.

****$$****

Long after the mixed couple was out of sight and out of my mind, Grace and I saw an interview with the two on Miami 12 TV, a local favorite. They said they were visiting from Switzerland and were interviewed on account of their experiences in South Florida. They talked about how the uncertain weather had "blown" their minds, and they mentioned they had met us, among other things. In response to a question from the reporter they said they only had one argument on their visits to five different countries and that was on their US, Florida stop.

"Silly," the lady said on the TV. "We argued when he told me the old woman was going on a date. "Silly me," she repeated. "I got so offended, not because of what he was telling me. Really, it was because he didn't want to marry me and I was so jealous. I asked him if he was telling me that only men could have fun at her age?"

"Yeah, of course," the Black man replied.

The lady said something about how Grandma should take a vacation in *her* home country, Australia."

"I reminded her I was not a male chauvinist pig," the man said in the piece, and he cautioned her not to go *there*.

"Where," came as a question from Grace.

Grandma can go wherever she wanted," I replied. "Africa. Maybe, one day the Sahara. You know they still have wild animals there. People shout and yell there. I saw it on Discovery, you know?"

Grace watched me strangely.

The Black man in the piece had the last word in the story. He said, "Overall, our five-country tour was swell."

They had visited Canada, Brazil, Turks and Cacos Islands, the US and Spain. As he placed his hand on the older woman's leg, he concluded, "My girlfriend here; Sam shouldn't be jealousy at all."

He looked the lady in the eyes. "Baby, you know, that lady at the mall has no chance with me; I might love older women, but me being that much a cougar? I love you baby. Happy Valentine's."

****$$****

The way Grandma moved and was stepping to her vehicle, you would think she was someone's Valentine. She looked young, a lot younger than she actually was.

The thing, though, our day was far from over. We still had to go to Shines! Our transportation was Grandma's seven year old Suburban, never mind age; it rode and looked like a ride, two years or less off Everglade Motor's new-car lot, not far from her house.

We, also, still had to eat our ice cream. And as far as Grandma was concerned, she still had to listen to her music. Almost every day I knew our grandmother, she took off at least a couple minutes of her day, a period she had coined "Music Moment."

She turned on the CD player to her beloved singer's Benny Goodman. He was perfect, singing "Shine."

We thought Grandma would be quiet now and listen but that was not the case.

"What you kids need is a good understanding of life," she said just when my mind was on what I would do with the rest of my life.

"Not just ice-cream, Gameboy, L-phone," she continued as she glanced at the gadget we had bought earlier.

"Grandma! I-phone," I corrected.

She didn't look at me but I could hear a strange sound coming from her; apparently she was irritated. She pressed heavily on the pedal as we headed to the place incidentally called Shines.

****$$****

I had never been to Shines, but she insisted that we would not go home without doing so this time as we had plotted ourselves out of going a hundred times before.

She had told us most of the people ended up there when they couldn't pay their bills. If I were turned upside down then, not even enough money to pay a bus pass back to her house would fall out.

Could I have said no? How would I have gotten back to the house?

****$$****

When Grandma insists on something, you say, "Yes," as she knew what we didn't. She said this is where we would learn skills to prevent things that have "befell" those before us. "No if's, and's, or but's about it, Soldiers."

As the Suburban went down Hope Street, Grace and I ate down our ice cream, and we found ourselves bickering about all sorts of unimportant things. It was soon though, there was the entrance sign. Shines was a real place, a brick and mortar kind of reality, a vapor turned solid for us. My new hope was we would get this over quickly, however. *Quickly*, I could tell in Grace's eyes as well.

The sign blinked "Shines Retirement Home" and for the first time I could vow Grandma was actually not wasting her time or money when she said she was helping others. Smaller writing below the name, spoke more about what the facility owners thoughts of themselves. The words were like "Service, Security, Smiles." Don't quote me on those for being exact wording as even I do slip up on things like this from time to time, and when the experience is like the one we had, memory on such small fish as a name comes secondary to other things. Nonetheless, I take those as close enough. If it was Grandma trying to remember something, she would have put it this way, "That's what recollect in my head, Tagg, and that's all that's going to come."

What I do have branded to eternity was the thinking that somebody was very proud of the facility. After all, they had called it Shines. They had the temerity to put the name in neon blue, and it was bright too. The words at the bottom were neon yellow.

Sadly though, what we saw at the home is more than I could stomach. I'll tell what's palatable. The women residing there were in a rowdy mood when we arrived, one saying if she was smart a long time ago and managed to pay her bills she wouldn't be in the old, messy home. There were about three or four of them in the kitchen chattering how the government wanted to cut money set aside for their facility to operate, and on and on they went, complaining about the difficult condition they found themselves in.

I have etched in my mind this part: in the center of the main room was a group of old confused looking ladies playing bingo, some knitting, some there, just drooling on themselves. One even ran under a table, I guess frightened, when she saw our young, virgin state.

Of all the people and things in there thought, the one that keeps coming to my head most often after all that time, was the hypocrisy of life there. I've not checked recently, but I hope the facility is no longer in operations.

There were many signs around: A moving, blinking sign in there reads, "Better Living for Our Seniors." A posting on the wall said, "Prepare for Your Retirement," and there were pictures of some people I recognized including Michelle Obama, Hillary Clinton and Margaret Thatcher. Grandma told us about a few of the others, including one Grandma called Golda Mayer. Next to her was Indira Gandhi.

Strange, I remember thinking, after Grandma explained who all the unknowns were: strong women posted everywhere; weak ones walking, limping and wheeling themselves from one corner to another. Strange. That part, I play over and over in my head even today. Now, every time I see a person crossing the fifty-year line, I stop and think. Humh?

I found my eyes surveying the entire place, and I wondered what were the prior life stories of the dozens upon dozens of ladies I was seeing now. What did they do with their lives before they got to the Shines? What did they think of the outside world? Did they have lovers, children, friends? If there was one event that caused them to land at this place, what is that event?

Those kinds of questions kept popping up in my head. I turned and looked, and looked and turned, and then one of them stopped me: What would be my fate when I am their age?

With that question I felt a freezing of thought for an entire thirty seconds. It was a strange kind of question for a kid. I had not even reached the point of kissing a girl. I had not made more than five dollars on my own, thus far, much less to say about driving. Hadn't driven anything yet! Not even a nail. Dad hadn't thought us that.

"Is this what it means to be old?

Strange people were all around.

I kept saying to myself, "Is this what we're living for?"

Instantly, I recalled our going to a swap shop in Fort Lauderdale a week earlier and a couple forty or fifty something year old men were talking. One of them, a long, gray-bearded limp, said to the other, "You live a fucked up life and then you die."

Was that the testimony I would hear? Should I ask?

****$$****

I kept my questions to myself, deciding to use my eyes to do my work for me.

Some old, some old and musky, including an aged Black woman with very white, shiny hair were looking at us. This one seemed like she had picked me out and kept staring at me intensely, to the point I wondered what her beady eyes were trying to steal off me. Grandma said she was the oldest person in the home and not to be feared. But after she apparently got to see what she wanted to see in me I began to trust her.

The old woman turned to a commercial playing on a TV in the corner, watching an oversized, rambunctious cartooned Latino male lawyer touting his service. She glued her eyes on to the commercial the same way she had them stuck on me a second earlier. I joined in with her.

"The Vargas Law Firm, *Winning* for You!" the old lady read aloud, spectacles free as those words flashed on the screen.

"Strange" I said loud enough to be heard. The lady's body was moving more than her mouth when she talked.

The cartoon character spoke the line, and the old lady finished it with him as if she had done it a thousand times before. "… And remember it's no cash *now*. When you win, you pay."

Grandma tried to get the old lady's attention but she would be intensely focused until she was ready to unglue from her momentary interest; that was halfway into the following commercial.

"Now, that's a nice man," the old lady said when she felt the timing was right. "Maybe he can help me and My Benjamin get our house and lodging back!"

At that point, the old lady did something like a bow from her wheelchair, something I would see in Grandma's persona as time went by.

But when the old lady lifted her head it seem like she saw something frightening in Grandma. "Sandy, Sandy," she said, her voice more like a cry than separate, distinct English words, her eyes jumping. "You! Only you can stop ..em!"

I had never seen any big adult crying before, but she did, leaving a squeaky, fearful chill romping in my body. I quickly would find out there was more to come: One frightened woman created another, and another, and soon most of the ladies looked horrified. The TV on the corner did not stop for them, though. Commercials were over, and the reporter had come back on, momentarily talking about a man who got 50 years for "Ponzying" investors in our town.

****$$****

Our visit did not end at this point, and in a way I was glad it didn't. Actually, ambivalent was how I felt back then. I was now curious, notwithstanding my memory that Grandma never failed to tell us "curiosity kills the cat, Soldiers. Always guard yourself!"

There was, then, a moment of calm, and I like that. I, and I know, Grace, needed that break too, regardless of how short it was.

When all were at ease, Grandma introduced me to the old Black lady, sharing names. Hers was Ms. Wonzick. Grandma said the lady was ninety-seven years old. She referred to Grandma as "Love."

Another lady, by the name of Ms. Diaz who apparently did not realized we were there, even though her eyes were on us all along, went "eeehaa! The little ones! Eeehaa," when it seemed she first registered us.

I looked at Grace who was gesturing for us to quickly finish passing out to the old ladies some of the items Grandma had bought earlier at the mall, including a couple of the more thick-threaded night gowns. We gave a desk clock to one of the ladies. We gave another a *Rich Dad Poor Dad* board game.

Even a portable piano was given to one of the ladies. This one got so excited she started to throw up on herself.

Grace and I, as well as a number of the women watched concerned, some ghastly, as the happy lady was scolded and dragged away to one of the rooms on the left side. We were not to see that in the first place.

On TV, the man with the Ponzi Scheme had a faint resemblance of one of Dad's friend, Mr. Caucius. He was in handcuff. The reporter's audio faded, but not before her parting words: "…other people are also involved."

With all the action and commotion I was thinking there couldn't be any more kooky thing I would witness before we got the heck out of there, but that was not the case. I turned around to the sound of a lady at the bingo table, screaming at me.

"Where's my giff," she said.

We had already given the lady in question a Logitech head piece Grandma had bought for her. Clearly, however, that was not enough, so she turned to Grace and screamed the same words at her, only this time louder. Grandma said this lady's name was Mom Saraplin.

****$$****

Grandma stood by Ms. Wonzick who was telling her that they were weary with Ms. Saraplin, but Grandma appeared uninterested in that conversation.

"Everywhere, they have that same nonsense on the television," I heard from Grandma.

Again, Mom Sarapin's gruff, old voice rang out, this time like a strange hurt animals in the wild. "Where's my giffs? You owe me!"

Grandma turned to Ms. Saraplin, and I could sense her kind heart at work. Her voice was no less compassionate, and at the time, I thought, refreshing. "With this shaky economy, just one thing at a time, Mom Sara," Grandma said. Her volume towards the end was almost a whisper.

Ms. Zenida Reid, an elegant eighty-something year old Asian woman who looked like she once had things going on for her, wheeled herself slowly towards us as she used sign language that surprisingly the other woman seemed to understand. I, myself, over time would develop some skills in this area from a three-credit "Art of Signing" high-school class I took and liked.

"Everybody's broke. Baby," One of the other ladies translated for me.

"Saraplin, you could help this economy recover. You have your talent," Grandma said to Mom Saraplin. "Sell them here!"

Ms. Wonzick began shaking again, like a just-started lawnmower, and then her mouth began to take over.

"They say no shekels," she said. "Nothing to jingle."

Grandma said things were getting almost like the "Depression" to which many heads showed agreement.

"My Benjamin says they still stealing people's mullah left and right, Love. Big mortgage, holy molly, late fees, my golly, and bills like sand." Ms. Wonzick, added, her body again speaking volumes.

I think for her, movement and words were synonymous.

****$$****

If you knew me back then you would expect me to be laughing or something like that. I used to be goofy back then. I was even know as a little comedian at times, but I wasn't this day.

I wasn't, and I sure was getting tired. I looked at my phone, and we had been there an hour; I was ready to take off.

As expected, though, Grandma was not ready yet, and it seems Mom Saraplin was neither ready for us to say anything like *until we meet again* or *see you later alligator*. She was on to a groaning noise in the background, and telling the other ladies that Grandma was selfish, mean and would need them one day, and just when I thought an applause was the end of her sad talking, there came another, "I want my giffs!"

Grandma reiterated with a longer but more slowly released version of what she had said previously. "You don't need to be hoarding all your art, Mom Sara. Sell something."

That's when I again began to think deep about what was happening around me. What did these people do wrong that I must avoid doing? What event or events would cause a person to leave her house to come to this? What did these people look like when they were young?

Ms. Diaz, who I heard had a very bad stroke asked Grandma in a repeated kind of way when Grandma would come to live with them.

"Silly idea," I mumbled, simultaneously pulling Grace away from the area, but evidently, Grace had already heard what I had.

She gave Ms. Diaz a severe look and then gave me one of like kind.

"Strange people. Why we here, Tagg…" Grace asked and grabbed my and Grandma's hand for us to leave, but we hadn't make more than three or four steps when a shadow of a very tall figure started coming towards us.

At first, the shadow looked so skinny, it made me hold tight on to Grandma's hand, but as it came closer, we saw it was that of a male. It moved closer. He leaned forward. He pushed out his hand. Grandma placed an envelope in the hand.

"With Congress choosing Big Oil and the Big Banks over us, we would be stranded without your generosity, Ms. Muley," the man said as he folded the envelope with great care. He placed it in his right shirt pocket and then stumbling at the task, he latched the button of the pocket.

Looking annoyed, Ms. Wonzick whispered to Ms. Diaz. "See, I told you. She not comin' here, Patrice. Love gives five-thousand dollars to this place a year."

One of the ladies noted that Ms. Wonzick's and her son also used to give money in the past, but added, "look where she is now."

Grandma shook the man's hand. "Mr. Sealey, hope it helps. Fix the plumbing. And it would be good to see them get good nutrition. That's vital!"

Mr. Sealey lifted his head high and brought it back down that his and Grandma's eyes would share in the moment. There was a peaceful look on both of their faces.

"Four years after John's gone you're as philanthropic," Mr. Sealey said. "Thanks to the Father for you. You had a good hubby, Ms. Muley."

I couldn't help but to look and listen. To the ladies, Grandma was undoubtedly someone they looked up to. One of the better spoken ones spoke for the majority: "Socially responsible….A God-sent lady," she said of Grandma.

Ms. Wonzick was very close to Ms. Diaz at the moment the money was transferred, and she said, "Love might be our age Patrice, but she's a player, rich business lady. She ain't coming here. You see who she hangs out with?"

I looked around at the place and the people and felt a conflict of sort in me. My awareness of what Grandma was doing, I knew was a good thing and humbling, yet I felt afraid she was giving away everything. Her bank, she would explain, was taking away her money, and she had said the night before, her issues with the bank had left her not feeling well.

She, herself, seemed in conflict.

Meanwhile, Mom Saraplin, who was now holding in her hand the gift we had given her, and who seemed to get jealous about the money transfer, growled out again, "No mo giffs? I deserve giffs!"

I found myself asking, how else we could bless this poor woman.

Just then Grandma decided she too. "Mom Sara," Grandma said to Ms. Saraplin in a strong voice. Ms. Saraplin returned a sharply reproving look at Grandma.

Grandma made a couple step backwards and asked Mom. Saraplin if she could call her by the shorter version of her name as she had just done. There was no reply, unless a dull look of hers was one.

Grandma moved on. "You know what," She continued. "I'll bring you something else when I come back. How about that?"

Following that, I could remember our waving goodbyes, Grace's hand moving left to right but in a rigid way.

She would later inform me she was instructing herself in that moment she would never, ever go back to that place; never again, and she never has.

****$$****

Later, I was to learn the ladies were not done with us just because we were not in their physical presence. They carried on an active and partly loud conversation about us after we were long out of their sight. One of the ladies, I was told, liked me. Grace had at least two fans.

In so far as what went on, Ms. Wonzick reportedly told the other ladies that Grandma thought she was the hottest chick in town. And she warned them, that could all end. Her only child, Benjamin was big in business one time too, and then life happened as Ms. Wonzick worded it, and things fell apart. Grandma would later use a single word of her own, "ephemeral" to explain what Ms. Wonzick meant. Over time, I kept hearing the concept. I like ephemeral existence.

Now Ms. Wonzick's son Benjamin couldn't help his own mother anymore. The tide had changed. A Tsunami of debts from costly medical bills, late fees on mortgages, and loss from a stock market fall had taken away her once "good life." Now, her Social Security money was far too little to keep her at her home she called "comfortable" for more than twenty years.

Fortunate for her, she loved to boast, she was unlike a couple of the other women who had come from nursing home in other states because they couldn't pay the fee, which had passed on to their children in what Grandma called filial responsibility.

"I hear she refuses her Social Security too," Ms. Diaz said of Grandma. "Social Security."

Ms. Wonzick said she had something to say but she didn't want to speak it when Grandma was there. She said she was ready and free to say it now, and the other ladies looked at her with great reverence as they told her to go for it. She said Grandma should be put in a straight jacket for not taking and using her Social Security money. She continued.

"They'll eat her up too, Patrice. Like me and My Benjamin," Ms. Wonzick said, her eyes holding on to one person at a time, but there was no doubt she was talking to everyone in the room. The attention level was as high as that at the last Democratic Party Convention in Los Angeles.

"You hear what she's up to now," Ms. Wonzick continued.

Ms. Diaz mumbled, "She, she, can live here. Can live here."

Enough is enough, the old adage says, and that was the case here. A Shines center's attendant came rushing in. She had a bunch of utensils in her hand; a cart pushing with more stuff held by the other hand. "Come now ladies," the attendant demanded of the group that for the most part ignored her.

They were more interested in spreading gossip. One was saying she heard Grandma was behind with her mortgage due to bad checks.

"She's a woman of pride," Ms. Wonzick said.

The other woman replied, "That explains why she's doing her best to keep it all a secret."

"Let's get ourselves ready for nap," the attendant interrupted.

The attendant looked up to the clock on the wall in a way that made her look like she was angry at the clock. In time, she would tell the women she was angry with them for not noticing the time and ignoring her. She had come to put them to rest since they had not done it themselves. "You know what you should be doing right now," she continued. "Nap hour! Now!"

# CHAPTER 5

In time, Grandma and Grace decided they too were entitled to rest and opted for naps of their own, something I have never been privy to have as often as them. I chose to spend the time cleaning the room Grandma called her Library as she was becoming too busy and neglected to keep it neat, like she was accustomed to.

She called the area her Library but it was in actuality her den, converted to our playhouse when we were younger visitors—converted to her bookstore over time. This was the only room in her house we were allowed to leave a book or pretty much anything out of place when we would visit or spend extended periods of time with her, like summer, the time Mom and Dad visited Uncle Dean in Nebraska for over two months, and the time the two went to celebrate their fifteenth anniversary in Greece and Rome. It was also the place at Grandma's that had ten thousand books lining the walls, some shelves packed to the point of bending. For Grace and me this was our sanctuary before Grandma turned it into part of her money plan. Now our adopted bedroom had become our new place for self, reflections, and most of our toying around.

Grandma had taken good advantage of the Library space and hanged pictures in every area that was not covered by shelves or boxes. The pictures seemed to capture our lengthy family history, even a couple of her and Grandpa John in Africa from a long time earlier. I think she said that was the 50's. One showed them sitting around, talking with a group of young Black children around Grace and my age.

As I dusted one of her two desktop computers, I came across her marriage record, to grandpa: Sandra Elizabeth Smucking and John Fredrick Muley. And then there were more pictures of hers, telling other stories we seldom talked about at either our house or Grandma's.

There was some showing her as a very sexy dancer, others of her posing with friends when she was young, and a group, of people even before our grandparents.

I looked at the pictures closely and moved around the room wondering why Grandma never talked much about her life as a young person. From all the pictures I had seen over the years it seemed like it was actually a good life, something to boast about. Maybe, it was as Grace once said, it was that she just never had enough time to tell us stories about that period in her life.

She had been busy all of our lives making money and spending it, Mom offered.

As a kid Grandma had sold newspapers to help her family make ends meet. Later she worked with a maids' service, cleaning large commercial buildings and banks. At another point, she had gotten smart and bought stocks. She did well with that, reportedly.

She had told us tips and bit about an even later time with Grandpa and how proud she was of being a businesswoman, but there were so much more I hoped for.

As far as her business was concerned, she said she learned it from her father whom she claimed got it from his dad. She said our great, great grandpa was the quintessential stockbroker.

"Or whatever they called it those days," I said.

Her grandfather had shown her long ago that as a nation we're blessed with certain core strengths that had made and continue to keep us the number one nation in the world. One was the effectiveness of our financial system to help build a robust economy, another was the value women contribute to our society.

"If we ever lose our competitive advantage, we're done," she would relay the words of the old man. "We'll be done Boboo."

That's what he used to call her.

I don't think Grandma went a month of her life without quoting some little thing of significance he had taught her. She thought he was the core strength of our family.

"And he had done pretty well for himself," she told us. She said he was a man who loved his family, his country, and his business, in that order. She was convinced it was from him whom she learned everything she knew about business.

She would sometimes go on this way: "That's from whom I learned the importance of making contact with other people. Making the right contact is the most important thing; Soldier, you hear me?"

She said she was very thankful and proud of what the family before her had achieved and passed on to her in life and in business. "They were good examples of corporate citizens." A good legacy. She said it was this feeling of respect that got her started. And it was she that impressed me so much that I wanted to pick things up when Mom and (so accused) Dad had dropped the ball. I just needed to get old enough.

****$$****

I went on to clean and dust for a while moving from desk to book shelf as I eyed some of the books nicely stacked before me. For some reason my eyes particularly liked one and stopped at it: "The Eight Characters of Comedy," and then there was another with the initials of the author being JC. I couldn't for a long time remember either the author's spelled out name or even the name of this one, but with the initials JC, I kept thinking that was Jesus' initials. Jesus Christ, King of Kings and Lord of Lords. Interesting. I remembered the subject as I had scanned the book for a long time. I would recall it to be mythology.

Soon, though, I was back looking at the photos and found myself in a quiet, peaceful place, my mind trying to create a fuller picture of Grandma's life when I heard footsteps. I looked up from the book and pictures. It was Grace. She was racing towards me. I sensed she was going to drop my laptop.

"You have homework. You have work, Buddy," she said as she looked at my hands strangely. I was holding one of the pictures of Grandma in my writing hand.

I thought she was asleep, and I told her so.

She pointed to the picture I was holding. "Even she was telling me I can miss out on a lot if I sleep too much."

"Really," I replied. I was still holding a good feeling in my head about Grandma.

I said, "You know anybody that can do what she can do, G?

Grace seemed like she was not really into me at the time. Maybe her autism was flaring up. She passed me the computer and darted towards the staircase. She said she would tell Grandma I was interfering with her pictures. I focused on my assignment. Grace was not my job nor my duty.

****$$****

A watchful security guard standing upright at a door with a gun graced the first three-and-a-half-seconds of this new video assignment. At about four seconds in, we were in a room with a large number of executives hashing out things. In it, I immediately recognized Corporate from my previous assignment. Not far from him was a lady that looked relatively young, and a bit playful, I felt. Another student would later tweet, that she was "hot but looked giddy." We were still teenagers.

The lady had a nameplate that read Marketing Director in front of her. There were also two other men I had seen before. They were sitting in front of a sign that read, "Inter-Banking Consortium."

Corporate leaned forward and placed his hand on a miniature replica of the sign in front of him. He ran his hand on the word "Chairman" that was included on the smaller sign.

He lifted his hand. Everyone surrendered to his gesturing. "Divide and conquer if that's what it takes!"

He ripped a piece of paper into two pieces with all the force he could muster.

"No one's going to take our bread or butter. PERIOD," he said. His palm came down "bang" on the desk. He looked at it.

Another man, sitting in front of a sign that read "The Money Bank" scratched his forehead as he spoke. "We think we got in late at "Money" on the $40 billion. The whole industry should be looking at $50 B, not retreating!"

A third man that must have thought of himself as very important by the way he held his head and talked, added something about how overdraft at the Friendly Bank was taking in twenty-five percent of that bank's revenue. He barely moved his body as he pointed his talk to Corporate, the CEO I had seen in the first assignment.

"We know the twelve percent squeeze you guys could have at $$ is going to crush like a rock on a soft ceiling. We know what it's going to do to you," the important looking man said.

Corporate pointed at one of the men from the previous video. "My operations manager here knows this as well as any of us," he said. "Over two billion and no more chi-ching."

"And it's my job to change the whole thinking about it," the marketing director lady said, proudly.

Corporate lifted his hand and chopped it to the table. "Not just our bank must fight evil. I may be the chair, but all of us have a sheared, a vested interest to protect our rights to earn. With all the guns we've got, we won't let them tell us what to do. We must fight."

A scan of the room showed full approval to whatever Corporate meant as he pushed on. Fuck! Fight anybody who envy our success, OK! As it is, we can do without half of our depositors, and that's the damn truth. Isn't that right, Andrea?"

"Empty pockets, trying to empty our barrels," Miss Andrea the marketing lady replied.

Corporate gave Miss Andrea a visual reprimand for something.

"We won't let anybody rip us off," he said as he looked around. "Get me what I need; you get what you ask. Corporate's watching... together with you!"

"They're on their way, though Boss," Miss Andrea replied in a fear laced voice.

Corporate shook his head. He was disgusted.

"How much fee they want us to take to watch their penance? Less than their pals?"

"None," the CEO from the Money Bank asked.

By this time, the man from the Friendly Bank looked very annoyed, and a whole plate of food, plus a bag of potato chips that was in front of him had disappeared into his greedy gut. He put on a new baritone voice. "The administration," he began. "They think they can goddamn, goddamn do whatever they goddamn want to goddamn do to us. Godamit! But there's a comeuppance!"

The people in the room burst into a flash of elation, some chanting, others nodding; things like that.

A fellow student would text, "That one looked like an Amway meeting."

"They're going to hell. To hell with them," the executive from the Friendly Bank touted.

"God, bless us all," Another executive joined in.

The camera moved to Corporate, and he looked contrite. He spoke solemnly but stern. "All I can say, anybody who tries to touch our safe will get their hand cut off," he notified them.

The crowd seemed to like that line. They chanted again. They waved. They nodded again.

# CHAPTER 6

"You're cute, Soldier, but if you're going to win the battles life's going to throw at you, you must start by taking instructions and following orders. Now, go get Grandma's laptop," Grandma said to Grace who had ignored her call not once but twice in the preceding ten or so minutes.

Grace sauntered off towards Grandma's bedroom with her mouth poked out like a pig's nose. She found that Grandma's laptop was on. She mumbled to herself that Grandma was a "stupid—an old fool, wasting money" by running too many computers at the same time—the laptop and working on a PC in the Library.

It was dark outside. Inside, the TV was on with a sitcom replay. A tall male actor tells his counterpart, a stocky Black guy, "If you were not so fat your bank would not have foreclosed on you!"

The audience laughed.

The Black guy replied, "If you were not so ugly, your mother wouldn't have had to try again, for a more handsome re-take!"

The audience laughed again.

Grandma laughed also.

She was sitting in front of a very neat and professional looking desk, thanks to me. On the desk and on the walls were here pictures, clean, dusted and probably most obvious, straight. On Grandma's desk there was a picture of Mom and Dad, their marriage picture, actually. Grandma had moved it to the side.

She stared at her desktop screen that showed the contents of her business bank account with an available balance of several hundred dollars. Grandma tapped her finger over the account balance and leaned to get a closer look at it. She turned her face to me, and as she did so, I saw a contented look, the kind we were used to—what seemed like long, long ago.

Ever since we were rudely dropped off at her house this time, I had noticed her face to look quite different. She picked up an album with newspaper articles about herself and gazed at her pictures. She turned the pages. She stopped at one of the stories that showed a picture of a young girl.

"That's you, ha," I said tilting my head to enjoy the picture. She gave an acknowledging smile as I read out the title, "9-Year Old Refuse to Leave Zimmerman's Till She Secure Food for Poor Mother."

"I was very different back then," she said abruptly.

I looked more closely at the accompanying picture showing her braced before an angry looking shopkeeper in apron.

"Young and foolish," Grandma said. "That's when you don't understand the world yet."

I nodded.

****$$****

On the screen Grace was looking on, was a webpage Grandma had left open on her laptop. Grace read aloud the heading on the screen, "How to Get the Most from Your I-phone."

"Dong, dong, Grace voiced, stopping at the refrigerator, the laptop in one hand. She searched inside the refrigerator, moving several bottles of wine, a bottle of vodka, and a bottle marked BV Georges Latour, to get to plastic bottles of orange juice, she brought to the Library.

On arriving, she pointed to the I-phone on Grandma's laptop screen, and then passed the computer to Grandma. She pointed at me. "*He* told me you want one too," Grace said. She simultaneously passed one of the juices to Grandma.

Grandma nodded in agreement while accepting the juice. "You know this is not what I drink. I need something to knock me out tonight, Baby."

"Granny," Grace exclaimed.

Grandma nevertheless began drinking from the bottle of O.J. "Remember the old, very old Black lady at Shines," she said. "The lady said I should have one. The one we bought, I'm keeping!"

Grace laughed hysterically as she indicated with head movement her disapproval. "Ah aah."

Grandmother shook her head in return, affirming her position was firm.

Seeing a serious look on Grandma's face, Grace looked to me. "You heard what she said, Tagg? And she doesn't even know how to use it!"

I could not say if Grandma was angry or sad. Sometimes such sensations are hard to decipher, and with Grandma lots of things are hard to tell. She stood erect and quiet for the moment. My thought for her was, "who cares?"

"Darling," she said. "You think I'm old?"

"You're not Grandma," I told her. "Grace's whose stupid."

****$$****

Later that night when Grandma was in our bedroom reading us bedtime stories like she did for so many of our nights together, I was still upset with myself for saying such a negative thing like the "S" word. Grandma taught us from we were a lot younger that negative was never the way to go. "Always hit above the belt," she used to tell us. "Never let anyone drag you in the mud. Hit hard, but hit high!"

I told Grandma of my upset as she sat in front of a large tropical picture of Grace, me, Dad and Mom in Orlando, taken earlier, when we had gone to Disney World together. I was holding a big snake, and as Grandma was ready to leave, she looked back at the snake in the picture. She turned around. She pointed at us.

"Soldiers, Sleep tight and you know what…"

Grace and I completed her usual saying, in unison as we used to do back then. "Don't let the bed bugs bite."

Grandma laughed, sounding good and exited. "Don't let the big *snake* bite. Soldiers!"

"Love you, Grandma," I said and placed my head on my pillow to forget the long day I had, but Grace would not give me the peace of mind I asked for. She began a vicious argument with me for not agreeing with her that Grandma was "getting strange" as she called it. I was tired and at such time could get upset easily. She wouldn't let me sleep, and I told her she was talking crazy stuff.

"Grandma's getting strange," Grace repeated.

"You're the strange one," I voiced.

"And I know why," she said in a teasing way.

At the time, I must not have been privy to as much information as I thought I was. I realized that. I had no clue. "Why," I asked.

"She went to see a professional and…" Grace said. She stopped abruptly.

"What? What, G?"

Grace said she would not tell me anymore about the "professional," except that Mom knew.

Grace continued. "Mom said, they're stealing her money, and she doesn't want to go into that nasty, insane home."

Grace said those words and then she looked at me sadly.

I asked. "Is that it, G?"

****$$****

Grandma had gone to her own bedroom and said she only had her TV light on. Beside her were the bottles of Vodka and wine, and on her bed, close to her pillow were a piece of paper with all her bills, as well as one with a list of her bounced checks. Next to those was her Maxwell Bible. She always liked Maxwell more than just a regular NKJV or NIV because it provided a lot of insight on how to do business the right way, she told me once.

It must be the same moment she was galloping the vodka or taking here pills because my heart began to beat fast right then. Back in our days, the abrupt heartbeats would have meant that Grandma and I were making contact even when we weren't in the same physical space. Grace asked me if I thought she should go to sleep with Grandma. At the time, my mind didn't know what it knows now. My heart knew.

The doctor had said Grandma took another shot, and then another with her pills, and it was that kind of reaction to problems that led to even bigger problems for her.

"I don't feel good about her, Tagg…," Grace said.

Grandma had taught us that week that we must just accept things we cannot change. We could only change the things we could. That was my thought at the time. Just pray. Let the Good Lord do the rest. When you are weary, pray.

"Sis, Pray for Grandma," I said. "If you want, pray for me. Pray for you. Pray for the government. Pray for everybody and everything. Just go to sleep, G. Pray."

That's what I did.

# CHAPTER 7

That night I had a dream that Mom and Dad had won a mega million dollar lotto prize and money was no longer a problem in our lives. I opened my eyes to our real existence just at the moment we were at a lawyer's office discussing the legal ramifications of having such a large amount of money.

When I awoke, I had barely finished breakfast to find my computer beeping with another assignment.

The first few moments after I pressed the play button the screen went blank, and then there was the badge of a security officer, which gradually got replaced by the officer himself. He was a heavy-set Black man, tough looking and with not one, but two guns—one on his left, and the other on his right, a modern-day Black John Wayne. He looked, he glanced, he stared.

He was keeping eyes on a male bank employee rushing from his rustic, broken down car in the night as the employee headed into brighter and brighter light, approaching a large building with the sign positioning it as a bank processing center.

As the employee and others enter the building, two other security guards kept watchful eyes on him and on everyone else. Then, the employee emerged into the large, well lighted space. It was one of hustle and bustle.

Computers and people were busy processing a bank's customers' activities, in an ultra animated, Wall Street environment. People moved and talked as fast, some inquiring, some shouting, "Supervisor, Supervisor," and on and on. To this date, I've not been to Wall Street, New York, so when I say Wall Street in this context I am referring to what I've seen on TV or read. Actually, I've seen a lot. Grandma loved to watch that business channel, CNCB.

Conspicuous signs and names of employees were on desks showing titles. Some said. "Relationship Manager," others, "Supervisor," and such like everybody there was in a high-up position; like everybody there did something super important. Without them, those of us out here were nothing, I conjured.

I kept looking at the video, which was by no means amateur made. There were other security officers walking around with guns, and then the video moved to a clerk looking very studious. He was rather short and was paying very close attention to some information he was reading directly in front of him. He mumbled out, "Madam Sandra" a couple of time. He studied the information more closely. He shouted out, "Supervisor! Supervisor! Supervisor!"

The man that had come from outside rushed over and looked at the items the clerk was looking at and at the clerk's computer screen.

"That's $35.00, Shawty," the supervisor said sharply. "And that's 35.00, that's 35.00 and that's $35.00."

Shawty dropped his head into his palm.

The supervisor upheld his position. "I wish they had allowed *me* to do a hundred, not four a day. They're nincompoops!"

Shawty pointed to the paperwork in front of them. "These are all under $5, Boss. If we don't pay that $922, we can pay all of these."

The supervisor laughed out loud and sudden. "They'll pay $40 for that cup of Starbuck, ha, ha, and if they don't cover this new shit by tomorrow, new shit will pile. You know how shit piles and stinks, don't you?"

Shawty, the clerk look like he wanted to say something, but the words from the supervisor did not relent.

"Thirty-five. Thirty-five. Thirty-five, and God, you, and me know the shit is not going to stop!"

Shawty shook his head. "God made us to take care of each other. Isn't that what we're here for?"

A voice from someone that was not in the picture came back. "You and your *Good Book* ideas again!"

The supervisor asked Shawty if he knew the bank was working on becoming the biggest in the country within two years and if he saw a communiqué from Corporate the month earlier.

Shawty again shook his head, this time briskly, and there was a loathing look to his face.

"I wasn't here yet," he said.

The Supervisor replied with a head action of his own indicating he understood.

"If we pay the smaller ones first, just one will bounce," Shawty continued.

The Supervisor placed his hand on Shawty's head. "Being new Shawty doesn't mean you have to be a moron. Does it?"

Shawty parsed his lips. He followed that with the dropping of his eyelids. He did not need words to show he was affected.

"What I mean, you keep bouncing those and you'll be the one bouncing to Mickidee," the Supervisor added.

"But that's not right," Shawty now countered. "That sucks out of the Customer's…"

I watched these actions and tried to make sense of them. Why did Dr. Erskine give us this particular assignment? What was in this for us? I rushed out a blog. Another student replied, "Edumacation, dummy!"

The Supervisor looked Shawty from down up, stopping at Shawty's pants that had a noticeable blotch of ink on it, apparently from a leaking pen in his pocket.

"Hay. Just do what I teach you, Pal and you'll be able to fix a lot of your problems," he advised, as Shawty said something about 'honest money' to which the Supervisor declared, "Lunch on me to-night.

All right!"

Around the large factory-like environment similar scenario played for our viewing.

****$$****

A new day had come, and I wondered out loud what Grandma was doing, to which Grace reported she was fine. Her feet were up and the bottles of liquor were replaced by bottles of medication. She was in her room watching TV. Grace did note that most of one of the bottles of Vodka got finished the night earlier; however, and now Grandma was into an infomercial talking about how women could be successful with their money. Grace said that was a "big deal" noting that Grandma was over the hill and all she had to do now was cut her costs, chill out, and enjoy her Social Security money. Why wouldn't she? She had earned it, Grace calculated accurately.

Grandma always liked to look at subject about money management on TV, saying it helped her with an affirmation of hers she spoke of whenever she thought about it—the one that success with money is not about how much you make; it's about how well you manage it.

Grace ran back up to check on Grandma as I returned to my class video.

The supervisor and Shawty exited the Processing Center in the dark of night and headed towards the supervisor's car.

The two men talked about what they were going to have for their lunch. They approached the supervisor's old, rustic 1980's 90's looking Ford. The supervisor placed his hand on Shawty's shoulder. Shawty jumped.

"If the company's successful, we will too," the supervisor tells Shawty.

Shawty's mind must have still been in a different place, even outside. "If we had put the lady's deposit from her sales, she would be OK now," he said.

"You got money you write checks," the Supervisor replied in a scolding-like tone. "You got no money you stay home. You know who got money these days?"

Shawty shook his head. He didn't have a clue.

"The Kardashians," the supervisor continued. "Don't you think they're melting hot?"

Shawty sounded upset for a moment. He didn't seem to want to go down the alley the supervisor was heading.

"If we released her deposit, she would…," he spurted out.

The supervisor was, however, quick to respond and explained to Shawty it was in fact the nightshift's responsibility to get *certain type of work* done for the company and Shawty had no right questioning how the company does its business.

"And suppose I do," Shawty asked; his tone was rude now.

The supervisor kicked the tire of his car.

"This my ride, Pal."

Shawty brought forth a crude laugh through which the Supervisor explained, "You see why I have to follow the rules? You must too. It's our duty, Pal."

At a later time, as Shawty sat in the passenger's seat, he told the Supervisor that what he was told was hard for him to swallow, to which the supervisor told him he understood. The supervisor said, though, he had to elaborate.

"A couple years ago I was right in your seat, Little Man," he said. "New and coming here on the bus. I'm working my pants off; I can reach a manager in three years. Here, you never know what you can become."

# CHAPTER 8

We had not been with Grandma for very long when I started to notice that she was seriously falling apart. On our next shopping to buy things for the business she told me she was interested in something they called a reversed mortgage to help her have "more than enough money" as she put it.

One day a man from the light company came thumping on the door, saying he was going to turn off her electricity for non-payment. Grandma said to him her check had bounced because her bank had taken her money via NSFs. The man chuckled and said that was not the power company's problem.

I believe that occurred in the same week she received a letter about foreclosure on her house. Her payment for the storage where she kept most of her books was due, and she had to go with another late fee. Not long after that, the T-Mobil lady had to grant Grandma a discount on top of her already senior discount.

Personally, the most irritating part, and Grace would go with me on this one, we no longer were getting to choose what we wanted when we went shopping.

We would worked our pants off helping to prepare shipments for Grandma book business, which was, by the way, fading because as Grandma put it, nobody wanted to read paper books anymore, and now we had to go and buy stuff for the business without our treats of our own choosing.

****$$****

Grandma, Grace and I were back at the mall. This time, I carried a small money chest in my hand for Grandma; Grace was pushing a cart of stationery. And Grandma? She was "supervising" us.

I wanted steak, and Grace chased for a shrimp dinner, but we were all now on a Big Mac diet, Grandma told us. I tried to question why at one point, but the store was so busy with lots of people in front of us. I stopped in shame.

On reaching the store clerk, Grandma pulled out her bankcard and flipped it to the clerk.

Instantly, there were reactions.

"Ma'am, do you have another card?" the clerk asked with the same upsetting voice the previous clear had asked the last time Grace was embarrassed at the mall. Now, it was after the clerk had ran the card twice.

Grandma looked suspiciously at the clerk. "What's wrong with my c-a-r-d," she asked.

The clerk started to try it again, speaking her action out loud. "I'm try ….," she said.

Grandma insisted, "Please do!"

****$$****

The clerk ran the card through a third time. "Not going through," she announced.

"It's fine. I'm not asking," Grandma responded in an agitated tone as Grace smacked me on the hip to look behind at an impatient looking crowd in line."Dejavu," she called out.

"It's not working Ma'am," the clerk emphasized. This time her voice was a bit louder than before.

"I checked it before I went to bed last night," Grandma answered. It's got to work!"

A Black girl probably about four or five years older than me in the middle of the line walked out and came closer to us and asked Grandma what she wanted them to do for her, including the word, "Miss" at the beginning and end of the question. We looked at her and wondered why she had come at us.

"Pay for you," the girl asked angrily as she looked at us.

Grandma took out another card from her purse, but first held on to it. She didn't look happy or for that matter, very healthy. She looked at me.

"How am I doing, Soldier," she asked me, her voice nevertheless as calm as the South Beach water on a windless day.

I looked at Grace who had become red in the face. I was concerned but probably not as much as Grace was embarrassed, again. "Fine Grandma. Fine." I answered.

Grandma was not done though. She lifted the card high in the air, and then she did something that was probably to her, acknowledging the weary looking crowd; it seemed like a bow, something like the old lady's at Shines, only without the wheelchair. It was the first of many times I would see her do this.

"I don't see why it's not working. I just don't see," she said.

****$$****

By the time the clerk decided to run the old card again, the people at the back of the line looked like they were up to something. I imagined their taking us away in straight-jackets: Grandma, me and Grace. Just get us from that counter. That never happened, though. What did come about, however, was a surprise we were all happy for.

It was the, "Hummuh!" that were going on.

"It works now," came from the store clerk after running the card another time.

A young Filipino girl close to the Black girl looked angrily at the Black girl, defending Grandma as if she was a member of our family.

"See," the Filipino said. "See. The lady's got dough in there! I told you!"

Almost immediately the crowd in line gave a huge splashing applause as they all looked relieved, and Grandma flipped the card out the hand of the cashier. They both went back into her purse so quickly and smoothly, I could remember her hands going like a machine: this, that and that, making sure everything was right where it was supposed to be.

A "you know I was right" smile replaced Grandma's new everyday face all the way as she drove us back to her home.

# CHAPTER 9

Dr. Erskine who told us she worked primarily from her home, had all the latest technology to work with, and sent us an e-mail stating the "WikiCreeps" assignments were case studies we were to use to get insight into the good and evil that exists in business. I, in my childlike view of human ways and things, thought they were simply interesting vignettes, and that's where my senses were failing me.

Case for analysis: In the next take, Corporate was wearing his trademark suspenders and red tie at a ribbon-cutting event at one of his branches. There was a big crowd, well over a hundred people in attendance as Corporate talked to them, with his VP of Bank OPS and the marketing lady, Miss Andrea at his side. From previous viewings, and our class communications we the male students had come to an agreement that the lady was not only elegant and charming....but if only we were old enough. On this occasion she did not disappoint any of us, the boys, that is. She looked fabulous, wearing a big colorful hat, her cheeks powdered, and her lips nicely *balmed.* Beside her, a security guard strolled with his hand on his gun.

"Mind me now, they're trying to get us," Corporate announced from a lectern with the emblem of his bank in front of it. The emblem read "UPPER CREEK BRANCH, 100 Years of Service." He looked out to the crowd that appeared anxious about something, maybe just tired; I don't know.

"Our responsibility is the allocation of capital, and I'm here to tell you by March 15$^{th}$ each of you will be seeing your reward in your account, checks, whatever" Corporate continued, projecting a sense of boastfulness.

I learned that was the part the crowd was waiting for as that piece flipped the faces and mood of the crowd from whatever they were in to elated and participative. For the rest of the speech there was a "living audience" a fellow student wrote. That's a term later used by a number of my fellow students.

Corporate rode on. "Last quarter, a home run. This one, we're on target! Thanks for going the extra mile, Guys!"

The camera panned the room for reactions, momentarily stopping on two men in the back of the room, wearing ties, but it was not well focused in on them before it went back to Corporate. He was now telling the audience that their future was secure.

Corporate added, "Not to say we don't have our challenges ahead, so we're counting on you."

****$$****

When we got home, I was pooped, knowing our work was still not done. There, Grandma insisted that we carry inside everything we had bought. She rationalized her overworking us by saying she was tired too and our young bones had not seen enough work for their age. She was not all negative, however, as she said she was glad she could count on us, which was exactly what Grace needed to hear. She stuck her hand out for recompense and Grandma gave money to both of us.

"You've been good, loyal Soldiers today," Grandma remarked as she transferred the cash with one hand and ended up ruffling both of our hair with the other.

Grace playfully tried to grab the twenty-dollar bill from my hand, asking what I was going to do with it.

"Different things, I offered. I lied. My mind was actually only on one thing—the bank.

****$$****

To say the least, I was finding the information I was learning about business quite fascinating. That attitude helped me to get back to my schoolwork with excitement and as quickly as I could.

I found out the two men at Corporate's meeting were actually employees of the bank branch Corporate was talking at. One named Sosa, was Latino; he was balled headed and moved around with an exaggerated swing of the hips; his shoulders swaggered. The other was called R. Paul by the first.

"You make all the difference," Corporate continued to the crowd as the two men kept eyes on the goings-on under the makeshift tent at the Upper Creek branch.

"Keep on doing what you do best," Corporate said.

R. Paul and Eduardo Sosa looked at each other and shook their heads.

"Funny money," R. Paul concluded. "The bitch's going to give us three-hundred pesetos like he did last year time around."

"Pesos! Hablas Espanol, Cuz," Eduardo Sosa responded. He gave a quick laugh, and R. Paul asked him what he thought was Corporate's take that year.

"Twenty mil," R. Paul answered himself. "And have us *steal* money from the poor, the sick, the old! You saw the lady that came in this morning? She isn't rich!"

"And let us think we're going up *in The Clouds* one day," Eduardo Sosa added, as he opted for a silly laugh. "That's my kind of guy!"

The crowd kept its eyes on a nicely designed PowerPoint presentation Corporate was flaunting, with revenue from different sectors: mortgage, credit card, interests, fee, and all of the bank's money. It showed a two-point-five billion from NSF's and a seven billion net income for the quarter. Next to the word net income, in brackets it claimed "Profits."

Below a column labeled "Investment Banking," a rubber-stamping said, "To Be Desired." In a column Corporate was now pointing on, referencing the NSF, it said twelve percent.

"Mind me now, we'll pay back the President's stimulus," Corporate said to the crowd. But what we have to do is to keep the momentum. Momentum is everything!"

This triggered in the crowd another one of those Amway type of shaking of heads and chanting. This time it was, "momentum, momentum, momentum." It came in a chorus-like way; one, that in actuality sounded good. "Catchy" is a nice way of seeing it.

R. Paul apparently did not like it that much, though. He shook his head in a way that showed his disposition.

"We're just a big racket," he said to Eduardo Sosa. "What you think about his last e-mail?"

Eduardo Sosa had a hand on his scalp that seemed recently polished. He placed a grin on his face, and then went for akimbo. "Why you think I left Cuba," he asked.

"Checking accounts? Liberty! Freedom," R. Paul answered.

****$$****

What I didn't get was why the tape got cut right at this point. This one, our class concluded was amateurish. I was just thinking, "these guys that run the banks are interesting and the employees know it;" when I saw what came next I was hypnotized.

They took us inside Corporate's office, a nice pad like what I was visualizing having for myself in the years to come. It had everything. There were the massage armchairs, glittering chandeliers; TV screens streaming Wall Street; even a pool table. A gold looking statue of the CEO stood in the center of attraction.

"A good thing," one of the men concluded.

"As of right now, all the arrows green and pointing upwards," another replied.

Several of the bank officers were present including the bank VP of Ops who sat across from Corporate. He was thanking Corporate for putting "a good stash" in his account the previous year but was concerned about the projected small raise this time around.

Corporate replied that he wanted to make some changes so all of them at executive level would see what he told them could be significant gains.

"What you haven't been telling your audiences, we're so close to being canned." The VP of Bank Ops said to Corporate.

Corporate laughed, nodded, laughed louder. "Always a cheetah, trying to run faster than their prey."

The VP of Bank Ops shook his head, "How bizarre can this Administration get," he questioned.

Corporate noted that the government didn't matter. "We're going the distance, Guys," he added. "You'll be working with Miss Marketing. Line up a campaign to get at least 90% of customers to opt in if they go crazy on that one," he said. He flashed a small red light on an area in a duplicate of the PowerPoint chart—the area that said "NSF, 12%."

The VP of Bank Ops waddled his finger. "You the cheetah.

Corporate grinned.

"Always ahead. Always ahead, Boss."

****$$****

In the relative short time we had been with Grandma she had also begun to show some age, and Grace and I wondered quietly if we were her problem. After all, our parents had just dumped us on her and went off into their own world. Grandma, however, insisted we were not what was bothering her and even gave us kudos for being with her in what she related was a difficult and crucial time in her life.

As reward to us, she took it on her own to make sure we learned everything she said we were supposed to know but never got, and one day she turned a run-of-the-mill homework question into what she called her educating us for the battles of life her "Soldiers" would one day face.

"What's the difference between a thief and a robber," she asked Grace in reference to the homework problem Grace was trying to solve.

Grace said, "a thief is someone who goes into your e-mail account and read all your personal information. A robber is someone who takes over your Twitter account like it's theirs."

These were in response to some accusation she was making of me a week earlier, and she found this moment a good one to spread it further. Grandma, however, was totally out of the loop.

"What on earth you talking," Grandma replied.

She's blaming me, Grandma," I offered, not then thinking of the whole different era Grandma smelled, tasted and chewed on even as she tried to keep up with us in our time. "I didn't do it!"

Grace came back swinging at me. "Yes, you did!"

Grandma ignored our back and forth for the most part as she kept her focus on what she was trying to teach us.

"OK, Soldiers," she proceeded. "Here's a two-second question to get your neurons firing the way they should. They need to be oxygenated, you know? A farmer has 200 cows, he added 50 sheep, he added 10 horses and then he sells 50 of his cows. How many animals he has at this point? Go!

I didn't even have to think it out. "*Pica cake! 210*," I said.

Grandma asked us if we knew why addition and subtraction were so important.

I laughed. This was ludicrous.

That Wednesday, on my way to class, I got what really happened. Grandma was the real student, the real winner, the real utility seeker. The concept of Twitter had triggered great interest in her, and like a child she couldn't stop saying the word. For a very long time we had to deal with her repeating the word like a young child going Apple, Apple, Boy, Boy, Boy, Cat, Cat, Cat, Cat."

****$$****

That week, many of my fellow students complaint of our having too much work to do. At this point for me, schoolwork was just a constant. I didn't care about its burdens. I was liking it, actually. It gave me the unprecedented opportunity to learn what was happening in corporate offices all over the country; some of the same students said, "all over the world."

To make things sweeter, Grandma made a commitment to me. She said if I graduated on time, and with a B plus or better she would be my number one fan at my graduation. All good I agreed. Good reasons for me to keep on studying, and that I did.

****$$****

In a new video, Corporate was worried that the bank's investments in mortgages were not adding up as they had hoped, and when the VP of Bank Ops got angry for having to attend a meeting on his golf day, Corporate was not so happy.

"What did you do last year," Corporate said to the VP of Bank Ops. "21? I know Fred was at 20.4. I was 34.2, but that was with bonuses and options. I know you guys are low but …."

It was fun peeking and listening in as the group talked about numbers that were so big they sounded made-up. After some hot-blooded exchanges they agreed that their numbers were not bad considering the high unemployment rate in the country, and so many people were losing their homes. Corporate reminded them that because they were still feeling the pinch of the slow economy, patience was in order.

"That's why we're here," he added. "We don't want to go to skid row. Do we?"

One of the men in the room said "not right now" as Corporate spoke of projections for the company.

"By the end of the year we should at least increase our NSF's by another ten or more percentage points. That will increase all of our assets," he said.

He continued by speaking of the company as being in a skirmish with its customers who "are disconnected and always want something for nothing."

"As with a story," he tells them, entertaining himself while trying to capture that side of them. "The most difficult part to tell what's going to happen is the end."

The crowd looked at Corporate as if this was some sort of a "Jeopardy" case.

He persisted. "If they're going to take away our NSF from us, let's get as much as we can get before it's too late. That's what I'm shooting for."

The group gave its attention to Corporate, listening as he plowed on.

"Cold and calculating," CFO Tolly concluded, removing his reading glasses to get a good look at Corporate.

"Cold and calculating," Corporate replied. "If Congress passes any of those senseless laws, we lead the fight."

A number of the people looked at the VP of Bank Ops who tried to laugh off what he must have thought would be a big task ahead for him. Every time there was a shift in policy, his duties would increase. He hated that, but that didn't change Corporate from being unrelenting.

"When the goings get tough Guys, when fire hits the roof, what have we done historically," he asked, to which there was no answer.

"What have we done historically," he repeated in a strong, rackety voice.

"The tough gets going," the entire room replied.

He looked at them. He shook his head. They were in harmony. "Thanks Guys!"

He left the room and headed to an elevator marked fittingly, "Executive Staff Only."

# CHAPTER 10

For Grandma, the goings were getting tougher and tougher. She would spend many hours of her day checking and re-checking her account to find it all right, but as soon as she blinked, there would be another charge to her. This made her frazzled over time, and even though we tried to get her out of an ongoing sinking mood by going with her on a trip to Cape Canaveral to see a shuttle lift-off and another trip to Tallahassee, we could not always keep her calm.

Some days she appeared more concerned with her bank and the associated struggles that were coming her way, than other days. Exhibit one was the day she quickly got out the Suburban almost slamming Grace's fingers as she closed the door. Exhausted and clearly frustrated about something, she dashed towards her house, Grace and I following as Mr. Saul stopped his lawnmower and waved.

"More troubles today, Ms. Muley," Mr. Saul bellowed. This came in the form of a question the whole neighborhood was becoming more and more concerned with.

Grandma waved so quickly she dropped a bag with eggs to the ground. "Hello Saul," she replied. Grace and I picked up the bag.

Momentarily Ms. Cynthia peeped out to see us moving fast and wiped some sweat from her forehead; it was a hot day even for Florida standard.

"Don't let anything get you, on a God-blessed day like this, Ms. Muley. Psalms 23," she said.

To that, Mr. Saul pulled his finger across his face, sweeping a scoop of sweat of his own to the grass. "We're here for you, always, Ms. Sandra," he shouted.

Before any other scripture, we were inside, and Grace was telling Grandma to relax. We promised her we would completely handle her book shipments for that day.

"It's not the orders," Grandma barked. She needed to check her bank balance.

Grace looked at me with her senseless smile. She opened her lips to make sound but chose not to go any further.

"You didn't have to rush us back home, Granny," I said. "You could have used your I-phone."

Grandma response was fast and furious. "How do you know I have one?"

Grace and I looked at each other as Grandma blinked, turned away from us and began opening her bank account on one of her PCs.

"I told you; she's getting old," Grace whispered to me.

"Can't keep a damn secret around here," Grandma said to me and Grace who now stood quiet, then stone-faced at the woman's words. We waited for more.

"To talk the truth," Grandma continued, appearing uncertain of where she was going. "One of the ladies at Shines. I kept your mother's," Grandma said.

Grace looked at me again and nodded. I responded in-kind.

****$$****

In truth Mom didn't care about getting a new phone anyways. She and Dad would be functioning fine in the mix of fun and play. With all that had happened with Grandma and us their half-of-the-world cruise seemed longer than it actually was, and the strange thing was they had been far from getting to the halfway mark. She, with Dad would tell us of their flowery Caribbean adventure: she in her swimsuit and he in a short sleeve shirt that put on display all the labor he had put in at Bally's and another gym called LA Fitness for years.

Mom said she could not tell if the water was blue or green as they perused the Barbados coastline. The food was "exquisite", I found out. I heard a female's voice in the background telling others about that amidst the loud music and talking. Mom said there were gambling, and drinking, and all sorts of activities that made me want to get big even before my freshman TRIG class at FSU.

At the time Mom called she told Grandma she was having a romantic moment with Dad; for them, that meant rubbing his head.

"Sorry, Son," she said to me for leaving us as long as they had. She said she was trying to make up with Dad who complained he was overworked and wanted to abandon us.

They had not gotten in contact with us for over two weeks, so I was pumped up. "It's Mom," I shouted, and Grandma won a race with Grace for the phone.

Grace and I observed Grandma who felt that every conversation was a family event and had me turn the phone into a megaphone for all of our listening pleasure.

Before long, the contention was back on. Grandma asked Mom why she had to call herself "your lovely daughter?"

There was no answer to that, but there was some piece about how Grandma had her bloomers on when Mom was conceived. To this, Grandma tried to no avail to wave us out of the room.

"I swear you had forgotten I told you about that," Grandma said into the cell that somehow got knocked off speaker. She tried to put the speaker back on but didn't know how to do it.

"Technology," Grace whispered as she stared at the cell phone. "Old lady doesn't even know how to use it, Tagg."

The two on the phone talked some more, and then I heard Grandma telling Mom she didn't need the amusement.

The conversation had moved to how Grandma was hesitant to sign Mom's college financial aid papers thirty-years earlier and how that one act had impacted their relationship.

Grandma said it had to do with money.

****$$****

Amusement was not what Grandma, Grace, or I was having. Work? Yes! Learning? Yes!

My computer beeping would leave me busy for the next hour, taking me through my twelfth video assignment in an incredibly busy season. Some students communicated they should have taken something with less time commitment. Philosophy was one suggestion.

I sent off a blog, “Take a look; this one’s cool!”

In this assignment, Corporate was getting ready to buckle up for a Disneyland ride with his children and wife. Everybody in his family had taken care to ensure an impeccable, clean and bright look which gave into a natural sense that these were people unlike us: people with money.

There was excitement everywhere. An attendant walked around telling a man and his group, in front of Corporate family to buckle up, the man’s wife having her purse protected securely around her neck, extending to her abdomen.

“Everybody! Buckle up,” the park attendant reiterated. “This could be the most bumpy ride of your life!”

Corporate’s wife gave him a fast kiss on the cheek. With the lift beginning to go up, she looked downwards to capture the world from her higher and higher perspective.

“They look really small,” she said to him. “Insignificant!”

He looked down to what she was seeing: a large number of everyday looking people hustling and bustling in the vicinity.

He laughed a sly one as he took another look. “They furnish our food, Baby. They give us what we have!”

Corporate’s wife appeared to instantly lose interest in the conversation. She was back about the kiss she had pasted on him, and telling him about when she was young.

“Alice told me, ‘stolen kisses are the best wealth’,” she shared, her voice girl-like.

“I like your sister," Corporate replied. "But not when you’re in a precarious situation like us.”

The camera moved to the man in front of Corporate and his wife. He was looking downwards when his face instantly got powder white. The man grabbed a stack of money from his shirt pocket as if he had forgotten it to be there until that moment. He passed it to his wife, calling her Sweetheart. He instructed her to protect it for him.

"You never know," the wife replied as she pushed the money quickly into her purse.

"Only Wal-Mart can top you guys at this point," Corporate's wife said to him.

Corporate smiled. "Some dozy lady's been writing. Writes bad check; Wants a bail out…."

"You said the returns last quarter was over the top. Tops The Salvation Army with their free inventory, I might say…," Corporate's wife said; she giggled.

Corporate looked to his wife and reminded her he was running a bank.

"Deb, you know we're not about entitlements. And we don't sell milk and butter, or old, stinky clothes for that matter," he said.

His wife did not react well to the way he spoke to her. She had graduated from business school as he did, and she was not afraid to remind him.

Corporate's voice changed to that. His response was personal and base. "You realize, Deb, you're just spending too much green as it is. We'll have to cut back!"

Corporate's wife had enough and found herself in a push-turned-pull struggle with her husband. She knew it was she he depended on to "humanize" him.

"The women at the auxiliary would hugely, *hugely* disagree with you," his wife replied. "Without us you look wild!"

# CHAPTER 11

It was another week before Mom called again, but we couldn't stay for that one. I wished I could as I wanted to chat with her and Dad. More importantly, I wanted to stay with Grandma, as the night before she had complained of a horrific headache she attributed to worrying about her bank account; I thought my staying would help.

The yellow school bus, however, had come to take us. And Grandma, had already accepted the call when she patted us on the butt, insisting that we gave her, her kisses before we left.

"Don't cheat, Grandma," she warned us and positioned her cheek for the catch, first from Grace.

Grace and I had followed this routine since we were toddlers; we surrendered; before we were out, we heard her going at Mom on the phone.

"Ah, ha! They're still with their Machiavellian moves," she said to Mom.

Mom said she had to ask Dad to explain, and then to give her a moment to handle the situation with Grandma, as Grandma's temper and anger had elevated high and fast. In Mom's words it was an intolerable barrage on Grandma own bank: anything and everybody that had to do with her banking situation.

"Humans must never be treated this way," Grandma told her. "But who am I to expect you to be thinking about that while you're gallivanting the world?"

Mom said she promised to give Grandma money to put back in her account if she needed it, but that was not the point Grandma was trying to make.

"Start by helping me. That's not to say your loan is not long due," Grandma riled.

Mom tried to stay away from Grandma's banking problems, but Grandma hooked her at every turn.

After all, Grandma would not go anywhere messing with the bank, anyways, Mom said.

Grandma ignored that.

"Mom, they make their rules and we have nothing to do with it," Mom continued. She covered the phone and whispered to Dad her thoughts that it was a risk they took leaving Grandma with us. It was not wise. Not good. Not this time around.

"They've been bouncing my checks, godamit," Grandma said forcefully.

It was a long time later that Mom and Grandma related their versions of this event to Grace and me. By then, the tension with the two had gotten to a boiling point that left Grandma very emotional. To her last days she felt nervy around Mom.

Mom told Grandma to keep enough money in her bank account and the bank wouldn't bounce her check, but Grandma was just "livid."

"It's not about enough," Grandma replied.

Mom told her it was, "No problem."

Grandma said she went at that too, calling her out.

"What's with you and this "No problem, nonsense? It's a problem!"

Mom said no matter how much she told Grandma she shouldn't be worrying at her age about what a bank does to its customers and things of that nature, Grandma insisted that people and institutions in which you put your money and trust has "no right digging out the eyes of the innocent."

"OK." Mom concluded Grandma was over her head. She asked Grandma to go on a cruise with her and Dad sometime. "Come see new places, a new horizon, Mom suggested."

Grandma was adamant about "keeping," and if "getting," was the right word, then getting her life in order as she saw it fit. She said she had already lived the extravagant and didn't need anything material to complete her passage here. All she yearned for now was to see people held above profits.

"Why do you give a damn," Mom asked at the peak of her own frustration.

Grandma's replied. "So I can end up at Shines?"

Mom told Grandma to take some time to enjoy life, but Grandma had long "refused to pile up bills and fall down over them." That's when Mom told Grandma of the ship and the food. Everything was incredible, and they had not quite finished their Caribbean leg of their trip. Puerto Rico, Belize and Barbados were among those scratched off the list. The Mediterranean sea was still a virgin, unexplored by them.

Mom told her, "Incredible.... The world's more fascinating than you think."

All that did not move Grandma's heart.

Grandma told Mom she had to stop *them* as she went into some far-out talk about her "elders." She stressed the kind of behavior that was coming from the bank was not what the forefathers had in mind.

"Ma. Ma. Ma. They mint the coin," Mom told her. "Banks and insurance companies own the world! We just have to be cool."

"Well you stay *cool*, Dear," Grandma answered.

The two did not talk for a while after that.

****$$****

If I had the mind I have now, the whole course of things would have been different. I would not have watched all of what happened to happen and said nothing, and that applies to everything—the whole gamut, the whole enchilada: Mom and Grandma, the CEO, the whole everything.

I began the next class assignment in this darkness. Miss Andrea was telling the men in a room, "All right, take a look."

They were at one of their executive building that made midgets of the smaller ones in the surroundings and Miss Andrea was referencing the comparative size of theirs to those in the surrounding. Momentarily, a secretary came by to ask if the room was cool enough.

"As cool as a cucumber," the marketing lady replied, breaking into a previously going conversation.

"What I'm saying is we can put a moratorium on accounts with low balances," an executive said, waving off the secretary and her interruption.

Another executive voiced a rejection. "That's going to take us right back to square one," he said. "What I see, is a charge for every service: checking, Internet, ATM, bankcard use, everything! What we need is to get paid."

Just then, a young executive tried to enter the room but a security officer blocked the entrance.

The officer pushed out his hand. "Your phone. All recording devices."

The young executive refused to pass his phone to the officer. "I was hoping it would be OK this time," he said.

Corporate approach the door to enter simultaneously as the officer instructed the young executive, "Zero recording device." He pointed to Corporate. "That's who makes the rules. Not this meeting."

The young executive looked to Corporate for help. Corporate looked beyond him.

"Sterile," the officer remarked.

The young executive insisted that he would need his "tool" as the officer pointed at the camera on the phone. "People can tap into that shit! Can even turn this on, even if it's turn off. The big man said this one won't get out under any circumstance."

Corporate seasawed his head to an approval.

Inside, the VP of Bank Ops boasted, "Our numbers are more lucrative than Avatar."

The group took that with smiles and nods of satisfaction. Marketing director, Miss Andrea told them it's not the company's *fault* they were doing well. "It's our job to get in there, kick asses once they make themselves susceptible!"

"Two points we must always keep in sight: the food chain follows the economic chain, and two, it's always a crime to write a bad check," Corporate noted. "They know the law, and we know the law. That's it! Freedom: Choice!"

Suddenly, a strong male voice came from nowhere. "Time to wage war," it declared.

Corporate raised his hand to get attention. “One more thing. Whatever they do at Congress, we will act. We’re not sissies. We’re not going to be bullied! We won’t let bullshit stick!”

Another voice at least as strong as the one that had cried out “time to wage war ”followed. This one was as swift as a speeding boat and echoed the sternness of the first, “Aggression!”

There was a quiet moment. Corporate looked slowly at every face in the room. Everyone was where the company had ask him or her to be. “Winning,” he said. He waved good-bye to the group. Two men escorted him through the exec elevator to the rooftop of the building. He entered a jet with the company’s name on it. He waved. They took off.

# CHAPTER 12

Inside a large training area they called the War Room at the corporate headquarters, the instructor up front flipped a presentation chart to a page with the title, "Winning with Customer."

He queried, "The question is, if you have a check that comes in to you and you see the opportunity to cash in on it, what are you to do?"

An older Latino lady from the front of the class lifted her hand. "Would that create the same effect like the hold-on-automatic payment for a day or two? Like you explained yesterday?"

The Instructor placed his hand on his cheek. "Think," he advised.

The video rolled and Shawty, the employee from the Processing Center appeared in the center of the frame. He ran his hands through his hair holding his mouth closed and his eyes as if to himself.

The instructor looked to the students. "We're not lawyers," the instructor explained. "And I'm not here to tell you, you should do this or do that, or anything. That would put me in the wrong place!"

"How do we decide," the Latino lady followed up.

"You know what to do," the Instructor said. He placed a wise guy grin on his face. "What I'm showing you, you already know. Wealth is fluid. It's abundant. It is here! It's up to each of you to see how money mints and how we can individually and collectively help to craft opportunities for ourselves, your bank and ultimately, your family."

Momentarily, Shawty sprang to his feet. “You call what we do *opportunity*,” he asked.

This led to a case of confusion in the classroom as Shawty continued. “Do you realize it’s real people and real money we deal with?”

There was no word from anyone. Faces had taken on a more conservative look.

“People like you and me,” Shawty added.

The instructor ignored the short, un-refined looking man who he saw as picking an argument with him. There must have been a reason he took on such a funky, screwy name, anyways.

Focused, the instructor approached a flip chart and started to turn the pages. In the process, he passed one that said, “When to Post/Not Post.” He promised he would get back to that one. He positioned his pointer to the content of the next sheet, “Customer Demographics & Psychographics.” He read the title aloud.

“A reminder, there’s a reward system here,” the Instructor continued as some of the students in class looked angrily at Shawty; the instructor moved on, pointing to a bulleted list labeled “Account Holder’s Strength & Weaknesses.”

“You as Customer Relationship Reps are at the forefront of knowing the Customer’s patterns and trends,” he instructed and then shook his head up and down to each of his words that immediately followed. “This is your most important tool.”

He went on to explain why employees must stand up for their employers, especially in bad economic times. He concluded, “We’re too big to go in, Guys!”

Over time, the class would be very focused, but there was a continual, definite out-of-the ordinary look of incertitude on Shawty’s face.

****$$****

In the meanwhile, Grandma remained busy working out life and “babying” her headaches that were coming more frequently and stronger. She told me she had never had the kind of headaches before she started worrying about her bank. She described them to me as generalized head pain occurring on and off.

Feeling frightened for her, I advised she give up on her overindulgence with her bank, and to that she said no. I suggested she go to her doctor, but she complained about the cost.

****$$****

That week, we celebrated what would have been Grandma's 60th wedding anniversary if Gramps was still around, by going fishing, and that Sunday we had Mom's friend Miss Bridgett over for dinner. I had boiled the potatoes for the salad; Grace and Grandma did everything else, and that was plenty.

A lot for an old lady, and a lot to say about good food. It was the most mouthwatering meal we had in a while. The get-together also provided Grandma an opportunity to lay out to a dear friend some of the things that were going on in her head and her world.

Miss Bridgett was actually a friend of Mom's who had gotten so close to Grandma and us over time, she was spending more time with Grandma than with Mom. She said she was of the impression Grandma had worked out things with her bank and suggested Grandma was now in the position to start enjoying herself again but Grandma made clear her purpose, as she sometimes called it, was far from achieved.

"It's just beginning," Grandma declared. "I didn't make the same mistake. I sent this one certified mail—directly to the big honcho's office!"

"You're a bold Mama," Miss Bridgett teased Grandma.

Grandma told her she knew the CEO would be delighted to know what his staff was up to.

"I trust he will—but I wouldn't bet what they're doing a mistake," Miss Bridgett said.

The two ladies engaged each other in a fascinating way, as when Mom was center stage.

Grandma told her that she sent the CEO "a complete, detailed account" and explained that her bank had her out twenty times at thirty-five dollars apiece of recent. "Seven hundred dollars," she emphasized.

Miss Bridgett, who usually had less money than Grandma was used to telling Grandma any amount over six hundred dollars was a typical Social Security check for a person Grandma's age. She failed at saying that this time.

"I told him to put it right back in my account," Grandma continued.

As this was happening, I noticed for the first time wrinkles in Miss Bridgett's forehead. They showed she was fully engaged in thoughts. She also was accustomed to saying in our circle that Social Security was a Ponzi Scheme, and I expected she was going to go there today, a favorite subject of hers, and yes on that one she hit it on the button.

"I pray in hope they put your money back. I hope they do," she continued.

As she spoke, she gave Grandma a spaced-out look, one I read as she was strong and Grandma was weak, a kind of condescending sad cornucopia of emotions dripped. She paused. "I'm sorry to say Ms. Muley but you can color me skeptical… Color me on this one!"

Grandma didn't say anything for a moment, but it was clear she was still in her head. It was tilted, her pupils were to the far right of the otherwise poignant white area of her eyes, and she was unusually motionless. When things like this happen, things that shouldn't have occurred in the first place, her everyday response would be to take a moment and think. This time she decided on a long gaze, "Why wouldn't they? It's a bank. Here to serve we the people, Dear," she decided.

Long ago, long before the bank decided on changing its policy to maximize profits at all cost, Grandma used to believe that banks were "our rock of Gibraltar." Everything good and helpful rested on them. "They will be the last standing stone of our system," she would argue.

"Holy," Miss Bridgett interrupted.

"I prefer them having my money than Gloria," Grandma answered. "But…"

Grandma did not continue that trend of thought; instead, she chose Mom's father, Grandpa John to talk about. Some believed her real father was different than this man; but he was who we knew.

"Her Pop, when he was here, used to think the bank was God. I trust they still are," Grandma said.

Miss Bridgett gave Grandma a fresh, invigorating look in the face. "You heard me say, 'holy', didn't you?"

"Yeah," Grandma answered.

"Well, should I be surprised," Miss Bridgett asked. "What I knew of him, he was different."

The two ladies carried on in their conversation, and I used every word of their talk to learn about Grandma, Grandpa and many of the other people and things Grandma had not spoken about much with us. It turned out that during the Great Depression our family had done well, but Grandma said she never had the conversation with Mom.

"Ms. Muley, I have news for you. It's a lot different now," Miss Bridgett offered after a while. "If there was anything good from back then, I can only tell you, it's over now!"

"They're the last honorable profession," Grandma said. Her voice was firm yet passionate.

Grace later called her out on that one saying she was confusing.

To all this, Miss Bridgett said something of Grandma living in a deep, dark hole. That took Grandma to reminding Miss Bridgett of years earlier when she was a child and Grandma was her Sunday-School teacher. Based on what was said, I gathered Miss Bridgett was a fast learner, and it was Grandma who had given her, her first Bible, which Miss Bridgett boasted she still had; it was actually inscribed and signed by Grandma.

Miss Bridgett continued, "But Miss Muley, when you hear me talking the way I just did, you know."

The two ladies ended late that night with a glass each of Napa Valley Cabernet Sauvignon, one with a nice, flower-like aroma. I know because I tipped my finger in and tasted it when they had walked away for a private talk in the kitchen.

Sweet and rich, I recall. Grandma said it was a berry wine from South or Central America. I think she had this one wrong.

# CHAPTER 13

A snapshot of Eduardo Sosa and R. Paul at the Upper Creek Branch introduced the first moments of my next video class assignment. It showed the two men looking older and more mature than the last time we had seen them. They moved around the bank as they engaged each other.

"You know, the old lady that came in and said we OD'ed her account, right," Eduardo Sosa said.

R. Paul nodded.

"Follow me with this," Eduardo Sosa instructed. "She said we took her medication funds Right?"

R. Paul made up his face, interrupting Eduardo Sosa's trend of thought.

R. Paul took the stage, expressing with frustration that they didn't have a choice but to carry out the orders they were given as employees.

Simultaneously, an older male employee passed by with some papers in his hand and shook his head to the bit he seemed to overhear.

Eduardo Sosa pivoted in the direction of the older man. "It's the photographer, Billy B." He acknowledge the man he called Billy B. "We don't have a choice, right?"

He turned back to R. Paul. "The shit is, if we don't' do what they tell us, they'll have somebody out there ready and willing to do it for us."

The two men talked, alleging some mean-spirited system they were a part of. They agreed they would have to do something about that.

In another moment they were questioning what exactly they could do and who would lead at their level.

"You do," Eduardo Sosa demanded of the older R. Paul.

"No. You the man," R. Paul responded. "All I know, we can't show up here every day being witness to them taking away people's money by force. Well, not quite force, but we have to start!"

Shortly thereafter the assignment ended with a security guard passing by the two men, his eyes never failed to secure his gun.

Eduardo Sosa's eyes were on R. Paul, meanwhile. "They carried that thing like my mother," he said.

R. Paul looked at him for clarity.

"She use-to carry a long stick, Bro!"

****$$****

Our next assignment was quick to come, and though the last one was short, the speed of this one caused another uproar among the students. Some complaint we were getting too much work, too fast for only a four credit class. Others said the stuff we were studying had no value in the real world. To these types of concerns, Dr. Erskine wrote back and said we could drop the class anytime if we wanted. A "W" was no longer an option, however.

That made clear, no student dropped the class.

The new assignment was in queue, and I set my goal on maximizing my information intake for the time investment.

Class was in the room I had viewed before, a different layout, but most of the same students and the same instructor. He had put on some muscles, looked better groomed, and talked with an occasional pause as if he had to review what he was saying before his ideas made their way to sound. He was in center of the room. A sign reading "Corporate Training" hanged from the ceiling to the area he stood.

"This time it will be different," the instructor said. It was about making connections, and that was what the exposed page of his flip-chart referenced.

After awhile of lecture the instructor asked a young, very attractive female student to the front of the class.

"You're Number One, Jesse," he said to the fine lady, who came across in dress more like a model that a teller.

The instructor then searched around for another student, which turned out to be Shawty, who at the time looked like he was admiring his khaki pants. His white shirt, like the pants, were with sharp pleats, and the pockets on both left and right breast gave fitting insight into his perception of himself.

"You Number Two," the teacher said to Shawty as he looked to a smiling Jesse.

"You really want to be liked by her," he tells Shawty. "OK?"

A burley male student in class asked loudly. "Who wouldn't?" That brought laughter and giggling to the room.

The teacher asked for and got the laughing, giggling crowd's attention.

"Wouldn't you say that she represents the kind of *ideal* all of us in society are looking for today," he asked.

The video rolled, scanning students in the class. There is a clear and obvious look of curiosity on the faces of the students. The teacher walked up to Jesse. He spoke in her ears.

"You're the essence of who we are. You must hate his guts," OK."

The instructor then addressed the class. "Listen to this," he instructed as he pointed to the individual to whom he was making reference, "You all make Shawty here know that Jesse, here is *really* attractive, pretty, OK!"

Again, the video momentarily moved to the other students in class. They still appeared with a high sense of inquisitive interest on their faces.

The video rolled. The instructor spoke into Jesse's ears again. "You're to reject him as brutally as you can–you have what he doesn't! You're not to empathize or sympathize. Got it?"

"Shawty, you come here." The teacher followed up with him in his ears. "You go man. Take on the world! She likes you. She really likes you!"

In due time, Shawty would be rejected and insulted by the young lady he was trying to charm.

The video rolled.

The class looked to the instructor. The students needed guidance.

"Class," the instructor concluded. "That was your experiment! The point is this: this young man here has got to work harder and that's the message we're hoping to get to you. We all have to do better every day we answer to our company's call to duty. Those people out there are out to get us; it's your job, my job, our job, all of our jobs to understand this simple reality. We're paid to provide a service; not to give away the bank! You've got to put your foot on the enemy until the enemy knows it's your foot!"

Years earlier, I was diagnosed with a sleeping disorder problem, and I inadvertently fell into a snooze. When I awoke two or three minutes later, the Instructor was outside the classroom waving to some of his students.

"Have a nice day," he said.

****$$****

Speaking of "a nice day," Grandma dreamt of having one of those again, and in the new day she found herself with such an opportunity.

April 1, was one of those days that changed everything; it was the day Grandma first put eyes on Billy, her so-called helper.

Since we got to know of him we called him Mr. Billy, but he preferred simply, Billy, even Bill worked at times when he got alert enough to know what his rewards were.

Grandma remembered him as looking "excited and interested."

Billy walked out of the Upper Creek Branch as Grandma waited her turn to use the ATM machine, a customer ahead of her, and a couple behind her. He tilted his shades and snapped a shot above them. He liked what he saw. Grandma returned his stare. She recorded his every move as he proceeds in her direction in the parking lot. Reportedly, he was moving with the energy of a young man; not someone his age.

Then it was Grandma's turn; she put her information into the ATM when her phone rings. It was Mom, still on her cruise. A security guard came from around the corner. He took a close look at Grandma and the other people at the ATM.

****$$****

Grandma said Mom described their trip as "just fabulous" and promised that everybody's souvenirs would be coming soon. Grandma was never much into such things and turned the conversation into asking Mom when she was going to pay her back money Mom owed her for a long time.

Grandma said Mom tried to avoid the question as if her "money didn't have *significance*" and preferred to ask her if she had gotten her banking problems all cleared up.

Grandma said she was in a good mood, all things considered, so she played along.

"At the bank as we speak," Grandma answered. "Don't want anything else to happen!"

"Hope not."

Grandma looked around again. Billy was still positioned in her direction gathering his load. He lifted his chest. He gave the hint of a smile. Grandma told Mom again about her letter writing project to the bank CEO, but Grandma puts it that Mom's tranquility was so high all Mom answered was, "Just calling to see how things going, Mother."

Grandma looked at her account balance on the ATM console and her face changed. She looked around, but Billy was long gone.

"They'll never steal from me again, Gloria," she stormed.

The couple behind Grandma looked concerned.

That's the point Mom picked up on the conversation. She told Grandma not to let *those people* bother her.

"Grace told me what Dr. Rostein said about your mind," Mom said to Grandma.

Mom recalled Grandma's saying, "Dear!"

Grandma said she took her money from the ATM, put away the phone and turned. She stepped off the curb and walked towards her car, finding herself in her head and at the bank parking lot—two places at one time—simultaneously dealing with the same problem.

The head experience was from her recent conversation with Miss Bridgett when Miss Bridgett told her that people shouldn't be messing with her.

"Miss Muley," Miss Bridgett asked, "How many people are there your age still working to make their living like you?"

Grandma's answer was a mere laugh.

Miss Bridgett continued. "Not those ones at Shines, and I agree with you. You keep kicking, Girl!"

As Grandma turned from the ATM, and the memories with Miss Bridgett kept coming back, she held her head up high with a gradual brighter look covering her face. "They're not going to mess with me anymore," she said loud.

Grandma looked around to see in the distance the security guard. He was still staring at the people in the parking lot. She thought momentarily, "I'm talking out to myself like a crazy woman. 'I'll work on them until they're put down!'" The people at the ATM looked at Grandma strangely.

Memories of her encounter with Miss Bridgett would persist, even as she dealt with the moment.

"You watch your penny like a hawk, Bridgett," Grandma had told the younger woman. "I should be the one watching every cent now."

Grandma looked back one more time. The security guard was shifting his head to get an even better assessment of whatever he suspected her to be doing.

She said she thought the guard was loony, even trigger-ready, but he was not what was dominating her world. It was the idea of her own money and the experiences and conversations that had brought her to this point.

Miss Bridgett remarked Grandma should be focusing on her every cent, because Grandma didn't have youth on her side, as Ms. Bridget chose to word it.

Grandma recalled telling her that nobody was going to destroy her life, and Miss Bridgett pointed to her six-sense, her knowing *that* would never happen. Her image of Grandma was too much of a soldier in her own right, one who would fight to her death.

"I know you for how long, Ms. Muley," she said. "But remember now, you're dealing with bullies."

The memories details were so vivid when the ladies related them to me, they ended up playing as if for my own eyes and ears.

Grandma said she was a bit weary and getting a headache by this time, but remembered her response was that she paid her taxes. "I carry my own," she said.

Grandma said that was one part she thought Miss Bridgett was nasty with: a, "So?"

"It's my earnings Bridgett," Grandma, replied. "This, Dear, is a free country."

Grandma noted Miss Bridgett saying, "OK."

Grandma turned the key in the ignition and departed the bank parking lot. "OK," she spoke to herself.

****$$****

It became apparent to Grace and me that something unusual was going on with Grandma, and we agreed to secretly monitor her behavior. With my schoolwork, however, so much could be said for how much I could do immediately. I was off almost instantly to my next assignment.

In this one, a guard was coming around the corner at Upper Creek branch when an armored truck approached. The Armored Guard took a bag with him and walked into the bank chatting with the clerks in the main area. The events moved quickly. In the vault Eduardo Sosa And R. Paul were working, using laptops in their work. Eduardo Sosa flipped to his own account with the bank and sees that his account was overdrawn.

Even his ATM withdrawals were stacked up over time, resulting in a number of bounced checks, he tells R. Paul.

"Shoot! You're always doing it to others! Your turn now, Amigo," R. Paul answered.

Eduardo Sosa rolled his eyes as R. Paul shared his feelings. "It's a bitch how we're 'f'ing and 'dicing' up the customer these days," he said. He questioned how they came up with the plan to pay the smallest first. The two men questioned which of them should be the last to be angry on the issue. R. Paul reminded Eduardo Sosa of their plan to do "something."

He continued. "There's no way to stop the momentum that's started."

The armored guard entered the vault and asked the two if they were ready. He referred to them as "Budds." Outside, two vehicles drove very close to the armored truck having the lone driver constantly looking through her rearview and then her side-view mirrors, monitoring the activities around her.

"I was just telling your friend here, he loves the system so much that when it screws him, all I can do is laugh," R. Paul tells the guard, as he pointed at Eduardo Sosa who looked infuriated.

The armored guard laughed out loud. "Hard to put eyes on moving objects, ha?"

R. Paul said, "I'm trying to figure out why it is when they rob him, he gets so uptight?"

"The goddamn bitches. That's it! They bounced the max, Cuz" Eduardo Sosa said.

R. Paul responded, "No shit."

Outside the bank the lone armored guard in the truck was now doing her checks faster and in a staccato-like way.

"The suckers got paid but they didn't pay my baby sister's immigration processing fee," Eduardo Sosa tells R. Paul and the armored guard, inside the vault. He concluded, "That's fuck!"

The armored guard butted in: "Listen to him there, Ron. Remember when you were telling him they changed the online statement to create confusion? Remember how he was indifferent? If… "

"Yeap. R. Paul replied. "We've got to think how a thing is bothering another person, not just ourselves. Don't we?"

****$$****

At this point, the sound on the recording got a bit unclear, but the picture kept good and steady. The armored guard began handing the bag to Eduardo Sosa. What he said sounded like, "C'omon, Wardo."

Eduardo Sosa's response sounded like "c'mon?"

R. Paul's response in the audio was improved. "We've got to start putting the right label on the bandits," he said. "And we'll need to get *that group* going."

Outside, the lone armored guard looked both intense and impatient. She glanced at her watch. She shook her head. She looked back and forth into her mirrors again and again as a third vehicle made its way closer to her truck.

"He used to enjoy taking other people's greenbacks," R. Paul tells the armored guard in the vault, as he pivoted away from Eduardo Sosa. "Not because he's the one in the oven now, he's got to look so pitiful, right?"

Eduardo Sosa said the bank's bouncing of his checks and taking of his money should be illegal, and while he and R. Paul tried to understand the bank's stacking up of accounts that paid the biggest withdrawals first, resulting in the bouncing of Eduardo Sosa's smaller charges, the armored guard continued standing with the bag in his hand. No one had taken it yet. He looked like a football player holding his helmet.

"Hay, you guys work it out. Work it out and let me know how it goes," the armored guard inputted.

I wanted to go for a leak, but the assignment was too interesting for me to step away from it.

The armored guard in the truck was now holding her gun in plain sight. She kept moving around her body frequently to try and keep abreast of the goings on in the three different vehicles that had surrounded her.

****$$****

"How many times you've seen me trying to let him see this?" R. Paul asked of the armored guard, on whose shoulder he had placed his hand for solidarity.

The armored guard shook his head two more times in a way I usually do when I can't believe something that eventually actually turns out a truth, or at least something that should have been easy for me to remember, yet hard. He addressed Eduardo Sosa. "They got your dick tied to the post, Brother man, and it's tied tight."

"They should tie yours," joked Eduardo Sosa, who had placed his attention back to looking at his account on the computer screen.

The armored guard laughed out again. "They haven't grown the twine long or strong enough for this one," he asserted.

With that, Eduardo Sosa threw his computer to the ground. He gave in to an over-pressuring of his valve. "Pricks." He didn't get what he wanted, nor a dollar left in his account.

Outside, two of the men did a hand signal to each other and then both began getting out of their cars. They would start towards the armored truck and bank entrance.

"Work it out," the armored guard inside the vault said to R. Paul and Eduardo Sosa as he received a now heavy looking money bag back from Sosa. He began heading out, towards the main banking area.

Inside the vault Eduardo Sosa reminded R. Paul he needed his help.

"Seriously!" His sister's docs, he reiterated. "She's young-pretty, and has her future ahead of her."

"Why haven't you helped all the old and poor folks who ask you to help them," R. Paul asked, his voice clearly on the side of those he thought of as the bank's other victims.

"Hand wash hand," Eduardo Sosa countered, a senseless grin included. "Cancel the charges!"

Simultaneously the armored guard waved goodbye to a teller in the main area and headed towards the exit.

"You know we shouldn't do that," R. Paul said to Eduardo Sosa as he began walking out the vault.

Eduardo Sosa responded. "You know what they did isn't right. We work here, Bro."

Momentarily, the armored guard with the money bag exited the bank. The two men, now with drawn guns appeared in front of him. Several rounds of gunshots were heard. The recording ended.

# CHAPTER 14

Mom and Dad had some personal knowledge (thought conflicting) about the bank incident. They were back in town and were in the area that day and happened to be crossing path with the players when the shots rang out. They said it was three. A police report documented two, both lethal.

Referring to the deaths, Mom told Grandma," They don't care who you are," and then Miss Bridgett, Grace and I heard about the adventure she and Dad had been on.

Grandma did not participate much as she was not interested. Her excuse was that she was swamp, filling orders and responding to her customer's query. As she got the work done, she warned us thought, not because there were many orders, things were good. In actuality, she noted, things were worse at times, many orders were so small in value, she was losing money on a high percentage of them.

By the time Grandma did start talking, she looked very weary from her work, and the conversation was not about what she insisted was our parents' "gallivanting" around the world.

"It's my fourteenth letter and counting," she said when the conversation was flowing. "They'll respond. That's moral!"

Mom mumbled out a piece about how decency flew out the door after Grandma was born, and how it didn't matter whether Grandma had sent her letters overnight, signature confirmed, or with the

CEO's name written in bold red type. Mom called it a waste of time and a waste of the "God-given little" Grandma had.

As this was taking place, it happened Miss Bridgett lost her bearing and said something Grandma had sworn us to secrecy on. She announced that Grandma was even going to the banks downtown on Kale Street, when she realized herself. She shouldn't have spoken this in front of Mom. She placed her hand at her mouth, but by that time Mom was already asking Grandma, "Why, Mom?"

"Maybe I'm just called," Grandma responded in a sudden, but calm, controlled delivery.

That ended in a series of back and forth, with Mom telling Grandma that not even John Paul, the Pope was made sainthood.

"Neither are you," Grandma, replied. "Calling me stupid?"

I looked at Mom and wondered if her coming back from their trip was worth it. When she and dad were gone the energy was different—mostly better, I noted. Now, again, the two were *at it* as if Grace, me, or Miss Bridgett were not there. But we were witnesses! Don't count Dad. He barely cared.

Mom demanded, "Drop it, You!"

Grandma look at Grace and me as if she was saying, are you learning anything about how your mother is treating her mother? She didn't say these words, but I was right a lot of time in reading her face and movements, and this time I knew that I knew what was happening with her.

Grandma reverted to her shallow thoughts. She asked Mom, "So I end up at Shines?"

Mom located Miss Bridgett. "She's going off on us," Mom complained.

Grandma glanced at Mom slightly askance. Who was going to take care of Grandma when Mom was always broke?

Mom said she was more interested in Grandma's present condition, keeping her house, keeping her health, and things of that sort. She spoke briskly. "That's low."

"Have you ever been to Shines," Grandma replied.

Mom did not answer, and it appeared she was afraid to come up with one, for which Grandma waited and waited.

"Well, I've been there. Not once, either. A thousand times," Grandma continued.

She explained it was never the outcome she thought should be of older people, people who had worked so hard and for so long, and now this.

"I'm not selling no art. I'm not selling no art," Ms. Diaz was repeating in Grandma's head.

Ms. Wonzick lifted her head from one of her drowsy moments. "How many times we've told you, you're good at painting. You don't have to be here, Patrice."

Grandma looked at Mom sternly. "The last time I was there, one of the ladies, Ms. Diaz was yelling, 'Thieves. Thieves.' Her dentures fall to the ground. But she didn't let that slow her for a moment. She went, 'Take car, take house. Take car, take house.' Those are God's people over there, Gloria. But I'm not going to be a part of that!"

****$$****

In that moment, memories and the moment were again taking the front and center as one for Grandma.

She said Ms. Wonzick was back shaking her head in "her jerky old way" as if to give herself a new head or at least some clarity in the old, spent one she had. She beamed at Grandma—Glued her eyes on to Grandma, that, is.

"My Benjamin says it's that criminal corporate culture, Ms. Muley. "Them damn thieves. Those ones," she pointed out.

Momentarily, she swung her head wildly. "Go get conscious," she squealed.

I shook my head.

There was a voice coming from one of the other ladies in the room saying, "You always say that, Mom Wonzick! You always say that!"

Grandma was holding her I-phone in one hand looking as if she was going to call someone, but gave her attention to the people in the room.

"As you all know I'm having problems with them myself. Still, we have the best system in the world, Ladies."

By this time Ms. Wonzick's head was right where she wanted it to be, or so it seemed. She was staring straight ahead. She now looked very alert, never mind her body playing like piano keys springing back from each pronged.

"My Benjamin say, when you get rid of the loan shark you get right into the mouth of the shark," she offered to the room of people who responded as if genius was in their presence.

Momentarily, the voice that had come from nowhere on a recent visit by Grandma, reappeared.

"Good golly! Good old golly!"

****$$****

"It's about greed," Ms. Wonzick declared as she goes over to Grandma. "Sandy, Love, it's not our age that's the problem; it's how they *weakened* the calcium out of all our bones. They got us *'non-players',* Love. Only if we could get anew!"

The other women looked at this in bemusement, some bobbling their heads; their wherewithal dancing. Everybody and everything were in agreement in that moment, whether they understood or not.

Grandma told Ms. Wonzick that what she had just said was "deep and profound," prompting more action in the room.

"Baby," Ms. Wonzick said, catching on to Grandma's hand.

"Remember this if nothing you remember, when you're dealing with shark OK, remember I'd tell you, you have to have a wire between, because it will cut your string! It'll cut your string, Love!"

Some of the other women burst into a laughter, but for Grandma there was nothing more, nothing less than the look of "wow!"

"Oh sweet Jesus. Remember," Ms. Wonzick besieged.

Grandma said she would, and then placed her hands on her head. "Everything you've ever told me is all packed... *right in here*," Grandma claimed.

Ms. Wonzick, behaving modest as Grandma thought she was, acted as if she had not heard a word of complement. She positioned her laser eyes on Grandma's I-phone.

"You see that computa you have there, Love," she said. "My Benjamin has one like you. He said it's the best thing he ever spent money on!"

Grandma replied, first with a smile. "I thought it was his house on the hill."

# CHAPTER 15

When Grandma returned, the discussion had shifted, with most of us in our cubby holes in the Library. Mom's spot was in front of the extra desktop, Miss Bridgett was in Grandma's lazy boy, I was sitting on the floor with my legs stooped into my chest as I listened. And Grace? She was sprawled in front of the Toshiba with Dad, whose only curiosity in life now seemed to be Mars.

Just a moment earlier Grace was moving around the room making sure we all kept refreshed with Coke and water; cranberry juice for Miss Bridgett who said that made her inside feel like new every time she had a half glass or more.

"The only person down there interested in your Mom is an old shrivel playboy," Miss Bridgett said in a voice that was not as loud or as bold as she usually talked. "What's his name, Grann? Grann, what's the curious lover's name," she said.

"I wish he was, indeed, interested... *in helping*," Grandma replied. He's nothing but an old bucket. Don't have authority to do a thing!"

Grandma placed her hand on her head and rubbed it. My mind queried if the act was because of a new headache or she was just trying to brush off the "old man" as insignificant.

Miss Bridgett who had called herself devil's advocate on numerous occasions, including this one, started the wiggling of her finger.

"You're the one who said he was cute," she said.

"No, I said handsome," Grandma replied. "And what does that have to do with my money?"

Miss Bridgett played with the words handsome and cute saying they were the same, as she looked at Mom.

"Your mother's got a gentleman."

This made Grandma laugh out in a way I hadn't heard from her in a long time. Whatever strain was on her face disappeared for at least a second. A second. And then she was back.

"At our age, Baby Girl we can't do anything anyways," she said.

"Talk for yourself," Mom engaged. "That's what happens when your man's been gone for so long. Four? Five years?

Grandma told Mom she had more Alzheimer than Grandma thought, reminding Mom it actually was going on a decade Grandpa John had left us.

Not liking to be corrected, Mom switched the subject as quickly as she could, and told Grandma that she didn't need to be working that hard.

Grandma came back saying that even a lazy, homeless person in New York worked harder than Mom.

"Well," Mom followed through. "If this is your way of not going to Shines!"

Grandma waved us out as she had gotten to love doing when she felt we were too young for what was happening with her.

She looked at Mom. "You've got my mullah yet?"

****$$****

Money seemed as important an issue at Bank $$ as I viewed my next assignment. It started with a conference room discussion. A reporter with his crew pointed his mike at one of a group of bank executives, asking the executive how he thought a stockholders' quarterly conference call with Corporate was coming along. The executive leaned over and asked the reporter to wait, as she wanted to listen in on another question that had just come in to Corporate, who began to answer it.

"Yes, we're makers, not takers," Corporate remarked to the caller's question. "And you're right—both revenues and stocks are up. I can tell you though, our projections and targets are viable. But, there's always avenue for growth, and we see that into the next four, plus quarters."

"What sectors do you see the biggest growth," the caller's voice came back crisp over the conferencing system.

"Sir, our business is dynamic; never seen it this good. Lots of greenbacks, jacks, cabbage, if you will. Lots to be made—opportunities in all sectors!"

Next, a foreign voice came over the communication system. A video connection was established with the caller.

"Any plans for expansion," the permed hair caller asked.

Corporate said they had a plan on the table for a new corporate center in Los Angeles. He said they were pulling together architects and engineers as he spoke; their "goal to build the tallest building in The City of Angeles," he said.

That was that because there was some defect in the video, and I had to go to another.

****$$****

In the new one, the bank employees were at their company's check processing center, processing away the day's transactions. It was just after midnight as indicated by a number of clocks on the wall. As the video rolled it came to an older and more mature looking Shawty in his work area with his supervisor beside him.

"This one's got megabucks, but he's idiot too, Boss," Shawty tells his Supervisor as he pointed to some of the items he was processing.

The Supervisor shook his head in agreement and read aloud the transactions were for $250,000, and $85,550, respectively. He noted that the night earlier the account holder's balance was over $3 million, and he was now bouncing his check. The Supervisor raised his head up, and then it went down. It went up and down a couple more cycles, and there appeared a look on his face like what is common when people are green-eyed of those more successful than themselves.

"Hell, yes! An idiot too. I would like to have the kind of money he's throwing around, but idiot too!"

Shawty placed a look on his face that made him look like he understood.

"I could get a car like yours, even a house. Who knows?"

The supervisors shook his head. He agreed.

Shawty continued. "How's the boat?"

Hay. Hay. You saw the pictures? My ride. My float ha?" "That's not just a ride, Sir. That's a cruiser," Shawty said as he tussled with another customer's transactions.

The Supervisor peeped over. "My favorite customer," he said, dragging out each word. "The 5, $10, $2" lady."

Shawty joked that over time those were the kind that had become his *favorite* too.

The supervisor pointed to his computer screen. "These people think we have time to mess with their two and three hundred dollar E-commerce ACH," he uttered. He made open and close quotes with his hand as he said the word "e-commerce."

"Hay. I'll just leave that for tomorrow."

"I'm glad you heard what the succession plan is" the supervisor replied. "In two months *you'll have it!* That's going to push me out of a job, but…"

Shawty clipped his boss' talk. "Manager Level I, ha?"

The Supervisor reminded Shawty in a teasing tone how a year earlier he was "freaking out" on the job. "You remember you back then going bonkers?" The Supervisor illustrated: "'Something's not right, boss. Something not right.' And then you would pull out your crazy calculator and shout, 'If we pay out all the puny ones first the customer will not punk out!' Remember that? Remember that? Huh? Remember Loony you?"

Shawty placed a grin on his face, the childish kind you bring to your face when another person catches you masturbating. You have nothing rational to say. You just look at them. *Well?*

He shook his head. "I have one principle in life now," he said: "Live and learn."

The Supervisor went speechless as he gave his full attention to Shawty. His head seemed to say what he was thinking better than he could with his words. He was contented.

"Of course, I see the stupidity now," Shawty, said. "And more so, it's illegal. It was right there…in his e-mail!"

Week after week, Corporate had sent e-mails and other communication instructing the management and staff on policy: customers were to be watched for their abuse of banking privilege, OD accounts were to be sent immediately to the banking credit agency for credit downgrade, and customers' accounts were to be reviewed on an ongoing basis for opportunities.

The supervisor plugged in, "Just finished reading yesterday's e-mail!"

"They write bad checks. They *pay* for bad checks," Shawty offered.

The supervisor was quick with his approval. "My boy. My boy. You read! Good man!"

"High school dropout makes big," Shawty responded as his shoulders straightened and chest got buff, and then… "How about a sign that reads, 'No Floating Here'?"

The Supervisor liked that. He again used his head to indicate he was onboard. "How about no flying blanks at Shawty?"

The two men giggled as Shawty moved back to a past assessment of his, "Idiots!"

When he was composed again, the supervisor talked about a recent communication from Corporate. "People *out there* were trying to demonize the bank," he recalled. Because the bank was prosperous, there were those who felt the bank owed them something.

"We have some of the most evilest people we call customers," he said. "Too many fricking takers!"

Shawty spoke. "Not bright, I might add."

The supervisor proceeded to tell Shawty that if he were to "stick it to them," he would never have to find another job in his life again.

Shawty leaned forward and typed some information into his computer as the supervisor pointed to the papers Shawty was working with.

"I now know what I must do for my accounts, Shawty said. "Boss! What grade you give me?"

"Well. Fireworks! It's like having *four Starbucks* yesterday. *That, My Boy*, is 35 times four, plus-plus-plus! She's got a few bucks today but more fireworks. You're right. They're lots of fools in this world. Real, bloody fools!"

****$$****

At 1226 Jack Street, Grandma had thrown in the towel on a promise to us, and that worried me. She had previously told us she would stop worrying about life and just live it to the best of her potential, but when I saw her looking bothered at one of her desktops, I knew she had reverted to her tension-ridden self. What was she up to? I knew it wasn't about her customers. She thought of them as the best in the world. Her sales? No. She was working on that.

Grace passed by and noted her act as I was doing, but Grace elected to ignore what she saw: Grandma again reviewing her account.

"Why is it saying, processing… processing… processing," Grandma asked out loud.

"Are you OK, Grandma," I asked; Grace had reached the dining room on her way to answering a ringing of the doorbell.

"God knows it's not Me to be bothered with this kind of worthless, senseless thing," Grandma said, her tone indicating her disappointment.

"They took more of my money, and why don't they just cash these ones?" She looked at me. She paused. She dropped her eyes. "Soldiers?"

Perhaps I wasn't the one she should have asked. I at the time had no clue, no answer, and I was not in any mood to make up something either.

That, however, was not the case with Grace. She shouted from the living room that the bank didn't like Grandma. "They don't," she stressed.

To this, I did not offer an opinion. I merely listened. Listening and watching are important tools for every living being, Grandma was accustomed to telling us.

She continued.

It was already Tuesday and the bank had not completed the processing of her transactions from the prior Friday. There was an entire page red, making her angry and hot. She said, it looked to her "like a hundred items saying, 'processing.'"

"Lord," Grandma said. Her word didn't come as a statement but rather, a question nevertheless emphatically asked.

****$$****

Momentarily, Mom entered the Library.

"You're, not the bank," Mom blurted out. She did not even say hiya or good afternoon as she normally would. She went straight at Grandma's business.

"I have here sixteen items they haven't processed so far," Grandma responded. She concurrently inputted something into her desk calculator. She whispered sweetly, "Sixteen."

If I wasn't interested in our family's story, I would have left then, but from the time I was tiny, I remembered everybody saying to me that I was not on this earth for nothing. My mind went fast—perhaps it was to learn as much as possible about my family and then tell what I learned.

I stayed.

Mom continued to bicker with Grandma; Grace was going "Granny, Granny" in her singing way, and when Mom saw she was not going to get her way this time, she slammed back, "Mother!"

There was no response.

Mom!"

I asked Mom why she was always bothering Grandma, but in the perplexity of the moment I don't believe the question even showed up on her radar. It was Grandma's time to twinkle, and she would do her best to get us to take a view of her star—her compulsion, that is.

"Look here! $2, $10, $12! For goodness sake, $4.29?

"Why pending," I asked.

Grandma answered. "They're just holding them to wipe me out again!"

Mom advised Grandma to make sure there was enough cash in her account and everything would be quite fine, she reasoned.

Grace turned her focus towards Grandma and then to the rest of us. Her eyes were deep—piercing, actually.

"Something's going to happen!" She said this and then began to head out. "I don't feel good. I'm going!"

Grandma stood there as we watched her fiddling with her bookstore selling account. I knew her revenues weren't where she expected or needed them to be. She had voiced that a score, plus ten times over the past month. The average sale was as small as most of the items she was now calling 'pending,' for her bank to cash.

She stomped her feet as she spoke. "Small!"

# CHAPTER 16

Outside a restaurant, June 13, Mom talked with Miss Bridgett about an elaborate getaway they had put together for Grandma to relieve her stress and get their help to re-organize her life and finances. Mom felt that in spite of Grandma's having the reverse mortgage she was in jeopardy of a grave financial meltdown. Mom reported they spent the first night wining and dining at the Fontainebleau in Miami, paid for thanks to a $500 gift certificate she had won on her recent cruise.

The next day they traveled up the coast to Daytona Beach where they went to a wild-animal show and saw a man put his head inside the mouth of an alligator, the man talking while having his head between the alligator's jaws.

"In a heartbeat, let's make that less, in a nano-heartbeat it can take my neck," the man tells the worried looking spectators.

The alligator eyed the crowd of onlookers; It rolled its round, shiny eyes. The alligator moved a bit. The man's muscle tensed. He held stronger onto something under the alligator's neck. The alligator's teeth dripped some saliva on to the man hair and head.

Reportedly, the man's head was spared and the show likely saw another day.

For Grandma, Mom and Miss Bridgett, things went on, as well. Their trip was completed with a nice meal at another fancy restaurant Mom promised she would take Grace and me someday—

sometime when she had the money. She claimed the entertainment was the best, and though she would ordinarily run around the house turning down our loud music, she described the sounds at that joint as “the bomb:” loud and wild.

The word out of there was they could barely hear what they were saying to each other as the shirtless Latin men and a tall sexy woman, lead singer who Mom said had the face and moves of Amy Winehouse entertained the house.

The main reason Mom said she would take us there was not the music though. A long period later she said her nose still relished the smell of the rice and peas they cooked there, with coconut cream. And the steak, she kept calling that more tender than ground beef. The food was what she wanted us to experience.

“One little slowdown,” Mom noted, however. Grandma was frequently dragging and threw tantrums when Mom and Miss Bridgett elected to take a break from talking about Grandma's banking situation. After every so many steps, Grandma needed a break, to which Mom ascribed it was due to Grandma's age.

“Your Grandma's running old and tired now,” she warned.

At the end of saying that, she added the word “period,” and it was from her I picked up the habit of liking to say that word sometimes.

“Look at her,” Mom said as she pulled out a picture Miss Bridgett had taken with her Sony digital. “Look at how drain Granny looks these day,” Mom said.

She expounded on their experience: When she and Miss Bridgett announced to Grandma that it was not just Grandma's birthday they were hoping to celebrate, but also to help Grandma get back on track, things began to go downhill.

Grandma's reaction was that nobody stops her birthday. She took cheers with them and then galloped almost half a bottle of red wine.

That made Mom and Miss Bridgett a bit concerned, and they walked away to go and talk about it.

The trip outside took them by a bathroom where people were waiting in line, as many of the youngsters, “too-impatient-to-get-back-to-action ones” danced with each other.

****$$****

Mom said she and Miss Bridgett were outside discussing what

they could do to help Grandma while Grandma, inside, was trying to work out other matters. The two shared their thoughts as to why Grandma was still concerning herself with the bank, why she was drinking so much liquor of late, and all the other strange behaviors that were going on with Grandma, when they said a short, sturdy man in business suit walking fast out of the restaurant jumped into a car with a woman that pulled up for him.

"Hurry, hurry. Why so fast," Mom said as the car sped off.

Mom shook her head to the activities as she made headway with a secret personal hope of keeping Ms. Bridgett as far away as possible from helping Grandma.

Ms. Bridgett spoke. "Why is she still refusing to accept her Social Security is a question not for you or me. That's where Heaven comes in!"

"She's just got to eat her peas and stop $ Mortgage from foreclosing on her," Mom replied.

She continued, "I probably never told you. She's stayed with her own insurance—refused Medicare!"

Miss Bridgett looked surprised but held on to her words when Mom mentioned mortgage as Mom had told her years earlier that Grandma had long burned her mortgage.

"I told her not to do the reverse mortgage, Bridgett," Mom clarified. "It all dumped into the stupid business."

"It doesn't work that way," Miss Bridgett offered, to which Mom just stared at her.

"It's her life, nevertheless," Miss Bridgett continued. "No matter what, you still have to help her!"

****$$****

Mom said it was when she and Miss Bridgett were heading back to the table that they saw a crowd around Grandma.

They began to move faster to find out what was going on, she said, and from a distance they could see additional bottles of liquor were on the table. As they got closer they saw Grandma talking with the people. She galloped more from a bottle.

"You sure you're OK," a man with tie that looked like a boss man or owner, asked.

Mom rushed to hug Grandma. "What's going on? What the hell is going on," she asked as a couple kids did their best to confer their view of what had happened, to Miss Bridgett.

"He tried to steal her purse," one of the kids exclaimed.

"Who, who," Miss Bridgett asked as a lanky still shaking young boy with military birth control glasses provided more meat.

"He was under her table. And he was a really, really mean one," the lanky still shaking young boy said.

****$$****

Moving ahead, the man in necktie explained to Mom that someone, another customer called Shawty by one of the other restaurant clients, had gone under Grandma's table and was running away with Grandma's purse. The man in necktie turned on the ball of his foot, a near army-perfect right turn, and illustrated with gestures. "She grabbed it away from him and lashed him across the face with it," he continued. "You should have seen the fool." the manager-looking man said. "He ran out of here—a frightened dog with tail stuck!"

"Let's get out of here," Miss Bridgett said to Grandma.

"It's my birthday and I'm here celebrating it, even if by myself," Grandma said.

****$$****

Grandma insisted the party would go on, and it did. One of the shirtless men sang happy birthday to her, a cake with candles was brought to the table, and Miss Bridgett teased Grandma that the old man, Billy, at the bank was indeed her man-friend. Things eventually pointed upwards, and Grandma was allowed one more snippet of vodka.

"Happy Birthday" was designed in chocolate on the cake the young smart-looking Black waitress of about eighteen took to Grandma as she placed the check on the table. Her uniform was built with a large flower resting contentedly on her butt.

"My name is Sheniqua, Niqua for short," the young lady said to Grandma's asking, as Grandma placed her hand on the check and drew it to her. The company's name on the paper partially showed; it was "Jimmy's Hot S…."

"Not this time," Miss Bridgett said, trying to take the check from a playful Grandma. "It's my turn."

Mom moved her hand. It was "no, no." She was going to pay this time. She was looking at Miss Bridgett and her hand was now pushed out for the check. Miss Bridgett's also was pushed out, and she was telling Grandma, she would do it.

Mom looked at Grandma with an unsettled face.

Grandma told Mom what she could do, and that was to help her. Mom had done nothing worthwhile, only reminding her that she had financial problems, she said.

"Don't forget your bad checks," Mom said.

The waitress looked at Grandma who was exhibiting signs of intoxication as Grandma struggled with the two younger women and fumbled into her checkbook for clarity on where her numbers were.

"I'm better than good, better than most," Grandma announced on looking up to the waitress, her eyes telling a different story. "You're a nice young lady. You going to school, Dear?"

Mom looked at Miss Bridgett questioning if they should just drag Grandma out of the place and put her to sleep, but the young lady was nothing less than congenial, and did not appear affected by the women's antics.

"Yes, Ma'am," the young lady answered.

"And what are you studying," Grandma asked.

Niqua, the young lady told her it was political science, and to that she added law, which seemed to ring a bell for Grandma. She asked the young lady who were the Congress representatives for the area, and Miss Bridgett cautioned the young lady not to get it wrong. Grandma kept up on this sort of thing. To say the least, Civics was an important interest of hers.

"She's not going for Senators," Miss Bridgett warned the young lady, whose mouth was already forming the answer.

"How about Rep. Neal and Rep. Hahn," the young lady replied. And for senators, I give them even thought you didn't ask. She spoke immodestly. "Senators MacNarah and Reid."

Grandma shook her head. Her approval was as emphatic as the young lady's answers were right.

"You look like someone that will make something of yourself," Grandma said, and she began filling out the check.

On completion, she passed it to young lady.

"Something's in there for you, Dear," Grandma spoke, her manner proud. "Make *something good* of yourself!"

****$$****

Miss Bridgett gazed at Mom, visibly holding her words, and then she looked at Grandma.

"Remember you will need some when you go with him too," she said.

"What," Grandma reacted.

Miss Bridgett shook her head; a sly smile was on her face. "You know what. What's his name!"

Mom was known around the house to sometimes act like Grandma's parent, and not the other way around, and today she did. She looked at Grandma, her face heavy, disquiet.

"I hope he's helping balancing your checkbook," Mom said.

"I hope Bill's "fixing my banking problems," Grandma replied swiftly. "He promised he'll make me happy again!"

"As fast as that Billy moves…" Miss Bridgett began as she laughed out noisily. "I'm sure he would love to fix more than your broken bankbook."

"Didn't you tell me he can't even use the computer," Mom asked.

Miss Bridgett now looked and sounded as if serious. "You mean to say he does it all by hand?"

Grandma slapped Miss Bridgett's hand playfully. She replied she never looked. "But if that's how he does it," she continued. "He better do it fast!"

****$$****

All indications were that Grandma needed to have things done fast as she had fallen behind in many areas of her life, particularly her finance, and periodically, fulfilling her orders. That said, she was telling everyone she met at the supermarket, at Church, everywhere, about her problem with the bank, and had found a throve of sympathetic ears to her concerns and pain.

She, to some, however, still did not seem to be wrapping her arms around what was the real source of her problem and would at times find herself telling people, "oh no, it's just a bank mistake."

Miss Bridgett referred to that as *Grandma's big gaff.*

Grandma had sworn not once, not ten times, but more than that, that once she got to the right person, *they would fix their error*. She almost always added that to any conversations on the subject, and she believed it no less.

"Or maybe not," I argued with Grace. "I'm not sure they would."

"Sometimes Granny seemed fragile, sometimes she OK," Grace said.

****$$****

When she stepped out her car and headed to the door of the bank to meet Billy, we had questions about her again. Billy had once told her that he felt the banks, like the very one he was working for, was at the epicenter of the bad economy the country was facing. And he promised, there was something he should be able to do.

But, would he?

Grandma noted her banking problem quickly took the back seat. He and she walked back to the parking lot where he automatically let open the top of his Porsche as a security guard with his hand on his gun looked at them. Billy threw his briefcase into the rear seat of the car. He pressed another automatic button and music was on.

"This' a really fast one," he said.

"I like fast," Grandma said as she eyed a couple cameras he had left on the seat behind. She adding that even she got caught up in the moment. Her favorite singer, Benny Goodman was on. The car was magnificent.

"I like nice," Billy replied.

Grandma looked at the silver convertible imagining how many eons it must have taken Billy to possess it. "How long," she blurted out.

Billy placed his hand on his waist, his fingers reaching his thighs. "Here? At this location," he inquired?"

"Yeap."

"At least ten," he said, a smile on his face.

Grandma shook her head and projected her lips on a closed mouth.

Billy continued. "All said and done, thirty-eight when June comes around, but…"

****$$****

In time, Grandma would be standing in front of Billy, touching and admiring his plaything like a kid's first moments with Mickey and Minnie.

"A man and his pleasures," she said, her voice soft. "I like that!"

Billy did not go for the shy act Grandma would overtime say he put on when he was mischievous. He kept his eyes surveying both Grandma and his toy as if they were one and the same.

"Since I was a boy I wanted to have one…always wanted *one*," he said.

Grandma shook her head the way people do when they were falling asleep but needed to keep awake. It wasn't a nap she was in, however. She said it was that's her caused had flashed into her head again for the first time in hours.

"I don't like what's happening with my account," she said. "I'm considering Chase!"

Billy told Grandma that banking is not about society any longer. He explained: "It's about who can show the biggest growth. "Let me show you," he suggested.

Grandma's head and eyebrows moved upwards.

He continued, "To get, to make bigger. Expansion. Evolution. That's what it's all about!"

Grandma eventually looked at him from top to bottom and then back up, the relatively small man with clearly a strong, firm frame and strength.

"With all your experience you must know what you're saying," she replied.

Humor must have been in that one for Billy. He was giggling as she talked.

"Thirty what you said?"

"Long," Billy repeated to which Grandma started to cough. She had gotten choked and had to take a deep breath before she could speak again. "That's incredible," she said.

"Back when I started, we used to help people," Billy shared. "That's before profits became the only motive," Ms. Muley.

Grandma told him he sounded like some politicians, to which Billy laughed and responded in a way that belied his own words. "These Washington insiders are just trying to screw you, Madam. But, I'm not like that!"

Billy stepped forward a couple notches, his shoulders and rest of his body upright. He continued. "You know Ms. Muley, that's not right. They may have planted their flag, but there's a whole group of us inside that don't agree."

"Inside?"

"Yuuup! They have it coming you know. Right inside, Ms. Muley." Pissed off as hell and before long something will come out of this!"

Grandma began to bobble her head as her eyes went along for the ride. Going with that, they were looking glazed. "How many more years do I have to live?"

Billy moved forward another step and he was in her space.

He later shared with me that he wanted to say "forever," but Grandma's problems were too serious for a joke.

"Not everyone's a crooked, Ms. Muley, he said, trying to get her to trust him. "*That* you need to know!"

# CHAPTER 17

Dr. Erskine had told us if there was one thing we should never lose sight of, it was that wealth could grant us a great lifestyle, yet that lifestyle is the same that creates envy in those less lucky. Money, in other words, is a good thing, but it has its place, and it was our job to learn how to turn it a leverage and not a curse. She noted this in introducing our next assignment, which began with Corporate exiting his multi-million dollar home.

Grace, for some strange reason watched this segment with me, and asked me if the house was in England where "Her Majesty" lived and I chuckled. Two hundred plus bed rooms was a far cry from sixteen, but still quite remarkable.

She asked me who the man was coming out the house with cell phone at his ear, and I explained it was Corporate, the CEO of Bank $$—"A shrewd but smart fellow."

"A man like Dad," Grace said.

I elaborated: "The money version." They had said in one of our earlier assignments that Corporate's father was also in that same kind of job one time.

Grace listened attentively and then said he looked like a person who had nothing to worry about. To that, I consented. I generally felt that way.

"So, that's not Dad," I said, and I began to put my focus back on the work.

In the far distance, there were three people coming into the spotlight, and as they came closer, I told Grace who they were, from some of the prior videos I had looked at, I had them nailed. They were VP of Bank OPS, Bank CFO Fred Tolly and Miss Marketing, the lady that so boastfully wore the big, pretty hats.

When Corporate saw them he removed his cell phone from his ears and waved them in his direction. Here, the video moved from their faces and bodies; their feet were traversing the dollar-green lawn.

The recording momentarily shifted to Corporate who began talking fast on his cell phone but kept note of the trio moving towards him.

"Well thank you Senator," he said. I have to run, some other money business. Don't worry, we'll be sure we speed that to you, Senator. Right away!"

Corporate looked into the distance, but the focus was on his face that held a heavy bias for concern. He shook his head.

He continued. "Yes. Yes. We'll do whatever it takes to help; just cut the red tape and regs!"

The camera came even closer on his face. There was an added look: impatience. "Yes, if you don't waver," he answered to some question. "But you and the clan will have to get that Congress back in control. You hear?"

The trio continued their parade towards Corporate, traversing a circular area with a half-dozen picture-book cars: a Lamborghini, a DeLorean, and two Bentleys glittering. As they passed by, they gazed, the way an interested person takes in an attractive other. Miss Marketing got the attention of the others. She said to them that Corporate should be thankful and stop being on their assess.

The VP of Bank Ops acknowledged her, then shouted to Corporate, "Sweet!"

"Not hard at all," Corporate replied. "You have the same shot at it. Overnight!"

In conversation, Corporate exhorted his team to remember, "the law's on our side." The group laughed out as CFO, Tolly asked the other two if they remembered some e-mail from Corporate.

The three of them spoke, but in each of their own characteristic way: **"Every time *they* write a bad check, it's a crime!"**

****$$****

Meanwhile, Grandma and Billy were working on their thing.

"I don't think that was funny," she said to him as he navigated his long, skinny dinghy, "Billy The Boy" up the intercostals at a point where it narrowed and the sea bottom was visible, through water as clear as crystal, more than ten feet down.

"I can end their crime with a CU," Grandma said introspectively.

"Ms. Muley," Billy said. "They're better, but with their membership climbing to a hundred million?"

Grandma began gliding her hand up and down a pole they were using to control the boat.

"Never thought I would say it—by a long, very long shot," she said.

Billy noted that a lot of people at the bank thought Uncle Sam's stimulus to the banks would fix the economy. He told her he was on a committee that had come up with the idea of asking Congress for a taxpayers' bailout the bank had been granted. He explained, "At the time we were optimistic the bank was going to use the money to help make people's lives better."

Now, he looked grim.

He looked at his watch. "Now I see it only strengthen *our own* balance sheet," he tells Grandma.

"Where have all the funds disappeared," Grandma queried.

Billy looked lost for a moment. He stuttered. He admitted he felt he personally owed Grandma and the rest of us an answer. "What I can tell you, Ms. Muley, is, they're sticking it to the middle as we speak. In all these years, never seen anything this bad!"

Grandma understood; her nodding said she did, as Billy forged ahead. He told her of a group he knew within the bank that did not like what the bank was doing to its customers. He painted a picture of a real battleground with weapons drawn. On one side was the protector of the bank and its policies, on the other, disgruntled staff and employees. He asked Grandma if she knew who was winning.

"And what can we do," Grandma asked excitedly.

Billy either did not hear the question or he didn't want to give an answer to it. He went on to emphasize what he was saying, adding that lots of people within the organization at his level didn't like banking anymore.

A few distractions, and Grandma didn't seem to remember she had asked a question. She just seemed to be taking in everything Billy was willing to share.

"Lots of my colleagues don't like what they have them doing either, Ms. Muley, he continued.

Grandma stopped in stillness for a moment, and there was another moment for pure staring at Billy, before she spoke. "Does God know?"

Billy looked at Grandma. He indicated without words that the answer was unquestionably yes.

"And that's why we come back to the pit day after day, Ms Muley," he added. "What else are we to do?"

As Billy made his point, Grandma inspected him, top to bottom, like a TSA inspector. She said it was the first time she got a sense, a feeling his heart was "contextual." She subjectively defined this as "his heart being where she wanted it to be." His sharp nose was quite fine too.

She said she opted to touch him and tell him that she felt his spirit, and it felt good. Everything could be all right one day. Everything. All the world needed are "honest people earning their honest day's pay." People like Billy.

That's what she said to see him stepping forward. He said he had been thinking about retiring for a while.

"Moving on to better things," Grandma quizzed him.

"I'm one of them—just don't feel right about things," Billy said shamefully. The more I think about it, the more…"

Grandma placed her hand on his shoulder. "Well, That's what' I'm talking about. "I'll call you Mr. Blue. How about Billy Blue?"

The two laughed.

****$$****

With Grandma moving her focus so strongly from her business to meddling in banks' concerns, as Mom framed it, her business performance had reached an all time low. Orders were coming in slower and smaller, and even when they were reasonable, she would let them pile up instead of shipping them fast as she promised, and was accustomed to doing during her better days. Sometimes, neither she, nor her Library I had made so neat, could be found well kept now. All this we took as ironic and sad as Grandma had a reputation as the most impeccable among us. Mom said she had lost the sense of how to maintain the space around her. Dad called her situation, "disenchanting."

One thing, though, she didn't change her love for Grace or me, and deep down, we didn't change ours for her. When Grace didn't correctly or completely fulfill some request of hers, she used the opportunity to draw us in rather than push us away. When I got in her way, as it turned out was happening a lot these days, she politely said, "Move on, Soldier."

She said she was only echoing the concept, "move on" from a time she was at Shines when a group of lackadaisical looking women stood complaining about their lives and an attendant went up to them, "No more lamentation you-all, move on," he said.

Grandma laughed as she elaborated, "the end-game was, the ladies got moving."

She kept moving on all the same.

****$$****

At Congress's Senate Committee on Finance, a weary looking Congresswoman says to the chambers and Corporate who was testifying, "We've been here a long time, not going anywhere. Let's move on."

I paused the recording for a moment with Grace who was being both naughty and nice. She had brought me a slice of lemon pie that I liked a lot, but the mischievous part was that she called me lazy, saying that I would leave the plate on the table unwashed when I was done.

"Not true, and not now," I told her. I had to get back to my assignment at hand.

A Congressman was already on the center stage. "Mr. Chief Executive Officer, I don't think I'm the only one here today who is not able to see how our citizens' money we loan you is helping our free-falling economy."

Corporate placed his hand at his chin. He gazed straight at the Congressman. He looked him down the way he had looked down a Congressman in a previous assignment. "With due respect, Senator," he began, "We're using it to invest and re-invest in communities all around the nations—to help both the disadvantaged and otherwise—to help—to ensure a more viable and robust economy, Sir."

Another Congressman called those "well spoken words," but he wasn't clear how they lined up with a promise of helping create a healthy, sustainable economy. He said he didn't think any of the executives in the meeting was of any help to anybody.

"Your bank has received over 4 Billion of taxpayers' earnings," the other Congressman maintained. "What specifically will you show us today? You're asking for more…"

Corporate chuckled, his hand covering most of it. He waited. He appeared to be making a new appraisal of the surroundings. "Again, Sir," he started. "We see sustainability of our client base as the basis of helping sustaining the overall. You know, corporations are people too."

In time, the men and women of Congress would be scratching their heads, some leaning their hands into their opened palms. One ripped into her own hair, and then looked at the hair in her hand. Surprised?

"We're doing everything we can to help ensure the viability of a robust and viable, sustainable economy," Corporate insisted, sounding and looking like he was hollering for someone in an empty room.

One Congressman who came into the video for the first time, placed his left hand under his chin, a finger extending on his nose. He looked at Corporate intensely. He shifted his attention to his colleagues whose numbers of head-scratchers had at least quadrupled. The Congressman looked at the palm of his other hand. He started to scratch his head.

The Congresswoman posed another question. "Sir," she began, "is it possible for us to get from you how the monies the taxpayers have loan to your bank is being used to help revitalize the economy?"

Corporate began to talk again as members of the Congressional panel started placing their hand on their head one by one; many of them snapped into a sleep.

****$$****

I told Mom about my schoolwork on another day she was meeting in secret with Miss Bridgett to discuss how they might have persuaded Grandma to stop chasing after a worthless goal. They said so far they weren't sure how much progress they had made as sometimes it appeared Grandma was leaning their way, other times she was right back "heading on her bridge to nowhere."

Mom said I was a good student and could learn anything this world threw at me. She didn't stay on that topic, however, and I'm not sure why. I loved the feeling of her telling me how good I was. Grace was getting a lot more of that from her, except when it came to her schoolwork.

She said her meeting was about what specific steps they could take to stop Grandma, and again made inquiry as to why Grandma wasn't cashing her Social Security checks. Soon, she was mumbling that Grandma should stop what she and Miss Bridgett were calling a "dog and cat fight with the bank, for the ball."

Mom went on to voice that Grandma was out of sync with the real world, to which I could not at the time tell where Miss Bridgett really was on that judgment. She was an odd-ball when it came to her position on the issues with Grandma. Sometimes she was with Grandma, and then before we knew it, she seemed on the other plane.

On this occasion, she was more a listener than a talker that I would have bet anyone ten-grand the meeting was not her idea. She appeared so bored, she was more into me. She said she remembered seeing me taken over to Grandma's long before I was big enough to know I was a person: "blood, flesh or mind." When I was at that level of awareness she used to bathe and dress me, I learned. She smiled as she asked me about school and what I was planning to do with my life, noting that I was now big in my pants and could even make a baby if that was the kind of stuff on my mind.

After a protracted distraction with me, she returned her attention to Mom. "You really don't think the system's rigged, uh?"

# CHAPTER 18

Growing up, one thing I wish I had gotten a better sense of is the way things change from moment to moment. For me, the world was flat and predictable, and, well, linear, so I expected everything I saw in a certain way would only change by a certain small amount when I saw that thing again. Now, that was about to shatter as the new days came. The ephemeral idea had revisited.

There was about to be great adjustment to what we knew. The start of the day, however, did not give any indications: Grandma was struggling with this and that. She was on her usual work schedule. She was in her everyday conversation: She had problems with Bank $$.

"The bank's making *their* headways. They know exactly what they're doing," she told me that day.

I was helping her in the Library, processing book orders and she was on the phone holding for a customer. A Bank $$ advertising was on TV momentarily with the ad selling the bank as being friendly. There was an account shown with some large, bold typewritten words on the sheet, saying "Understanding Customer's Statement." A young, very eye-catching lady came next, moving her body like she was the ware up for sale.

"We're your friendly bank," she said in a cute voice as she threw her chest to the camera. She blew a kiss out to the audience. "We make banking *simple!*"

I turned my head towards Grandma who also was taking note of the message. She never liked that kind of hot 'n heavy approach to business, and I wanted to see her reaction. She had said it over and over: "The Corporate world is sacred; sex has no place in their commercials. It was stupid!"

She shook her head signaling her disapproval, and then turned to the phone; her customer was waiting.

Grandma responded to the customer. "I get it; its Campbell's 'Power of Myth,' you ordered—the soft cover version."

There was a pause, and then Grandma continued. "Exactly! That's why I'm giving you your full money back. No complications. Wrong is just like it sounds: 'wrong.'"

I gestured I was leaving for a glass of water but Grandma gave me her right thumb up. Things must be going well, I figured.

I listened further.

"I know you don't want a refund," Grandma said to the customer. "I know you just wanted me to know you got the wrong binding."

Later she would point out to me that I had put the hardcover version of a book in an envelope to this customer, one valued $18 more than the paperback one the customer had paid for.

"Nevertheless wrong," she told me, and went on to explain why this was such a big deal for her. It was a pet-peeve: "Customers should never fall victim to those who get to spend their money on their hair, their children and their homes."

The customer said something to which Grandma answered, "You keep saying that, but I'm old-school. When you make a mistake you do whatever it takes to correct it."

I ran to the kitchen for my water, and when I was back Grandma was still on the phone with the customer, but now she was slumping. Her voice, also, had changed.

"Yes, I know that also, and I appreciate your going to give me good feedback. But that's not what this is all about, Ma'am."

Grandma added that she was in the process of sending the customer the promised refund as they carried on.

This was one of those rare times Grandma did not get her phone on speaker, so I could not hear what her customer was saying.

Grandma shook her head as if the person was directly in front of her. Her lips were bitten in. Her face was as if she had just won that lottery prize I had dreamt about.

"That's my policy; the final answer," she said, and then as she turned as if to re-acknowledge me, I saw in her a new slump. The smile was still on her face, though.

I asked her if she was well, and she lifted her open arms as if in stretching. And there again was her smiling. "I just made a customer's day," she declared. "That's what money making should be about, Son!"

She asked me to do a few errands in the house, like going to tell Grace it was time to turn off the TV and switch to schoolwork, getting her glasses from her room, and then she asked me to go to her desktop and open her bank account for her.

At first I was resistant for reasons I don't even know. What I do know is we had all gotten tired of her checking her bank account two, three times, and sometimes more, a day. Our problem with it was that she would complain about her bank another hour or two after she got any bad news.

Eventually, and only after she addressed me in her formal way, the one when she use the word "Soldiers," I began to fill her request.

"Grandma. What's the number," I asked.

An abrupt and very strong lightning and Florida firecracker thunder happened through the house simultaneously, leaving Grace shouting, "Whoa, you guys. Heard that?"

When Grace was getting calm, she said she had just pushed in one of Grandma CD in her laptop and she thought it was something going on with her computer.

"Grandma's music," I asked.

"Take a look at this," Grace said, simultaneously pushing out the CD from the computer. She waved it in front of my face.

"It's called 'Dizzy Spells,'" she said.

# CHAPTER 19

In so far as my question to Grandma pertaining to her password to access her account, she gave me "Biblestories 123," which I used. Immediately on entering it, I found there were lots of items that were red and many $35.00 charge, also red. I have not yet stopped apologizing for what happened next. I excited Grandma.

"Something's not right! Look here, Grandma! Look," I had alarmed.

Grandma slumped a last time, and as she turned her face was powder-white, now as it slowly commissioned itself for me.

She got up but stumbled.

"What? Soldier," she questioned.

"They're red! You're bouncing! Red," I said.

"Again? Again? Bouncing again," Grandma said as she made another wobbly step.

I held on to her and tried to find out what was going on, but I was late.

"My Lord! The thieves got me again," she yelled, instantaneously falling from my grip. She had fallen into a fit.

For a split, I could not talk, and my feet were likewise put out of action. I felt myself a person being strangled, and yet my head was fluid. In there I could heard "What!"

What had I done?

I spoke it out, and the neighborhood heard. “Grandma! What have I done?”

****$$****

When the man and woman paramedic team was preparing Grandma for the ambulance she appeared half disoriented and half conscious to me. At one point she grabbed for her I-phone, but the woman paramedic at once took it away from her.

“I need Billy—know,” Grandma cried out. “Call Billy, Tagg!”

In the fast-moving seconds, the woman paramedic reviewed a paper from Grandma’s purse and passed on her findings to her partner.

“David Rostein’s, General Care,” she told him. Momentarily, she again moved her attention to Grandma, instructing her to relax. She mentioned the number “three-hundred” in reference to Grandma’s blood pressure, and called her cholesterol level, “out of whack!”

These may or may not have been the trigger s that sent Grandma into her mad woman wailing. Her voice was now deep and husky as she did it.

“Thieves, thieves. The sonofabitches, ‘fricking’ thieves,” Grandma screamed.

I looked at Grandma and remembered when she was normal. I knew there was nothing I could do; not with the anxiety I felt storming through—trashing protons and neutrons, blowing out the windows and doors of my head. I got steady to find myself numb, looking away; it was too much. That’s when I saw Mr. Saul and Ms. Cynthia coming into my view. They were running over and transformed from midgets to giants as they got closer, both aged from the last time I had seen them, both sorry-looking themselves; she with a Bible in her hand.

“Oh Heavens. I told her to just spend her Social Security,” Mr. Saul shouted. “Half the country’s on something!”

He continued. “If they’re going bankrupt, that’s not her problem, Darl!”

Ms. Cynthia was looking at me with a mean face, but got to knock her husband on the head with the Bible. “You never give anybody credit, you! Sandra *creates her own JOB!”*

Momentarily the male paramedic placed his hand on Grandma’s shoulder to calm her down; I found myself wiping tears from my cloudy eyes. Through them I saw the male paramedic quite different now. He was coming across as frightened as well as too busy for me.

"Please don't let my Grandma die," I said, thinking about Grandma. She had told us just a month or so earlier, one of her other neighbors, a strong healthy looking Ms. Luz had gone to the hospital one night and by next morning her doctor pronounced her a goner. I told them just like the deceased's niece had done that tragic Saturday morning, that Grandma was a hard-working lady and beg them again and again to please not to let her die.

In all of this, Grace was quieter than I had ever seen her. All I could get from her now was an off-the-wall glaring that made me wonder if she was about to break down too.

Was this the end for Grandma? And the end of us?

The questions commanded my whole mind for a minute, and seemed answered "yes" when Grandma, jumping and jerking shouted again in a perplexing and fractured way, "Thieves. Thieves. If you let…, you be next!"

The male paramedic, who was at the time working with adjusting the medication, looked like he was drained.

"Ma'am, Ma'am you, just had a stroke. Calm down! Now," he shouted. He then moved his sight on me and asked if we had seen any signs of this coming.

I hadn't before thought about this kind of thing, and I don't recall supplying an answer. My thoughts and heed were on Grandma who had taken on to foaming from the mouth.

Another second and she was shouting as loud as she could, "We have to stop them. Stop them, now!"

To the rage, the male paramedic informed that they would have to sedate her.

"Hell! Hell come high water," Grandma reacted.

"Grandma," I cautioned.

I could see her turn her head a tad but it stopped, and what I was able to see of her eyes was that they looked stationary, like a glass marble, a motionless, opaque cat's eyes.

"Why they take away our living," she mumbled.

The male paramedic announced to us that Grandma was "losing it!"

Whatever that meant?"She's our neighbor, and she's a child of God," Ms Cynthia interrupted, lifting her glossed over face from a page in her Bible.

"…elp," Grandma said in a gasping manner.

The two paramedics looked at us, and then to each other, shaking their heads as if in passing a secret code.

"She was a strong person," Ms. Cynthia said. She had a heartrending expression on her face. "Just don't bring her back dead. You hear me? God loves her too!"

Momentarily, Grandma again moved her head, very, very slightly this time, and as her eyes were going shut, she forced out one lasting word, "Terrorists!"

****$$****

We watched powerlessly as Mr. Saul stood over Grandma in a prayer-like position as if he had finally stopped resisting his wife's call for him to come in line with Christ.

"You were a good neighbor, Ms. Muley," he uttered. "We'll do whatever it takes!"

The paramedics had done everything they could. They had arrived in less than two minutes. They had moved fast. They kept focused from the get-go. To me, they had done their job, but there were no guarantees. The woman paramedic had said those words the minute they arrived.

"A few more moments give or take and the whole outcome could have been very different," she said.

Now they prepared to leave.

****$$****

The machines Grandma was hooked up to were quiet when the woman paramedic closed the rear door with the male in the back.

For me, my head was in my hands, and my hands were wet from my eyes.

Inside the heavy round ball I call my head, was still the inquiry: "what had I done?"

The woman paramedic headed towards the front, leapt into the driver's seat, and speeds into traffic just as a truck full of watermelons and oranges cuts in front of them. This action sent a ton, of the fruits crashing to the ground, some rolling, others smashing immediately on impact.

I looked at Grace. She was no longer just gazing at the activities; her eyes were heavy, sad.

Suddenly, she pivoted her foot in the direction of the moving ambulance. She had found her voice.

"Granny! G R A N N Y," she yelled.

****$$****

My having to do schoolwork was a weighty distraction for me for the first time especially with Dr. Erskine warning us that business never stops, and there was no excuse we could give her other than our own death, that she would accept. To make her point "see-thru" as she called it, she noted the difference between a corporation form of business and the sole proprietorship counterpart. She said corporations exist beyond the life of the owner. Sole proprietorship goes in when you know who does, she went on. She recommended we form corporations when we were ready to start our gigs.

To a request from me about Grandma, she wrote back, "You must have sustained energy to get every assignment done well and submitted in a timely manner. Thanks for asking, Dr. S. Erskine, P.h.D," the e-mail read in excerpt.

With that clear, she directed the class's attention to a large conference room at the bank's corporate office where an organization was giving an award to the bank. This was our next video assignment.

It's was a big, happy event with tons of big wigs strutting around. A representative from the organization made her way up to the lectern and announced her pleasure in awarding the bank, "an institution that fulfills our society greatest need, the organization's 'Sterling Award.'"

The recording proceeded. In it were Eduardo Sosa and R. Paul again, in their own corner, as if they were in some special category. They were afresh giving commentary on what was going on.

Eduardo Sosa said it was, "Another great day at Bank $$."

This assignment, like so many others, provided the details that could have stopped me in my tracks, but I was living too much in the bubble and missed the signs and signals that were coming at me. If I knew and understood what I do now, what eventually turned out for us would have been quite different.

Corporate received the award and then stepped to the microphone.

"Thank you," he said. "Thank you for noticing how tremendous our help is to the communities we serve. We're the producers, making the world a better place…."

Eduardo Sosa and R. Paul, who I had gotten to know from the previous class work, did not appear particularly happy about what was happening, though at times they too did not always come across as confident in their position.

"Just listen," Eduardo Sosa said. "The bitch knows how to bribe even them. You heard what he's up to, now?"

"You keep coming at me," R. Paul replied. "You remember way back when he was your hero?"

"You must have heard it by now. The bitch's new scheme's 20% increase in NSF by end of fiscal," Eduardo Sosa said.

R. Paul knew. He shook his head to say so.

"That bonehead we have as CEO. You heard his "parasite joke? He's something else," Eduardo Sosa concluded.

R. Paul agreed to that, expounding that Corporate had used the "P" word in one of his famous e-mails referring to his customers.

"More of my Sis's immigration money, Paul," Eduardo Sosa said. "You should head this, thing. You should be president, Cuz!"

****$$****

Moving forward, the Rep gave her all into enjoying Corporate's company. His bank had served the community well and had served the country likewise, she noted. "You should be more than proud!"

Corporate received the complement with a smile that seemed to improve his whole thinking of self. He declared, "We're going to have a party!"

To that, the crowd lifted hands: glasses of Champaign, whatever they were holding. They cheered. Some waved.

R. Paul looked to his partner as the two men wagged heads. "If they only know what happens in the back room," he said.

"Incredible. We know the truth," Eduardo Sosa replied. "What's up with the plan?"

R. Paul didn't answer, so Eduardo Sosa took back to the center.

"Don't you think it's time we consider another line of work?"

"Eastside's heading-up the attack. Heard 'bout the wrong customer statements going out?" He winked at Eduardo Sosa. "Slow but methodical. Slow."

Eduardo Sosa laughed, but there was a fox look to him. "Cuz, I once heard someone say… 'if you mess with tiger, you end up inside!'"

R. Paul laughed, himself. "Really?"

****$$***

With all that going, on the other side Corporate stood at the lectern with the organization Rep placing a Hawaiian lieu around his neck.

"For all you've done, for the good of human kind, for the love, you deserve this too," the Rep said. "Not only a plaque."

The Rep raised her hand to the audience. "Wouldn't you agree with me?"

To that point, the audience gave a thundering applause.

With that, Corporate gave the organizations Rep a kiss on the cheek.

"This is a high honor, a reflection of how much we have helped communities all around this nation to live the dream," he said to his receptive crowd of employees, clapping and waving at him. "And everywhere I go I'm glad to say how the government STIMULATED us!"

One person in the crowd shouted "bail out," and then from another it was "stimulus." The crowd seconded the stimulus one in a quick church-like three-prong chant, "Stimulus! Stimulus! Stimulus!" A loud hand-clapping followed.

On stage, Corporate lifted his thumb in a "yes, we are great," position, and another round of applause came for that.

"I'm glad to say it again, you all," he belted out, his now open hand moving swiftly and parallel to the ground. "We brighten communities! Our plan's to create the greatest financial solution this world's ever seen!"

And for that, the crowd went wild one more time.

****$$****

Grandma was still at Upper Creek Memorial when a letter came in the mail giving her notice that her mortgage lender was coming after her with foreclosure proceedings. I intercepted the letter, got frightened and hid it.

Meanwhile, at the hospital, a weary doctor sauntered into a waiting room filled with family members who stopped what they were doing to check in if the doctor was coming to talk to them. The doctor made it up to a Chinese family as the wife grabbed the doctor's hand. The man placed his hand on his wife's arm, and their young daughter, fifteen years or so, burst into a big cry.

"Yes, I repeat, I'm sorry," the doctor said, speaking slowly and in broken English. "We did everything we could. We lost her."

Momentarily, the whole room of people looked sadly at the family as crying broke out from another family with another doctor talking to them.

The doctor with the Chinese family said she was sorry to be the messenger of the bad news.

I found myself talking to Grace about this hospital and the kind of news it was finding so appetizing; they were scooping it out fast like they do popcorn at Sunday matinee.

# CHAPTER 20

The party promised by Corporate was nothing short of a Vagas extravaganza, and they made a video of that too. In part, an employee dressed as a clown gave jokes about how the company had so much money it was going to build its own shuttle and take all its "higher ups" to space. In another, the women in their pom-poms were pointing their butts to the men, primarily, one of whom joked they were like "Alaskan bears unfed for all six months of daylight."

Corporate had joined most of the other men in tux that made The Rat Pack looked cheap that night. That night, he danced every opportunity he could with his wife.

That night also gave us great insight into the world of Tolly the CFO. We learned he was a man who could overdo his liquor intake when there was no one to tell him he was going overboard. He also at one point revealed great distaste for Corporate.

For the marketing lady, Miss Andrea, she too danced the sweet night away. She was adorned in her most elegant dress yet, something from the Liz Taylor collection, undoubtedly. Talking about elegance, her wild, big hat was talked about by everyone who set eyes on its intense, beaming colors that were bouncing off the party lights, ricocheting from wall to wall. Even those of us discussing the event, including Dr. Erskine felt it was a "pretty dandy hat."

"Hell of a party," a lady on the dance floor in a gypsy style ballroom gown said to her partner as they made way to a Nutcracker ballet. The lady said the piece was from the school of Vaganova.

Oh yeah," the MC's voice came singing over the music. "The best of the best. And now for a mood swing!" She turned to Frank Sinatra, and he sang, "Anything Goes."

# CHAPTER 21

Unaware of the situation with Grandma, the woman at Shines found themselves in ongoing conversations about her.

On one particular bad day when their conversation was about bedsores, poor diet and the hospitalization of three of them after receiving wrong medication, they switched their lasers to beam on Grandma.

"Not here. No money," one of the ladies said to a new asking of Ms. Diaz about when Grandma was coming to Shines.

"They said she was dead," Ms. Wonzick replied to the other women at the retirement home, gesticulating from her wheelchair, her eyes piercing as usual.

Ms. Zenida Reid, the closest to Ms. Wonzick replied signing that they sent back the priest.

"That's what I was saying. I didn't say she was *dead*. They did! She's close though—really close," Ms. Wonzick supplied, as Mom Saraplin groaned in the background for gifts.

For a moment the ladies ignored Mom Saraplin, and Ms. Wonzick gossiped about Mr. Sealey's saying that Grandma must have been going insane "trying to mess with them banks."

Without notice, Ms Wonzick began to shake again, her finger as pointed as Grandma's old ice pick. "Get a life, Sarah! No more freebies!"

Ms. Zenida Reid signed to the ladies that the attention should be on her now and went on: “They thought she was going in last night and the night before, Baby Girl.

Ms. Wonzick said that’s what she had heard as Ms. Zenida Reid signed, “Sarah needs a gift.”

*“Love* as we know, *is over,*” Ms. Wonzick said in a slow-motion way and in a voice that sounded more like scolding than pure talking. “No more gifts coming. Sandy said the economy’s going up shit creek!”

That was a strange idea.

“What’s shit creek?”

Ms. Diaz had told the other ladies a day or so earlier that whatever was happening with Grandma was plain and simple, sad. Now she looked doleful herself.

“She was my good friend,” she forced out, tears revealed. “My very good friend!”

****$$****

With time, the living area at Shines had gotten messy, as it usually would in those days, and most of the women had gotten knocked out from high heat, high humidity, and one of the many days the facilities air conditioning was not functioning at its best. In one area there were ten of the ladies, another had twelve, and in the center were Ms. Diaz, Ms. Wonzick and a smaller crowd. Throughout the room there was the sound of snoring not the nasal zzzzzz one—the way Grace does it, but in a strange, thin sssshhhhkkk sound. That is what I think woke Ms. Diaz. She started to move around her head, bouncing her eyes off the other women one after the other, and making her way to Ms. Wonzick. She stopped there for a wink and more. Ms. Wonzick’s head was swaying, now, forward and then backwards, forward and then backwards it went again. Ms. Diaz reacted with a nodding of her own.

Ms. Wonzick made another jerk and then her eyes unlatched . Ms. Diaz smiled.

“I was dreaming,” Ms. Wonzick announced, goose pimples blanketing her arms as she turned on her gesticulation channel. “I was dreaming and she was just jerking and jerking, and there was a large group of Black boys, and they were jerking too, and it was all in black and white!"

Ms. Diaz tried to put her hand on Ms. Wonzick to calm her down, but they were too stiff to reach and what she brought out was the sound of her vegetating reality: "Ouch."

"I know suffering too," Ms. Diaz claimed. "Every woman does!"

"Yes. It was strange, Ms. Wonzick proceeded, jerking her body so much her wheelchair kept moving out of place.

"It was in Africa in the Safari."

The other women began to pay attention, some intrigued, others confused, as Ms. Wonzick kept the ball rolling hard and fast. "A large group of half-naked Black boys and men in a ceremony. Mom Diaz, me, Sandy was right there, too!"

Ms. Diaz started to look at Ms. Wonzick as if she had farted and it was a real stinky. "You OK, Pet, she asked.

"The boys were," she said. "I think, like eleven, twelve—children like that—and they were having like a ceremony; they were tired of being boys; they wanted to be man!"

Ms. Wonzick added emphatically, "They had giraffes, kangaroos and all kinds of things like that. Love...."

By this time many of the other women were awake and were listening to Ms. Wonzick who continued to relay her strange experience when she was in the bubble, the essence of which was that their dear friend Sandy was not dead. She was right there watching in the crowd, watching as a group of half-naked young girls and women came with drums. They formed a circle enclosing the males. They began to sing.

One of the ladies, a very pale and skinny Caucasian woman who I had never noticed before threw herself in front of Ms. Diaz and Ms. Wonzick. "Were they rich," she asked.

Ms. Wonzick looked at the lady, annoyed.

"Were they good looking Africans," the lady asked in a demanding voice, as if still waiting for the answer to the first question. "You know, the ones with big—large feet? Were they rich?"

Ms. Wonzick and the others ignored the lady. The dream-telling was too important for both speaker and listeners to put aside for a distraction of such small magnitude.

Ms. Wonzick continued. “It was scary, you ‘all. The drums were like shrieking, changing, the sound, and then a young man at the front of the line of men fell into a trance. It was scary you ‘all! And then the Group of naked young African women and girls, they started beating the drums faster and faster and faster and the shrieking, and the sound! That kind of thing frightens me, you know?”

Ms. Wonzick took a pause and an audibly noticed deep breath as if she wanted to let everyone know she was not over whatever her dream had done to her.

“It was all in African but somehow, I have not been to that country, but I understand,” she said.

The skinny tall lady sat on a nearby chair and started to smile as she looked Ms. Wonzick in the eyes.

That brought about an important question. Who was stranger, Ms. Wonzick or she? I don’t go around day after day expecting to see either at the local Publix supermarket, the nearby Balboa Park, or at Sunday service. One thing I know, the tall lady knew Africa was not a country, and she kept clarifying, even if only for herself: “Country! Country!”

“Momma, so what were they saying,” the lady mocked thereafter.

“It was in African,” Ms. Wonzick repeated angrily and then stopped in mid air as if someone was feeding her with her bizarre message. At a point where it seemed she was running on empty, she looked up to the sky. “Kill the boy and bring forth the man,” Ms. Wonzick said. “‘Into the womb and then back to protect the land.’ That’s what they were saying! That’s what’s they were saying! ‘Kill the boy and bring forth the man.’”

The skinny, pale lady stood up and opened her arm as if to address the crowd of women that had gathered.

“And what was dead Sandy Muley doing,” she again mocked.

Again, almost no one paid attention to the skinny lady. Their world was temporarily consumed with the words and sight created by Ms. Wonzick who was imitating the shrieking kind of tone, like the one she had described earlier. Her gesticulation made her account of events even more absorbing.

“L-o-o-o-o-loose. Loose. Loose. L-o-o-o-o-loose. L-o-o-o-o-loose,” she went, saying this is how an older man who looked like a tribe leader was going. “Loose. L–o-o-o-ose!”

Before it was all over, a couple of the women said they always knew Ms. Wonzick problems for being in the home were not only physical. One went as far as to ask that Ms. Wonzick be committed that day. This all came to the disregard of Ms. Wonzick who blurted out the word "divine!"

There was something fateful indeed in what she was saying, and there was more to come.

"The young boy that was in the trance came out of it," she claimed. He and the other young boys were going, "Sing, sing, sing. I dance. Sing. Sing. Sing. I enter. Sing. Sing. I climb. I am!"

When this piece was over, The skinny, pale lady put a very frightened look on her face; she began walking away. The other ladies teased her that she couldn't take anymore.

"And you want to tell me you understand all of that, ha," she said to Ms. Wonzick as she looked backwards, through wide open eyes. She had already made it to an exit, and one more time before slamming the door behind her, she looked back. "Ha?"

# PART 2: FIX IT

*"When an empire fears for its survival,*
*its time has passed"*
Martin Dansky
(Actor, Artist and Writer b. 1952)

# CHAPTER 1

Inside a large hospital room at Upper Creek Memorial, Grandma was hooked up to "a snake pile of wires." That's the term Grace coined to describe the many wires and tubes, each extending to its own and distinctly flashing or beeping machine as Grandma laid in what her doctor said to us was "a dreaming state." I pushed out my closed lips and shook my head at the sight of Grandma fighting for life. To me, she looked more like someone who was already gone, not someone in a dream.

Day after day we visited to see her looking the same, in her drowsy, drifted-away state, and then one sun-lit afternoon as we were saying goodbye, her chest made a sudden and noticeable jolt. Again, though, that was about it for another week, until her breathing started to improve and her doctor declared her to be more in a "meditation," no longer a coma as was written on a previous report. Not a dream as the doctor had called it on a previous visit by us. Now, "a meditation."

In time, the doctor shared with us that he was "not just a doctor," MD, DO, names like that, but he possessed additional training and skills—qualities he called ESP and clairvoyance. He said he knew what was happening in the inside of Grandma. He determined she was in some sort of a "cave mode," unable to focus and upset as Mom, Grace and I stood by the bed watching. At one instant the doctor looked at Grandma who was motionless, and said she was in a phase of telling herself to get quiet.

"OK." I went that far.

He reviewed her blood pressure and her other vital signs and showed us some charts and numbers that Mom seemed to understand and gave good feedback to.

"See, see," the Doctor followed through. "She's beginning to go into the zone right now. She should be left in quiet."

That was that.

The following day Grandma would make new jerks of her chest while we sat by her. These were smooth lurching moves, if there are such things, more like adjustments than the kind of shifts you see in an earthquake, for example. They came like Jello shakes and appeared to help Grandma to look peaceful, more like someone alive, almost like when she was up and out, and with them, a halo came forming around her head.

In a blink the glow grew brighter and then bigger, and soon it was overwhelming.

****$$****

We looked and some found themselves dumbfounded.

I would later learn that for over a week Grandma was coming and going out of this state. She was seeing herself sitting in the lotus position, as in yoga. She saw some poor-looking people in a gathering like a church with a few playing steel pan music as the song "Kumbaya" came from the drumming and humming. A man in the audience, a very rustic looking one stood up from his seat momentarily as the music played.

"I know you will be OK Sandy. You're no longer a girl; you're a big woman now," the man declared, his voice revenant.

Grandma lifted her head to the utterance. She wanted to know who the stranger was.

"You know," the man said in a demanding voice.

She looked the man in his face and recognized him as her first lover, Long Gone; with him were two other friends, Stiff and Vivid.

Grandma moved backwards. She was fourteen and it was her first menstruation. Fifteen came and with that, the first hint of the "S" powers came to her, and now it was all there, all flesh: It was the summer camp, the ocean, Fort Lauderdale, the early 1900's. Her school had taken her class and the three higher-level classes on a trip to South Florida with the older boys, and as they swam in their swimsuits and trunks, one of the older boys did her in.

"That's when I lost my innocence," Grandma declared. Stiff had taken advantage of her. "That when .... When."

Things happened so fast that by the time Grandma was seventeen she was known on the circuit. Vivid, Long Gone and many others had gotten to know her well.

By the time she was twenty she was busy with Mom's older sister from whose namesake Grace came. When she was twenty-one she had uncle Ed.

This is how the dance became a part of the whole: Mister T, Uncle Ed's father was a chorographer. He had taught her how to move her body, which she did so much and so well, so, she decided why not move it for the world to see. The world did see it, and for that she won numerous accolades, not to mention a dancing scholarship in due time. She maintained from that time any child she had would have to earn their own degree. She had done it. They should too.

The story of the scholarship even appeared in a Detroit daily. The article was in her album, the third leaf, brown, old, and crimpled—a good read, nevertheless.

In 1927 she had been pregnant for a couple guys, one half her age of whom the article quoted her saying she had the sweetest of sex. That was bold for that era and that was until she met Grandpa.

With him, Mom is said to have been accounted for, and then there was another uncle, but Mom said he passed when he was very small from something she called SIDS.

****$$****

"She's having good memories now," the doctor, whom I never got his name, said.

I asked him how he knew what he was professing to know, and he advised, "trust me!"

He said he could see through things and claimed he knew I was Grandma's favorite grandchild, and was actually named by her and not by Mom or Dad. My name had something to do with some odd attachment I had with Grandma: "to learn, relate and tell about her."

"She will live on starting with you," he said. "She will tell you *everything* one day."

I was somewhat intrigued, and at the same time confused. Goose pimples started building up on my skinny arms. I asked him if his medical training taught him the kind of stuff he was dumping on us. He never answered that question; he just grinned until his pink gum turned to a frightening red, and then he spoke slowly and in a whisper-like talk, "Your grandmother's moving data from the unconscious to the conscious. This is a very important phase!"

I thought in dept: He was the doctor, the one with the degree and all the fine training he had already stoned us with; He understood diagnosis and treatment. He knew about categories of diseases, types of patients, methods of treatments, and the like. For me, I was just a relative of the sick. In my capacity, they saw me as nothing more than someone with an affinity or similarity to the patient. I was not the doctor.

The doctor spoke. "Anthropologically, speaking you have a social relationships with your grandmother, one that makes you a part of each other."

Wasn't it our biology he was supposed to get into?

I recalled one of the paramedic saying Grandma had gotten a stroke and a list of complications. Was I going to get that, too? Biologically, I wondered. I wanted to know what was next for me.

The doctor looked at his paper. He mumbled some more madman stuff about the degree of genetic relatedness—something about the "coefficient of relationship shared."

I looked at him. I ran my hand above my head and told him he was too much—somewhere above my hand. He needed to come down to my level.

He indicated he would. He began to smile in an assuring way.

"Your grandmother's a remarkable person," he shared.

Momentarily, I remembered a show on TV. It was named, "They Called them Quacks."

I said, "Well Doc. Just get her out of her… as soon as you can. OK. Doc?"

****$$****

With that, the doctor's countenance turned to serious as if he really knew what was going in my head.

"There's somebody somewhere," he spoke slowly.

He pulled backwards and his face took on a wise-guy grin I had seen somewhere before. "It's a lady!"

I eyeballed the doctor hoping he would see in me the pain and confusion he had already imparted; I was thinking, "Oh, no!"

"She's old. She's in a nursing home," the doctor plowed on.

Mom and I squeezed hands and the doctor gave his attention to Mom.

"She's synchronizing with your Mother!"

The group looked at me as if I was the adult in the room. The word, "wonk" surfaced, but I wasn't one of those. The only thing I could think of was to sneak out as quietly as I could if the doctor was what they call a quack.

The word "quack" came loud, however, and the doctor heard. He looked at me as if we had come to the end of our knowing each other. He proceeded to tell Mom that Grandma and some lady thought they were in the same room.

"They're having their conversation as we convene," he declared. "Be quiet!"

He explained at a whisper's level that they were completing something he called a transition. "They're looking at a young African boy in a trance. Foam's pouring from the boy's mouth!"

The old lady translates:

"If you don't get out, you're dead. You're dead if you stay in. Out! Out! Out..."

# CHAPTER 2

What was happening at Shines was probably not what the doctor had said but was nonetheless of note. For one, the place was as messy as I can recall ever seeing it, and two, it looked as if most of the women were in their thing.

Ms. Wonzick had gotten fatigue wheeling herself around and talking about how she was getting her exercise. Bored with all that, she decided on her strange obsession: Grandma.

"I think I was dreaming," Ms. Wonzick said. "We should go and see her. Bad stroke."

"Stroke. Stroke. Come. Come. Here, Here," Ms. Diaz said, her voice sounding as annoying as when she was voicing to Ms. Wonzick her desire for them to go and see Grandma. In the world of Shines Grandma bore significance not because of what she took to help them out, but rather because no one in their right mind seriously believed she would ever have to live the way the women lived there. She was above the fray, or so "the wise" of them said.

One of the other ladies complained that the attendants wouldn't take them on any field trip to go and see anybody, anywhere, which came in just when Mom Saraplin again was asking if any more gifts were on the way to her.

That greatly annoyed Ms. Wonzick this time around, and she screamed for the "Lord," followed by alerting Mom Saraplin that she would not be allowed to go on any trip with them, even if there was one.

"Not going. Not going," Ms. Diaz echoed.

Ms. Wonzick started her gesticulations anew, this time, increasing its intensity. "Too crazy," she suggested. "If she want gifts, why don't she just call the Salvation Army. There're St. Paul's. Call the President of the United States. He'll write you a personal check! For goodness sake, Saraplin! S-T-O-P!"

The commotion was so great, a Shines Center attendant came speeding in. "Ladies we can't be idling," the attendant warned as she bounced around the place. "Got to clean up this jungle."

One of the other ladies replied that where they came from was the real jungle; Shines was paradise.

The attendant, seeing that no one was in the mood to listen to her this day, left as Ms. Diaz addressed the group.

"Coming here! Muley, Coming here." She did her hand like a jockey speeding his horse, "Giddiup, Giddiup, Giddiup. Eeehaa!"

"She doesn't have any more Benjamins," Ms. Wonzick said. She placed her hand over her mouth and sighed. "No more gifts. She'll have to live here."

Ms. Diaz brought tears to her eyes. "Soon? Soon," she asked the best way she could.

****$$****

Grace and I went to bed that night wondering if Grandma would see sunlight another day. One of Grandma's few fears was "going over" as she so pitifully would put it. Now, Grace tried her own hand at putting fear in me that what we were witnessing was: "Bank $$ sending Granny over the financial cliff."

They think she is game, Grace said.

She continued, "And they're waiting on the other side to eat her up!"

I shook my head firmly. I didn't want to go there.

I was thankful for what Grandma had done for us.

"She'll never sleep in her own bed again," Grace said.

I had my own doubts, but I didn't want to show my hand, knowing Grace: *Much less ours home!*

The stress led to Grace bursting out in an outcry, leaving me to do everything I humanly could to console her, which meant I had to replay her favorite move, the Hurt Locker.

We sat on the edge of my bed for probably an hour-and-a-half in our pajamas, and then amazingly she was fast asleep.

****$$****

The next day when we visited Grandma she was still asleep, and sadly to a new infection, she looked frailer than when we had last seen her. Mom was the first one to walk up to her bed where Mom paused, looked, pause again, and then lifted the sheet, exposing Grandma's gray hospital gown. Mom looked at Miss Bridgett, paused, and then looked at Dad. She looked up at the TV that was on, faint with sound.

"Benny Goodman's. 'Body and Soul.' That's what her spirit needs right now," Miss Bridgett said.

I was going closer to check on Grandma as I did every time we went to the hospital, when a weak but raspy voice seeped out of her.

It said, "Right now, I have a picture in my head and it's different than what is…"

"Ms. Muley, relax," Miss Bridgett reacted.

Those were Grandma's first words back, and she was not even given the decency to complete them.

Grandma opened her eyes partially, her voice still weak. "Any, anybody that can start the process?"

I was not sure why these words irritated Mom the way they did, but in all my life I had never seen her respond that cruelly.

"Not now! Not ever! Not Mom," she said. "Relax!"

Miss Bridgett reminded Mom that we were in a hospital and cautioned the staff would throw us out if they thought we were not helping the patient in the healing process.

I looked around and listened carefully to find that none of that would change our privilege. And none of that would stop Grandma either. Her voice and volume were improving with every syllable, every word she was releasing for our decoding and analysis.

"We the people," she claimed.

Again, it was Miss Bridgett attempting to keep Grandma calm. "Ms. Muley! Ms. Sandra," she demanded. "You're frightening!"

Grandma disregarded her.

"There's got to be a lawyer, somewhere," Grandma exclaimed. "You think I don't know what's going on? I know out there. I know the lay of the land!"

I glanced at Mom and Miss Bridgett, both of whom had gotten to look irritated, and I wondered what they were going to do. Would Dr. Quack help now? How? Was it another ghost? Would these concerns kill gray, old Grandma? I could only speculate, and I knew I didn't have privy to such questions of providence. Mom had a way to telling Dad and us, "Don't speculate, don't guess. Don't be a quack." That's what others do, not us.

Grandma insisted for a lawyer.

"Damn shit," she said. "Is there one within a thousand miles?"

Mom made an attempt at being nice and held on to Grandma's hand. "Mom, you don't need a jurist," Mom shared. "I'm trying my best to keep the priest from coming back. You're sick, Mom!"

Grandma gave her body a three-second jiggle, the way a soaked dog shakes off water on emerging to dry land after being tossed into the ocean. Her face took on the look of a happy Halloween pumpkin, "I am?"

"You've opted out jury duty not once, not twice, a trillion times! You're so damn scared of big, tall buildings!"

Grandma move her lips a small bit as if there was something between them—something that should that should be exposed, but it never met the outer space.

Mom beamed at her, concerned. "Mom. What cause have you to do with the law," she said.

Grandma's voice came even stronger. "You keep rubbing dirt in my face, Gloria!"

"Even if I try to, I can't! It's already been there—front and center," Mom said."

****$$****

In the past I had heard Grandma tell Mom that she couldn't believe she had invested so much in a fool, and I thought she was going there this day, when her next words were clipped by Mom. She began, "If I had a choice…"

"Simple," Mom interjected. "People in the court have college degrees."

"Gloria," Grandma's response came sharp and clean.

Mom tried to convince Grandma she would not do well in front of a judge, but Grandma's response was as quick as "wow," which was echoed by Dad who had long been there but had been as invisible as he became when he first lost our five-bedroom waterfront to foreclosure. We since have live in a smaller two-bedroom, one-and-a-half bath dump, just north of West Palm Beach.

"You'll kill yourself with this stupid thing," Mom argued.

And that's when Grandma's voice came fully alive. She said to Mom. "Miss Graves, tell me, who cares about death? Who cares about foolish things like that?"

"For long, you haven't been yourself," Mom exclaimed.

With those words I could feel my heart leap. There was something in what Grandma said that connected to me. I've felt a greater connection to her from that day. I felt like her son, not her grandboy, her Soldier—all that bullshit. *Son.*

That said, I knew Grandma was back. *Grandma's back, I just know it!*

Mom, Dad nor anyone else in the room did not seem to have the keenness I had though. In truth, they were devastated, frightened.

Grandma spoke more softly and methodically now.

"Gloria," she said. "I've been thinking and thinking all this while. With or without your help, I'll see this thing through!"

Mom was mad and the breaking of her voice said it. "G-oo-d!"

Dad turned his head swiftly at Mom and like Mom, he again spoke only one word. His was "Gloria!"

****$$****

It happened that my computer started buzzing just this moment, and I found myself tossed at what to do. Grandma was making some progress, so, should I stay and witness more, or was that the warning I should get back to handling my and Dr. Erskine's affair? Should I do it in the room or should I do it outside? My mind had become so misty in the moment, I felt beaten, but then things began to clear up for me: the woman is merciless. I didn't have a choice. Not only that, but we had just witnessed what I thought was a miracle for Grandma. She was doing things I hadn't seen her doing since she had fallen sick. Mom, Dad and Miss Bridgett were watching over her. It would be wise of me to get to different room and make Dr. Erskine happy. She would love me for that.

****$$****

In the associated assignment, a short one in comparison, the Congressman Roper was talking to a journalist on TV about financial reform. He told the journalist that the country was in "a financial jungle" but predicted an eventual recovery—"a temporary situation," he named it: home prices down, unemployment up, deficit exploding. "It'll be OK, …, even if it takes another election."

The journalist responded by asking Congressman Roper how he saw businesses factoring into helping to repair the economy.

"We see the financial sector at least as a partial cause of the financial crisis the country's facing, and we see them, in a measured way, mind you, at the center of the solution," Congressman Roper replied. "The more they are corporate citizens, the quicker the turnaround, Steve!"

Steve, the journalist presented another question. "Are the banks, in your opinion, up on their part?"

I'm proud to say I got full grade on this one, and all but one other assignment up to this point. Dr. Erskine said my writing was better than good, and my ideas were, to quote her, open quotes, 'strong and convincing. Brilliant!' Close quote."

Congressman Roper never answered the question.

# CHAPTER 3

With Grandma, we had a couple rough days in between as we heard Dr. Quack saying Grandma would be discharged from the hospital soon; her appearance to me at times suggested she was not ready for that. We were often walking away with opened mouths. Grace said that if Dr. Quack was a meteorologist and his sun forecast was anything close to our 4:00 pm weather caster's accuracy, that would take at least thirty percent of our chance. I liked the seventy percent hope for Grandma.

It was on the day we had this discussion, the fourth or fifth day after she was removed from the critical unit, Grandma looked at me and said with no uncertainty that I was her "joy, Tagg," and I loved her for that. Like a glutton adding sugar to Kool-Aid, she said I was more than that to her. That day she named me her "Dependable Soldier," and I trusted her instincts.

Another two days came and went and then Grandma was home, but not tightly wrapped as we hoped for. That, however, did not stop us from singing to her, her preferred church song "Jesus Loves Me This I Know" and others.

The family tried to do everything we could to make her comfortable. In the little extra time I had, Grace insisted that I re-watched the *Hurt Locker*, and that's what we were up to when we heard Grandma voice calling.

"And you, Bridgett. You're always going off into some other place," she screamed.

Mom would later replay those shifting bits: Grandma was hooked up to almost as many pieces of equipment as she was in the hospital and was making changes quickly and unexpectedly.

"I think at this point you should just relax and take it easy, Ms. Muley," Miss Bridgett suggested.

"Relax," Dad offered.

Mom said, Grandma ignored all warnings. She had her eyes pierced on a TV commercial. The law firm ad she saw at Shines was again on, talking about how small people could fight back against big companies.

Mom noted that the lawyer talking was not the cartoon version of the Latino lawyer that was on in the past but what she described as "the real flesh and hot blood version" of the Attorney.

His name was Vargas, Mom recalled, with relative ease. She called him "an arrogant finger-pointing bastard who shouts at his audience."

"...Don't be the little guy that get cremated," Attorney Vargas, advertisement went. "Just call our law firm and we'll get you back on track!"

Mom said Grandma became "a stupid woman" when the attorney said the middle-class in this country was suppressed. "You've lost your self-worth," he claimed. With those words Grandma went grabbing for a piece of paper from her bed table. She lifted herself quickly and forcefully, ripping herself from her hookups.

"She looked like a woman with a purpose," Miss Bridgett said, and I asked what she meant by that.

"Anybody got a pen," Grandma yelled.

She looked at her toes and they were wiggling.

Mom was so frightened, she jumped to help. "Mom," she said.

Dad tried to help as well, and so did Miss Bridgett. She was going, "Ms. Muley! Ms. Muley! Ms. Muley! Stop!"

They had no problem agreeing Grandma was excited at this point.

"I need this lawyer, and I need him now," she barked as her feet began to move to the side of the bed and her hand braced, as firm as the Navy Seal in Push-Ups 101.

Mom said she and Miss Bridgett tried to hold Grandma down, but Grandma was "with a new, strong self that came from nowhere, and she fought back with all she had."

"She's always been rogue," Mom said to Miss Bridgett."

Grandma would end up brutally fighting off Miss Bridgett and Mom in a brawl that left some blood on the floor, and several of the equipment broken on the ground as she got up to her own surprise. She looked at her feet and toes a another time. She shook her head. They were fine. They were dying to do the work she required of them. She placed them on the ground and yes, indeed, they were brilliant. She made a couple steps and everything was A-OK. She smiled at them as she darted away from Mom and Miss Bridgett, panting, and calling the two captors on her way out, passing by a mirror that reflected to her, herself looking a couple decade or more younger than she looked the moment earlier.

****$$****

It was later revealed by Dr. Quack that when Grandma left she had not fully gotten over her headaches. Added to that, he noted, what she saw in the mirror as she was heading out was "not herself as she was."

I said, "that's interesting."

"Instead," he elaborated, "the image she saw in the mirror was a message to one's self. Don't' forget. That's important!"

Even her clothes were brighter. They were brilliant, now, he noted.

Perhaps, what deserved a polychrome shot, was the way Grace looked at me. Her face was full with bewilderment, her pupils a dime or bigger and deep blue.

"Why we still here," she asked, her voice coming across more like a spookie-movie jingle, than like a normal person just wanting the answer to a straightforward question.

"I keep saying, something's not right!"

I sensed the urgency, and without another word we darted down the stairway in time to experience the tail of the commotion.

Mom had her hand in the air and she was dashing after Grandma who seemed to be on a glide being ushered away.

"This is getting outa hand," Mom shouted.

Grandma looked backward, and I recorded a smile on her face. "Am I really doing this," she whooped. "If I can do this, I can…."

I found myself shouting inside, Fly Grandma! Fly, Fly! Fly!"

# CHAPTER 4

At an almost wall to wall, mirrored bank conference room with silver and red lining, Corporate was meeting with his Counsel.

The Corporate Counsel joked that Corporate, who looked like he was aging fast, was not as virile as he used to be.

I listened in. Men talk.

I stared at the video. A line at the bottom weighed in: "Assignment 36!!"

The video clocked 45 seconds with a blinking blue-on-yellow display.

The office was lavish with mirrors on both sides letting the men see themselves in their own reflection and reflections of reflections.

Corporate, however, looked unsettled. He rubbed his hand on his head. Whatever they were saying we could not hear but fingers had taken on the shape of pistols, and there was a clear-cut look of antsiness between them. In a flick, there were faint words coming from Corporate, asking the Counsel, what was wrong with capitalism.

The sound faded away again momentarily giving way to a reporter talking on an off-volume TV. The logo of Wells Fargo bank appeared. Corporate reached for a remote control and ramped up the volume. The reporter's words were that, Wells Fargo had lost some case against them.

The reporter noted that Wells Fargo would have to pay out over two hundred million dollars to account holders in California for something that was incomprehensible.

Corporate shook his head, and it's clear that he is disappointed about what he had just heard.

The video presented a view of him in the reflection of his reflection.

He joked, "Mirror, mirror on the wall, who's the wickedest…"

The Corporate Counsel made public his views: "The crux of the matter—the only truth, "we're never immune," he offered. "Consortium chairman."

Corporate rubbed his hand through his hair as the Counsel kept on truckin'. "Enough judges sitting on the bench as we speak, willing to entertain those punks."

"You hit it right on the dollar bill there! They love to hate us; that's one thing I know for sure," Corporate replied.

The Counsel shook his head in agreement. Corporate forged ahead. "Another thing I know, they can't do without us! What are they to do? Put their money in some mom 'n pop's, back alley credit union?

The Counsel looked at Corporate, shaking his head. "Yeah." He replied, "Well, that won't be for long."

The video continued for another five-minutes-twenty-four seconds. It ended with the two men shaking hands and heads.

# CHAPTER 5

As for Grandma, she said she needed to tell her story and find help. She had made it to Attorney Vargas', the now real, red-blooded lawyer's office and was sitting in his front area, waiting, as the receptionist looked exhausted from repeating, "Hello, may I help you. Please hold. Please hold, may I…"

At one point Attorney Vargas passed by to go to the copy room. On the way back, he looked at Grandma, and shook his head. He smiled in a way as if he had known her before. She smiled back with like intensely and as pleasantly as if she knew him likewise.

As he disappeared, two ladies in suits who also came across as attorneys from the office passed by, lunch in their hands with one of them telling the other something about someone at least having "the social responsibility to do the right thing."

****$$****

A series of rushed assignments would start with Corporate again with his Counsel exploring ways to build their bank.

"How can we foil against the threat of the same kinds of lawsuits coming against us. I mean what do you see as our weaknesses," Corporate demanded of his Counsel.

The Corporate Counsel moved slowly and methodically to an answer: He looked behind himself, to his right and then to Corporate who this time sat more to his left. "Like we always know, it's illegal for the parasites to create the NSF draft on us. Not illegal for us to charge them though!"

He shifted his head, neck and shoulders as one does when releasing stress. "Is it ethical how we're lining up highest to lowest? Is it ethical how we conduct business," the Corporate Counsel asked rhetorically. "Is it ethical how we train? *Those* will be important questions going forward."

****$$****

"Go forward. Room 126," the Receptionist at Attorney Vargas' instructed Grandma as she simultaneously answered the phone to another of her irritating "hello, may I help you."

She pointed Grandma to Attorney Vargas's office.

"Right there. The one with the nice door," she aided.

Grandma used the word "thrown" to describe herself on entering. This had "thrown" her. That had "thrown" her. Everything had "thrown" her. At an earlier time of her life, among her many jobs previously unlisted, she had worked as an appraiser for the Sotheby's company in New York, and had learned a lot about the value of things. Here, everything was bigger and grander than she had imagined and absolutely nothing was a misfit, not the gold plaque on the wall, not the Ziegler Mahal carpet at the entrance, not the gold framed family pictures on the attorney's sprawling mahogany desk.

She took slow breaths, taking in the atmosphere, and then she positioned one of the pictures for her better viewing. She was looking at a thinner, more healthy looking Attorney Vargas in shorts, and she liked what she saw; she read out aloud an inscription embossed into the frame, below the picture: "26.2 Finished!"

"It's amazing," the attorney said to Grandma. "At your age you make over a-hundred-grand. That's attesting to something when young people can't even get a hundred greenbacks in their pockets these days!"

Grandma went into a long session about how good that was, and how she never had much time for herself anymore. She ended sharing she had to do what she had to do.

Attorney Vargas looked at Grandma as he kept un-blinked.

"I'm just curious why you spend your time working so hard when you could have been anywhere and the government foot the bill?"

“Me? A government check? Do I look lame.” Grandma said.

The attorney explained that he didn’t think it was an issue of lame as his own mother was *on it* when she was alive.

“You paid into it,” he said, giving emphasis to his last word.

Everybody he knew had done *it* when their time came. He made that known as well.

That was what led Grandma to tell the attorney about Grandpa. Grandpa John’s last gig was as an auto interior specialist who owned his own shop, and as small as it was, he never missed a day of work. And even with all that on his plate, he wanted Grandma to go to grad school.

“I never thought that was right for me to do either,” Grandma said. “He was such a good money handler. To show him my commitment, I never stopped working all these years!”

In time, Attorney Vargas was describing to Grandma his take on things. In his words, the banks had “loosen their demons on their customers,” and he asked her, what made her think she could put a retreat to a dragon that vicious.

“Let’s put it this way,” Grandma replied. “My grandson said if I can work a computer, and I can have a business that gives me a middle-class living, what can’t I do?”

Attorney Vargas placed a look of doubt on his face. He started shaking his head, and with that came the rubbing of one hand with the other. He looked like a person who was caught off guard, but that was not the case this time. His skills of being a former Boy’s Scout and Toastmaster saved him.

Hanged pictures of him giving a speech at a Toastmasters meeting as well of pictures of him as a Boy’s Scout were highly visible, and Grandma did not miss them, nor did she missed the one with him getting a “Prosecutor Of The Year” award. That too must have been a long time earlier; he was a fit looking man back then.

“Admirable but those are not necessarily the competencies needed to win a case,” the attorney said. “Let’s try it another way. What do you think would be your greatest weakness going forward? Keep in mind the giant $$!”

Grandma smiled and leaned forward, looking like a more beautiful version of herself, comparing with her own youthful dancing pictures. Perhaps she was feeling cute and, God knows, sexy is En

Vogue; her whole self was into it. "Well, I can't think of any, but my daughter does."

"And what's that," Attorney Vargas asked.

"She would be quick to say I'm not smart, or funky, a diva, or even strong," Grandma offered.

She moved her head as if she was all of those things. "She thinks I'm too weak. I was in the hospital and she swears on the Bible it's because of this."

Attorney Vargas, "Well… is it?"

Grandma brought forth a new smile that the attorney said made her look half the age of the woman who entered his office.

With that, she shifted her body closer to his, and she said that made her feel more like a young woman on a date than some eighty something, "gray, spent dame trying to bring down some evil empire."

"Why don't you tell me Mr. Vargas," she asked. "What do you think?"

"Well, well," the attorney began, being alert, as a pilot fighting to keep her plane on course. "Ms. Muley, what I see is you wanting to shed white light on a very dark issue. I understand that, and I appreciate that. And let me not fail to point out, I see your charm. You have intellect. I'm excited. But …."

The "but" had barely come out the Mexican's mouth, when Grandma, who was again eying pictures of him on his desk and coming across one with him in fine red necktie in Louisiana helping oil spill victims, cut him off.

"No buts about nothing" Grandma stated. "Right?"

This time Attorney Vargas was taken aback. He looked at the Toastmaster's certificate given to him, hanging next to the picture of him giving what was his best practice speech. He shook his head.

"You see," he started to explain. "Going full circle we must also deal with threats and weaknesses as well, and….

"You know, my grand-boy showed me you on Facebook," Grandma interrupted.

"Facebook," the lawyer replied, raising his head. "One day, the attention on them will be huge!"

"I saw your ad on TV too. I didn't come without the highest endorsement of you!"

Grandma pointed to one of the pictures she was looking at.

"You defeated big oil! Didn't you?"

The attorney shook his head, "Exxon! Yes! BP…"

Grandma interrupted. "I know. I told you I didn't come here a blind girl!"

Attorney Vargas began shaking his head again, first towards his left and then it was all over. He knew he had to get out of this.

"My mother was 79 when she passed, Ms. Muley, and she was nothing like you! That said, I'm still questioning whether you can have stamina?"

Grandma said she wanted to slap him. "You don't know what I can do, Sir. Do you?"

Attorney Vargas response was that he knew how taxing the process could get, and then he lifted his heavy hand the way a woodcarver works his hatchet. He used it to shape out his words, the air standing for wood.

"I don't see how you can do it!"

He proceeded to ask Grandma if she realized how much paperwork was involved. How about the hours? The cost?

With that, his face took on a harsh, serious look. "And you realize the scrutiny on one's personal life?"

"What the bank's forgotten, our account is not their property," Grandma rebuked. "And I'm here to let them know!"

The attorney made a quick and apparently intended up and down motion of his head.

Grandma continued. "Is there something wrong with that?"

Attorney Vargas signified *no*.

He added, "But that's not everything, Ms…"

"Sir. Sir," Grandma stopped him as she pointed to the picture of him in shorts. "When you run a marathon, tell me Mister, do you break down at mile one?"

****$$****

Our next short assignment in line was beeping in queue. It would have Corporate with some of his surrogates strolling by offices, passing cubicles and talking about how they had a long way to get to where they needed the bank to be.

"Yes, this is fourteen percent, but we can't stop now," Corporate said to the group.

Miss Andrea, who was wearing one of her oversized fedoras, advised it would be foolish to let Congress take anything from them without a rumble.

"I'm doing whatever it takes for us to get the profits we deserve," the VP of Bank Ops contributed.

Corporate asked the group to give "pity to the leeches" for they knew not what they were doing. They did not even knowing that the bank was not taking half of what it was supposed to take in many cases. In fact, the bank was already generously returning $35.00 once a year to any patron who had an NSF and asked for it, "a gift back to the customer for allowing us to serve them," Corporate explained.

Corporate looked annoyed as he continued. "They get the gold and what do we get? The shaft, he asked. This question led the VP of Bank Ops to agree, fittingly noting that it was in the bank's prerogative to bounce as many checks as it wanted each day.

"We could do six, eight, How about ten, twenty a day? How about mortgages?"

The crowd laughed, leading into $$ CFO Fred Tolly's talk that "If a customer eats the hamburger, they ought to pay for it."

"Of course we can do six, but we need the trade! Why kill em?" Corporate queried. He noted he was interested in a superior "end game!"

The crowd took notes.

"Mind me now," Corporate came back. "We're a bank with a conscience. We can stand up for ourselves, but goddammit. We have to give back something. That's doing our share. Sacrifice! Isn't it?"

He squinted at Miss Andrea. "Big-hat, be sure to include in future communiqué, 'Thanks for giving us the opportunity to serve.'"

With that, he asked for an excuse, noting he had to take off to a "consortium" meeting.

# CHAPTER 6

Inside Attorney Vargas's office things were heating up as the Attorney spoke with one of his secretaries on the phone.

"Are you definite we can't do it? Just one more time," he begged.

The woman replied that taking on another case would push the company's expenses over the edge.

"Sure," Attorney Vargas asked. His voice was whimsical, and he was biting on his fingernail.

The woman's voice came back. "Verified twice and confirmed!"

Attorney Vargas knew this, yet looked disappointed. "Very well. And thank you Lydia," he told the lady on the phone as Grandma swung her head for a full meeting of the eyes.

"Ready to testify," she declared.

The attorney was not so sure of the future nor thrilled.

"What we're dealing with, Miss Muley," he began, "is a financial lightning in a bottle."

Concurrently, the light on Grandma's I-phone blinked indicating a text message had come in. She picked up the phone, but did not look at it. What she had to say was more critical.

"Circuit court? Federal court? Congress? Where do you need me," she said.

The attorney flipped through some papers. "The record shows they took over 30 billion from your wallets in just the year" he said.

"Seems like you're on their side, too," Grandma countered.

"You haven't included anything about credit cards. And you think—home loans not messed with?"

By this time, Attorney Vargas looked like he had ran out of time and his dealings with Grandma.

"Where do you get time to worry about all that," he asked.

"Me? I make time," Grandma answered. Her words were snap and came with a lifting of her hand. Some wrinkles from age, close to her arm revealed themselves.

****$$****

In time, the attorney told Grandma it could take months or even years before a case of the kind would probably be heard, and he asked her if she realized that.

Grandma pushed her chest forward.

"With due respect, Your Honor," she said.

"No. No. Reserve that for the judge," Attorney Vargas replied. "Now, let me explain…"

Grandma told the attorney there was nothing more to explain. She was excited to get started. He, however, interrupted her, reminding her she was in his office and not the other way.

"Ms. Muley, so you see," he kept moving forward. "At this high profile level there's a large initial investment on our part."

He brought out that over the past six months his firm had put large sums of money into a number of cases and he didn't think his company could take on another retainer of the scale of Grandma's case for awhile.

"Don't try to pull that on me," Grandma reacted, as she got to her feet. "After I've been here with you for the last ninety minutes, I'm not going anywhere!"

Attorney Vargas seemed to try and find the calm voice a man of his education and experience is expected to bring to the world he found himself in. At first it was craggy.

"Just got off a call," he elaborated. "Even though I believe in my heart, this is a good thing and a good case, I think we'll need the kind of bankroll we don't have for your monster."

Grandma slammed her right fist into her other palm. "What happened to your no-cash-down broadcast?"

Attorney Vargas joked that nobody was expected to read the fine print as Grandma glanced at flashing news that was on her I–phone. It was headlined, “Charity CEO Grossly Overpaid.”

She looked crossly at the attorney.

“Are you telling me you’re no different?”

“Different?”

“Different than the dirty crooks! The world’s worst actors,” Grandma replied. “You all should be behind bars!”

Attorney Vargas had long moved from the calm sounding voice; now he endeavored for it again. “You said you saw our commercial, right?”

Grandma began laughing. She admitted she was acting like a child carrying out a prank.

“Yes I did! Now it’s interesting to see where you stand,” she said. “You’re a young man. You don’t want to screwed up your life like so many goofballs before you. Do you?”

Attorney Vargas seemed to be in a period of amnesty; he leaned back in his massaging seat.

“Those are serious matter for us, Ms. Muley.”

“I came all the way here,” Grandma replied. “Is this all you can do for an *old* woman?”

In the face of all the trouble Grandma had caused Attorney Vargas, he noted he did not have a personal gripe with her.

He took a slow, full breadth and then he addressed her. “You know Ms Muley, you’re a very likeable person, and I have an idea,”

Grandma yawned.

“I have a friend,” he continued.

“And she trusts you,” Grandma countered.

“It’s a him,” Attorney Vargas said.

“Good,” she replied.

“With the tough economy, as it is, he might be in a better position than we are right now. I’ll get you hooked-up.”

****$$****

Attorney Vargas went on the phone telling a secretary to follow through with Attorney Barrow because “Ms. Muley’s a nice lady,” and he wanted her to have the best representation. The secretary’s voice came back over the phone to Attorney Vargas. “You know how Sir Fredrick is; 'he likes horses that can run fast and win races!'"

"I wanted you," Grandma protested, yet projected her hand to Attorney Vergas.

"But as you can see, we're not in a perfect world," he replied.

Grandma tried to take her hand back but skin was already feeling skin, and Attorney Vargas was not about to change a thing. The deal was sealed.

"I'll settle for your, whatever. Sidekick," Grandma said and kicked her own foot sideways. She was not a horse, a donkey or a mule, but generally would not let the attorney get away without a fight. She was not happy.

Attorney Vargas looked cautious, tight lipped. He is focused.

On the phone, he instructed his secretary to tell Attorney Barrow, another local lawyer, that he *highly endorsed* Ms. Muley.

"I know if resources weren't down, you would have taken it," the Secretary said.

Attorney Vargas concurred. "There's a time for everything," he noted.

****$$****

Everywhere things were changing. In her car driving, Grandma was on the phone talking with Mom. "Change," Mom said was on the way.

"Gloria," Grandma said. "He doesn't have the time for me."

"Change, Mom. You have to change," Mom said.

Grandma replied, she would never contemplate abdication.

****$$****

At Shines a young woman in suit was teaching a class to help the women deal with their financial life, a picture of Suse Aman, a financial guru, projected on a screen, and a label above read, "Time, Change, Wealth."

At the bank's Corporate Training Center things were changing as well. My quickie next assignment started with a financial analysis, teacher looking up at a clock. The time registered 1:49 pm.

The Shines teacher told the students to keep focus as they were beginning to drop their heads and with that their attention.

"What I'm saying is you must know what time to act and when to sit back and observe," the teacher instructed.

****$$****

"Nobody, nobody likes the time they spend here, likes being here all this time." Ms. Diaz blurted out from a slumbered position in a newly minted wheelchair placed close to a bathroom door at Shines.

On the other wing, the women were in a revolt, one telling Ms. Diaz, "Patrice stop it." Others chatting at the same time, some complaining, some mumbling to themselves.

"We. We. Sick and tired. Sick and tired, all the time," Ms. Diaz said.

Ms. Zenida Reid, using her way to language, told Ms Wonzick, "I heard your friend going to lose her house. No more rich lady."

Ms. Wonzick spun her wheelchair to look at Ms. Zenida Reid.

"It's time we help her," Ms. Wonzick asserted. "She needs our Jane Henry now!"

Ms. Diaz asked in her do-again speech pattern if Grandma was going to live with them soon.

****$$****

At the Corporate Training Center the teacher now told the students they would have to do their class another time. She noted the class was too inattentive. Why not go home?.

# CHAPTER 7

Grace and I had a bet out on which of the lawyers had the fancier office, Attorney Vargas or Attorney Barrow. I won; Grandma served as judge. Not only was Attorney Barrow's office with more unforgettable things, it was also housed in a better building.

When we were there, Grace went for the large globe on the attorney's, desk while my eyes explored a larger-than-human sized Black Madonna hanging on a wall lined with solid wooden bookshelves. In a way, it was like being in a moneyed version of Grandma's Library.

Grandma believed the shelves were antique as she thought of many things old. They seemed to be made from the same mahogany log Vargas's came from. I since have gotten to learn a lot more than I cared about the wood. I preferred the books themselves. I wanted to smell them, but I didn't have the audacity to do so; nonetheless, they filled the shelves, and Grandma called them "incunabula."

As she sat amidst the niceness of the law office, I began to see something others had been pointing to for a while. She was indeed looking younger and more vibrant than before.

In our face-to-face view, she looked younger than I had ever seen her in the past, even when I was a kid. To add color and elegance she wore a dress with pastel roses, a bullion lining around the sleeves and neck. The light in the spot was warm and made everything illuminate perfectly. This was the mixture that made me see Grandma as able, even as she graced herself before the lawyer; his face and demeanor I now see best in Doctor Murray, the accused manslaughter doctor of singer Michael Jackson.

Well dressed and full of good posture, he was as much an ornament to his office as he was the living being that evidently had matched the yin and yang to come up with such a comfortable setting.

Now the office served host to a vibrant, restive woman who had told us when "the big, fat lawyer" had turned her down, her focus went to one place and one place only: She would "not stop until the bank's "evil is exposed and they pay for their sins."

Here was her new opportunity to begin that process.

She was not in Attorney Barrow's office ten minutes, however, when he was rubbing his hand across his forehead..

"Ms. Muley," he said from a throat long-waiting to process sound. "The point is, the banks are too strong. They have the monop…"

"And," Grandma countered. She was determined not to let this one slip out her hand.

She looked at him: handsome, tall and perfect in skin tone, texture.

He spoke. "They have the big guns, and I might add, they'll use it without impunity!" They have their blue-chip lawyers, Miss Muley."

"They want blood," Grandma replied.

The lawyer waited for more, like a lion awaiting its zebra's sprint.

She felt the game so did not speak.

"It's just not right for us right now," he followed up.

****$$****

Grandma placed her hand at her mouth. Her face noted her level of disappointment. From the time Attorney Vargas had recommended Attorney Barrow, she knew he could help her. To get attention, she called the powers the banks held, "weapons of mass destruction," and she insisted that Attorney Barrrow hear her and help her to make the bank's wrong, right.

The lawyer placed his palms under his chin as he looked at Grandma flirting with her eyes.

He said, "For one, I agree our government gave away the citizenry money to the banks and these guys just stole it."

"I knew you would understand," Grandma replied. Her response was fast coming, her hand hurrying towards her head.

"Let me tell you something, I voted for *this* president," she said.

Attorney Barrow looked meditative for a moment. He parsed his lips for a second. He reflected: Grandma was playing with his race."Indeed, they've crossed the red line," he said, to which Grandma's was, "I told you!"

"A year or two ago this would have been right down our alley, and I would like to do it," the attorney picked up the conversation.

Grandma looked him straight through his brown eyes and he into hers. Hers were blue, and in them were a fight.

"I won't give in," her words came out.

He continued. "Recently, Ma'am, the banks have become bigger and with that, too big," he said. "Not even Washington can keep a lid on them now."

Her eyes searched for his, that had wandered a bit, but he chose to let his words do the job. They had won him many multi-million dollar lawsuits in the past, and he was not going to let this lady's moves change his game.

"They're adding gasoline to fire, not even giving us loans," he said.

Grandma began shaking her legs and stared at one of many pictures on a wall not far away. Momentarily she leaned forward to look more closely at one of the group pictures to see what came into view as the young Black girl she had given the tip to at a restaurant earlier. She was now older and looked in full bloom, but Grandma did not forget her. She was one of about ten people in the pictures of what seemed to be staff members of the firm, she being the only other pictured Black person, counting the attorney.

"We're the clients. We tell the banks what to do," Grandma said.

Attorney Barrow stretched backwards, swaying his head on the way.

"Whoo, Whoo. Where you get your spunk from?"

"Use it," Grandma fired back.

Attorney Barrow rolled his fingers over his lips and then to his chin. "I would love to, but a class-action like what's necessary requires more than just a tough personality or our anger at what they're doing to us. What it really calls for is …."

"Is that your daughter," Grandma interjected, still having the picture on the wall, in her trail of sight. She pointed to the photograph.

Attorney Barrow grinned. "I wish! You know Niqua?"

"Niqua?"

For a split Grandma went quiet as she re-winded and replayed in her head the day she and the other women were at the restaurant Jimmy's Hot Spot, and it was a $10.00 tip to Niqua that had the next day caused her account to go overdrawn.

Niqua! That's her name! Jimmy's, Bald Road. NSF!"

The attorney stared at Grandma with a question.

"Jimmy's," she said.

Attorney Barrow said something to the effect that he had been to Jimmy's and something else relating to how the food was good.

"The best steak in a hundred miles," Grandma shared.

And I *gathered* you're the best in town!"

"Yeah," attorney Barrow answered, in fact not taking note to where the conversation had gone.

He went on to tell Grandma that Niqua, the young lady, had done summer work at Jimmy's a few semesters. "If I'm not wrong, she's back there. Her last semester," he said.

Grandma called Niqua a nice kid, and Attorney Barrow said it was sad they could no longer keep her hired.

"When the economy turned we had to slice her and eight others," Attorney Barrow shared. "That's when we started to know we can't do everything we want to."

"Time to turn her back on," Grandma put forward, her voice strong and authoritative.

Attorney Barrow believed in the powers of the moon and sun, and things of that sort, and he looked up to the Black Madonna. "The stars are not lined up for that right now," he said.

Grandma said she wanted to lay out her feelings right there and then that corporate bandits were taking consumers to the poor house, but before she got to that, the Attorney was telling her something about how his own mother had also become leery of the deals big banks were making among themselves and with the government.

Grandma marveled at the thought of the attorney's mother having some of the concerns like herself. Not only that, but he had a mother, and for some reason unknown to her, "mothers" were bouncing up everywhere as Grandma went around talking about her banking problems. He should understand, even if lousy Vargas, who, by the way, claimed one also, couldn't.

Grandma decided she would take on the new lawyer tactically.

"What is it about everybody claiming a mother these day," she asked.

Attorney Barrow spoke kindly, "Yeah."

"So, you understand," Grandma replied.

She put on a happy face.

The attorney put on one that was stoic.

"You've got to help me. Do something!"

Attorney Barrow got up, started to pace and then sat in a chair on the same side of the desk as Grandma. He spoke as if apologizing, telling Grandma he would love to help her, but said he really didn't think he was in a position to do it right then, which put a mean look on Grandma's face and her snatching of Barrow's hand.

"Let go," he demanded, but she kept possession of it.

"It's heavy lifting! You've got to lend a hand!"

"Ma'am. Ma'am," the attorney begged, but Grandma could not let go. Her mind was only holding one idea in that moment, and that was herself, 9 years old, Zimmerman Grocery and Produce, a tense moment. "I said. I said you *must* help me," she stipulated for a release. "You're not leaving here till you do!"

Attorney Barrow did a hard, speedy pull and freed himself from Grandma, but even though he released himself, he was instantly recaptured.

"Ma'am, Ma'am, I have another appointment," he lied

"Damn outright greed and thievery," Grandma responded, loudly as she released the attorney, pushing him away from her in the process. "If not now, when? Aren't you going to stop them?"

Attorney Barrow inspected his hand momentarily as if it was someone else's, and when he saw it was not bruised, he brushed it off and placed it in his pocket.

"I'm sorry Ma'am. I've got to go," he said.

Grandma looked around and said she conceded this was his place, not hers. A soldier doesn't give up his quarters that easy. Does he?

"You! You and your slippery cohort. What's his name? You're nothing more than sorry lawyers," she barked, nevertheless. "It doesn't take me to tell you that, though!"

Attorney Barrow was standing now, this time holding his face so serious, his shoulders upright; he had become the rightful tiger in the room.

"It's over Miiis." It's over!"

Grandma, also standing, began to walk away but turned aback, pointed.

"You need to hear this, you sorry jurist. You sad …sapiens," she said and then began to slur. "You've not seen the end of me. You hear me. You hear me, you Weakling!"

# CHAPTER 8

For the next few days we did all we could to keep Grandma from falling ill again and tried to convince her to use her energy in her business that was going through a period of decline presumably due to her busy focus on her banking problem.

To say we got it right, would be wrong, but that doesn't mean we are quitters. She stayed off the streets, even though she didn't make it easy for us, nor did she relax.

By the end of the first day she was in full career planning out what she was going to do to Bank $$, and by mid morning on day two, even though still in her bed, she was on the phone talking to a reporter from a local TV station about what she called downbeat behaviors that kills the American spirit.

The lady TV Reporter, who insisted that Grandma stop calling her Miss, but rather Toni, pointed to Grandma that AL Graham was the reporter who handled that kind of story for the station, but he was not in right then.

"When do you people work," Grandma inquired.

Toni, the TV reporter overlooked the question and told Grandma she knew tons of people who had the exact problem Grandma was having with her bank. She hinted that the real problem the banks had was that they were copycats. As soon as one does something awful to you, another follows because they were afraid their reporting to their god would look bad, she said.

"Whether that's true or not, it's our job to stop them," Grandma followed up. "Isn't it?"

TV Reporter Toni said she agreed one-hundred-and-ten percent with Grandma and shared that she was one who felt if they did enough stories on the subject, they would be able to help change what she believed was a culture of Corporate Greed. "I was at Bank CashCash today, and they had problem with a lady and her fourteen-year old boy. Can you believe that? She was trying to get back $400 they took from the youngster's pop tarts, Wendy's Double Stack account!"

TV Reporter Toni continued as she burst into a laugh. "A Coke. You believe that can easily cost a kid forty dollars today?"

"I'm all game," Grandma said, offering herself.

The TV reporter asked Grandma if she had seen a piece her colleague Bob Frost had done on Bank $$ just two weeks prior.

"You guys interviewed them?"

"Yeah, a really conceited man," TV Reporter Toni replied. "He didn't tell us much about anything! Corporate, you know?"

Grandma spoke. "If I ever talk with him I will ask him if he's human like us."

"Well," TV Reporter began but was cut short by Grandma whose voice seemed to be going at the speed of a car's screeching sounds.

"No, no, I would just the…!"

TV Reporter Toni told Grandma that Corporate goes to their station often, and the last time he was there another of their reporter, Shirley Smith tried to tie him down on a slew of issues from credit card fees to mortgage, and the overdraft issue in question, but she described Corporate as being as vague as the night wind.

"You think he gave us any reasonable answer," she asked; her voice telling of her own frustration.

Grandma noted the whole system started to go lopsided twenty or thirty years earlier, but she could not have dreamt it would go down to the point it had gotten.

"I see it's 11:45 right now. AL's going to be in, around 4:20 to prep for his program," the TV Reporter Toni said.

"I want it on today," Grandma said emphatically.

"How fast do you move?"

Grandma responded. "How fast do you want me?"

TV Reporter Toni told Grandma that if she got to the station by 430, they would have adequate time to get her on the 6:30 newscast.

"I like how AL takes on consumer's problems," Grandma said.

TV Reporter Toni said AL Graham was the best in the business—the best in the contiguous United States—"The best from Minnesota to Florida and from Maine to Washington," she said sounding like she was standing in for their ad reps.

Grandma responded that she liked that.

"Timing is everything on TV, Miss," TV Reporter Toni followed up. "Be here or be square!"

"AL and I going to get them," Grandma boasted.

TV Reporter Toni replied that Grandma would be doing a grand, good thing for the middle-class if things went well. She continued. "...saving a lot of the viewers "a mint; they'll love you for it!"

****$$****

Grace and I could not remember seeing Grandma preparing as fast as she was going that day. Grace said she was moving like Speedy Burnette. I remembered Dad's term for the same was Speedy Gonzales. In fact, I recall there was something about him in cartoons we used to watch when Grace and I were younger. Speedy Burnett could never sound as good anyways, I noted.

In spite of a all the hustle and bustle, however, and even an admonishment of us not to interrupt while she was readying herself, Grandma had not made herself completely ready after a couple hours. With that, Grace saw an opportunity to go at her.

"And you always like to tell us that haste makes waste," Grace said to Grandma.

I knew Grandma was doing her best and did not need to be bothered, so I told Grace not to "mess with Grandma." She was going to be on TV, I told Grace and proceeded to hug Grandma who I encouraged to look as good as she wanted.

"Grandma, wear a hat like Elizabeth of England," I suggested.

Grandma became energized. "Soldiers," she said. "Which one you think will make me look like the woman I am?"

She speedily drew several of her many hats to what was already a crowded dresser, practically dancing as she moved around. She put on one and Grace and I gave her two thumbs down. She puts on another and got the look of one thumb down from Grace. She puts on another, a pink one with a large fuchsia rose on it, but I didn't think that was her best look then and likewise gave her a thumb down. That's when her hand reached for and placed on her head an orange Cha Cha's Jena hat that matched her Nordstrom dress. Both Grace and I were thumbs up and excited.

I momentarily looked out a bedroom window to see Mom and Miss Bridgett stepping out of Miss Bridgett's Volvo, both looking unusually unkempt as if they were responding to an emergency. Who told them? I later found out, Grace.

"Sometimes some of the best folks have rough edges," Miss Bridgett was telling Mom as they rushed to the house. Miss Bridgett answered that Grandma thought she could dance her way into getting people to do whatever she wanted them to do.

The two stepped in but were instantly halted by a stare from Grandma. "What's wrong with you now," Grandma asked the two with the readiness of a waiting snake, her eyes recording their choices of dress.

Mom tried to move beyond all this and began to open her arm for an embrace. "My Mommy! My, my, my. I came as soon as I heard," She said.

"And what did you hear, Dear," Grandma asked, a sly smile on her face.

"I thought you were going to quit this foolishness," Mom replied.

Grandma ignored mom and brushed off the hug. She was preferring to admire the way she looked from a nearby mirror, which was quickly transforming her into the youngest looking grandmother she had ever known.

Mom repeated the piece about Grandma quitting.

"At what point was that," Grandma asked of Mom's question. She continued, "Gloria, you're nuts!"

"No! You're nuts!"

Mom lifted her head to the ceiling. Like Grandma, she was not up on the many tools, machines, techniques, crafts, systems and methods we were using to make our lives easy and fun, but whatever she was doing with her ears and eyes was my view of a radio or television station streaming live events to a computer.

Still looking upwards, she spoke.

"Well, let's see," she began. "You were far ahead before you got sick, and you were ahead of that before you started."

She proceeded to check our Grandma for cracks and spillages as the volume and pace of her voice overwhelmed us. "Mom, when will this stop? Why is this even happening?"

If there was one thing that stimulated Grandma, it must have been the combination of Mom's questions and the look of she and Miss Bridgett. I had never seen Grandma more resistant and happy at the same time.

She moved her head slowly and gracefully, and with her chest lifted, and her feet in a fine pair of shoes, she glided to her make-up kit on the dresser, her hand waltzing over to her lips.

"How is my lipstick," she asked. "My face? My hair?"

"Mom. Are you nuts," Mom barked back as Grandma reached for her purse. Mom continued, "You think you're Miss It! just because you're …"

Grandma was dancing towards Grace, which interrupted and disappointed Mom, but didn't change a thing for Grandma who chose to be our entertainer of the moment.

"How does my chain look," she asked of Grace.

Grace looked at Mom first in hunt for approval, which she did not get, but gave her views nevertheless in a faltering-like nod back to Grandma that her chain was OK.

Grandma then decided to get my final seal of approval as she did one of her "young-girl" dancing spin towards me.

"And you my handsome Soldier, my Dear and loving grandboy, you like my dress?"

Of course I did. And of course I loved her too. I loved everything about her. "I love it Grandma and I love you too," I said, disregarding what anyone else said, thought or would do.

I could see that Mom was not happy with our answers, but in that moment, I don't remember caring, and most of all, I knew Grandma got what she wanted from me.

She was looking towards Mom and rubbing her hand down her dress, and she was Marylyn Monroe!

"Not even in blue have I ever looked more beautiful," she bragged of her dress that had some small blue stars on it. "Gloria, my dearest. Why should I drive through those busy streets all by m *little* self," she said as she looked at Mom. "To *wrinkle* it all?"

I know that if someone had taken our pictures in that moment we would have all, except Grandma, looked odd. Mom looked like a mad woman, lost in the happenings around her. Miss Bridgett looked like someone caught in the wrong place at the wrong time. Grace, well, she just had the look of something bad happening, and for me, I had a wild, silly grin going on. I thought I knew my Grandma, so this just tickled me to the bone.

"My ride of the day. Come on. Come on, Dear," Grandma said, holding on to Mom's arm. "I'm running late for Wall Street!"

My grin turned to a laugh when Miss Bridgett rubbed her hand on her dress to try and make it neat.

"Are you with me," Grandma said to Miss Bridgett in an off-hand way.

"My opinion's evolving," she announced, yet speeding to secure her spot. "I'm coming too!"

# CHAPTER 9

In my life I have had the benefits of many treats, and one was to get a peek into the wild and murky world of banking.

It is one filled with glamour, shears-sharp minds that can turn a penny into a hundred dollar coin without even asking a mint's permission, and it's one where machines can easily be the boss of man. The last words are not mine. If I were to claim them, I would be called a "thief" by the very one who first spoke them, the one who despised thievery so much: Grandma Sandra Muley. Over time, she had found many creative way of telling us that once the machine takes a customer's money it's the hardest thing for the employee to get it back to the customer. Thief, rasscloth thief, was another way she had put it, herself borrowing the "R" word from a Jamaican man we once heard cursing out another man on Miami Beach.

When I took on my next class assignment, Grandma was front and center, consequently: The "wild and murky were on exposition."

At the corporate office a plasma screen flashed moving words across, about city executives in a California municipality that were highly overpaid while providing pitiable service in a bad economy. Another screen ran a story about a wealthy man putting billion of dollars of his money into a nationally known bank, noting his view on the un-likeliness that the country would go back into a recession.

Inside the company's Boardroom, Corporate gathered his usual executive staff and referred to them as brilliant. He told them they were called to tackle the next assault on $$.

Both Wells Fargo and The Money Bank had lost lawsuits against them, he reported. He went on to explain: "A certain bunch is picking a fake fight with our industry."

The audience listened with keen awareness.

He plowed on. "What we need to worry about are the new legislations coming down the pipeline. Left unchecked, these criminals will take everything—leave us destitutes!"

One of the executives in the room stood up and spoke. His voice and manner were in opposition with a smile on his face. "Nobody can take a $2 Billion hit and still be grinning with their customers," he said.

Corporate leaned towards Miss Andrea, who he kept calling his marketing mind. "Make sure we're ahead of the curve," he tells her. "What you need is a hand-grenade in your hibachi. Mind me, this is not a slaughter. This is the work we live to do!"

Ms. Andrea looked at Corporate. Stared. "I believe we all got your e-mail," she said. She pulled a sheet from a stack of paper in front of her and began reading it.

"It may be Operations job to 'F' them, but don't let them 'F' us. Do whatever it takes to keep the customer on our side," Signed: Corporate."

****$$****

The group took a break and when they got back they went straight to a bi-monthly report on how the shifting of processing ACH was increasing profits. Training was coming along fine, according to the report. The report highlighted, however, they would have to find alternative sources of income soon if Congress kept crafting new rules that cut into their profits.

One executive noted it was a "damn shame" what was happening to them and informed, "there's no time to idle."

"But what's after that," another asked.

"Not a problem," Miss Andrea answered. She was flipping through some of the other documents she had in front of her, and she took some notes into a tablet next to the documents. "We'll sell, they yell!"

Momentarily, Corporate lifted his head to one of the TVs and sees news pertaining to banks having to allow people to opt out from overdraft.

"That damn thing's still on," he said. "Change the channel!"

The group carried on with a lengthy discussion about how the bank and the industry were just bouncing back from the steepest financial losses in a generation and now Congress and the President were attacking every attempt they made at trying to make a profit.

"What have you got," Corporate asked Miss Andrea who was still reviewing her notes.

Miss Andrea face came up from her gadget with a wild, out-of-this-world smile on it. "Let's frighten them," she suggested. She dropped her head back down.

"By letting them know we will not authorize their ATMs & debit card purchases when they don't have their *chips* on the ship, they'll flip," she continued.

One executive declared a resounding "Excellent!" For another, it was "Damn Good!" Even the term "Genius" surfaced from another to ricocheted to a group ovation.

For a brief moment there was doubt as to how things would play out with Corporate as he was stoned face.

"We need more than some rhyming solution," he said eventually.

One executive suggested that if customers opted out, "we can always opt them back in after a while."

Corporate flashed a look of discontent, or chance it was boredom. "Every day I think about your bonus," he said. "You like yours. Right, Tolly? How about you Andrea? Trevor? We all do, and we all know that!"

The group's gaze at Corporate was keen, a distasteful look covered the room of faces. For Tolly, there was the sense he would get up and slam Corporate with a fist.

"I'm already under," Tolly said, his voice cracking.

Corporate studied the faces to get some consensus. He moved ahead. "If you're going to continue asking me for a raise, we'll need something better than what's been presented. Now! Get the hell to work! Do it now! This meeting's adjourned!"

****$$****

Meanwhile, at the Upper Creek Branch the tempo was business as usual. Two of the managers had just finished coffee and returned to their seats when the mail courier trekked in with a large stack of mail and places it on a manager's desk.

"Pretty soon you'll need another assistant," the courier joked and tapped her fingers away from the mail. She then departed, leaving the bank manager to sort and opened the mail.

A few minutes into the task of sorting and reading the mail, the Upper Creek Manager got to a customer's letter that irritated her.

"We have the weirdest douche bags as customers. They think they will be irresponsible and we're just going to keep putting *our hard-earn* cash back into their accounts," she said holding the letter in her hand. She crumbled it and "basketballed" it towards Eduardo Sosa's trash bin. Eduardo Sosa reached and caught the letter on the way to his basket.

"What you think, Wardo," she asked Eduardo Sosa, whose response was one of those kind of head shaking a person does when he or she is upset and simply doesn't want to be a part of a conversation.

"Jackass," the Upper Creek Manager concluded.

Eduardo Sosa now shakes his head. "If I had a dime for every time you do that…."

The Bank Manager created a new jeering voice. "Dear Sir/Madam, I am writing to inform you…"

Eduardo Sosa began to open the crimpled letter.

"Yeah, I know 'it's *one of those again*, but we should at least scan it into their file."

"Can't be bothered," the bank manager said. "Corporate policy…."

"You should," Eduardo Sosa interrupted as the manager asked back for the letter and began sending it through the shredder at her desk. "Just don't spend greens you don't have! Ha, ha, ha, ha, haa!"

# CHAPTER 10

Grace and I sat quietly as Mom sped onto I-95, passing areas of heavy greenery and then small to larger and larger buildings. Along, Mom kept questioning Grandma why she couldn't be like other women her age. At first, Grandma laughed it off, but when Miss Bridgett, who sat on the passenger side, second row, got into the mix, Grandma found herself in full swing of another fight.

"You know my heart's good," she replied to a question that bothered her. "Why you' all keep messing with me?"

"You don't even know why you're doing it," Mom countered. "I know you don't know!"

Grandma eyed Mom as if her occupation was one in surveillance, her stare without-flicker.

She said, "Children obey your parents for it is right…."

Sensing a moment of strain, Miss Bridgett said she knew she had to change the conversation. She looked at Grandma, admired how she came across, shook her head and then looked at Mom. "The first movie star in the family."

"Not a movie star," Mom returned. "And she's not your family!"

Miss Bridgett's face instantly turned red, and her head pivoted away from Mom. It turned out she was trying to find the right words to respond.

"All these years, Gloria," Miss Bridgett began, "All these years she's been in my life. Your mother and I are more than family."

Mom's forehead was wrinkled, her eyes squinting, and her hand theatrical. "Don't spoil her anymore, then."

****$$****

Soon, Mom was turning on to a wider street called Commonwealth, then Occupied Street, giving a good view of the now mostly soaring office buildings and Saint Thomas Cathedral, less than quarter mile south. We proceeded, passing the stop sign and turned on to Wall Street as Grandma and Mom continued to go at each other.

"Sometime she feels more like my daughter than you," Grandma said to Mom. "But you weren't born a normal child. You weren't even…."

"Don't even go there," Mom retorted. "We need to get to the address."

Grandma lifted her hand and held it in that position for all to see. She was as chippy as she was on the day when she was nine and went to get help for her family from the Zimmerman storekeeper.

"I go where I want," she answered.

She then looked to Miss Bridgett, "Am I not a big lady?"

"You *are! Definitely are,"* Miss Bridgett answered.

Mom chose to work it out her own way. She gave Grandma a hard look as the one that was coming from Grandma. She paused. She moved her attention full circle of Grandma's face and then went for her eyes.

They were running out of time. They had reached their location, however. They were now in a new setting.

Pulling into the parking lot of the TV station, Mom put an evil eye on Grandma. "You don't have to call me daughter. Anymore," she said.

****$$****

At WXB Channel 4 Grandma met with Toni, a young, nervous-looking TV reporter who kept putting on her reading glasses and taking them off as fast as she got them on, giving Mom and Miss Bridgett an on-the-side raison d'être for humor and gossip.

At this point, everything was up for talk.

Coming from all corners were people talking, some walking fast and discussing events in the world at speeds that seemed un-human, others just every day.

"It was so important Ms. Muley that you made it in on time, "TV Reporter Toni complemented Grandma. "You know, *everything* in the media is based on time."

I kept glancing at Grandma as she herself seemed a bit uneasy. Was she nervous, or was she just impatient to get on the air? She held one hand into another and swayed her body, left, right, left right.

Momentarily, TV Reporter Toni pointed to a man in a glass studio thirty feet or so, along a path of other padded, glassed-in areas filled with microphones, electronic equipment and busy men and women doing whatever they were doing.

"The thing is," TV Reporter Toni started to tell Grandma, "I actually forgot to mention to him about you—something came up."

The reporter grabbed the glasses from her face and without another look at us, took off towards a man in one of the studios. "Just give me a minute," she said.

Left alone, Miss Bridgett told Grandma that she knew Grandma was going to "kick things right where they're supposed to go."

Mom had never been anyplace close to the inside of a radio or TV station before, and that had her looking very uncomfortable. Neither Grace or I had had this experience, either, but somehow we were at home with all of it.

There, Mom twice complained of feeling claustrophobic and wanted to go back home. When no one listened, she complaint the place was too cold. Then, once she seemed to remember who she was, she started firing all over at Grandma.

"Mom, you should quit right now! Right here," Mom told Grandma.

Grandma did a spin like the one she had done at home when she was putting on her lipstick, a kind of move that only a dancer or ex-dancer could make. She pointed towards the studio. TV Reporter Toni was in there sitting.

"Look, Dear, I haven't come this far because I'm made of cob web," Grandma said. "I'll be in that studio. I'm going to go live!"

What was Mom to do? That was my dollar question of the moment. She curled up her nose. She stared. She looked like Grace would when Dad would tell her "no" to TV viewing; she needed to get her schoolwork done.

Mom kept staring.

****$$****

The action inside the studio was separate and different from what was going on the outside but would be observed by and reported completely to those of us on the other side.

AL Graham's hands were flying in the air in short, up and down movements.

"Not possible. No. Not me. No, no. Not presently, he said to TV Reporter Toni.

"Here he looks older than on the Toshiba," Grandma remarked to the other ladies.

"From here, we get the real view, Grandma," Miss Bridgett contributed.

Grandma looked to Mom who was still recovering from their latest fight. "Not like you," Grandma said.

Mom was in a childlike posture, but when she talked it was bold and with even more energy than she normally drew on in her contests of words. "Even a broken clock is right twice a day," she said.

****$$****

Behind the glass, AL Graham's hand was back up in the air as he and TV Reporter Toni tried to create an arrangement acceptable to them.

"No. We cannot touch them," he said to the reporter.

She told him that she understood but followed up with the "but" word that she had promised the lady and she couldn't just let Ms. Muley go back home without the interview.

"Sacred cow, Toni," AL Graham barked. "Sacred. As sacred as they come!"

TV Reporter Toni came out of that as disappointed, her reading glass back on her face but pulled down to give her an uninterrupted view of the man that could let her look like a crackpot. She pointed to a sheet of paper in her hand.

"Lots of reasons to do it, AL…."

AL Graham moved his hand to the nix sign as she hasten on.

"How am I supposed to do this, AL?"

He said, "Figure it out."

"I've never set you up wrong," she retorted.

As the two carried on in the studio, Mom and Miss Bridgett looked at Grandma and at each other with questions, the big one coming from Miss Bridgett, and it was, "What's going on?"

The answer pointed to a disagreement: a to-and-fro, a breakdown of communication.

"AL, I assumed I could count on you."

"You thought wrong on this one, Toni." He moved closer to her and she stepped backward.

"Here's your chance," AL Graham said sounding like his mouth was full. "Maybe if you didn't marry that chump I would put my head on the chopping block, but…."

The request had nothing to do with that, and TV Reporter Toni said it.

"Everything does," AL Graham replied, his arms opening to her.

TV Reporter Toni spoke some more with AL Graham in quiet and after a noticeable moment of ongoing awkward behaviors she left, heading out towards us on the other side.

****$$****

Grandma said she was concerned when we saw TV Reporter Toni dawdling out with her head down, but that did not get our complete attention. We were already looking at a group in the distance coming in our direction. The group seemed so involved in whatever they were up to, and who they were, they even drew the interest of others, including a group of media persons that were filming their every move.

Miss Bridgett and Mom, when all was said and done, spoke of the cost of a missed opportunity that occurred right there and then.

The group that was in the distance was now within speaking distance of us as Grandma was being escorted into the studio by TV Reporter Toni. Grandma turned her head in position as Lot's wife did way back then. She stared. Her pace decreased momentarily. TV Reporter Toni placed her hand on Grandma's shoulder, signaling her to move forward. She did but only after she mumbled, "fee-fi-fo-fum, I smell the blood of; I smell blood."

Mom and Miss Bridgett momentarily looked at each other. They shook their heads.

As the group approached, two of the people were identified as reporters, one writing as they went along. A third would be Corporate, and a fourth, one of his surrogates. They incidentally had a TV station taping on mortgage meltdown that very day. As the group edged Grandma, Corporate said "hello" to her and Grandma returns it; at the time, neither making any connection about any common concern.

Then, as the groups step in their own direction, one of the Reporters said to Corporate, "I bet you, you don't know who she is?"

Corporate pulled on his suspenders. He looked backwards. He laughed. "Somebody's grandmother." He kept looking back and took note. "Yours, mine. Could be anybody's."

The reporter talking with Corporate shook his head. "Not quite so," he said. "I heard she's one of the grass roots—the ninety-niners"

"You mean forty-seveners," the assistant with Corporate offered.

"What does she want," Corporate asked. "That we steal from the rich and give to folks like her?"

The media recorded that line and played it on TV that entire week, causing a firestorm nationwide. This resulted in the President appearing on 60-Minutesf that Sunday and CNN claiming he was for all citizens, the middle-class included. He said, to fix the broken economy, he wanted to see the rich pay more.

At the TV station, the assistant looked at Corporate; every emotion was managed.

Corporate continued. "Reduce our fees on large deposits? Is that it?"

The group with the reporter found that humorous.

That line was likewise picked up by the media.

"Mind me now, I just remembered something," Corporate said to his assistant who without being asked, pulled out a pen-sized tape recorder and flashed it at corporate. Corporate spoke into the gadget: "E-mail this to all Tier One today, 'We may be the one percent, but that doesn't mean we don't love our country. We just want to see everybody contribute their fair share. Be sure to include the closing, Signed: Corporate.'"

I also saw this part in the local paper and on the TV.

****$$****

Mom and Miss Bridgett kept on with what they were about.

Mom said Grandma was nothing more than an "obsessed old woman."

Miss Bridgett replied, "When we first met….," but Mom butted in.

"You love to go backwards. I know that. But don't do that today."

"Until she started to do this, you thought your Mom was some genius, and the most frank person you knew," Miss Bridgett said.

"So," Mom inquired. "People change!"

Miss Bridgett glared at Mom as if she didn't understand something. "You felt that way not very long ago. What's making you such a crazy ant, Gloria?"

Mom explained her feeling that Grandma had lost her axis, her head to be true to her word, and cautioned that Grandma couldn't afford to get sick again. Grandma's getting sick, she rolled out, was why she was so concerned.

That did not stop Miss Bridgett. "She's always stood up for what she believed, and I got to tell you, the more I see where she's going, the more I believe in her," she said.

Mom asked Miss Bridgett if she was losing her marbles like Grandma, to hear Miss Bridgett tell of her bank causing her headaches likewise.

Miss Bridgett said she was sadden as she told of her own experience.

"Just this week," she said. "What do you expect?"

Mom made a comic's face. She was disappointed, actually. "You not going rogue too? Are you?"

"Yes! They did," Miss Bridgett said empathetically, her head in step with her words. "Your Mom's right, Gloria. They're real scoundrels!"

# CHAPTER 11

Grandma's getting served tea in studios by the British accented AL Graham hinted some degree of geniality by the man they called the best, but there was no sureness to any other good deed by him. Almost immediately after the serving of tea, Graham presented his side, which was that he could not run an interview on the subject with Grandma, and for that matter with anyone. He pointed he did not see a story in what Grandma presented as her problem with the bank.

"I told it to you," Grandma responded, hoping to continue the narrative.

I looked at Toni, the TV Reporter who had fallen sadden for Grandma. We listened in on AL Graham's elucidation:

"Banks make policies and that's just one of them, Ma'am," AL Graham said. We don't tell banks what to do. We're a television station."

Grandma moved a bit closer to AL Graham. "Mr. AL," she began. "What I need is a dance partner, someone with the right moves! Someone to help me stop the bastards from emptying our accounts," she said. Her words were unusual but came in an earnest begging way to them. "I'm not asking you to protect what they're doing."

****$$****

On the other side of the glass, Mom's frustration had raised, again questioning Miss Bridgett if the bank's taking Grandma's money gave Grandma the right to madness?

Miss Bridgett answered, "Yes it does," which coincided up with Grandma giving the same answer to a question of whether the bank owes its customers a reimbursement and an apology, from AL Graham.

"Oh Lord," Mom replied to Miss Bridgett.

AL Graham placed his hand at his chin momentarily. "You have the ability to stop them though… by balancing your account!"

Grandma opened her hands to AL Graham, her brow wrinkled, her eyes fixed on his glabellae. "My God. It's unfair! You have cataract?"

She said when she looked at AL Graham she thought, how handsome, yet weak; how disgusting. What kind of man is this?

"Do men have no power anymore," she asked.

AL Graham noticeably searched for something to say but could not find acceptable words.

"Do we just leave them to steal our *nothing*? They didn't earn that!"

AL Graham reached to placed his hand on Grandma's shoulder. He knew her heart was right. She had given up a lot, and yet he couldn't see a path to help her get to where she wanted.

Grandma noted his hand on her shoulder was no help. What came next was also of no good or use to her.

"When you have a bounced check, Miss," AL Graham asked politely, "Don't you pay a fee?"

Grandma told AL Graham he was pivoting away from the subject, but AL Graham was not in any position to do anything, any way differently.

"If you were the bank, how would you answer that question," he asked as he stop himself from folding his arms.

Grandma stared, her eyes were wide now, nose flaring. Her lips were opened as well, but just enough to show she still had good front teeth.

"Let me set the scene for you: I bought a wallet under three dollars with my debit card and made an overpriced $14.00 purchase for paper with the same card, it takes four days to cash and then suddenly they lined them up with new charges, pay my last written check, a twenty-one hundred-dollar mortgage first, take out $35 and $35, time after time for themselves and then bounce my $2.95 Made-in-China plastic wallet. What's so good about that?" She had said all that in a single breath that had TV Reporter Toni shaking her head in respect as Grandma kept with her storytelling.

"You know what they told me?"

By this time, AL Graham was tapping his feet and moving his body like an on-air radio DJ taking pleasure in the music she's blasting to her happy listeners.

"Let me tell you," Grandma continued. "They'll give me back one $35! And that's once a year! You see anything wrong with that movie?"

AL Graham turned away, looking as if he was of another planet; Grandma pointed to Mars.

AL Graham now had his arms folded. "I don't' see a story," he said, echoing what he had earlier announced.

"Are you hard of hearing or just allergic to reality," Grandma replied.

"Well, madam," AL Graham said, "I don't see why we're still beating the dead horse.

Grandma mimicked Graham. "I don't see why we're still beating [a] dead horse."

"Even if there was a story," Al Graham continued. "Why would we turn the hose on a patron like…"

"I felt I was bowling down you alley," Grandma interrupted.

"I mean. I mean….," AL Graham said.

Grandma bent her neck towards the ground, her eyes fully in that direction. She made a step towards the door. She knew what he meant, and she said it to him.

"Sir," she began. She lifted her head to show her full face now, daring, her eyes directly on AL Graham, and her mouth going fast. "You're one of those stinking rats like so many. Just another pretty suits," she told him.

He moved about his shoulders suggesting a high degree of uncomfortableness. "You trying to lecture me?"

She continued as if there was no talking in between. "You're in it too? You! I can't take the smell of your odor, you know?"

****$$****

In the meantime, on Corporate's yacht, "Lady Betsy," Corporate and his staff sat down to a grand meal as CFO Tolly profusely apologize for being "un-team-like" as it related to his salary and benefits.

Corporate accepted and went on to playfully fan the smell of the turkey leg on his plate, towards his nose.

"Exquisite," CFO Tolly said.

Marketing Director Andrea fumbled with her hat as she nibbled on cheese and crackers, and as the waiter brought to her table a new bottle of 1978 Montrachet, there was a clear look of anticipation in the faces of everyone.

"Bon Apatite," a lady in an elegant red dress responded.

"I am glad to be out of those suit," CFO Tolly said as the camera moved to a stage in the yacht.

This I elaborated on in the assignment paper, but the "video" was rolling fast:

A group of woman dressed in leotards were doing a pom-pom like dancing on the stage.

"I'm, too, glad to be out of those," Corporate said. His words were clear, but his eyes were not on the subject of his talk; they were going for the skimpy-dressed women on stage.

One of the executives thumped his hand on the outer fiberglass surface of the yacht. "You won't be the proud owner of this baby much longer if we don't do something," he tells Corporate.

"Let's make it that if they're overdraft for five or more days, we slam them with that nice fee," the VP of Bank Ops contributed.

The video rolled: The women on stage kept entertaining. The executives went at throwing around numbers. How about twenty bucks, one asked. Another was, "No, thirty-five-ninety five." There was even an idea of sixty-five that enlivened Corporate and had him saying that if they didn't fill the silk stocking now, "houses would get smaller, cars would get fewer, and jets would be non-existent."

"This time it's not going to be my pocket that gets hit," the VP of Bank Ops notified.

Corporate squinted at Miss Andrea, his marketing head. "Let's go at it again," he said.

Miss Andrea snapped a picture of the dancers, one of whom was saying, “write this off too,” as she wiggled her perfectly shaped butt with the words “You Build This”, to the executives. Miss Andrea smiled but swayed her head from side to side. Women are supposed to be more than that.

“Your banking relationship is important to us, she said. “Here’s how you can avoid overdrafts.”

“No. No. That’s too nice,” Corporate interrupted, and as he prepared for a dictation that brought a tape recorder to his mouth again, he supplied the words. “Get this out and get it out quick, verbatim: ‘There will be occasions when your activities may still result in an overdraft charge. If we return the item unsettled you will typically end up with an NSF. …’”

The staff onboard immediately got to work.

****$$****

That weekend Grandma set out in her own way to solve her problems as she saw fit, she sitting in the front seat of Billy’s white Porsche Carrera GT, Miss Bridgett in the back.

Grandma explained her plan as getting Billy to help her, but the motive, considering her choice of a skimpy, Caribbean top and shorts, still leave our minds searching.

Even before she left out, Grace and I talked about how she had increased the regularity she was getting her hair done. Moreover, this day, she was in one of her shortest of shorts.

In my eyes, Grandma looked like she was going through something they call age-erasing on TV. Why she took Miss Bridgett along, we’ll probably never know that part. What I do know is that she explained her purpose as nothing but business.

They gathered Billy started his career at Union Bank in California. He had held many positions within the bank but had not known of any job outside of banking.

“If I did,” he said. “Who knows what I would be today?”

Miss Bridgett placed her hand under her chin as she and Grandma listened to Billy chronicling his own path to senior citizen. When he thought he was done, Miss Bridgett jumped in.

“Well, you’re still here and you’re going to help her,” she said, referring to Grandma. “Am I right?”

The question was direct and important, but the look on Miss Bridgett's face was calm and pleasant. She was not interested in the charade.

Grandma smiled, patted Miss Bridgett on the hand. Even she, Grandma, was not that pressing on Billy, at least not yet.

Even though, Miss Bridgett was right, Grandma's time with Billy had changed things to a not-the-end-of-the-world set-up for her. And though her talk was about her pains, there was an overall sense that if she lose another day, that would not be a big deal.

She turned to address Billy. "This might seem like a stupid, everyday things, but it's now out of hand. I gave birth to Gloria and we barely talking now!"

Billy who had previously told Grandma about problems in his own family, laughed.

Family life can be great drama at times. He was no stranger to that. He began a drumbeat on the side of his Porsche.

Miss Bridgett stood by, her hand on her lips. "Looking for more," she asked Billy who was still tapping his fingers on the car.

"How you think I got this baby," he asked the ladies. "The boys… all five thing I should have given them the dinero instead." He evaluated Grandma, head to toes. "Senility doesn't come that easily though."

Grandma stared back at Billy with an excited girl's smile on her face.

"You don't give your mullah to nobody," she said.

Billy took a couple seconds to process the face and words, and then spoke. "No matter how many beer or cigarettes they consume, they think I still owe them for bringing them into this world, Ms. Muley."

Miss Bridgett was just starting to know Billy, and she took a hard look at him. "I thought your boys were old."

"Five adults! Enough to have wives and pups," he answered.

"Pups," Grandma said.

"That's what I call *their* young ones," Billy said. "They're suckling too."

Grandma looked at Billy, her eyes deep and her face curious. "You think we are old, ha?"

"I wouldn't say in the sense of physical," Billy replied. He found himself straightening his shoulders and tightening for a strident display for Grandma. "But to be trying to get revenge on someone who has done you wrong, I would say yes."

"What are you afraid of," Grandma asked.

Instantly, Miss Bridgett turned, revealing a waking set of eyes from a disconnect she had made, and now she repeated to Billy that he needed to help her friend. To that, Billy replied that he kind of like her "friend" and would do anything to lend a hand.

"She thinks you have the connections to do it," Miss Bridgett added.

Billy placed a playful but trustful smile on his face as he addressed Miss Bridgett. He told her that from all he had gathered, Grandma was good with the computer.

"Use it," he said emphatically and then he sped up.

****$$****

Several hours into the moonlit night, the three returned to the parking lot of the bank where Billy worked. He stopped and stepped out, made it to the back door where he took Miss Bridgett hand to let her out. He then made himself over, in a happy, light hearted walk to Grandma's area. He released her door. He escorted Grandma out. He gave her a kiss on the cheek.

Miss Bridgett looked at him from a straight face. "Billy," she informed. "It's not about helping yourself. Remember, Ms Muley needs *your* help!"

"That was a good time," Billy said.

They giggled like children and waved goodbyes to each other.

****$$****

Grandma had a couple up and down days following that. On one of the down ones, she did not want to go and get her scheduled medical checkup, saying she was disgusted with the way things were going, and on two of the ups, she rang in her best and second best business numbers of all times.

That meant "specialties" for her assistants, Grace and me.

One of the good days meant all the Haagen Daz Grace and I would devour; another that started good found Grandma in the kitchen in her Betty Crocker apron, our meal—beef stroganoff with bake potatoes and dressing. Grace and I teased her that if she ever cooked up one like that for Billy she would never again be around to cook for us; she said she was no Julia Child.

****$$****

"All's well," she said at the end of the meal, and then she was off in her Suburban, her phone dialing the local Chamber of Commerce, "Music Moment" in the background.

In the back seat and on front passenger's she had a half dozen or so post office containers filled with packaged books we had readied for her customers.

"Has anyone else ever made this complaint to your branch," Grandma asked a lady on the phone.

Momentarily a popping sound came back over the phone to Grandma. She queried what it was and the lady begged for a pardon saying she was blowing her chewing gum into bubbles and it accidentally popped.

The lady went on to explained to Grandma that her job was not to resolve problems like the ones Grandma had with her bank, but simply to take note of customer calls.

"But who gives answers to the complaints you make note of," Grandma asked, looking exasperated.

Concurrently, another bubble popped into Grandma's ears. "Ma'am, *that*, I believe is incidental," the lady said.

Grandma replied with an abrupt, "OK," and she was off mumbling and punching another number into her I-phone.

"State attorney's office. May I help you," the new person answered as Grandma looked up to see a truck trying to get out of her way.

"Yes, my name is Ms. Muley, Sandra E. Muley, I'm calling to make a compla....HOLD ON!"

The driver of the other vehicle swerved to a long, loud squealing of tires to prevent an accident. The other driver looked out her window with a foul look on her face. She gave Grandma "the finger."

Grandma grabbed on to the rear view mirror and saw herself a stunned lady who could not even respond on the phone that flew to the seat on the other end.

"Hello Ma'am. Hello. Hello? Are you still there," The State Attorney Secretary's voice came through.

****$$****

For Billy, he was back at work. "Back on the saddle" as he jokingly referred to himself at work, but now he had some new thoughts to be with.

For one, he turned to being a lot more cordial with the people he was dealing with on the bank's behalf. He also found himself paying special attention to the security guards who themselves were as wide awake as ever. Most of all, he found himself thinking a lot more about Grandma.

He headed from his desk towards Eduardo Sosa's, passing by a guard who took a prying look at him.

"Wardo. You there?"

Another security guard passed by and took an even closer examination of everything and everybody, including the guard that was around already guarding.

"Wardo," Billy repeated.

Eduardo Sosa lifted his head from the counting of money.

"Billy B., what's percolating?"

****$$****

Alas, Billy had made it into our school work. A couple students wrote that he was a part of the problem customers were fighting with. Many others differed.

He glanced up at a clock at his bank and noted the hour with a head and eye endorsement. "I think it's about time you live up to your words."

"Depending on which ones," Eduardo Sosa replied.

"What do you mean, which one," Billy inquired.

"You know you can cash my word in any day," Eduardo Sosa said. He flashed some money he was counting, above his head.

"You promised, and a promise is a man's' honor," Billy said.

"C'mon Billy B, spit it to the *piso*," Eduardo Sosa said.

Billy reminded him, that they had prior arrangement to a computer training class for Billy. Eduardo Sosa owed him that.

Eduardo Sosa shook his head in surrender, his words coming fast, "Billy B, Billy B my man, ready for his computer schooling. Ha?" He lifted his voice. "Billy B's ready to take on Billy the Big Willy 'Kahuna' Gates, ha?"

Billy whistled and shook his head. "How long have I been steering at that bald skull of your?"

The answer was nine years.

"Good, that's how long you've been my debtor," Billy replied. He went on to remind Eduardo Sosa of his early years in America, when Eduardo Sosa first went to work for Bank $$ and how out of touch he was.

"I taught you finesse. Remember how your English was, should I say, rustic when you came here," Billy continued. "A promise's a promise, Senor."

Eduardo Sosa remained quiet.

"I put English in tu cabeza, Senor " Billy said.

Eduardo Sosa shook his head. Smiled. "Cuz, so you speak Spanish now?"

Billy lifted his head, his attention fully committed to Eduardo Sosa. "In this town, in these days, even a guy like me have to 'habla poco' to survivo mucho, Senor Sosa."

"Not bad, Espanol," Eduardo Sosa replied. "You see Amigo, you didn't know mucho Spanish when I first met you. You learn the computer, and I eat for one week. Sloppy's OK?.

The two men shook hands, and then there was a minute with the two as Eduardo Sosa showed Billy something on the computer.

****$$****

That entire week Billy fulfilled on his promise of taking Eduardo Sosa to Sloppy Joe's, a noisy downtown hideout for corporate executives that made them feel they were in Hawaii rather than still on the mainland.

On the last day Eduardo Sosa and Billy recollected about the holdup they had at the bank the day he and R. Paul were working in the vault. The "lowdown" was that it was some sort of inside job. The Armored guard in the truck was killed. Over $1.6 million was involved. That day's headline included, "Heist Led to Guard's

Death," "Robbers Took Over $1 in Bank Heist," and "Police Investigating Alleged Internal Plot."

Billy told Eduardo Sosa he had never before seen anything like the holdup. He blamed it on the "health of the environment we find ourselves in."

Eduardo Sosa noted he was proud of Billy's progress, and to that point Billy remarked he was "feeling much better."

He claimed the more screens he was getting through the more confidence he was gaining.

"I'm impressed how some of you old folks get this new thing so quick," Eduardo Sosa continued. "I used to think only the young would get this shit! Technology, Cuz."

Billy smiled with Eduardo Sosa. He trusted him with some things. "And I'll tell you my little secret," Billy offered.

Eduardo Sosa skipped over to Billy and placed his hand at his ear.

"But if I hear it around the job, I'll cut off your you know what, Billy said. "

Eduardo Sosa stepped backwards, his hand in his version of the Muhammad Ali ready position. "I'll have to introduce you to my wife's sister."

"Ah, ah," Billy replied.

"I'm telling you, Old Boy."

Billy braced his body and lifted his two thumbs in front of himself. "I was seeing a forty-nine year old Black chick you know."

Eduardo Sosa stared at Billy with a sly smile on his face.

Billy dug in. "She's dropped me now, thought. She used to by my private mentor. She had me all over the keyboard!"

"I bet she did," Eduardo Sosa responded. His voice was now teasing. "How 'bout the lady that's been visiting? I get the up and up around here, you know."

Billy shook his head telling Eduardo Sosa that "when you work in a place like this," referring to the bank, "you have to be respectable." He said everybody at the corporate office knew him to be a man with a wife but *his* and her's marriage had gone down the "d" road.

Eduardo Sosa approached this as one who wanted to be considerate and asked if Billy knew anyone who hadn't been there? He himself was once married. Now the person her called his wife was actually a guy.

Billy shook his head. "Five years ago, Wardo. Five weird years."

Eduardo Sosa placed his hand on Billy's shoulder.

"Cuz, stuff happens," he said. "But what are we here for? Another day, right?"

He told Billy that he was weary from work. He was going to California and Vegas for a week, and he would like to see Billy quadruple his learning in his absence.

"Master that computer and you'll understand the lady of the new land," Eduardo Sosa added.

Billy brought a salute to his forehead. "I'm the master of my destiny; I'm the captain of my soul…."

Eduardo Sosa accepted that with a small bow. "Old Boy, Billy B," he said. He wrote some information on a leaf of paper and passed it to Billy. "My password to everything I know—You master the safekeeping of this, or else…."

Billy told Eduardo Sosa that what's good with Sosa, was good with him, Billy.

"I know that," Eduardo Sosa replied.

Billy shook Eduardo Sosa's hand. "Just don't do what I wouldn't do when you're out there in Sin City."

Eduardo Sosa laughed as he answered. "Look this up if tu Espanol is not yet up to par: 'Lo que pasa en Vegas, se queda en Las Vegas.' Look it up, 'Cuz!"

****$$****

On a nice, warm Florida days Grandma was back in action. She was earlier given a nice boost by some people she had met at a Church event when they told her that what she was doing was noble, and now she was back in her routine. That meant, in part her catfights with Mom. That's the kind of reality Grandma would ease herself into in the next chapters of her life.

Grace and I were out for the first part, fishing at the Everglades, returning at Grandma's to see her and Mom preparing the customers' package as Grace and I would normally do. The first thing I notices was that the two were wearing the same kind of shirt, a black T-shirt with the name DanceLab on it in bright colors. The two nodded in acknowledgement of us, but that was about it for us as Mom told

Grandma that Grandpa (if he was alive) would think Grandma and Mr. Buck would make a great match.

"I know he would disagree," Grandma answered.

Mom tried to compare Grandpa with Billy saying Grandpa was kind, "a little old eccentric collector of things like Billy."

Yeah, they had that in common—Both engaging fellows and with their nuances. Grandma admitted to that.

"Can you believe, he's just making his way into cyber world," Grandma said.

"How many people your age, you know *that's good at it* like you," Mom asked.

Grandma told her that Grandpa was one. She placed a sly grin on her face. "Your dad was faster and better than anyone in his time!"

"Really?"

Grace and I watched each other, she with her palms opened, her face tilted as with a question. It didn't come though. Grandma kept speaking.

"Yes. He could do things I've never seen anyone done," Grandma said. "And I miss him for that."

Simultaneously Grandma's hand began to go to brush us out, but by this time we were used to that and we did not budge.

Mom's reply was "she too," but it had been so long. To that, Grandma stated that "long has nothing to do with it."

"Depends," Mom said in a dreamy kind of way.

Grandma rubbed her hand into her hair, and turned to Mom looking like a young spoiled girl. "Who would want a man who can't even go online and book her a nice hideaway, say a weekend at the keys. How about somewhere on the French Rivera, Gloria? Who would? I should have taken you up on those cruises. Even a nice restaurant? My Lord."

Mom smiled. She shook her head. "He seems to have an interesting take on life."

Grandma replied that, "Billy's just helping me with the banking situation," to which Mom inquired if he was nuts too.

Grandma did not seem to take what was going on well and responded that it was her "duty and responsibility" to help to get things right.

"What makes you think that's the part of you he wants," Mom said, and then realizing her words she now tried to brush G and me away. We still did not move; Mom took our no for an answer.

****$$****

It was Grandma who had Grace and me thinking that day, though. She stood up, wearing a kimbo as she began stating and re-stating that she would never live at Shines.

To that, Mom asked her if she was OK.

Grandma walked to her desk and returned with a newspaper article; she pointed to the story, "The Hazards of Modern Banking."

"I read this story, Dear," Grandma continued, shaking the newspaper at Mom with a strong force, and in a disenchanted way. "They've broken the contract, Gloria!"

"Things have gotten outa hand," Mom said.

"Ain't that a …"

Mom shook her head. "Mom!" "You've got to get pass it, MOM." She pushed her hand in front of herself to help her do the talking for as much as they knew how to carry on. "Remember you taught us as kids, how to get 'over the hump? Get on the other side?' Now, it's your turn! Mom, you realize how much you've lost,"

Grandma replied, "You realize what I've learned?"

These banks' emptying pockets, Gloria" She said. "And Billy said …"

"Ok. OK… OK," Mom interrupted. She began to leave and not hear the whole thing.

"WAIT," Grandma demanded, claiming she called her bank again, including and emphasizing the word "today." The lady on the phone was rude, she said.

Mom stated she as well would be mad if Grandma was calling her everyday with "the same silly argument."

Grandma ignored the harsh words and went on to explained that she went back and forth for half-an-hour with a bank clerk who called herself Eggy and still she did not resolve her problem. To that, Mom asked her if she thought the bank was purposely doing things to her.

To Grandma this was a shallow, disrespecting question, so she began walking away, towards the garage.

"I urge you to hear what I have to say," Mom demanded.

Grandma placed on a coverall and turned around just in time to see Mom coming at her.

"You stick with me, and I'll stick with you," she said.

Mom had followed Grandma and was imitating Grandma's bumpy head movements as they went towards some gardening tools that Grandma began to gather. In Grandma face, now, Mom tells her that the people at the bank were just doing their business.

Grandma continued to ignore Mom and headed outside, raked some leaves, asked Mom to leave her to do her work, but Mom told her she needed to understand her point.

"Gloria, they raked another $140 from my account—and that was last night," Grandma said as she pulled her tool from a stump in the ground.

Mom stood upright, her mouth parsed and with no words.

Grandma dropped the rake momentarily and threw her hands open? "Do I have to do this alone?"

I don't know what all this meant to Mom, but her lips dropped and her eyes chose a fixed spot for what I sensed were more than a few seconds; this actually seemed like many minutes.

"I asked for Corporate's number and the lady asked me if I was out of my mind," Grandma picked up.

"You are," Mom said.

Grandma appeared attacked with that one, and I thought she was going to fire back. Maybe she was going to hold on to Mom's hand the way she had done with the Black lawyer. Maybe she was going to fire an insulting word, maybe even a bad one. After all, she was not perfect to her own teachings at times. I had never heard her do the latter, but she was really irritated this time around, and I expected anything.

Instead, she chose to ask a question I thought was simple and significant. "You think I am?"

Mom walked closer to Grandma with arms lose. Maybe it was time to make up. Maybe it was time to pluck a hug out of her heart and make Grandma's all the better. Maybe she was tired of making Bank $$ setting the agenda between she and her own mother. Maybe, Mom had finally wised-up.

Maybe not.

She said, "Mom, you don't have to be Al Capone for us!"

"You think that's what I am," Grandma asked. And Mom began shaking her head indicating that was her ardent belief.

"You do? Ha," Grandma's voice raised.

"I'm saying you're not God," Mom said. "What they're doing may be a sin, but is it a crime?"

Grandma stayed quiet for the instant as if she was actually asking herself what she was or wasn't. Maybe now she was getting to reflect on what was happening with her. Maybe this was the first opportunity *she* was getting to give thought to how much this thing with the bank was crushing her life and those of us who loved her so dearly. Grace and I chose to do nothing more than stand by, to watch.

What Grandma came up with was not in my book.

"What I'm trying to figure out, is what has gotten into you, Gloria? You don't talk to me like that!"

Mom responded with a statement about how she was a woman herself for long enough, and she had every right to have her own view about God, man and banks. She had children too, she reminded Grandma.

"I know that," Grandma gave as her answer. "And God knows I do as well!"

Mom bellowed back, "And I balance my account correctly!" That was the difference as Mom saw things.

****$$****

Grandma would go into questioning why Mom was always borrowing money from her and others and called Mom a sponger. Mom got back at her saying that Grandma should just fix her finance and she wouldn't have any problem.

"It's a manufactured problem," Grandma said in a voice that sounded more like a reminder of some universal thought than a personal opinion.

Mom accused her of faulting others, claiming this was Grandma's custom for having alibis throughout her life of "weaknesses."

"Gloria! Gloria," Grandma rang out. "How did you get to be like this? Dumb!"

Mom's answer left my heart skipping. It suggested to me that we had a heredity problem (my worst nightmare), and I am one who continue to believe if your Mom or Dad has it, you will in time get it too. I wondered if I would be next in line. Do boys get it before girls? Would I be the susceptible one? How about Grace? She's a girl!

Mom claimed Grandma had lost her mind. At my young age that sounded like a grim future. No kidding.

She went on and calculated, "I'm looking at the seed!"

Grandma responded with what she knew and what was liquid. She asked Mom, "When are you going to pay me back?"

Your sales down Mom, and you're messing with this nutty bank! I'm trying to help you. I am only trying to help!"

"Hay, You! Let me lay this down on you," Grandma replied. "I've been handling life long before you were. Not because you're here now, I'm 'dead.'"

"Mom, that stuff doesn't happen to *me.*"

"What bank you have," Grandma demanded.

"The Money!"

"And," Grandma asked.

"You're just going ballistic! You're going to explode," Mom said.

Grandma now held on to the rake with both her hands. She began chasing Mom around the yard, the rake going at Mom, but banging into the house, right in front, catching between the paste on address and the house itself.

Mom thought that was comical behavior. She giggled. She laughed. She kept on mocking.

"The next time, it's not your heart that will go pow," Mom said. "It's your head! And you think there's someone out there that can love you? Ha! Ha! Haa!"

****$$****

At Upper Creek Branch, Billy took a moment from his busy work to wave at his co-workers as they were leaving for the day.

Ralph, a fellow bank employee, asked Billy if he was going to be watching the Lakers playoff. The Lakers had defeated the Piston 102-99 in their match a week earlier and the upcoming game was expected to draw a crowd.

Billy, lifting his cup of coffee to his face, said he wished he couldn't and then dropped back his eyes to the business on his laptop. He said he had to catch up on some important work.

Eduardo Sosa approached right then and looked at the screen with Billy. "I see you've got a good hold on it now. Aren't you, Big-Bad-Billy?"

At the branch, a clerk passed by on her way out, her pocket book clutched beneath her arm, her stride on purpose. "He's making us look lazy," she remarked to which a Co-worker responded, "Don't get jealous, Boss. "He's going to be so good. I'll leave him some of my work soon."

As the group reached the exit, the manager looked backwards.

"Don't forget the alarm tonight, Mr. Buck," she said.

****$$****

In step with Billy, Grandma was out and even thought she would not meet up with him physically, they would have shared experiences.

Short on ink and paper, she decided her last stop would be the Staples on Northwest Grand Avenue next to our Chinese restaurant of choice KowLoon. She had barely gotten a good look at where she was heading when a white-bearded Indian clerk, Rashid, with a large tattoo on his forehead walked up to her.

"Another late night, Ms. Muley," the man said, his voice silky, almost music in the way he drag it.

Grandma agreed.

He told her that he had heard she was not pulling the blinds at five in the evening anymore to which she again stated her agreement.

"Well, buy your heart out," Clerk Rashid said, waving Grandma in towards some items with large sales tags on them. "Lots to excite you tonight."

*****$$****

At Upper Creek $$ Branch, Billy was in his own world, getting himself a new cup of coffee, yarning and looking like a man that should have been in his bed. When Grandpa John was his age he would have likely been getting a Swedish "rub-down" as he used to call his massage sessions, or at least having Grandma putting some lavender or geranium oil on his back to get him through his forty winks of the night.

Billy chose work and introspection. In actuality he was not the kind that shut down at five, dinner at six; he preferred to be out slapping backs and wheeling and dealing.

Now, he returned to his paper-filled desk and placed on his spectacle. He pushed some of the papers and his writing utensils out of his way, spilling a can of coke to some of the pages. He drew his spectacle and looked at the content on one of the sheets. He laughed at what he had done. He looked closely at a paper that had a number of names and phone numbers written on it. He read from the sheets: "Help Ms. Sandra Muley," it read. He removed his spectacles from his nose and cleans the mess, and as he did so he moved his two cameras out of the way, to a dry place.

Soon, he was back at his main task, looking very intense and renewed. His energy was upbeat.

*****$$****

"What a night," Grandma whispered to herself, standing in the greeting cards area, a heap of office supplies in her cart, and her eyes deep into the words of one of the cards.

Rashid circled the area taking note of an impish look on Grandma's face: a playful, girlie stare as she scanned other cards in the "love" section. Rashid stood in silence. Inquisitively. He smiled.

Grandma turned around and returned the smile. "Aren't these nice cards," she asked.

"I've been thinking about giving one to someone, but I'm not sure," Clerk Rashid said, his voice lacking the steady and calm flow it commanded earlier.

Grandma shook her head. It was saying "yes," but her spoke words were not in conformity: "We're never always certain about such things. Are we?"

Clerk Rashid pushed out his lip and with that came a tilting of his head. He was not sure either.

"I just want to encourage someone to help," Grandma shared.

Clerk Rashid couldn't help himself. He smiled, his face lit, and his hand went into the air.

"I knew there was more to you than banking problem. I knew there was a Mister somewhere!"

Grandma leaned towards Rashid, looking closely at his name badge. "You have me all forgetting your name—'Rasheed', ha? It's not like that, Dear."

Rashid carried a tricky grin as he waved. He shook his head again, this time affirming.

"The sansara, Ms. Muley," he said. "It's never like that!"

****$$****

Still studious and deep into his work on the computer, Billy took one of the sheets he had looked at before, from the stack of papers in front of him, the one with his handwriting. He brought the piece close to his face to admire the name—Sandra Muley he had written it large and with a special lithe to it. He shook his head; he rubbed his chin; he smiled. He shook his head again, this time up and down, the way some pulleys jerks up a pale of water or a cement block for construction work, only to fall and having it pulled up yet another time. Was it, "Sandra Muley? Sandra Muley, Sandra Muley" he was dreaming. That's my Grandma, I might say.

Billy got up, inadvertently brushing the front of his pants with his hand. He departed to the kitchen where he poured himself a new mug of coffee and looked up, taking note of the time on a clock above. It was 9:21.

****$$****

A clock at the Staples office supply store simultaneously registered 9:21. It coincided with Grandma unloading her two baskets of office supply at the checkout. She looked at her purse and then at the cards in it.

"Debit or credit," Rashid the Clerk asked.

"The next person that asks me that question, I'm going to shout," Grandma said in a voice that caught Rashid as a surprise. "IT'S DEBIT!"

"I wouldn't wrong you, Miss Muley," clerk Rashid replied after he quickly composed himself. "They're stinkers. They get me all the time!"

Grandma dropped her head to the ground briskly and as swiftly brought it back up. "Ditto!"

Rashid told Grandma a story that his uncle, a merchant back in India, told him a long time earlier. "The purpose of it," he stated was that, "cash is best."

"'Cash is King," he recoiled, making fancy the idea. "That's the concept Uncle Abdul would say. My country was not even with much technology back then!" Rashid spoke this part in his sharp, proud accent that Grandma said can make a man sound attractive.

****$$****

At Upper Creek Branch, Billy continued to work and then looked at his wristwatch as he spoke on the phone. "Long night," he said.

It was indeed a long night. He had spent a good amount of his time working and thinking. It happened he was consumed with Grandma, and that is what he attributed to the spilling of his soda on his papers.

She was the Polaroid in his mind most of that night. As an amateur picture-man, he had taken many hot shots over the span of his life. Here, he was picturing what she must have looked like before so much happened.

For him the shutter was open: curly hair, a pretty daring face—he positioned himself as she placed her hand under her chin, now, and stared. Nice snap, he thought. How about an older portrait of her. A new hair style for Queenie, same daring face, a gold neck brace, rings on her fingers, and her semi-fisted hands close to her lips. She gawked at him through her stirring blue eyes.

Billy liked these shots, but there were far, far from his best. There was no dancing, no hips or legs, nothing in them for him. He picked up his camera and examined it. How about one of her, the blond. She's dancing, now, in a soft cloth nude pants, her navel and body exposed by her bra-sized sleeveless top as she placed one hand on her hip and the other in her hair. A half a dozen to a dozen bracelets for each hand?

A dozen more images before he began to see the magnificent performance he wanted to see. That's when the image began to develop and his eyes got lighted.

Sandra E. Muley. She was twenty-seven, in *his* hot shots. She was on the verge of something, he knew. She had thrown back her locks and threw off her top, which happened to lie on the floor and in the picture. She's now standing in front of a duotone—a red-black background, her eyes towards the heavens—one hand crossed the other, the first covering the bareness of her "hush-hush."

"Oh wow," he said, and shook his head. He began gathering his personal belongings. He looked frightened. His own mind has taken him to a strange, new place. He picked up his briefcase. He began heading out.

Remembering something, he turned back. He walked to the alarm switch; he turned on the alarm; he closed the door behind him; he stepped out into the night. He walked erect.

****$$****

We were all up early the next morning, filling customer orders when Mom turn up to do something she had promised Grace and me she was going to do for months: apologize to Grandma for being "rude" to her even in front of her own children.

To me it seemed that Mom had finally come to realize what I knew all alone: Grandma wanted to be respected, and she wanted help. She felt she deserved that much. After all, she did not only care for Mom and her siblings but for us as well. And to be straight, Grace and I were finding it a lot more fun at Grandma's house than at our own. This was due to Mom and Dad. Even though they had come back from their trip that was supposed to bind them together in love as they put it, it didn't seem like things were working the way they should have. Mom was still telling him that his good money days were long gone, and he would take that hard, retreating to the living room with his trademarked type of response like, "Good!" "So!", and "Well!"

For months, I along with Grace had been asking for the treaty. We even had off the cuff talks with them individually about how their behavior with each other had left us questioning the inheritance they were handing off to us.

To soften things, I had even left the front door ajar for Mom to come in without too much interruption, to fill her promise. How she went about it could be the topic of many of our later debates.

Mom was early, and the door even slammed behind her, causing Grandma to drop her checkbook that she was reviewing at the time.

"Hi. Bridgett gotten here yet," Mom asked all of us at once.

Grandma who was going at picking up her checkbook, stopped halfway down. "How you got in?"

Mom evidently did not care for the question and kept asking, "Bridgett hasn't come yet? Bridgett here?"

With that, Grandma inclined her head to see Mom from her down position. "When I see her I'll breathe better," Grandma said.

Mom moved closer to Grandma who swapped her movement for a backward step of her own.

"I came to apologize for what I've been," Mom announced.

Grandma reached and got the remote control from her nearby desk. "I was just getting ready to hear something on the Toshiba."

Meanwhile, the TV was on and Grandma and Mom were both looking at it. The President of the United States was again on talking about changes to be rolled out on banking and financial companies reform. He talked about a consumer agency watchdog.

Grandma threw her hand to the heavens claiming, "This is what we need."

Mom looked at Grandma. She shook her head in a way Grace and I knew well. It was her darling left to right motion, the one that cured me and Grace of a thousand tantrums long before I got to ten and Grace, seven.

The two watched and listened. The president talked. He mentioned in other words that a stable and reliable banking system promotes sustained growth.

"What we have seen so far is an army of lobbyists descending here on Capitol Hill trying to block basic and commonsense reform," the president maintained as Miss Bridgett, whose presence was undetected up to that point moved forward by way of a dishy Cha, cha, cha.

"I'm with you all-the-way, Mr. President," Miss. Bridgett announced. We need it!"

Mom looked troubled at Miss Bridgett.

"That's what you came here for?"

"Yeah. I agree," Miss Bridgett declared. "You know what I'm talking about? And you need it too!"

Grandma would snap into an eye-resting moment, looking as if in a meditation, one hand on the other and wobbling her head.

Mom, though, was in an entire different energy, scolding the guest.

"Don't even go there, Bridgett," Mom alerted.

Miss Bridgett leaned to Mom and placed her hand on Mom's arm. "I know you told me not to, but you're acting like…."

"Like what," Mom questioned.

We would never know for sure. Mom placed immediate breaks. "Bridgett!"

"Why don't you help you mother, Gloria," Miss Bridgett asked.

Mom feasted her eyes on us in the room reminding me of the way the lady at Shines, Ms. Wonzick, had taken me in the first time I went to their home. Mom kept her vigilance a bit longer. And then she asked, "What business do I have to do with this?"

Miss Bridgett stood tall with upright shoulders, making midgets of the sitting adults as well as Grace and me. She turned her head gradually to put her eyes on Mom, head to toes.

"They're bouncing your goddam checks too, Gloria. You said $80 fees this week and you're not smart to call a bull a bull? A cow's a cow? A pig's a pig, Gloria, and you need to stop acting like hurt doesn't hurt! Stop casing in your feelings. A rat's a rat, a cat's a cat!"

Grandma's lifted her head somewhat from her meditative state. She didn't need any of this right now. She placed her hand at her mouth. She closed her eyes again. She placed her head back downwards.

# CHAPTER 12

At a bar with a roller-skating rink half the size of a soccer field and a with a lot of young people skating, Grandma, Mom and Ms. Bridgett found themselves drinking almost to the point of full intoxication. They said their goal was to go and hash thing out, but the task turned harder than they anticipated. Grace noted: "every time they attempt to fix a thing, they end up in a deeper hole than before they attempted it."

Now they were drunk.

Grandma was slurring and she was not alone. All three of them had crossed the red line.

Grandma leaned towards Mom. "You shouldn't just sit there and let them rape you. A thief will always be that," She whispered.

Miss Bridgett began to talk and ended up giggly.

"Let me tell you how we used to say it when I was young in high school," "A thief is a thief is a thief. Even if they're your bank boss-man. Your friend, even your family can be a thief!"

Grandma kept her attention on Mom, and told a story we had heard a zillion times before. It was about when she was growing up, back in the depression. Accordingly, things were very different. She said, there was a certain family, a wealthy one who used to hold money safe for people because some of the folks did not have faith in the banks of the time.

Mom was by this time showing strong indications of her tipsy self. "Yeah?"

"And these folks actually got their chump back," Grandma said to Mom. Grandma said she knew because one of the persons was Grandpa John.

A waiter stepped up to the table.

"A Malibu Coconut for me. One for her and one for her. Add to that, a really tall glass of Silver Dog, for meow," Grandma requested. She pulled her head up from falling. "Be generous on the tequila, Dear."

The waiter took in the sight of them.

Grandma continued. "Your bank steals your money too?"

The waiter did not speak or give any indication of interest in Grandma's question or financial situation.

Grandma moved her focus to Mom and Miss. Bridgett. She made note that she would pick up the tab. Mom said that was not going to happen. Miss Bridgett looked to Grandma and told her that she worked too hard for what she had.

Grandma placed her hand atop the check as she loved to do. She looked towards Mom. "You always have to be a step ahead, right Ms. Graves?"

Momentarily, Mom was waving at one of the muscular waiter. "Handsome," she called him. "You like cash or card?

The shirtless waiter placed his hand on Mom's in a compromising way. He smiled. "Depending on what you're paying for."

Miss Bridgett said to Mom that the waiter wanted personal service. "Look at him," she added. "Just another broke one!"

The waiter was courageous and kept his hand on Mom's as Miss Bridgett questioned his action with her eyes and hands. "Look at you," she continued. "Her husband will prosecute you!"

Grandma laughed at the shenanigans. She joked. "Not if he takes the check on himself."

The muscle waiter dropped his shoulders at that and began walking away without the check.

"Don't forget to add a nice tip," he said, and promised he would be back soon to take care of them.

# CHAPTER 13

Frustrated that she was not getting the kind of help she envisioned either from her family or others, Grandma began a new campaign directed at Bank $$. She posted a sign next to one of her desktop with the heading, "Every Thing I Ever Wanted." Next to the number "1" she wrote the words, "Get New Letter to Bank CEO."

She altered old letters and scripted new one. In the latest she sent, she spelled out her request and her dissatisfaction:

> Dear Mr. CEO;
> I am writing pertaining to my bank account #4862X45X3712XX. In the past two years it has been over-drafted on numerous occasions not because of the absence of funds at the time of specific transactions, but because activities have been timed to create overdraft that result in a domino effect and an ongoing collection of fees.
>
> I have sent you many letters about this issue, but have not heard a word back from you. I am a senior citizen of limited means. I have lived in this country all my life, and I have never had this problem before.

My previous letters, which I know you have received, delineates my full and complete struggle with these issues, so I hope you will review them and follow up with me. I hope and pray you will return my money to my account. I'm middle class; I need my money to live.

Please also refer to the statements and other documents I have included.

I hope you write back soon, and thanks for cooperating.

Sincerely,

Mrs. Sandra Muley (mc/sc)

On occasion Grandma even hired a courier service to hand deliver some of her mail, but all of them, including this last one went unanswered.

"So, phoning doesn't work," she said.

Eventually she decided something more drastic was necessary. That meant showing up at one of her nearby branches to talk to a teller about her problem.

"I called and called and they refused to help me," Grandma told the teller who she described as being as close to hearing her as California is to Florida.

"They bounced four checks on Thursday and four more this morning."

The teller looked at Grandma with a mean expression, her eyes fixed and bulged, her lips clamped for an instant. She looked a bit longer. "We've told you we'll provide you with $35.00 this year."

"I don't want $35.00," Grandma countered. "You took $280 in one swoop!"

Grace and I turned our heads at the same time, Grace's slightly, not to be linked to Grandma. Some people in the bank were speaking with each other in a hush, hush tone. They understood what Grandma was talking about. Some were just gazing.

The Teller banged her hand on the desk in front of her, “I’m sorry Ma’am. That’s all we can do.”

“Well, who’s the supervisor?” Grandma asked. “Let me talk with someone who can do more.”

****$$****

In the Supervisor’s office, Grandma would come up against the same system.

“Unfortunately, Ma’am, these fees are not going to go away,” the branch manager said.

“What I want to know is why you process the large one first and you waited four days till I had penny transactions and then you bounce those and paid the big one and your fee,” Grandma said to her.

“Ma’am. I’m sorry,” the Supervisor said. “Based on feedback, our customers prefer having us pay the larger one first.”

Grandma’s eyes directly went half-closed and her mouth took on an ugly opened shape. She stomped her foot to the floor. “What do you mean your customer,” she said to the supervisor who elected to have a side chit-chat with another staff member about a walk on the beach than with her face-to-face meeting with Grandma.

Grandma waved her hand in front of the manager’s face as if to wake her up. “Am I not one of your customers,” she said.

“Ma’am,” the Supervisor said again, now in a admonishing tone. “Are you listening to what I’m saying?”

Grandma reached and grabbed on to the supervisor’s shirt collar, causing some noise and the tumbling of things to the ground. “Let me see that damn feedback you're…,”

The Supervisor at once shouted for “Security!”

Immediately, two guards darted to the commotion, and Grandma was consequently handcuffed and was hustled out of the bank by two police officers.

On the way to the door, Grandma glanced at the people inside, many of whom now appeared more frightened than she, the bank staff taken in account.

“I know what I’m going to do,” she warned. “Don’t worry. Everything will be quite fine!”

# CHAPTER 14

The hopes and dreams in Grandma's heart would come to surface in bits and pieces over the course of the ensuing weeks and months; the part she was immediately ready to share was that she was "ready to become completely savvy." She was ready to learn all the things Grace and I had been trying to teach her about technology. She said she was excited to be a technician as she called me. She had seen Grace and me Twitter, Face-book, Skype and you name it, and she said it was her turn to get in the game. The old Black lady at Shines kept encouraging her, telling her that if she didn't she would be a "non-player," and there was a place for people like that too.

Grandma said that at every turn she would hear the lady's voice: She was saying, no doubt, "we are all of the same family of man!" We're all of the same. "Love. This is Ms. Wonzick, Love—I'm just checking in to remind you. Remember to use every bit of those computa to advance your life. Remember, this is Mom. Wonzick…just checking in, Love!"

At first we thought Grandma's request was no more than a joke. Grace theorized the voice in Grandma's head was just one more warning she was losing the little she still had. After all, it was this same woman, Grace reminded me, who had told us following her stay at the hospital, that while there she was of "another mind." Whatever that meant, Grace and I had that on our *pondering* screen also. What we did know at the moment was that her behavior had changed considerably from the day she returned home and unspeakably for some from our earlier days with her.

Grace was saying that Grandma was acting like a young girl.

She tried to convince me that there was more to Grandma's relationship with Billy than Grandma had ever told any of us. Grace even implied Grandma wanted to learn all the new tricks on the computer and otherwise solely to make an impression her male friend.

"Buddy. He's her boyfriend," Grace avouched.

"No. He's not," I told her. "Period!

Grace laughed at me.

"Just a good help, G."

Grace went through a whole run of events in Grandma's life to try to convince me, and when I told her she was being disloyal to Grandma she chose to give me what she called evidence.

"Mom said he's not there to help her do the *"Lord's"* work," Grace said. "He's her man-friend!"

"G, that doesn't make any sense! Her banker," I said, feeling infuriated and so angry at Grace for being so dumb. "Old ladies don't do stupid things like that," I offered. "Her bank-man. That's all G."

I remember being the laughing stock for the flash. Grace darted towards the den singing, "Tagg is a blind boys! Tagg is a blind man. Granny's got a boy friend! Granny's got a boy-man!"

For a second I felt like a bullied child, and I dashed after her to find ourselves in front of Grandma. She was studious and unquestionably focused. Her head was moving through the standard path she taught us in reading as her eyes traveled across her computer screen. At first she did not give attention to us, but when she did, her eyes were sufficient. They cried out for the incongruity they spotted: "Soldiers!"

Immediately, Grace tried to make me the evil one, saying I chased her, but we swiftly realized the severity of Grandma's reprimand and tried our best to get back in line.

"Soldiers," Grandma voiced, now in an acknowledging sweet tone. "Tell me, how you think I should change this …."

Grace and I looked at Grandma's computer and saw she was log into her Facebook account, reading responses that had been sent to her by others.

"She's going social, Tagg," Grace alerted. "Damn! Shit!"

Grandma gave another of her castigating looks.

I suggested she go for the radio, too.

Grandma switched for what was a mischievous smile.

"Yeah," she said sounding confident. "And you'll show me how to put it on Twitter, Soldiers." She got up from her chair and did her darling bow, as if in recital; as if Ms. Wonzick was revealing herself through her. "Listen here, first."

Grace may have been jiving but all I heard next was her going, "No!"

My mind was stirring, "Go Grandma. Go," and that's what she went for as if we had a direct connection. And there was no resistance, no distraction, no fear of being seen or heard—just a calm—a calm attentive audience, appreciating.

"Ok," Grandma began, and we waved our approval; it was OK.

She pressed on, "Tired of your bank ripping you off?"

We both gave our thumb pop-ups.

She carried on. "Strike back!"

"How about, 'stop your bank from making you sick,'" I offered.

Grandma shook her head in consensus.

"Making a fool of you," Grace said.

Grandma again approved our contents, noting them as contributed text.

"Use their money for free," I appended.

Grandma seemed to like that line more than any of the previous as she took a longer than usual time shaking her head in thankfulness for it, and then she wrote it down. She ended with the words, "Here's how."

****$$****

Essentially, we had inadvertently helped to come up with a script for Grandma. One that would have ordinarily got me in trouble, like Grace, for going, "Damn!" on finding out.

"You realize what we just worked out? That's it, Grandma! That's it," I said.

There was no trouble for me this time. Grandma straightaway pulled out her I-phone and made some calls, one to the local Miami Herald to which she flaunted her use of technology and simply called out the name "MIAMI HERALD," and the call was placed on her behest.

Another was to some other paper called The Sun Sentinel; a third was made to The Florida Times. For the last one, she composed an alternate script that was essentially, "End to bank stealing. Use their money for free. Call us for details." With that, she included her I-phone number.

Grandma spoke. "What I'm here to do, is to reach heart and souls!"

What I did was to stop with my hand on my chin and listened before going, "Go Grandma. Go. Go. Go." And that she did. She bumped fists with me, and then in a playful way, spoke. "Now you two midget of Soldiers," she said. "Show me this Skype thing!"

Grace went over and sat on her lap. "Facebook, first Granny."

And they worked.

# CHAPTER 15

Over the period of a week Grandma had developed the skills necessary to make "Friends", albeit, Grace and I got irritated teaching her hardened brain. She, however, promoted her cause so well, she brought a crowd of several hundred out to Balboa Park to rally with her.

The weather-lady on WFOR-Miami had forecast a twenty percent chance of rain, but thanks to God it didn't happen, because, if it did, a lot of cardboard placards and posters would have gotten wet, not to mention all of us.

One woman who lived in the neighborhood and called us nothing short of disruptive, shouted at us, saying the rain should have come and send us all to where we came from. A man hollered back at her that, "What you see here will spread this country; the world!"

Just about everyone else was kind to us during the first hour, however, like the man with the sign that read "YOU'RE WHY I'M ALIVE, MRS. MULEY." He left from one side of the park to greet Grace and me after someone told him who we were. He reached to shake my hand, knocking into a lady with a placard that almost fell from her hand. "Human Dignity Cannot be Denied," it read.

"Is that your Grandma," the man asked us elatedly.

My answer was "of course," to which he said, "She's the right girl at the right time."

"OK!"

****$$****

When Grandma was on stage with her cause, Grace and I were front and center, and for me, there was no one I fashioned more in this world in that moment. My Grandma on stage: eloquent, smart, in control. In the year that passed, I had heard different stories about her: who she was as a child, who she was as a young lady, how she had problems with reading up to the point she got married, and now this: The lady standing on stage was beyond all I had ever imagined. She was Grandma Smart. Grandma Courageous. Grandma something inspiring. Glittering and imposing. Something along those lines.

"It seems like something here has resonated with a few people," she tells her admiring, energetic, crowd. "And that's kinda neat!"

I shouted the "Go Grandma, go," line, and the crowd made those words its anthem, which drove Grandma to coming off the stage with the mike in her hand as she revved them up.

"We the people, middle-class and all will prevail their vice," she declared. "We're not going to take it anymore!"

She threw her hand to the crowd and they cheered, whistled, and some throwing back kisses.

She upped the ante, "Let's go and get them, Soldiers!"

I shouted the "Go, go" thing again and the crowd picked up on it yet again, this time not only in song but also in dance.

****$$****

Not long thereafter, Grandma was leading the now noisy, raucous crowd across Yellowback Street to a Bank $$ Branch as people in the group went one by one to the various ATMs and retrieved money from them.

I kept soaking in the goings-on.

One man lifted the money to the crowd like an award. "$250 over balance. Won't pay it back till late Sunday," he said boastfully.

Not far from us a boy of about my age grabbed money from the hand of one of the bank customers that had gotten out his money, but a crowd was instantly after him.

The little gazelle must have done this before as he knew how to get through the crowd for a minute, flying by placards with everything from, "Eat the Bankers" to "Bust up Big Banks!"

I wasn't on the hunt. I was more into the thinking aspects of things, the observer's outlook, reading signs and making the most of what the world was teaching me in my youth. In time, my eyes had reached a sign that stated "Capitalism Isn't Working."

In time, new things happened—the crowd got the little bandit and banged him up.

"Three hundred and fifty dollars! Free," another money waving account holder claimed simultaneously to a group shouting, "beat the rascals… Beat the shit out the rascal!"

Right then, from a nearby street a car approached, speeding, and a lady in the passenger's seat push out her hand to the thumb-up position.

A reporter jumped out of his van, immediately, antenna up, a camera lady following; they hurried to capture the events.

A man was at an ATM and asking out loud, "What's the maximum you can get?"

The reporter pointed out to the camera lady an up-coming truck with a group of men on the truck's flatbed stretch.

"Get them," the reporter instructed. "That's contrast."

One of the men on the truck, who came across as the leader, sprang to his feet, threw his fist in the path of Grandma and yelled. "Find something better to do you Jackwagon. Get the hell outa here!"

They were quickly gone and would circle back after a while but their return did not garner the same attention or troubles.

What took my greatest interest was the potpourri of signs in the area. "I am a combative person; I love to crush bastards!" one claimed. Another was that of "Sandy Muley For President!!!!!!!!!!!!!"

My favorite was "MARRY ME, LADY. I'M SINGLE." This one was carried by a man of about 40; he came across as one of those dedicated souls who came at the slightest called for a rally.

Everybody, including a no-teeth woman, were out to prop up Grandma. This one was a noisy fast-talker who said she saw the "notice" on her computer and knew that if she didn't come she wouldn't get some blessing she was seeking out, and so she showed up so that she would be in the right "energy." She too was waving money she got out, a sign reading, 'Thieves—Bitches' in her other hand wielded above most of the others. When the sign was knocked around by a wind that had begun, I saw its other side. It read, "Remember Lilly Ledbetter!" She gave me and Grace high-fives!

"I might just not pay this back," the lady shouted at the top of her voice to a spontaneous applause.

****$$****

At the end Grace and I concluded the most fitting sign—the one that captured what Grandma was trying to accomplish was one bore by a man in suit and tie. He was standing right next to Grandma when she was telling the crowd "Big banks would be on the run soon." The man's sign was large and spoke volumes, "Stop The Bank—Save Society."

I passed by the man as he moved through the crowd and got much notice, then stopping to talk with another man, an old gray-headed one, probably what Grandpa's age would be if he had still been here. The gray-headed one erratically waved a handful of money into the air. "The fuckers have been fucking us for years," he shouted to find a friendly audience.

"Now's our time," he continued, and threw the handful of money into the air, sending the crowd into a scramble for it.

"Horray! Horray! Horray," the gray-headed one shouted.

At once, another man pointed from a distance, towards Grandma. "You' all go home. That bitch's dangerous! You' all go home!"

****$$****

The important moments that captured the emotions of the park event were echoed at the studios of radio and television. Many of the local papers also cashed in on it, parading the story on their front pages. Even Bank $$ boardroom got its taste of things.

Even thought the executives did not schedule a special meeting to discuss the happenings, they played a clip of the Ladies of "The View" take, asking the financial guru Suse Aman her views about Grandma having the event at the park.

"Everybody knows a good thing when they see it," Kevin Michael Smith, the Co-host of the program Entertainment Tonight said.

"Yes," Suse Aman replied on The View. "She's a genius, a role model I know I can use to help educate us Women."

Co-host Smith spoke. "Even "Lady O" had her praise for it. Let me show you what she had to say. "

They showed a screen with the two co-hosts and an inset in the background with Oprah Winfrey talking about Grandma.

"I wish I could get her for my show, but Pierce Morgan already got the deal."

The two co-hosts looked at each other.

****$$****

Abruptly, Corporate looked at his staff. "Do they need to be doing these things? Why taunt us?"

"Well, let's see what Dr. Sill has to say," Co-host smith said as the inset screen came in from the background.

"What a good exemplar of what we should all be doing," Dr. Sill said. "I can't believe we still have to be protesting this crap. I think we'll have to get her on the Dr. Sill Show!"

# CHAPTER 16

On receiving an insider's report about Grandma's success of the day at the park, Billy invited her over to his house to discuss the next move in the ground game. He told her he wanted to show her how he could help her to take on the bank that even he had gotten upset with. A few days earlier Corporate had sent out a circular to management and staff affirming the organization had acquired all it needed to crush anybody and anything in the path of their carrying out the bank's mission, expressed as "financial mediation work." Within, the organization, however, some had taken that mission to mean siphoning money from account holders and that was the basis behind a growing dissident movement. These were the ones that called themselves "The Insiders."

One day, a group of them held a meeting at one of the local Marriott to voice their concerns. Their conclusion? "The people at the top had created a system to privatize profits while socializing losses."

Billy was among these so-called insiders and in some respect he was a head. He was furtively responsible for many of the people who showed up at Grandma's event at the park. And this is how I concluded he was a friend and not a opponent.

He had heard about the planning of the park event and rallied a crowd of insiders to join Grandma to take the streets to show their discontent. It worked. The man with the sign that referenced his reason for being alive, and the other one that claimed, "I love to crush bastards" were among a group of almost five score who were actually employees of Bank $$.

From all reports, however, things at Billy went differently than planned, a new normal for Grandma.

Grandma found the house as cozy and elegant, and it was not until after seven in the evening that they even arrived. This, however was only after she had spent more than an hour at the flower shop where she had ordered a dozen of their freshest and prettiest red roses.

At the entrance of Billy's, a TV was loud, and what was on? The reporter offered, "Same 'O', Same 'O'" and promised that after an upcoming commercial, he would be talking about a CEO that had just been taken into custody. Corporate Greed, he said.

Billy looked disgusted with himself that he brought Grandma to that and he grimaced. "Old nonsense," he said, and he asked for. "Music!"

To get it, he pressed a button on his cell phone and instantly the TV was turned off. "Music! Music," he said as if craving, and he pressed buttons on his cell phone again to Benny Goodman's "When My Baby Smiles At Me."

Grandma was clearly excited as she lifted her head with a smile. She did not say a word though. She paced slowly with Billy admiring his wall of paintings draping the entrance, including one of three young ladies, charming and exciting, each doing her own thing, one of which is dancing.

"This is for you," Billy said, sounding like an introvert. He shook his head to the music after a moment of silence that placed him and Grandma directly in front of a large Chinese watercolor. Billy gave the artist's name as Chiang T'ien-Hsi.

Grandma shook her head. "You know my taste," she said, pointing to one of the two paintings with young female dancers.

"I know this one. My step-mom owned Number 42."

She walked closer to the picture and smelled the canvas whereupon Billy made an over-sized step and position himself intimately behind her.

"Wonderful," she exclaimed. "Still fresh. The oil, that is!"

Billy placed his hand on her shoulder. “Like a freshly plucked lily.”

Grandma’s blushed, yet her hand reached for his, giving it a teasing slap. “Oh, silly.”

Billy pointed to the other picture with a dancer. “I bet you, don’t know this one.”

Grandma mumbled out that she came to get his help in learning how the bank works to help people get their money back, but she kept her eyes on the picture, looking closely at it. She leaned closer, trying to cheat by reading the signature at the bottom.

“You should know this one,” Billy said as he pointed to the vibrant, colorful piece in front of them. “This one’s contemporary. Come, now!”

Grandma brought her eyes close to the image with Billy standing now even closer behind her.

“It’s like I’m blindfolded, Bill” she called out. “Can’t identify this painter,”

“If you come with it in five seconds, I give you 5% of what it’s worth,” Billy exclaimed.

“Quickly, quickly,” Grandma begged, trying to decipher the words on the canvas. “Bodacious, Courageous, Delicious? Something like that,” she answered.

Billy reached for and held her hand in that flash. “Come now! Come now! Three. Two. One. Over!”

Grandma looked at him, her eyes half-closed, her index finger waving at him. “ Ah ah. That was too fast.”

Billy shook his head to say, “no it wasn't that fast for him.” As a young man he was known for his speed: sprinting, getting girls, getting things done. In fact, he’s been good at these as recent as when he was with his own Black Madonna.  The only thing he was slow at was learning the computer and keeping up to speed with technology.

"You cheated,” Grandma said.

Billy elected to give Grandma a clue to who the painter was, and with that, three more seconds. “He died less than ten years ago. He was from Overton.”

Grandma smiled at him. “We have good ones right here, ha?”

Billy shook his head indicating “yes”.

“A good part of his estate was sold to the Rubell family.”

"Peter Busby," Grandma said like she knew what she was saying.

"Far from it."

"Janet Cardiff."

"Wrong gender. It's a he—An African American," Billy said. "Come now!

Grandma studied him as she sniffed at the smell of the food he had prepared for them.

"How fast can you come," he inquired. "Go for it. Three, two. C'mon. Four, three, two, one. OVER!"

"OK my Dear you won this one; that doesn't mean I don't have what it takes," Grandma replied.

Billy began to glide with Grandma towards the dining room, to the meal that was apparently making them ravenous. It looked delicious, the naked chicken, the wine, the salad, all waiting.

"I know you do," he said as he pulled her chair for her. "You may have just lost that chance." The answer was Purvis Young. "But you haven't lost what's planned," he said, spreading his arms open to the table of food and wine.

Grandma smiled. "Young,". He was the Black guy from Miami.

"Overton. Liberty. Same "O"," Billy replied, again opening his arm to display the work he had prepared for her. "And what's more scrumptious and exciting than what you have here?"

Grandma shook his hand to which he placed his other on top. "You sure move fast, Dear B I L L Y. You DO," she said.

# CHAPTER 17

Grandma said the night at Billy's was what led her to open up, so she went all the way  relaying to me in details the problems she was having with her bank. He and she had discussed me, and they concluded the class work I was doing would serve well in helping her with her lawsuit.

Up to that point I had no idea how central I was. The videos I was studying in my class were yellow gold. They were about the people and system that were giving Grandma, and so many others among us, hell, as Billy would later put it. He explained them better than I ever would in a thousand words, even a thousand years: "Your work, young chap is priceless." He went on: "It's at the core of your grandmother's problems and solution."

I would have a change in how I saw things from that day, even though sometimes I pretended life was still standard.

# CHAPTER 18

Over the coming weeks I shared with Grandma many of the videos from my class, and she made a promise to God, me and everyone at a concert we were at who cared to hear, "to fight greed with every tooth and every nail" she had. *That*, we would find out, was a commitment that was much easier said than done.

For the most part, Grandma's commitment in pursuing the lawsuit against Bank $$ fluctuated as she would not get the constant, steady support she needed. For a part of that time she invested a lot in us, in another period it was her business, which continued to hinge to the seesaw.

She said that in spite of all the time and everything she had done with Billy, her problems were far from worked out. In fact, there was a period, she admit to secretly losing faith in everything. In this chapter she believed she was wasting her life and her time. She had given all she had to what she perceived as bringing justice for people she felt were knocked around by Corporate Greed, but felt alone. There were times when she thought she could be the voice for the movement, but no one would be there to do what she needed them to do. There was no support from the people she cared about the most: not Mom, not Miss Bridgett, not Dad, not even the lawyers.

Not until today.

****$$****

Today was a better day for Grandma, and on her better days she tried to do what she could.

We were at the local library learning new things when the first of a good change came.

"This one has in samples of the different financial statements. Ratios galore," the Librarian said as he passed Grandma a book.

"And has in galore of legal forms as well, to help you with what you're doing."

Grandma told the librarian the only business professional she cared for at the moment was her accountant. "He thinks I have a good turn-over," she said.

The librarian passed another book, a heavy one, to Grandma, telling her something pertaining to her wanting to see how she was doing in the different parts of her business.

"You'll get a good dose in that one and in this one too," the Librarian said. "Current assets, ROI; the chicken and the eggs."

That's when an announcement came over the intercom in the library:

"Mrs. Sandra Muley, If you're in the building, you have a call. Please come to the front desk. Mrs. Sandra Muley you have a call at the front desk!"

I called the front desk, and with the help of a very clever clerk they transferred the call to Grandma's Cell phone.

"Yes, my name is Juana from Barrow & Vargas Law Firm," the caller stated.

"And…," Grandma answered.

"I'm calling for Ms. Sandra Muley. Is this Ms. Sandra E. … ," Juana said.

"You don't have anything better to do," Grandma replied.

Juana on the other side of the phone line, gave details she had Attorney Vargas on hold, and they had news for Grandma.

"Is that the fat, mean one that stood me up," Grandma demanded.

Juana turned out to be the receptionist Grandma had talked with the time she went to Attorney Vargas's office. The one that kept saying "Hello, may I help you." She laughed out loud. "Yes. That's him. Still likes his quesso con carne," she said.

"And," Grandma interrupted.

"We have partnered with the Barrow Law Firm and we can help you with your case now."

Grandma stated she didn't know what to feel; there was anger, happiness, even guilt; she was still unsettled.

"Are you serious," she asked.

The librarian signaled at Grandma who had completely ignored him.

"Ma'am," Are we done," he asked.

"Got other fishes to fry," Grandma said, shaking her head and stepping away. You know it's not a so-so call when it comes over your intercom machine, right?"

****$$****

For the moment, Juana, the attorneys' secretary made headway. She thanked Grandma on behalf of the attorney's "for the beautiful bouquet...the dozen red roses you sent them. They loved every last one of them! And they love how you signed the card, 'Maam!' They got a kick out of it! Ms. Muley?"

"I'm here."

Juana continued, "When you're finish talking with Attorney Vargas, I'll give you the address for our newly combined exec suite. Hold on for your friend."

"I'm spring loaded," Grandma replied, jumping so high in the air, the Librarian asked me if the lady was on something.

"Next, Attorney Barrow," Juana said.

# CHAPTER 19

Grandma maintained the ride to the new Barrow & Vargas, LLP in Tampa was "as smooth a ride you can get from point 'A' to point 'B.'" Armed with all the information she had gathered from me she felt she had an excellent chance as she readied herself to take advantage of every moment.

She found out the lawyers had won some other cases; everything in and outside of the building showed it. Though they were only occupying two or three floors of the thirty-two story building, their name could be read miles away with the whole building flaunting their name, even affixing the word "Plaza" to ensure no one missed their accomplishments.

Grandma couldn't tell if the building was new but communicated it smelled like it was, starting at the entrance, the elevator and the main gallery that led to the consultation room they met in.

Grandma sensed the company's nameplate on the wall was made of solid gold, and I believed her. Yes, I did. She once owned a little machine she used for years when she was out and saw garage or rummage sales, to test if something was gold or not. I don't recalled seeing her testing this piece, but she had gotten to know gold so well, I don't think she needed to do any testing. I had never seen or hear of her making a mistake with gold, with or without her little set-up. Her years with Sotheby's were not that far removed. She kept reminding us of them.

She called the new team "golden."

When the attorneys were delivered to the room by a junior attorney, they found Grandma walking around admiring their achievements.

Attorney Barrow started by extending his hand to Grandma but then held back, visibly hesitant for a moment. He proceeded. "Never thought we were going to meet again," he said.

Grandma chuckled, but took his hand with great care this time and made bow-like motion as if to the charisma of royalty. When she emerged, the residual smile on her face had a sincere businessperson's look to it.

"I hope you re-hired the young lady that used to work for you," Grandma said.

Attorney Vargas answered on behalf of his partner. "How you know we did? And she'll been doing some of the research for your case! Ms. Niqua has come a long way. She's a junior partner with us now!"

"I don't want any junior anybody on my case," Grandma replied as she positioned her hand as if pulling a trigger at the two lawyers.

She said, "I want the big guns, you guys!"

Attorney Barrow brought himself to a firm and attentive position as Grandma continued.

"We don't want any pint-size case, here. Anybody who has lost their savings with Bank $$ *must* be a part of this! I know what they're doing," she said. "My grandson showed me!"

By this time a group of people including other lawyers had gathered around a sprawling meeting table and found themselves in conversation about Grandma. They inarguably had never seen their office ran over like this before. These were lawyers whose names made the headlines of the big papers and electronic media month after month for winning the coveted cases in town, and from time to time, the whole country.

"Stringent operations" one of the lawyers stated. That's how a Channel 2 reporter had described the firm two days earlier.

"You know that could mean billions and billions of dollars," Grandma said, uninterrupted by those talking about her.

Attorney Barrow exhaled gradually as he positioned towards the staff that looked startled. He addressed his partner, Attorney Vargas and then again looked at Grandma who was in a state of antics as far as they were concerned.

"This is for we the people of this country who've been victimized by greed and corruption," Grandma announced. "This is for the middle!"

Attorney Barrow, who was standing, leaned over, his fingers on the conference table holding his weight.

He was not in the middle. He said, "Ms. Muley, we're not going for billons of anything!"

Grandma inclined towards him. "Yes you are," she declared. "We'll stop them from fleecing our beloved…"

Attorney Vargas who was sitting in front of a flag of the U.S., thumped his palm on the table. "Calm down, Ms. MAAM," he said. "We know it's about a red-hot financial fight, but we shouldn't have to…"

Grandma struck her hand on the table in reply. She stated she wanted to change the direction of things. "I shouldn't even be here right now," she kept on, and then switched to a calm voice, her finger moving to people around the room. "You illustrious, fine men and woman can do anything!"

She pointed to Attorney Vergas. "First I met you." Then she pointed to Attorney Barrow, "And then it was you. You're giant killers! For God's sake, *now*, go and slay them beasts!"

Attorney Vargas placed his hand at his chin. " My Lord," he blurted out as Grandma started crushing some paper she had in front of her.

"What I want is for you to decimate them," she said. "Crush them with the biggest class action ever!"

The group waited, thinking she was ending. They were wrong; she only got stronger.

"Crispy," she exclaimed and glanced at the paper in her hand. "Cream em!"

To us, Grandma was clearly not posing a danger. It is true, however, she was wasting their costly time. At her best, she was entertaining them. They looked at her foreseeing the worse.

She pressed on keys of a calculator on the table in front of her as Attorney Barrow stated that between himself and Attorney Vargas they had a combined forty-six years in the law business and said he couldn't recall ever seeing anyone quite like Grandma before.

"Have you," Attorney Barrow asked of Attorney Vargas.

Attorney Vargas began laughing, his belly tumbling in rolls.

"She thinks we're slayers of dragon," he said to the room of chucklers.

Attorney Barrow looked towards Grandma, a more solemn look for her. "Ms. Muley, our goal is winning."

Grandma kept plugging information into her calculator as she spoke. "Let's say for example there are fifty million accounts at $$, and each account has illegally been stolen an average of 10 times in a non-leap year," she said. "That's 35 times 10, times 50 million. How much is that?

No one cared to answer that.

Ma'am," Attorney Barrow said.

"whoo ho," Grandma replied.

Feeling he was losing Grandma again, Attorney Vargas cautioned, "Ma'am. Ma'am."

Grandma chose to disregard the concerns. She was losing them. She gestured as she spoke. "Can you visualize it," she asked. She opened her arms to the group around the table, the way a flower opens to take in the sunlight. "And I'm not even talking about penalty."

# CHAPTER 20

The attorneys would soon have gotten enough of Grandma and talked about going into private to discuss how to move forward.

Niqua, the young lady Grandma had given the tip to, was called in to help. She joined. Attorney Sheniqua A. Pahram, was on the name holder in front of her as she sported a sharp looking low hair cut, and donned a swagger of poise and focus.

Some years later at the christening of my first boy, Grandma would, tell me my eyes were heavily on the lady, and I went on to admitted that was the case. Grandma said she thought I would go Black. My wife laughed.

"Not back, *Black*," Grandma said emphatically.

"Even at that age, your thinking about certain things was advanced," Grandma said.

I nodded as I thought back. The young lady was less than seven years my senior. The part I couldn't figure out then, though, was who else on planet earth would think our ever being together would be cool?

Miss Law, as I felt of her back then, stood in the receptionist area of the new office with Attorneys Barrow and Vargas as she took notes. I gawked, visualizing things as fast as they would be processed.

"Here's the deal for you, Ms. Muley," Attorney Barrow announced. "We're lumping your case with Feinstein vs. Bank $$."

Attorney Barrow began walking as the group followed; Attorney Sheniqua continued the note-taking.

"By Friday you get three to five people to join you in filing the lawsuit," Attorney Barrow continued. "I spoke with Judge Shilling, and she said we must—I repeat, must get all filings in by five on Friday, no exceptions! Did I say must?"

Attorney Sheniqua shook her head in the direction of her agreement but with a kind of stylishness that had me shaking. She must have been from some African upper classes. My moment brought goose pimples on my arms as she talked. "Is Friday the ultimate cut-off," she asked Attorney Barrow.

"One-hundred percent," he said.

She continued the notes taking.

"One minute later than four and we won't be able to do it,"

Attorney Barrow added, and reached over to shake hand with the Princess Niqua, his face and entire disposition at ease. "Thank you, he said. He departed.

****$$****

At the end, it was Juana the secretary who broke down the plan to Grandma that the attorneys *would* take on the case, to which her reply was softly verbalized: "Thank God!"

"Attorneys Barrow, Vargas and the panel have every confidence in your pulling this through, Ms. Muley," the secretary said.

With that, Grandma's voice sped from bland to excited. "Anything else on my part?"

The secretary snickered. "Can't believe you with your already tall order to fill," Miss Muley. "Get in those name by Friday. Before four, OK?"

"You bet," Grandma promised.

"We must fax them in by 5. Judge Shilling's not the kind of judge we like at this office. Hear?"

# CHAPTER 21

Feeling extraordinarily well, Grandma found herself doing more things than she could handle: Things she had neglected when she was not fighting-fit—Things that were left undone when her energy was not as good. One of those was to fulfill a scheduled medical checkup with her physician, Dr. Rostein, a Jewish Doctor, about 65, title on name badge: Md. DO.

Over the years Grandma had taken Grace and me to Dr. Rostein's office on many of her appointments, but I had not yet paid attention to him as closely as I did this time. In spite of the age Grandma said he was, he did not look aged, nor was he broken down—he probably was just where the good living had set him—rested in life and career.

He was handsome, tall and with a swagger that Grace said came from him having what most haven't. Neither was he fat or wore thick glasses, or in any way looked like someone who had gone through rigorous studying and reading, the kind that must have made even Grace and my personal physician, Dr. Williamson look tired and slumped.

Going over Grandma's chart, he at the same time held his hand on her wrist for a pulse.

"Eighty-one and counting," he said.

He noted he was very impressed at the strong force flowing through Grandma arteries and veins and then made mention of

Grandma's doctor from Upper Creek Memorial, the one I named Dr. Quack.

Dr. Rostein said he and "Quack-Quack," as he dubbed him, were once co-chair of a "medical panel," while he referred to the force in Grandma as "valoric fire."

Grandma told him she wanted to get rid of her headaches that had resurfaced.

He told her he wouldn't.

"I know what you're doing," Dr. Rostein kept on. "And I have to tell you, if you want to win, you've got to keep things the way they are."

Dr. Rostein leaned to Grandma. "How you handled the surgery, the belly tuck—cleaning up your whole health situation! God's watching over you, Ms. Muley."

"Oh Doc," Grandma remrked, coming off like a young girl in thrill. "You know how that shi butter just makes me exfoliate!"

"Well, I have to say, your aroma therapy's really working," Dr. Rostein said. He was tapping Grandma on the shoulder, now. "Whatever is happening in you is encouraging!"

"It's ironic, you know," Grandma replied.

Dr. Rostein leaned his head. "What?"

"It's a lady at Shines Retirement," Grandma offered. "She's given me so much insights from how to deal with the rascals at Bank $$ to beauty tips, you know," Grandma said.

Dr. Rostein held out his hand to lift Grandma's chin. He wanted to see her tongue.

"They say the best knowledge is either in the grave or at the old folk's home," he said.

The two looked at each other with Grandma shaking her head. "Wonzick. Something Wonzick," she said. "That's the good lady's name?"

"I've taken care of so many of them over the years," Dr. Rostein said. He shook his head, this time as I do on occasions when I want to unstuck my gray matter.

Grandma wobbled her head; her headache had intensified.

"Wonzick," Dr. Rostein repeated. "Doesn't ring a bell."

"Jess T. Wonzick! That's how she addresses herself," Grandma said. "Short. Black. Very talkative too! Very knowledgeable; everybody knows Mom!"

Dr. Rostein rubbed his palm over his forehead a couple times. "Jess T.? You telling me Jess T's there now? Jess T, you said, right?"

Grandma said he was right.

"Oh my God! I haven't been there in a while," Dr. Rostein called out. "I know that lady from high school, Ms. Muley. She knew me before. My mother tells me she was one of the mid-wives that brought me into the world. Oh My God. You sure, Jess T.?"

Grandma nodded.

"Yep, still kicking! A better heart than mine's was, and a good mind with that, Doc," Grandma said. "She promised to bring the crew if I need her help."

Dr. Rostein appeared not to understand what Grandma meant by *crew* or *help* but didn't make that an issue as he had another thought in his head. He went on to speak about what he called "a pity" the people at nursing homes were ending up with "bed sores, bad drugs" and the like. He threw a finger in the air as he spoke, "they even fight in there sometimes."

Grandma said from under her breadth something to the point that the people at Shines would not be able to help her.

Dr. Rostein spoke, "John used to tell me you were the hunter in the family, but…." He ended that thought abruptly as he saw Grandma was evidently not interested in talking about Grandpa anymore.

"You name it. Not surprising at all," Dr. Rostein picked up. "Bad treatment's happening at lots of these homes. But thank Heaven for healthy you Miss Muley."

Grandma accepted the compliment with a smile while the doctor progressed with his speech. "Good to see you the way you're now. You and I, God's willing, will never have to go to a place like that!"

He went on to tell her he could not detect anything physically wrong with her and her headache was nothing more than evidence of a personal struggle within herself.

****$$****

Soon, Grandma was admiring herself and shaking her head in agreement, to something of Dr. Rostein when he started to check her waist.

She spoke, "I'm glad about how I'm keeping but…."

"I'm so proud to be your doctor," the doctor said cutting Grandma's sentence short.

Simultaneously, Grandma's phone rang and she lifted her hand, her finger signals to the doctor to wait a minute. She had to answer the call.

To the caller who turned out to be Billy, she asked, "How about later?"

"We can't make ourselves too busy," Dr. Rostein said as he indicated with his eyes and hand for Grandma to turn around; he wanted a closer look at her back.

"If you say so," Grandma said to Billy. "Later."

Grandma turned in the direction the doctor had asked her to. "I'll tell you one thing. The only one thing I would improve at this point Doc," she said.

Dr. Rostein dropped his long neck downwards, his eyes to convene with Grandma's.

"Remember the vagina replacement we had talked about?"

For the jiffy everything was quiet. Billy was off the line. Both Dr. Rostein and Grandma were staring. He looked up to the ceiling and then his eyes went to a poster he had on his wall, behind Grandma. He nodded as he spoke softly the words. "You create your own universe as you go along." He looked to Grandma.

"You're single, Ms. Muley," He continued. "Foot-loose!"

Grandma chuckled.

"I used to think you were kidding," Dr. Rostein said.

Grandma added a jiggling of her head to her chuckle. "The mind's the last frontier!"

# CHAPTER 22

Knowing that my graduation was that week, I kept waiting to see Grandma get our the way her list of co-plaintiffs to help her prosecute Corporate, but she maintained there was nothing to it. Rather, she took off, going to meet her Billy.

Grace might have been right on this one, Grandma held her phone in hand talking to Miss Bridgett as she sped on what are still not some of the widest or best paved streets and roads in her neighborhood. She told Miss Bridgett that Billy had promised to show her something, and then off she went, flipping her disc over; the music was Benny Goodman; the song, "The Man I love."

"So why you going to see him when you should be busy lining up your 'so called soldiers.'" Miss Bridgett asked.

I thought the question was perfect and rightly phrased considering Grandma's timing and her use of the term Soldiers that she was using more and more for anyone she expected to help her.

Grandma again admired the way she looked. "I might be an eighty year old woman, Bridgett, but that doesn't mean everybody I know is dead."

Miss Bridgett replied that she understood what Grandma was saying, but she also "got" that Friday deadline was only a couple days away.

Grandma looked around at the traffic that was heavy, and there was clear concern in her face. Maybe it was she felt she was neglecting her obligations. Maybe she remembered her last near mishap. She placed her phone on her jack in the auto.

"When again am I going to rev up this much steam," she asked as she was in the act. "Bridgett, he said he wants to see me again."

"What does he want to do," Miss Bridgett asked.

"I can't think of a better time for me to mount and ride the flames," Grandma replied. "The world needs we win this case!"

Miss Bridgett told Grandma that she was at home in a daydream about Grandma and Billy when the phone rang, so it was a coincidence she was on her way to see him.

"You and Billy won,," Miss Bridgett said. "That's what I was dreaming."

"For the life of me, I hope we don't get burnt." Grandma replied.

"The thing is," Miss Bridgett spoke again, "You had a strange name. You were Gaia. That's a strange name, Gaia Muley!"

"Not Sandra," Grandma asked.

"You and him in one boat! He was your helper, and you were as affectionate of him, like the night we went driving. Remember that?"

"I hope he mans up," Grandma replied.

Miss Bridgett went on tell her daydreaming of Grandma and Billy in Washington, DC testifying before congress. Billy was standing, more eloquent and smarter than we had known him in real life, giving them a piece of his mind. He was telling the men and women of Congress that he, being someone who worked in the banking industry for many years, knew exactly how the banks were going about getting so rich on other people's earnings, as he put it. Miss Bridgett said she saw Grandma and Billy on one side of the Congress men and women, and what she called the "rambunctious suits," on the other side. "They had a huge team with them, you know," she added in such a voice and with a kind of passion that placed a wild but vivid picture in my own head.

In me, it was sort of like the story of David and Goliath, but not faithfully to the text. Grandma and Billy were like little dots fighting against a whole page of big dots. The big dots took a swing at the page of little dots, trying to grab the little dots. The little dots moved backwards and took a swing of their own at the big dots, but the big dots grab after, caught and swallowed the little dots.

Now, inside the belly of the big dots the little dots consolidated into one gigantic dot, a bigger dot than the previous little dots, but not as big as the big dots. The new consolidated little dot opened its eyes to find it was trapped. "Oh shit, it said. "This ain't right."

The little dot turned and churned, and it thought. It blinked its eyes the way Bambi did when I was a child and Bambi was my superman. "Oh, shit it said again." It blinked over again. "This is a big fxxxxxx deal," it said.

Instantly, a aura began to form around the dot with its colors shifting and the little dot became an active little dot. The big dots snarled at the little dot and grabbed at it, but it's "hand" began to burn. Soon, the big dot began to die and the little dot sprang out of the den it was in. It jumped to the center stage and began to boogie.

To Miss Bridgett, Grandma said she was liking what she was hearing and she wondered if Miss Bridgett had "nice" dreams like the one she had shared, all the time. She never got to ask, though, as Miss Bridgett kept her excitement full blast.

Yeah! You were so overconfident with your Billy," Miss Bridgett continued. "And when a Senator, I think her name was Watson threw some hard questions at the CEO, you and your Billy did not 'crack up' like the rest of folks said you would.

You were focused, determined, and you won!"

Grandma gave an abrupt, "Girl!"

"I wish they were that easy to defeat," she continued.

"No question, they've mastered the art of ducking, wobbling and weaving. But, Ms. Muley, I know you," Miss Bridgett said.

Grandma claimed that's what she was waiting for: that "glorious moment" when someone would agree with her. So far, she had not worried too much about finding fellow petitioners, thinking she knew people would come around when the moment was really urgent. There were enough people she knew who felt how she felt, understood what she understood, who had been hurt the way she had been; shown the urgency, they would jump at helping her.

In fact, "No one is immune to the wickedness of other" had become one of Grandma's new tunes. In her new thinking, One only had to live long enough for truth to come her way. The problem she had with most of us, then, was that we were too young—Mom, Dad and Miss Bridgett included. Just consider Grace and me. Grandma grouped us this way, "the whole lock, stock and barrel has got to grow up!"

Grandma looked into her rear view mirror to see herself looking anxious; she noted the traffic as flowing well.

"And that's where you come in, but they have heavy wallets and lots of time to deficit the lawyers," she said to Miss Bridgett. "Deficit our retirement savings; we really have to act and you could be one of the four I need to trample them."

Grandma read Miss Bridgett's response as swift and piloted for no other reason than to end her asking.

"Well, well. Well. I'm not surprise you would be coming at me."

"My question is, are you with me?"

"Still evolving," Miss Bridgett answered.

"You understand what I'm doing," Grandma replied. "The lawyers and I need you to take just one teeny-weeny step. That's it!"

Miss Bridgett replied in a witty way that she would be happy to count Grandma's winnings if that day ever lifted its head, but Grandma insisted on needing help. She said she was looking for three or four people to put on her "dance suit."

"Lawsuit. Me? Ms. Muley! Not me," Miss Bridgett replied.

"You're the one that told me they empty your wallet too," Grandma replied aggressively.

"Yes. But me," Miss Bridgett asked. "My name in law files? Thought you knew me, Ms. Sandra."

Grandma voiced she was very disheartened and found herself in a grave state of frustration mixed with confusion.

People are only your friend when they want something from you, her old mind played out. "Just let it be your turn to get something back and see how *they* act," she said. She looked up for help, clearly begging. I estimated she was about to cry, but not her. Maybe she would just end the connection, but that was not the case, either, at least not yet.

"Yes. Yes you, Bridgett," Grandma said.

"I see you can know a person for a lifetime and still not know them, Miss Bridgett said. "Not in this life, Ms. Muley!"

Miss Bridgett went on to tell Grandma that Grandma should have know she doesn't like to make a circus of herself. "And that's my final answer," Miss Bridgett said with an abrupt halt.

Grandma noted trying everything else she knew, telling Miss Bridgett she needed her help but it was to no benefit.

Minds were made up, and all that was heard after that from the other side was, “Oops. I’ve got to run.” Miss Bridgett was on her way to lunch with Mom.

Grandma sat, thinking she was very sorry. She placed down the phone and stared. She didn’t mean to upset Miss Bridgett. Her whole presence told what was happening now, and it wasn’t good. She would have to live with it, however, and it was that self-disappointing thought: “I can’t believe this is happening to me.”

# CHAPTER 23

TO keep herself from "cracking-up" however, Grandma promised to meet up with Billy. They would work together hard and fast and come up with answers quickly, easily… together.

But as it was when the two got together, work was put on the back seat. The two had decked themselves out in beach clothing and stopped for some knick knacks at a party shop where they changed what was supposed to be a strategy session to help find Grandma some helpers in the lawsuit, to something else. Billy's laptop, strapped around his shoulder as he drove, turned out more to be for decoration than for work.

"Your friend shouldn't be against you; she should be with us," Billy replied to Grandma telling him about Miss Bridgett's unwillingness to help her.

Grandma said she should have cancelled her trip with Billy and work on her problems from home.

Billy said she was unsteady and was not sticking to one idea at a time.

She said that now one of the biggest problems she had was dealing with Miss Bridgett.

To that, Billy reminded Grandma she was already having problems with Mom because of her banking problems. "Now it's your best friend?"

"She and Gloria were on the same cheerleading team," Grandma explained.

"My God," Billy replied.

"And to see, I've been to all five of her weddings," Grandma said cautiously, as one crossing a road she shouldn't.

Billy smiled. "Five? Even for me, a guy with accounting background, that's a big number to count!"

Grandma placed her hand on her cheek, gave him a good look down. "Not for an accountant like mine," she said. "Maybe, thirty five!"

****$$****

The two reached Fort Lauderdale Beach after a drive and chat that took them from what I had taught Grandma about her banks, from my assignments, to what they surmised Corporate was up to now.

The average debit card transaction in those days was $17, and Billy threw what he called a rhetorical question to Grandma, if she knew what the overdraft fee was.

"When good people do nothing, evil wins," Grandma retorted.

On reaching, the two stepped out his Porsche looking cool and collected as if there was no work to do.

Pretty soon, Billy was looking at a woman in her early 30's in a scant swimsuit as the woman promenades through the white sand to the water. Billy couldn't keep his eyes off her.

"Is that what you want to show me," Grandma asked.

"Nice trunks," Billy noted, still staring at the face, and body in the suit.

Grandma told him that she bought one the week earlier to which Billy merely shook his head; instead of falling for Grandma's line, he kept focused intensely on the woman in swimsuit. She had begun wiggling her way into the water.

"Want to see me in it," Grandma asked desirously.

Billy began tapping on the case of his laptop.

"Com'on! You know you want to see me in it," Grandma persisted.

With that, I thought he would have wanted to change the subject, but he didn't.

"Oh Dear," he replied. "Does one still have sex at our age?"

Grandma moved closer to him, and there was virgin princess's smile on her face. "If one gets lucky, Sure bet they do," she replied.

By this time Billy had the laptop opened and was fiddling with it, trying to show Grandma something on the screen that was made private to them with the glare of the sunlight.

"I guess eighty is the new forty," he said.

Grandma looked closely at what Billy was showing her on the laptop.

"I can't live without it," she said in a tender voice that came with a chuckle.

Billy replied in the male version of her soft tone. "I wouldn't have thought so."

"I thought you were scared," Grandma replied.

****$$****

Billy changed his voice for a stern, businessman one as he typed on the laptop, and chatted.

"Very well. Very well," he said. "Here's what you do, keep printing out your statement at least once a day. There's also an end of day report. Make sure you keep an eye on that as well. OK?"

Grandma told him she was already doing that. She noted she studied her account closely and knew every activity on her statement. "They vary—manipulating how they do things," she complained.

"OK, Billy said. "Keep on keeping track and see what else you see."

Grandma laughed nervously like a kid. She caught him looking her down.

"Stop it," she said.

"This is hard," he replied. He was thinking about the project Grandma was working on.

"Ok Daddy 'O'," she said.

Simultaneously, the woman in swimsuit was splashing water on her chest and Billy looked on.

Grandma tilted towards him, "Is that what you wanted to show me?"

# CHAPTER 24

When the day came, Grandma tried everything she could, not to go to my graduation, citing commitments like her business that was not doing well, she had not gotten the people she needed, and even that I had not been enough a help to her.

We argued about the last point and when things came clear to her, she apologized. She had wasted a lot of valuable time, and now her deadline was closing in.

With my persistence, she kept her promise made to me more than a year and a half earlier; she surrendered and did the right thing.

****$$****

The crowd was more than fifteen hundred, and my guests including Mom, Dad, and Grace, proud and thankful for me and what I had accomplished.

Around, the place would be festive, happy, and as the graduation got into full swing, we the grads prepared for our parade onto the makeshift stage. The venue was UF Global Academy auditorium.

Grandma, Mom and Dad were sitting around one of a hundred-and-fifty or so occupied round tables.

Our school Principal was Mr. Rosado, a conservative Cuban man who had come to this country on a boat sometime in the early 70's and now boasted of living in the best country created by God.

He was now on stage.

"In due time many of you will be solving the problems of our world," he claimed. "You're in line to become the next successful entrepreneurs, inventor, lawyers. Any doctors in the house? Future engineers? Bankers? You get to name your future!"

Next to me was the student who had text me saying the system is rigged. He told me his name was Siri and he reminded me how we knew each other: from our computer encounters-online blogs, chats and e-mails. He said he had sent a certain text. I recognized his talk as it was the same way he wrote.

"The system's rigged," he said again.

"My Grandma said it wasn't always this way," I replied.

I looked and waved towards the table where she and the rest of the family were seated and showed Siri my gang. Grace waved back, a full-sized smile on her face (not sure if for me or my new friend). She seemed to be saying, "Love you. Good job."

She later imparted, Grandma, Mom and Dad were talking about what they thought I should do with the rest of my life.

Mom said I was just a kid.

Not what I was thinking of myself, but that's what she held as her belief. And if she thought so, then what should I have done? For me, her skewed views meant more years of pocket money, a car, and how about all the money I ended up using on travelling?

The news said China and India were good places to explore if one wanted to learn a thing or two about business. International travel was on my list, and Grandma would help making even that a reality. A trouble back then, however, was that after I showed her my WikiCreep assignments she began to suggest that I change from wanting to be a businessman to becoming the first lawyer in the modern family. To try and convince me, she went as far as to demand I go on Ancestry.Com to see my great, great grand uncle Simon. We were proud of him as he had become one of the first trial lawyer in Loving County, Texas. She said that would have been a better fit for me. If she knew back then, what she knew now, she would have taken that route herself, she said.

Mom spoke on behalf of Dad, who called himself a reticent human being, and said Dad was hoping, a physician. Interesting, I said, as he never asked me in all seventeen years of my life, what I wanted to do when I grow up.

One thing, I was getting nervous. My having looked at so many videos of what the people at Bank $$ were up to had left me very concerned about going into business, as I had been dreaming for so long. Mom said that since I looked at a particular assignment, I had become stiff, and to give her description integrity, she clarified the concept with "frightened." The way she summed me up: "My little boy looked more frightened about his future than I wish I ever see him again!"

That video in mention was one with Corporate and his staff at his office as they made a last ditch attempt to stop anyone who was trying to get in the way of their efforts.

Corporate was inclined towards one of several laptop computers in front of him. He looked straightforward at the screen that was opened to e-mail, but he spoke as his head was down. "I'm completing the draft of my views as I speak."

He began typing. "Pertaining to the young man who goes out and get information from *suspects*...."

A male's voice called out, "Shawty."

The CEO continued. "*He's* a ten; a promotion is earned! We may be in the one-percentile but that doesn't give anyone the right to steal our money. Finally, Guys, never lose sight of our goals.

Remember to keep them separated, and constantly change the date credits are posted to accounts; nature dictates we stay afloat."

****$$****

When Corporate was done with his script, he lifted his head and thanked his staff. "Everything's packed and ready?"

Miss Andrea reached over and *shook* Corporate's hand. "I don't see any gun that matches up with ours."

Corporate shook his head. He approved of her this time. "Damn fishes. We've got more than enough nets."

I told Grandma about the exchanges and she shook *her* head in a kind of let down way, I sensed was in line with her new shattered view of "the great system" as she from time to time had previously thought of our way of life.

"Grandma, I agree they are not here for you, me, any of us," I said, remembering what happened the last time I told her a truth. Tears quickly welled up in the corners of her eyes.

Should I continue? I grilled myself. Should I lie? Just tell her what sounds good, whether it's right or wrong? Which would she vote for?

I tried to recompense with a compassionate hand laid on her shoulder, but that didn't do a thing. A hug, however, helped and when she was well again to talk, she said the events as I told them to her were warning signs that the world was coming to an end.

"Coming to an end?" I chewed on that for a moment. "Really?" What an overstatement, I thought. I looked at her and I, myself, felt lost from reality. I saw Ms Cynthia, Mr. Saul's wife. "This was the sign she often talked about, that Jesus is coming back soon. She was shouting as she ran exposed, her hair crazy. "If we're not ready, it will be really bad!"

****$$****

On Corporate's side, the conversation was that Satan was behind the people who were working [so] hard to make big corporations fail." It was Ms. Andrea who tabled the idea, and thought the executives did not come across as Believers in any way, the Satan thing got its full fifteen-minutes.

CFO Tolly shared how he once had a near-death experience abroad and that had made him a good Catholic when he was a young missionary man. Another of the executive in the room talked about how the devil could spin webs that no human could untangle.

Grandma had since come to tell me that what the banks were into was "false profits" that resulted in the little guy getting screwed, and she noted she would do everything in her power to stop being their ATM. She called their behavior "a craven act."

Now, it was all about me and my fifteen minutes as she kept her promise for my graduation.

"It's amazing how you get to be fourteen and then it's seventeen, then twenty-one, …a wife and then…," Grandma said to the family and friends seated around the table.

"The problem's the world he's going into," Miss Bridgett said.

"And then you just owe everybody and nobody owes you!"

Dad replied, "life," to which Mom's found some funniness, both in words and act as she begged, "Flow honey. Flow."

Grandma response to Dad's talking was "So pure a word. I guess,"

Grandma continued. "And there's so much more to it."

"Grandma," Dad exclaimed.

Grandma said she didn't quite know how to say what she wanted to say.

"Maybe you should just practice what you taught us. Hold your tongue when you don't have something good in your heart," Mom replied.

Dad looked angrily at Mom. "Gloria!"

Mom responded with an unusual surrendering tone to Dad, "Yes?"

"Twenty-four-hours and counting. Is anyone going to help me," Grandma said.

"Why," Mom replied.

"I need you, a joint petitioner with me," Grandma said.

Mom turned her face towards the table and swing her head as fast and as far as it could go to the left and with the same rapidity to the other side. She repeated the cycle. "Will you stop bothering?"

****$$****

As the ritual moved forward, Grandma noted she became more and more impatient knowing she had not done her homework of getting the people she needed to help her "stop the disarming of the middle-class." She looked at the hundreds and hundreds of people in the crowd. Why bother, she considered. She had just shown me an article that day in the Florida Wind, a bi-weekly, talking about people not wanting to join class action lawsuits; small claims were more lucrative.

All other targets dead, she threw her pitch at Mom in a long discourse that ended in she telling Mom it was time the two became a family again. It was high time they put their old differences to rest.

Mom shook her head up and down at first, and Grandma took that to mean that they would actually start to like each other once more, as Grandma returned a smile, but Mom's words were not the kind you would expect of someone you care about, less to say of a daughter.

"That doesn't mean I'm going to start anything new with you," Mom pushed.

Grandma tried harder to plea her case, beginning to state that, "When your family needs you…"

But a, "For what," by Mom ended all activities momentarily.

When Grandma picked up, her voice was thin and weak, not even Grace sounded like that when Mom refused to give us pocket money.

"Please help me, Gloria" Grandma solicited. "For long I've been wanting to ask you, but you're so hard to reach!"

"Glad you didn't," Mom replied strictly.

"Dad looked at Mom in a condemning way that left both Grace's and my face with smirks. This was the second time in a single day he decided to say or do something manly, something we were not granted often. His eyebrows looked stiff and his eyes daring,"

"Honey!"

Whatever Grandma must have felt at the moment, I will never be able to tell as she passed away last month, many decades after my graduation date, and at a rightful age that made her one of the longest living persons the modern earth has known.

Her passing called back in me all that we were together—years and years of Grandma and grandson, Tagg, the young surrogate of his "Grandma," Grandma and Soldier, Tagg and Newgrandma—a handsome relationship that became more and more like two people of the same age sharing each other's journey, each others joys and fears, learning from each other and becoming the best for the other.

In that last month or so, we became *fully alive* and that's when Grandma with her javelin-sharp mind took me through every bit of what she said Phil, Ellen, Wolf and Oprah, my four children, should know about the family.

"My Dear," she began with her last words to me, on her last night, replicating words she had said to me the day of my graduation, "I'm sorry, Soldier. I give you everything."

On that last day she elaborated: "I helped to pay you and your sister's tuition for college and your Mom's fully. Not my fault or anybody else's your mother ditched college. Now you go and make the world proud. You. Soldier. Tagg."

Those words I would also trace back to my graduation night. Even at that late hour, Grandma was still cheering on Mom to go and get her college diploma, to which Mom was answering, "I'm not interested, I'm not interested. I'm not interested." She also was not interested in Grandma's lawsuit, Grandma pointed out. In spite of all this, Mom turned out well—she went on to bring us here and up…mostly.

On my high-school graduation night she returned to Grandma all the money she owed her, bragging there was nothing else she possessed that was Grandma's.

I think back often and clearly, Grandma had her hand rested on me and she was holding the money Mom had returned to her in her other hand. She wielded the money in the air.

"This is my fortune. This is what we work for in life," she said.

That's when her cell phone rang and it was Billy to whom she was telling, "It's hard to say I'm love right now."

Grace looked in my direction and snapped her fingers at me. "I told you." I told you," she said.

"I told you what?"

My mind immediately went to the Black man we had seen at the mall eons earlier, the one with the lady that looked like Kate Gosselin, on TV. There was something he had said that I was trying to remember, and now it came back so crisp. I felt lucky I had lived long enough to retain things of the past. Sometimes you experience an event in your life and then time swoops by and you don't remember it—it has no significance; it's meaningless, you say. You continue to go on and on, and you live out the new experiences you come faced with day after day, then suddenly you remember the old day, and you feel so first-class you get to remember and even re-experience that aged thing. That's how it was for me. You end up thanking God for giving you life, long enough to be able to go back to that unfinished business, and that's how I was about this one.

The Black man had told Grace and me that even though Grandma looked old to him, there was a certain twinkle, a shine of sort in her eyes. He had said this with a high level of energy, himself. He said there was something magical about the spark and about Grandma.

Grandma, a week later laughed it off, saying that since the magic had not manifested itself up to that point in her life, the man was "a talking twaddle." A month or so later, she called the man a "channeler."

# CHAPTER 25

Later, Grace and I found Grandma short of time and breath, frantically searching through the drawers and purses in her room to try and find the name and number of people she said would come to her aid, but that was not to be her luck—her "blessings" she would have corrected us. What else Grace and I found when we happened to be playing and I chased her in the room was a state of confusion.

There were papers scattered on the closet, purses and clothes on the floor, and what turned out to be more than a hundred pictures from the protest event she had held at the park, pictures of people at events she had held at her house long before us, and even some of her friends at Shines, scattered around the room.

I was shock and asked her what she was doing, but before she could explain herself, Grace tried at giving her take.

"Mom says going nuts," Grace offered.

Grandma looked irately at us. "Soldiers! Not here," she blurted out. "Not now!"

****$$****

A bit later Grandma would be in her Library in the same kind of mess; now on the speakerphone, moving from one acquaintance to another.

"They're cutting and dicing us, Margaret," she said to a lady who spoke of her gratefulness to Grandma for giving her now adult children years of free dancing lessons. "I was really counting on you coming through this time for me," Grandma said.

I don't know who Ms. Margaret was in person, but for years we used to hear Grandma refer to her as a friend from when they were girl guides, and Grandma talked how they used to go on double dates later when they turned young women. Grandma looked at the phone on her desk as if she wanted to break it, saved for Ms. Margaret was still talking.

"I know I promised," Ms. Margaret continued. "But if I didn't have this cretin of a man. He's having an affairs, you know?"

Grace and I stood by, listening to Grandma with sympathy, and even though I thought about something, I didn't go with it.

Grandma ran her eyes by Grace and then by me. She spoke speedily. "I don't' know what this kind of behavior came from. I've lived long." She pointed her finger in the path of a couple hundred of her books on the shelves. "I read books you know."

I was still out of words but Grace was not. She stared at Grandma, her whole demeanor now solemn, and I could tell something was worrying her. She moved closer to Grandma.

"I'll sign the paper for you Granny," she said.

Grandma placed her hand on Grace's shoulder, and in her eyes I could spot her sentiments. "That's so sweet of you, Dear Soldier," she said. "But you're too young."

"I knew *I was too* at seventeen and nine months. More importantly, even though, both Grace and I had our money at Bank $$, they were under Mom's command, as our guardian. Would she put the brakes on me if I were to try? This though did not stop my mind from going in circles, "Grandma, Grandma, I'm big enough!"

"Then I'll have to go to law school and help you," Grace shared.

Grandma hugged both of us. That was a nice gesture and Grandma knew that we knew it.

"But you're still 'baby' soldiers," she said.

At this point in my life I was somewhat self-conscious about being called baby, and I could see Grace was likewise, but Grandma's speech was wrapped in a kind, sweet tone. What was not gentle, or sweet, or kind was Grandma's bellowing that came after.

"What I need are adults with guts, balls and an active Bank $$ account," she said. "I need them now!"

With those words she hastened for the phone again, this time for Mr. Saul, the neighbor that loved to cut his yard, the one with the lovely Christian wife, Miss Cynthia.

Grace and I took notes as we heard in the background Ms. Cynthia's calling, "You see what type of dirt she's made of?"

I, for the most part, kept my spotlight on Grandma; she had sprinkles of spit on the phone from the speeding out of her words.

"Saul," Grandma said after going around and around for about a minute-and-a-half with him. "I know it's been a decade, maybe more, but you're the one that got the free microwave when you made me open the account."

"Yeah. History," Mr. Saul responded. How time flies. John was still with us then, ha? Now, that was a really, really good man you had, Ms. Sandra."

"I know it's kind of late to be asking, Saul, but…" Grandma interjected, to which Mr. Saul did not hear or understand as his words that followed showed.

"I don't think we'll ever find another kind-heart like him. Ever! Not in these quarters," Mr. Saul said.

Grandma, by this time looked more tired, and I could sense impatience boiling up in her. "He was a darling," She offered, followed by, "But will you help?"

There was a moment of silence, then three important words came out from the other end of the line. "I would Patrice." They actually sounded like "I will."

The rest of words came fast, and Grace and I saw Grandma spin from elated to frustrated as quickly. Grace said that maybe Ms. Cynthia was again standing over "poor Mr. Saul" with her King James to smack him on his head or something like that, that he quickly scooped up the "but" word, and then it was that, "with this arthritis and cholesterol problem, and now the doctor said, diabetes..."

Grandma described the experience as one that made her "heart heavy."

"Lord Saul," she said after failing at even more pleading. "You've been a whiner since you moved here. 1966 Saul! When will you do something for mankind?"

Even in the strain of it all, Grace and I found the line as funny, and we found ourselves in a spontaneous chuckle as much as we could without drawing Grandma's attention on us. Somehow we knew if she saw us, it wouldn't be a good thing, but if you had ever seen the picture Mr. Saul and Ms. Cynthia displayed on Jack Street, you would appreciate why this would bring us or anyone unattached, a laugh: We remembered Ms. Cynthia as always chasing after him, calling him hilarious names, and he would be running with his oversized tummy telling her to remember scriptures they had read previously. This time it was him referencing the Word.

"Remember what proverbs 31 says. Remember Proverbs 31," I remember him saying the last time we witnessed their stage-show. That one climaxed with him tumbling to the ground as he attempted to escape from her and her quick hand, he used to say not even Federal Express could surpass.

Finally, Grace and I could not stop our laughing with Ms. Cynthia standing tall over him.

"I told you, you can't even run," she said.

He placed his hand to protect his head that was laughably small for his body, but that did not stop her from doing her thing. "And moreover, there's no place to hide," she pressed on.

So, as Mr. Saul tried to explain himself to Grandma, I was more than fascinated to learn about what was happening with them. I was also feeling a great sense of compassion.

"Ms. Muley," Mr. Saul went on, "My wife and I've been friends of you 'all since we moved here. You said since seventy-six, right? As far as the Good Lord will let me go to then. You and your whole family have always been good to us. I like how you and Mr. John and the children use to put off the fortnight Bar-B-Q's but ..."

Grandma began shaking her head in a way Dad would do his when he didn't believe something we were telling him, and I sensed that was not good.

Grandma said, "I don't need a story Saul. Can I bank on you?"

Mr. Saul's response came with a earsplitting cough. He asked for an excuse for being uncharitable, and then he explained his position. "Ms. Sandra, you know I would say yes, but you know Cynthia as good as me."

"I don't," Grandma responded instantly.

"Of course you do," he replied in a hobo's voice. "She doesn't like me to meddle in affairs I have no right to be in."

Yet again, I could see that Grandma was afflicted. She had made her world of just a few people whom she kept very close to her heart. When the holidays came she would share goodies with these "special friends." And don't let them have a need, like when Ms. Cynthia's oldest daughter from a relationship long before Mr. Saul, got a concussion from falling off a Mayan ruin in Central America—Grandma got known all around town for nursing her back to health, like the girl was her own. That particular story had made it in the Local section of the Herald.

Now Grandma was going, "Saul! Is this the same Saul?"

Mr. Saul coughed again and said something to the sounding that if he could he would, to which Grandma told him, he never let anybody stop him from anything.

Grandma, in her last days, would tell me, she knew she was insincere in making that statement to Mr. Saul, as she knew his situation, but, then, she thought that was the only way to further her case.

"Ms. Sandra," Mr. Saul replied. "Since she won the scratch-off, you know I can't tell her a thing."

Grandma made a goofy sounding giggle of her own. "Then get her to join us," she pled. "If we don't, the system's going to swallow us!"

"They already doing that," Mr. Saul offered in a sudden, brisk way that moved Grandma's attention from the path of going to the clock, to one with her ears closer to the phone.

"I know they have to learn a lesson," she said.

Mr. Saul began his coughing again. "Ms. Muley, I agree with you, but....*ME. I can't Ms. Sandra!"*

With those words, Grandma right away began to look exhausted and her movements showed she also was not in good spirit.

"We're against the clock here, Saul," she said, giving a glance at the timepiece.

There was no sound from the other side.

"Are you there? You still with me," Grandma asked, but the pause was only more apparent.

Grandma held her hand on her chin, appearing not to know what do next, but as with Grandma that was not the case. A comeback was brewing, and she delivered the goods just as we had come to expect she would.

"Even you can make a difference, Saul," she said.

Mr. Saul let out a blistering gush. "Ms. Muley, I've got to go. Bye," he said. "She's right here listing on the other line to see who I'm talking to."

Grandma looked at me and I at her. I could feel something move inside of me. She turned back in the direction of the phone.

"I want you to stop! Listen," Grandma's response came.

****$$****

Time, that great commodity Grandma was using as if overflowing was running amok on her now, and according to my notes from Mom and Grace, even if Grandma had more, she would have wasted it anyways. They said she was losing contact with reality, and on my way to the kitchen one day, I overheard Mom telling Grace, Grandma was becoming "crazier and crazier by the hour." I didn't feel that way, but my feelings, opinions, thoughts and ideas were not always the ones that changed the day in our circle.

Nonetheless, I knew time was limited, and to add some meaning to that, we had heard of one of the ladies at Shines passing away, and I was fearing that would put a bigger dent in Grandma's plan. Grandma said she was sorry to hear the news and hinted her heart and mind would not be at peace if she could not go to the funeral. I reminded her that her other responsibilities were pressing.

****$$****

I heard Grace swearing she had not interfered with a pile of papers and pictures Grandma was insisting had to be touched by someone, since they didn't have feet of their own and some were missing.

"They had some numbers; they were on my desk," Grandma said categorically.

I approached as Grace said her last, "No Granny." And then, the spotlight was on me. If it wasn't' Grace who created the century's biggest confusion, then it must have been me. Right?

Grandma gave me a guarded look-down.

"No Grandma," I said, and I instantly realized for the first time how differently we addressed our grandmother. I would spend all the years since to pay close attention to this distinction that appears so subtle yet ended up with our having two very different views of our grandmother's life.

Grace, now, no longer a spring chicken, has been married for years to one of my high school friend Mikel, from Russia, and they have two boys and a baby girl to whom she loves to sing. She tries to teach them everything anti-Grandma. I taught my four about all of our relatives, on both sides of the aisle; Grandma Muley has been right there on the list! She was my hero; I pivoted and pivoted my way through life until I became just the person she had imagined I would become.

****$$****

"I had a bunch of papers right here on my damn desk. Where is it," Grandma said, referring to a listing of phone numbers she had tried to keep near and dear to her heart.

"The one where you were trying to reach the bank," Grace asked.

"Where is it," Grandma demanded.

I pointed to the piece of paper that was directly in front of Grandma who had gotten to her boiling point but would have had a drop in temperature if Grace was better practiced at dealing with people.

Even when Grandma was moving on, picking up the phone to do what she needed to do, Grace had not left that spot where things were and instead inflamed the fire.

"Mom said it doesn't matter if you call them ten times or a hundred," she said. "They're not stupid to give you their boss's number or nothing!"

Grandma halted for a moment, swinging the cell phone in her angry hand. "Young lady!"

Grace scurried towards me and held on to my waist, implying I was some grand barrier that would stop the forces, the raging disaster that could put her down.

I chose obedience, my head playing something Grandma had told me when she first decided she was going to fight her bank: She was clear. She would *stick to her thing* to her last breath.

"She said you should leave them alone," Grace said of Mom, and then darted to, I don't know where. What I knew at this point, Grace would not stay anywhere near to find out what Grandma now had in her head.

# CHAPTER 26

"Yes, I don't want your machine again, and I don't want Eggy," Grandma said to a bank clerk on the other side of the phone line. "I've been trying forever. Get me your CEO!"

I listened as the clerk, who I couldn't settle on whether a man or woman, spoke back. Grandma and I later concluded it likely was a woman acting like her converse, the voice seek to make itself resonant, yet still a bit thin as if coming from the head, rather than the chest, and almost as high pitched as Grace's.

"Ma'am, Is there anything else I can help you with," the voice kept asking.

"Only if you're the CEO," Grandma replied.

In the background we heard the person snicker and then there was another, and even another, and then there was an incontestable female voice.

"Ma'am, may I help you," the new person inquired, but as soon as Grandma got to say "Yes," the original voice came back. "May I help you? This is Eggy!"

Grandma shook her head in the slow motion of disappointment and left her face positioned towards me. She place her finger over the microphone. "They're really evil! I have to hit everyone I know to get on board with this," she said.

I gave her the best appearance I could come up with, considering some doubts that floated in my own head. "Aren't you afraid of Bank $$?"

She sized me up for who I was then: 5 feet, 10½ inches, 116 pounds, handsome, the girls said.

**"Not Sandra Muley. Not Sandra Smucking Muley,"** Grandma said. "This not right. This' how they treat us? And think about it, *it's our money!* It's not a credit card. It's our money, Soldier!"

I looked at her feeling a heart full of hurt for her suffering. I should have been a better sounding board. I could have been.

I felt somewhat miserable for her and unhappy for me, as up to that point I didn't know what to do. I had not known what I know now. In those days as it is now, life is transient.

****$$****

Grandma said life has always been changing. It was up to me to put one and one together.

"Two", she added sharply, like she was revealing some unknown.

In fact, she was referring to she and me as a team.

"If you had paid keen attention to what I was telling you all along, you and me would have made the difference when it could have made a huge difference for me," she said.

I wanted to get up but she requisitioned me, "Be still," she ordered.

She said she was going to teach me to get as quiet as she was when she was in the hospital. If I were able to do that, she stated, a lot of things would come my way. She went on to clarify: "When I was there, yes, I was still, but that doesn't mean I wasn't stirring up. My mind was everywhere, Soldier!"

I looked at her, pondering.

"Not just a scribe. A real helper—A soldier, Tagg," she said. "If long ago, you understood the world, what people do, and things as they are now, You would have shown me your schoolwork much earlier! If only you were not so much in your head!"

"My own way of doing things? My own worldview," I questioned.

Grandma had struck a wrong nerve in me again.

# CHAPTER 27

One of my last assignments had come, beeping its way to my attention. The video began with Corporate at his office, holding an unlit cigar in his mouth. It was the holiday season, somewhere between the start of Hanukah and Christmas, and Corporate was with some of his subordinates, and they were having one of their many lighthearted moments.

At the time, what made this viewing a significant study for our class was the fact that the economy in the country was at its lowest in a generation, according to reporters on some of the major channels, CNN, Fox, MSNBC.

"Down in the pits," I recall a journalist talking that morning. "Unemployment rate of nine-point-one percent, falling home prices, and a big concern that middle class society is quickly being replaced by poor folks."

By and large, people were having a hard time, a higher than normal percentage struggling to make ends meet like Grandma, and there were so many people that didn't understand enough to care.

Now, much more mature, I'm clear I've been guilty of that same mindset. A lot of what Grace and I wanted to do back then was to spend Grandma's money. Whether it was ice cream, a new laptop or trips here and there; we accepted, and sometimes even demanded, stuff like they came from nowhere. Grasping what was going on with Grandma, and helping her to bring speedy justice to those who were wronged would have been much more a lofty purpose.

****$$****

The video moved through Corporate's office, with the VP of Bank Ops stumbling from drunkenness while the others threw cotton balls and rolled-up paper at him.

"You'll have to stop so much trying to build the most expensive office building in the world and put a bigger investment in those of us who make things happen," he said to Corporate, who himself looked tipsy.

There was the sweet ringing of colliding Champaign glasses, and then an "I ditto that," followed by some "me too's."

Corporate got his wallet from his pocket and raised it to the crowd while giving special consideration to the VP of Bank Ops and CFO Tolly. The marketing lady, Miss Andrea, who I found out from an Internet search, was Corporate's niece, stood not far away.

"I bet you combined are doing better than a small country," Corporate said as he pointed to the two.

The VP of Bank Ops again stumbled, spilling some of his drink to the carpet. He stared at the spill for a split second and then at his viewers. He chuckled.

"Just get a new one. No big deal," he offered. He lifted his head enough to pick up sight of Corporate again. "You still expect us to be at third-world wages. I know…"

Corporate drew some money from his wallet and paraded it at the crowd. "What you see here," he said, "is going to spread!"

Some people from the crowd playfully pushed their hands out for the money as The VP of Bank OPs said, "Let it fucking spread, then. We haven't seen it yet!"

"We spin straw into gold," Corporate continued, his temperament unchanged.

One of the executives in the room giggled. "What you'll need to do is to spin that old witch into straw, then," he said.

The crowd it seems knew what was meant. A chuckle ensued.

****$$****

What I retain of that period can sometimes be blurry in my head but with Grandma at my side during her last month with us, everything got clear again. We went back and forth, to this and that, and by the time we were in our final meeting, Grandma claimed I had made her feel young, going back to all that life we had lived; for me, I felt more mature and a lot older than I actually was. Both of us walked away grateful to each other for sharpening the other's saw. From this exercise I came clear on a point Grandma John was famous for making: Two minds working in harmony could really create a third.

Grandma harked back to her bouts with Bank $$ and particularly the one with the bank secretary, Eggy who didn't want to connect her to Corporate's office.

The he/she kept telling me "'Yes Ma'am, I understand,' until I fired back," Grandma said.

"I remember," I said.

"You don't understand a damn thing," Grandma recalled. "If this was your Mother's account what would you do?"

That must have upset or probably more appropriately frightened poor Eggy. Grandma think the he/she cracked in that moment. The only words that came from the other side after that were, "I could lose my job, Miss. I don't' want them to send me home!"

Grandma said when she walked away, she felt more than ever, she needed to stop what she called immoral acts carried out by the banks.

"No one," she said, had every treated her the way she was being treated by her bank.

****$$****

Another time, Grandma reminded us her conscience would not be in one piece if she didn't go to the funeral service of her friend Mom Saraplin, who Grace and I found out was the person from Shines that had passed away. In the midst of things, we also found out Mom Saraplin was a nun for about seven years before she got married and brought children.

Grace, who likes to go to funerals, and I, who hate them, arrived at the picturesque, small Baptist church early, just when Mom

Saraplin's daughter was giving the eulogy. She was calling her mother, not only a great artist whose work had reached the pages of Art Critic and Harper Bazaar, but also a good mother, and once, a good wife. Her former husband Teddy, according to his daughter, was an avid outdoorsman who did a lot less work than the departure woman, but she nevertheless loved him, though the daughter suggested he was in there for her money, and she alluded, "fame" at one time. She said she knew her mother better than anyone else, and she asked that there be no sadness, just a celebration.

And it was during the so-called "celebration" I got to find out who Ms. Wonzick's son was, the one she named Benjamin. He was eying Mom Saraplin's daughter as she lifted her head, exposing her long, bodacious neck. Her hands were in the air to give thanks for her mom's life, and to give pleasure to me and Benjamin.

A big shocking for us was that he actually looked more like us in complexion than his mother. He was waving his own hand to an uplifting song that was put in, replacing "Amazing Grace," printed in bold letters on the issued program. Grace was the one who Id'ed him and gave me an elbow to take a close-up. Yes he was a Wonzick—features, mannerism, the way of staring. The one difference was his skin.

Coming, following the elbow, Grace whispered to me that "*things* been going on a long time, Tagg."

The younger Wonzick inclined to his mother who seemed much aged from the last time we had been in the same space, especially when compared to Grandma who was strangely doing the opposite, in front of our eyes. Benjamin placed his hand on his mother's leg. He asked his mother if a Mr. Roberts got some vehicle ready. She lifted his hand from her leg and told him, "not now, Son." He brushed her off with his hand and a simple, "Come 'on Mom."

She cared less.

****$$****

When Grandma arrived, I could see people taking long stares at her as her looks had perked up greatly since they last saw her. Grace and I were sitting between Ms. Wonzick and Ms. Zenida Reid who that day had used her perfume like it was a penny a bottle at K-Mart. She seemed particularly more determined to stay alive that day than at any time I had seen her at Shines. Was it because she was outside the walls of the facilities and finally felt free, or was it because her friend had died and she was trying to drive away the same fate from being hers soon? Like many other questions I have pondered trying to understand these folks, this one probably will never be answered, and the truth is, I don't care, anymore. I'm tired and weary as this story has had great impact on my life as it has for so many others.

A sit down in Grandma's armchair allowed me a moment to ponder. Who am I to be bothered by these folks anyway?

****$$****

When Grandma entered the church, solemn, and with a veil on her face, I waved at her to take an opened seat Grace and I had reserved on her behalf.

At first, she did not see me, maybe because I wasn't giving it all my efforts. I was long nose-round on what was going on close to me. Ms. Wonzick was tittle-tattling about Grandma to Benjamin. I suppose she didn't memorize our faces and felt at the time we didn't know what she was talking about. We, nonetheless, could feel there was something very real about her words.

I didn't hear everything well as she was mostly low voice, but there was a part how Grandma did not pay Mom's financial aid and that was why Mom did not finish college. Ms. Wonzick even said that act, "which Love had no control over," was what spun Mom against Grandma.

For the jiffy I stayed quiet and with that motionless, except for my waving at Grandma, giving no hint to my active ear.

"That's the lady you got the 'scoop' for," Ms. Wonzick said.

I found my eyes wandering for a split and saw Benjamin Wonzick acting like a big kid. He wanted to play—and even thought the service was going on, he rested his hand on his mother's leg again.

"Big mortgage, holy molly, late fees, my golly, and bills like sand," he said.

I knew I had heard something of the sort before, but I couldn't remember by whom, where or when. Nonetheless, I kept my spotlight on Grandma who was approaching us as Ms Wonzick added for her son that she heard our mother was out and around telling people that she would never let her mom end up at any "old-people's" home.

"That's loving your mother," Ms. Wonzick continued with her son who became a bit worked up. "She will give up everything it takes to care for her!"

Ms. Wonzick went on to say "That's why she was so adamant Love kept herself healthy."

I looked at Grandma as she headed towards us. I looked at Ms. Wonzick as she continued her hearsay.

"She's even got a gentleman now, you know," Ms. Wonzick added.

After Grandma sat down, showing off her hair, dyed her natural color, I heard Ms Wonzick saying to Benjamin, "I told you she's more than a dogface skirt!"

I believe then and now she was referring to Grandma and not the dead Mom Saraplin, lying in state right before us.

I for one was weary of the diversion though and was glad when Benjamin attempted to end it. He placed his hand on his mom's hand.

"Mom, let's talk on the other side," he said to his mother.

I grasp the distractions were not over yet, though.

Ms. Zenida Reid reached across us to Ms. Wonzick, using sign language. "Think that helped," she asked to answer herself. "No."

"They're always trying to shut us up. They think we don't have a say," she said.

"This is not about death or destruction of the human soul. This is our ritual, a celebration today," Mom Saraplin's daughter, on stage said. She looked down at the coffin in front of her. "In death, life comes!"

"We'll miss Sarah," Ms. Zenida Reid at once signed to Ms. Wonzick and a couple of the other ladies.

"She always acted old," Ms. Wonzick replied.

"Old, old," Ms. Diaz said.

Ms. Wonzick looked at Grandma, tears falling to her cheek. "That's why I like you Sandra, Love. You've got that I-telephone. You young. *You know!"*

Ms. Diaz bent to get more into the dialogue. "What's that? What's…"

# CHAPTER 28

"Hunny, you see my I-phone," Corporate's wife asked him as he played around with their dog at the family's mansion.

"Not now," Corporate replied to his wife, while he secured himself in his scarlet bath robe.

He notified her he had another letter from a lady who said she was charged dozens of times over the past year for bad checks.

Corporate's wife inquired. "Why did she write so many bad checks?"

Corporate smiled as his head move in the direction of a pack of two-and-three feet sterling silver greyhounds the family had on display. "Humans!"

"I'm sure she's one of the 'ninety-niners as they call themselves," she said.

"If you're lazy, you pay!"

Corporate's wife ran her hand in her lengthy, curly hair. It was blond today, and silky as well. Appealing, actually. It usually would be designed to rest on her shoulders; today it dropped behind her neck and back with a young girl's knot at the end. "They can only take so many punches," she offered.

Corporate responded, "We're all in the same boat!"

Corporate's wife shook her head in concurrence.

He said, "They shouldn't be destroying; they should be helping us!"

"My I-phone. Gotta call Captain Joe. Have you seen the seats in Betsy, recently?"

Corporate did not answer. She kept on. *"The seats in Betsy's falling apart!"*

"The lady keep saying she's a senior citizen..." Corporate went again at his original problem as he moved his hand to scratch his head.

Corporate's wife chuckled and threw her hair to the other side of her shoulders. "In twenty years you'll be sixty nine—forty, eighty nine. What does age have to do with..."

Corporate, clearly confused, called out to his dog that came, wagging its tails but right away began snarling at the statuette greyhounds.

"Tttthief. Ttthief," Corporate called to the dog. He placed his attention back on his wife who was now holding the letter in her hand. She began hugging him in a consoling way.

"We all have hearts, kids, jobs. We all live, love, die. "You're not Warren Buffett, for God Sake! You just run the bank!"

****$$****

At Shines, concurrently, Ms. Wonzick tried on a hat, to which the other ladies nodded.

Close to the bathroom, Ms. Zenida Reid shook hand with a stranger. "Is it a big enough bus," she queried.

****$$****

For the moment, at Barrow and Vargas, LLC, Attorney Vargas and Barrow were in a conference room along with a number of other people including Niqua, the Black young lady Grandma had tipped.

"Niqua, she said she knows you," Attorney Vargas remarked.

Attorney Barrow fleetingly looked at the clock on the wall; it showed the time as 2:48.

Simultaneously, Niqua replied, "Mr. Barrow told me."

Attorney Barrow, "It won't matter who she knows in a short while."

****$$****

At Billy's place, Grandma was telling him, he was wasting her time. Billy threw himself on a couch and picked up a jug of coffee. He avoided looking at her.

"How delicious," he said.

"Are you out of your mind," she asked.

"You were the dancer, weren't you," he said as he took a sip from his cup. Do a dance for me!"

Grandma moved closer and looked down at him. "Billy, this' not a joke," she said. "When we're called to do something we must do it."

Billy close his eyes to her. She was already dancing in his mind. It was a concerto from her childhood, namely Scene de Ballet Op. 104. She was in her leotards now, and her hips were swaying this way and that way. She set a smile on her face and began leaning to the left; her hands briefly went above her head bringing attention to her firm stomach and chest.

Billy smiled.

Grandma looked at him irate. "This system has put a sixth of its people in poverty. Look at them ones at Shines, Billy!"

****$$****

The people in the attorneys' conference room appeared drained and began playing with their hands, some looking at their timepieces.

"I agree she's a charmer," Attorney Barrow said, addressing the others.

"Feisty! Brave too," Attorney Vargas contributed.

Attorney Barrow shook his head in frustration. He no longer was buying the idea that Grandma would come through.

He had a gray cast to his face. "It's not going to happen!"

****$$****

"The truth is I spent the past month, almost two trying to see what I can do," Billy exchanged with Grandma, as he sipped coffee with the Dunkin Donuts label on it.

Grandma placed her hand on her head and began pressing on it.

"Well, what are you going to do," she asked him.

Billy began playing in his own hair.

The consensus in our neck of the woods at this point was that Grandma should give up on her disagreement with the bank and give her focus back to her business. Things were too chancy, Mom and Miss Bridgett warned. Dad described Grandma's experience as "perilous," and Grace, by the ways she looked at Grandma, was saying Grandma was insane for giving up everything she had for what she was getting. I felt the experience was too draining on Grandma and her recourses among other things.

"The reality at this point," Miss Bridgett pointed out, was, "her business is slipping away from her." Her feedback from customers had gone from bad to worse. Sales was at the slowest crawl I had ever seen for her. Yet, Grandma would not quit. The last time I spoke with her on the subject, she asked me to stop and listen. She said, "Soldier. Soldier. I'm the voice of those who can't do it themselves for whatever reason; I'm the voice of the middle-class!"

She tried to convince to me that the low sales she was having was due to problems in the economy and not her actions. Unhappiness on the part of her buyers, she blamed for her sliding feedback.

I saw where she was going but didn't quite agree.

She stressed that all over the world people were suffering financially and were more quick to say and write negative things about sellers now than any time in the life of her book business.

I thought about this, but questioned aloud what she was doing to get the names she needed over to the Barrow and Vargas Law Office.

Grace said that at the point we were, the folks at the law office must be staring at each other. "Nothing to do," she speculated. "Granny's copped out!"

****$$****

Not long after, at Billy's, Grandma and he worked busily trying to find the people she needed to follow through with her lawsuit.

He noted he had reviewed over a thousand accounts with the problem Grandma was having.

"I was so angry I called every one of them to get their opinion. They could have fired me!"

Grandma looked in annoyance at him. "So. So what," she inquired.

Billy immediately took on his own look of frustration. "I started a non-profit to….."

Grandma threw her hands in the air. She had only a couple days earlier told Mom she expected "the bank and people out there" to be against her but not those in her inner circle, and now this.

She cried, "Oh Lord! You know what time it is?"

Billy came out not to be trouble about the time. He looked slowly at Grandma, fidgeting, his hand trembling as he reached for his coffee.

Grandma was not one fond of coffee, nor did she like what was happening, yet she did not know what would be a fitting response.

She reached for the sky, throwing her head in that direction. "Lord, Lord, why have you forsaken me?"

"Calm down," Billy demand. "Nothing in the world requires this kind of nonsense." He pushed his hand in his pockets and began pacing like a small drug dealer on duty. "Ms. Muley, I have a posy that will take it to them!"

Grandma stared at him. He was out of his element, and worse, squandering her time. She was heated. "How are we going to do it," she demanded.

Billy studied Grandma, his eyes moving down her body and slowing up as they took pauses on those parts that made him so different than her. He wondered what goodies she must have stored up in all the years she had been around. What's still there? Grandpa John was gone more than a decade earlier, and even though she was known for frequently visiting him at the morgue, he could not physically alter what was happening on this side of things. Billy got up and stepped towards her. He stopped. He looked at her chin. And then it was her lips that were loose and damp, which came from spewing her aggravations.

"Ms. Muley. Ms. Muley," Billy said.

****$$****

Later, when Billy felt his relationship with me was good and firm, he relayed his experience to me, telling me her lips were "salacious," a word I will never not remember as he proceeded to define it when he told me the look of Grandma's lips made him want them all the more.

"Why are we here today," he asked in a cheery way, and then he made other steps towards Grandma. The thing was, I knew something was not normal. His walk was not his everyday foot-in-front of foot, upright gait pass through. It was something new: A kind of grate-the-mate, on-the-date stride. I am evermore mortified to say I witnessed what was going on. None of it was intended for my valuation. It belonged all to Grandma.

"If things comes through, and I trust they will, then we don't have a problem, Billy picked up.

Grandma looked at him and told him he was a some reckless: "a psychopathic frolicking" and it was not even full-moon.

She took on to shaking her head in displeasure, but it had not yet made a full sway when he placed his arm around her.

"I love you, Sandy. I love you," he said.

# CHAPTER 29

At the law firm of Barrow & Vargas, the crowd was quickly getting wiped out. The clock on the wall was no friend of Grandma, either. It was 3:16 and Attorney Vargas was crabby that they had given Grandma more than enough time, and they had wasted a lot of time thinking she would come through.

"CANCEL! Cancel it," he instructed the assemblage.

"It's not just black or white," Attorney Sheniqua broke in.

"What are you talking about," Attorney Barrow intervened.

The crowd in the room looked earnestly at each other, some through wide eyes. A couple picked up their personal items to leave as Attorney Sheniqua answered, "Gray matters."

People in the room gave their consideration to the new, young attorney as she took center stage. "We're talking about an old gray woman," she said. "Not some nobody! And she possesses the armamentarium to do it!"

The group focused in intensely.

"We're not the only ones deserving of success before we die!"

A female office secretary, walking over to a fax machine in the room, stopping at Attorney Sheniqua.

"She's going to die?"

Attorney Sheniqua overlooked the secretary. She was stuck with on question of her own. "Why can't we help her?"

"Maybe, she'll fax it in," the secretary offered and then she stepped away knowing in herself that she was important.

In all of this, Attorney Barrow was beaming at the clock. He briefly got up with a sudden jerk and turned as abruptly. He began pointing. "There's the clock, and *there's* a picture of the courthouse," he noted, his finger moving in the direction of both items.

****$$****

There, at Billy's house, Grandma and Billy looked a bit less strained. They had made some progress. They bumped their fists in a mischievous way.

"One in five, twenty percentage in the bag," Billy announced.

"All right. An accomplishment. Now what," Grandma said.

Fleetingly, a lightning came through the house followed by a loud and horrific thunder. I looked towards Grandma, but the power was lost.

"Oh my Lord," Grandma shouted.

I could hear her running. She said she was in search of her cell phone.

Billy sounded frightened himself, and started to rehearse the Holy Mary, and with that I saw his hand moving to the sign of the cross. He had his own way of doing so when he recited the good gem. His finger would start at his forehead, dragging across his chest and abdomen and back to his forehead. With the second touching of his forehead he let us a big sigh.

"They pursue their foes in darkness," he stated. "They do!"

Grandma was still in a panic when she asked Billy if he had his phone with him. He didn't he told her. He had left his at his office, and that didn't play well as time was seriously short for them.

****$$****

At Barrow & Vargas', the crowd in the room said time had ran out, so they acted like employees ready to resign their jobs. Attorney Barrow called for documents for him to sign, giving up on the lawsuit.

****$$****

At Billy's hysteria was now taking over with Grandma making an echo of herself, "Oh my Lord. Oh my Lord. Oh my Lord!"

"Where is your blackberry," Billy asked.

"I-phone. 'I' as in indifference, Grandma corrected as if correct naming was what was important then.

"No," he said as he turned towards a window and saw the happenings of the outside.

Here's to a simple climax: A very old school bus with tinted windows and the name "Mid-Class Bus Co." written on the side was inching up from in front of Mr. Saul and Ms. Cynthia's house and then stopped in front of Grandma's.

A man stepped out the bus, and then the bus driver, in uniform, followed. The two said something to each other, looked around strangely, the way bad people do when they are up to something. The two marched to the back of the bus, and the taller of the two abruptly pulled the doors unlock.

Grandma and Billy ran outside to the surprise of seeing the ladies from Shine coming at them, some walking, some pushed in their wheelchairs, others maneuvering their personal transportation as a song "All the Single Ladies," by the singer Beyonce, blasted from the bus.

One of the ladies that was moving fast said they tried to come sooner, but their bus had broken down.

"But you can't sign the petition," Grandma told the lady.

Ms. Swazey, a generally reticent, mostly Spanish speaking lady from the Dominican Republic, spoke, "If Saraplin was here right now, she would!"

Immediately, Ms. Wonzick sped through the crowd. She laughed with a screechy sound to it. "My Benjamin said we can! If we couldn't make it here we would have done a virtual show-up!"

The ladies spontaneously went into a hugging of each other and a dancing with wheels, feet, crutches, whatever they used to make it in their world. The music was non-stop. In fact, it was blasting now. And the moment was like what they call a spiritual moment at a Full Gospel Fellowship church I'd attended one fine Sunday mornings with Dad, Mom and Grace. One of the ladies spun so fast, some of the others had to hold her up. They said she was about to have "an equilibrium mishap."

****$$****

Meanwhile, at the law office, Attorney Barrow was holding a piece of paper in his hand and telling his partners and staff his worry that the case was not going to happen.

"That doesn't mean we never believed in the case," he added, his whole demeanor dipping to his frustration.

He shared, "We had a better than ninety percent chance with this one!"

****$$****

At Billy's, the mood was likewise that of disappointment. The discussion was that the women's bank accounts were either expired or they were with some other bank and as a result, none was qualified to help Grandma with her problems.

I looked around at everyone, and what was a dancing and celebratory moment not much earlier was now a serious, even desperate looking environment.

Election's lost! Now turn off the cameras, trash the un-eaten hor dores, turn off the music. Our candidate will not be the next president—my mind was in a scramble.

I, however, remembered Grandma used to tell us that in difficult situations we should put ourselves in other people's shoes so we could understand things from their viewpoint, and I began to imagine I was her with her load to bear.

"Me? Not President," I said to myself. "I'm here to help those who cannot help themselves! I'm here to end *their* envy and division!"

Was Grandma reading my thoughts? Something sent her to the phone, that she flipped into the air and caught face up, ready to call.

"Crunch time," I said.

She did not answer me. Maybe she knew she was at the end of her rope.

****$$****

"Banks were not designed to destroy us; they're here to help," she said to one person on the other side of the phone.

I passed by the man who was with the bus driver and he acknowledge me. He was Mr. Sealey, the manager gentleman from Shines. He was talking with one of the ladies, commenting that Grandma was getting younger and younger every time he got to her recently.

The lady, who had but just a couple teeth in the front of her mouth, all brown, was one of the younger residents at Shines, smiled with Mr. Sealey as he talked.

I estimated the smile was more a flirt than anything else. That proved true as the conversation went on and the lady told Mr. Sealy that he too was getting younger. Her eyes were all over him.

"You look like a boy scout ready to prune some tree," she told him.

Mr. Sealey seemed to like the "boy" part—to the rest, he appeared un-flattered.

****$$****

For much of the next half hour Grandma was "*out of it*" according to Grace. She sauntered to an extra old armchair, from the garage, she had in the corner of her kitchen and placed her hand on her forehead, her elbow latched to the handle of the chair.

I looked at her first from a distance, judging she was behaving like a "brattish" child. I moved closer.

"Just want to take a moment to reflect on life and things as they are in this moment," she said.

"You' don't have time," I advised.

"I'm dealing with the feelings, the emotions inside of me," she said.

She moved her hand towards her belly. "I'm feeling in my lower abdomen a feeling of worry. I'm frustration, Soldier."

I looked at her. I remembered the ambulance, the paramedics. I looked at Grace who was walking away, throwing her hand to show she was tired of Grandma's problems. I remembered Grace's face when she was crying out for Grandma when the ambulance was taking her to the hospital.

The last time Grandma got sick was not good for any of us. I hoped some new spell was not upon her.

"I'm trying to put into words the physical manifestations of things that are filled inside of me," she spoke, to which I asked her if she was OK.

Maybe the things that Mom and Grace and some in the neighborhood were saying about her was true. Maybe she was indeed cracking up. Maybe her work was finished here.

I temporarily found myself wondering why she was doing the lawsuit if it was so hard? Should I pity her or help her?

Grandma spoke again of feeling a sense of frustration. And then, "So! Physically I feel in my body and it seems to be in the left side, some physical, stirring up of things that I'm not yet able to put into words, Soldier. It's not dead yet. Not freed yet. I have not yet able to formed into words to explain the actual feeling, this thing. This thing that's happening!"

I repeated my question pertaining to whether she was all right. Physically she appeared fine, but her words contradicted anything as normal to me. Could it finally be her mind? I hated to think that.

"But what else are you to think, Tagg," I deliberated.

"I'm just trying to explain my emotions," she said slowly. "They have done some things that are very outrageous and left me in great questions of how and if I should go further.

I noted that her head fell towards the ground and back up three times, but I would not make any movement except with my eyes. I was not prepared to contribute to or against what she was saying, particularly when the next line was just another punch into the belly of the family.

"Your mother—nobody can help. You've all been disempowered!"

****$$****

As I continued to look at Grandma I could feel a certain energy crawling through my own body, and my thoughts began to change. She was not stupid, or crazy or even getting sick again. Something big was happening inside of her. There was something important happening, and it had to do with Grandma having big ideas, I conjured. In a strange way she seemed in pain; in another, it seemed like he could move mountains—build colonies on moon! Momentarily, in my head, glittering was another pearl she had deposited in our trinkets: "The real battleground of everything is between your two ears, you Soldiers. That's where it is!" She had told Grace and me that many times, and as recent as the first week after she had left the hospital.

Grandma repeated she was still trying to sort out her life, noting this time "for the future," and what she should do to move *forward.*

She repeated the "F" word several times, which gave the sense it was the theme of her talk, so I kept looking and waiting. She had already made the amazing comeback from being so sick in the hospital. Maybe, there was something new to come.

As I looked I felt a certain calmness and a feeling of connection to Grandma that was stronger than what I think could ever be

matched. She was send out to me all this information as it was coming to her so I would get a sense of what was occurring inside of her. She said she was trying to find out how and where she was blocked in so she could create an "avenue" to move forward with her "life and things." She looked fiercely at me without a blink, and I supposed she didn't want me to miss any of what was happening in her world.

"I started with problems, and I did my best. Now forward."

"Very well," I said.

She upheld her flow. "I do hope that my mind hearing my words as I bring them to you, I will get clarity on where I am stuck. Tagg! I will be able to un-glue myself so I will be able to go forward, fully well."

I didn't want to interrupt, but my mind was in turbo, "Go Grandma, go, go, go. Tell me. What are you trying to articulate, Grandma? Why are you mumbling. I don't know you to be a mumbler."

She smiled but the stiff skin below her lunules told a different story. Maybe she knew something I didn't. Maybe her age and wisdom had trumped everything I had so far achieved; even what I could conceive.

She plowed on. "It seems that I operating in a small circle these days particularly and more specifically as it relates to my relationship with teams," she said. "It seems I'm going nowhere."

For the next moments she spoke again about her breathing. She said she felt herself trying to take control of her breadth, and then it was back to the rambling. "I trying to control my emotions and physical things. I'm trying to get a smooth breath, Soldier" she said.

She continued: "I hear myself asking. I'm dealing with the feelings inside my belly. It feels like I am not able to think out visually how to change things. How to change my world of things."

She gave me another smile, this one looking a lot more wholesome, as a result for me, more trusting.

"I used to be able to do this, you know, She said. "I used to have the mind of moving pictures!"

I shook my head to indicate my thoughts within: "I see."

"Why am I sitting here," she asked out loud, but did not do just then what I thought would be her self-created natural answer: Simply get up and get back to finding her helpers. Instead she reverted to the distorting world that she was in earlier, again speaking that her breadth was still stuck in her body, and she was not able to see what she wanted to see. She then questioned, to my feelings of fear, whether her body and organs were working correctly, and proceeded to question whether she wanted to continue to be friends with the people who she thought were "disloyal" to her.

She told me she remembered back in her past, in the old days, as she put it, when she felt that things were not working out for her, how she handled her problem by sinking herself into the finding of solutions.

She snapped out of that as fast as she got into it, and started to tell me how she could be evil. "As evil as anyone else," she said in a voice that brought with it an echo of her words. "I can tell my enemy's' secrets to my enemy's' friends. How about that for revenge, Tagg," she said to me.

I placed my hand at my mouth. It was thinking time. I was wondering what I could do to help when I heard her saying again that she was trying to deal with her breath and an idea at the same time. It was hard, really hard, she said. She went on to describe that the experience she was looking for was, "like a swing, a lever, a pulley."

"Something I'm trying to push down, and something I want to come up," she said.

By this time, I was feeling two things: excited that something seemed to be happening with Grandma, and weary that whatever that thing was, was not happening fast enough for her or for me. I eventually found myself wishing I was still a student having a legitimate reason to skidoo, something like those beeps that used to come to tell everyone, “Assignment! Assignment! Leave Tagg alone! Tagg got school work to go to!” Remember those WikiCreep assignments I used to get, the ones that use to interrupt me from some of my most sacred tasks? I hoped for one of those at that appointed moment, but class was done now. Grandma, Grace and everybody else were squarely back in my face. The only beep I was dealing with now, was one in my head that came with the thought, “you, young man, you have an interesting family, look at this. Look at that. Beep!

Will I turn out to be just a fruit from the old trees? I hoped not. Beep!

Will I become a man of substance when I grow up? Beep!”

The long and short of it was, there was no beeping assignment and so no openly justified reason for me to leave, and it seemed like Grandma understood that at least as clearly as I did. She was on how she had visualized starting over: getting new friends, a new environment; she even toyed with the scheme of having a new family.

She lamented; all this was on her mind. Her problem with this though, was all this seemed like too much work for her. Not at her age.

“The new one might be as screwed up as the ones I already have,” she weighed.

She crossed her arms and placed them behind her neck. She leaned backwards. She looked at her tummy. From her shirt, it was thumping. She claimed her heart was on fire.

“It’s a team I need,” she said even before I could ask her about the heart on fire statement she had made.

“I spent all of my life trying to help people, trying to bless them,” she continued. “I was hoping one day, maybe the day I needed them, maybe they would bless me.”

I felt a sinking feeling in my own heart, a sullen, cold one flashed through my body. I didn’t appreciate her including me in the mountain of people she said were users, but this didn’t stop me from needing to continue to help. In fact, I found myself wanting to be even more useful. I needed to help. The tears that showed up in the corner of my eyes, I hoped would serve as evidence to my faithfulness.

"There's no sign of help," she bellowed. "…A thousand miles if you look, Soldier!"

****$$****

When we got back inside all the folks had left except Billy who had turned on another of Grandma's favorite songs, Benny Goodman's "Blue Skies."

He was sitting with his legs crossed and appeared to be doing nothing more than parking himself and letting the music sink in; maybe thinking. New consideration, maybe decoding the music.

I looked at him and he seemed to smile. Grandma looked at him and he smiled at her. That one was for assurance.

"It's a gonner," Grandma said to him. "I'm sorry."

He got up and gave her a hug. "You're not alone," he said soothingly.

"I'll need more than that," Grandma said and began moving closer to him.

"Everybody," he said.

****$$****

Three-forty had come and gone and we knew it was impossible for Grandma to make it to Barrow & Vargas, LLC, so with her insisting, I use my skills and set up a face-to-face conference for her to make her presentation to the attorneys.

Grace and I stood on the sideline as things progressed.

"We've known it's a hard one to touch Ms Muley," Attorney Barrow said. "We've been putting together this case for years."

"Sure have," Grandma said.

"Ms. Muley, You see, this is not about you," Attorney Vargas cut in. "Long before Attorney Barrow and I merged, we started putting together a case on this but we just couldn't get it together for one reason or another until now."

Attorney Barrow eyed Grandma in a direct way that produced a warm feeling in me, like we were all in the same physical setting.

His voice came across in a strong and hearty way. "You're a bold person to help us take it through the courts."

Grandma placed her hand on her forehead. "Little Me? Can you imagine, little me cyberspacing with you?"

Both attorneys said yes.

"I never knew I had the power. Me doing all of this stuff," she said.

"We'll have to make the changes through Congress too," Attorney Sheniqua interjected.

In a relaxed and expensive looking chair we saw Attorney Vargas as he talked with another man telling the man that Congress was only interested in protecting Wall Street and Hedge Fund managers. He told the other that "Ms. Muley" was the right person to help them change that too.

Attorney Barrow proceeded to tell Grandma that he felt she was the perfect person to lead the effort the first moment Attorney Vargas' office had called him about her. "We just wanted you to know you can," he said.

"I know who I am," Grandma replied. "I'll go to the big fish, the President of the United States, if you want me!"

****$$****

At the white house, Grandma and Billy moved closer together. He placed his hands to bring her face nearer to his, and they positioned themselves for a kiss. He took a closer look at her face as something had changed: her philtrum looked unusually deep. His eyes brought tears. He turned a tick to try and hide it.

He turned back to Grandma. "Oh Dear," he said.

She gave him a smile and as she did, she cried out. "Oh, Bill!"

She looked at Billy and Billy at her; they both had transformed into teenagers. The two looked and stared at each other for a jiffy, she shy but smiling.

"You think I should update my swimming suit," she asked.

Grace and I looked at the two and Grandma directed a new smile at us.

"How am I doing Soldiers," She asked.

Billy gave Grandma another kiss.

I was answering her query.

"Doing fine! Fine," I said.

Billy lifted her into the air, and what I saw was a sultry, sensible woman, reveling in what she had become. Now she would have even more energy and vitality to speak for people across the oceans and around the world, I thought.

That wasn't what was on Billy's mind, though. He looked as strong as a yak but spoke like Romeo: "So you want something more?"

"What a question," Grandma answered. She gave him the look. She wanted him!

# CHAPTER 30

When we entered the courtroom on the court day, Corporate and his team were already sitting in their places, nicely dressed even though being ill at ease. Grace pointed to a strained look in their faces and later whispered to me her idea as to why they looked that way: “They know what’s coming at them, Budd,” she said.

Newgrandma, the *pivoted, evolved* transformation of Grandma Muley described the experience as her “best dance yet.”

What we all had to face was that we were in a space of total uncertainty. Either side could walk away the loser at this point.

Grace’s eyes hanged about on the defendants. “To me, they looked very old,” she noted.

To that, I pointed out they had changed indeed. For sure, the entire team I could identify on Corporate’s side had aged greatly as compared to the last time I had seen them on video.

Pertaining to Grandma’s promise to kick Corporate in the ….., the new person she had become did not see that necessary. She said no matter how many sticks and stones they threw at her, they would not be able to break her bones.

What was shocking, a real knockout of them, though, was how the main plaintiff looked. They kept waiting and waiting for the old woman to show up, the enemy, Sandra E. Muley, as one of the defending lawyers referred to her, but there was no old, tired lady, nor man on our side. What they would come up against was a group of young, bouncing, well informed and ready-to-fight Soldiers, as Grandma used to call us, Miss Bridgett being a stalwart among them.

Newgrandma, I called Grandma in her young self, and the name immediately stick. She had enlisted the ready squad.

She had brought her I-phone with her as well as an I-Pod that Attorney Barrow had given to her for the occasion. Mom and Dad were there too, looking incredibly relaxed from Swedish massages from a local massage parlor, Massage Ecstasy, and makeovers they had gotten in preparation for the event. Even Mr. Sealey from Shines looked a couple decades younger than just a few days earlier we had seen him rehearsing for the event. He had put on a little weight and no longer had a skeleton frame. Now he walked with greater liveliness and carried two briefcases containing paperwork he said would show the court many of the women of Shines were victims of the same crime Newgrandma was claiming victim of. For Miss Bridgett, she too had underwent a big conversion, a degree of change she called "the finishing of my evolution." Her testimony later showed she had made the full three-sixty in support of Grandma.

****$$****

Prior to our arriving, there were notes all over the house that Grandma had written, and Grace and I had been helpful in preparing Grandma in all aspects of her ground game. She had done well, leaving us to think the Corporate goose was cooked even before the first word was voiced in court. Grandma's performance in our practice session were on the money, and when she got to her big event, we thought likely, no less.

Behind us, Ms. Wonzick, the old Black woman from Shines sat, looking prettier than ever. She had converted into a striking twenty-something year old and dressed perfectly, making her look like what I would have expected of a grand or even great-grand daughter of hers. Her legs were long and straight, her frame curvaceous, and she was with the kind of chest, only a paid model would be able to maintain. In all of this new skin, it was she, who looked the smartest among the Shine crowd, as she reviewed her Mac tablet in front of her. She said she was looking for "updates," anything that would give Love the edge.

About two months preceding, it was found that she actually qualified to be a part of the court case. Now she had come to help Love with all she had.

Sitting on the right side of Grandma was Billy. He was challenging me in youth and charm, and I heard myself letting out a long, troubled breath at what he appeared to be up to. He was sitting next to Rozanne, my girlfriend at the time and seemed more into her than I had ever been.

I overheard Roxanne calling his name and pointing to him as an older, more experience "dude" than me, and with the shrewdness Grandma told of him, I visualized him effortlessly being more a draw to Rosanne than me. At the time, she was twenty-one—pretty, smart, and fairly intelligent, but as people usually are, no one is perfect. Over time I found her to be too bossy and too easily emotional; I ended things with her less than a year later, on one fine Valentine's Day. I say all this, not to decrease the threat Billy posed in that crucial moment we had at the courthouse. He had a great impact on me there, then, and even now.

****$$****

The case itself started slow but lasted for three-and-a-half days. It was dubbed by a national medium as "Corporate Revealed: The People-The System." On the first day, several of the additional plaintiffs and plaintiffs' witnesses, including Ms. Bridgett were allowed to present their side to the case, which they did to the endorsement of everyone on our side, counting a number of the ladies from Shines who themselves had gone through some exciting changes. Many of them that were before in wheelchairs and on crutches were now in much better shape—an evolution, I deduced—some walking, some jumping out of their seat, others even shouting to Newgrandma to "whip their 'asses' in their own backyard," when it was Newgrandma's turn.

As things would go on, though, Newgrandma made what Attorney Vargas called a "a personal gaff" when she stepped away from the testifying boxed in area and talked directly to the audience, demanding of the court to "do something to Corporate and people like him who are stealing our country away from us." She called the people on the other side "bad" and looked towards Billy. "They would have raped me if *he* didn't come along."

The defense objected to what Newgrandma was doing, stating that Newgrandma's remarks were prejudicial and her behavior was unbecoming of the respect the court required. The lead defense attorney asked Judge Shilling to strike Newgrandma's statement from the record, and beseeched the court that Newgrandma "go back to her box."

Before Judge Shilling could say a word, however, Newgrandma hurried to the audience on the other side, and the people in the court stared in wonderment.

She pointed at Corporate, "He's not fit to run the bank," she barked. "He's turned a blind eye, Your Honor!"

Judge Shilling sided with the defense, scolded Newgrandma, and told her that inflammatory statements would get her thrown out of the courtroom. To this, the defense gave its approval with an explosion of applause and a harsh attack on Newgrandma.

"You claimed you have been an upright citizen all your life Ms. Muley, but have you not broken the law by writing bad checks," the chief defense counsel engaged while looking suspiciously at the plaintiff.

Newgrandma got red-faced and was blunt. "Your Honor," she begged.

In a stern voice, Judge Shilling told Newgrandma to answer the question.

Newgrandma began drifting to the audience again, discernibly for assistance, but yet again in her demanding voice the judge instructed Newgrandma to keep her eyes on the plaintiff or her, not us, her help.

The defense side laughed loud, and the judge admonished them with contempt citation.

"I, like most of the people he overdraft, used our debit card, went over by a dollar or two, and we ended up with his two-and-three hundred-dollar charges. His fraud, Your Honor!"

The lead defense lawyer, who Attorney Barrow told us had crossed path with him at UM School of Law, yanked a pen from a holder in front of himself and took some notes. He visibly thought about something for a second then started to ask Grandma why she was so different, but backed away from that. He slipped his hand in his pocket, positioned his mouth for a new delivery. "My question again, have you not broken the law?"

Before Grandma answered, CFO Tolly put up his hand and ask the judge that he be allowed to say something.

The judge waved him to go to the testimony box, and when he got there she had him raise his hand to attest that whatever he wanted to speak was "the truth and nothing but the truth."

He did all that, then he went ahead to tell the judge he had broken the law.

It was him who had illegally released the WikiCreep videos. His quest to be the top man at Bank $$ had manifested an impossible dream when Corporate refused to leave as he had promised Tolly would happen three years earlier, allowing Tolly some time to live "the good life" before "the country got enough of them."

Now he was tasked with both sorrow and revenge and wanted to tell his full deeds to one that turned out to be a strict judge. Mom called it, his conscience catching up with him.

"You leaked this information," the Judge asked.

CFO Tolly disgracefully lifted his dropped head and answered yes. He wanted to expose corruption and abuse of power, he added, to which Judge Shilling said that would have to be handled differently—another case, another day.

The judge then returned her attention to Grandma.

Grandma drag her eyes back up to the judge. She didn't like the question that had come at her.

I remembered my little saying that had worked so well for so long with Grandma to go, go, etcetera, but I sensed saying it aloud would only get me handcuffed by the court marshals. Moreover, I figured that likely even wasn't what Grandma wanted to hear. She looked like someone begging pardon for something.

The judge lifted her hand, waving Grandma again to answer the question.

"I'm sure you have overspent before," Grandma said to the attorney. "I know of your lavish lifestyle and big pay; I know you have..."

The chief defense lawyer slammed his hand on the desk in front of him and that got the judge's attention big time. "She's not answering the question Your Honor. She's…."

Grandma pointed, starting with Corporate and moved her finger along the path of his team.

"They're the ones who don't answer questions," Grandma spewed out.

Judge Shilling looked at both sides singularly. She was undoubtedly not in the mood for anymore of what was taking place in her courtroom.

"Order," she demanded as Attorney Vargas leaned over to Attorney Barrow and then to Grandma.

Without another word from either side, the judge ordered a break.

****$$****

Mr. Saul and Miss Cynthia, both of whom looked aged and weary, showed up during the closing argument. They had sneaked in the back but came to our attention when Ms. Cynthia demanded that Mr. Saul sit on a long bench next to a man I had seen at Grandma's park extravaganza. She wanted the position next to the isle, leading to the turning of many heads, including that of the judge.

"Your Honor," Attorney Barrow kept on with a statement he was making to the court. "My clients know there's light somewhere—sometimes it's not even a large beam—but it's light. We trust that they see that light today."

The judge looked un-phased, and I found myself asking what was in her head. Our side had done a great job, and I was not even a lawyer to figure that out.

"Banking and these bankers have gone wild, Your Honor," Attorney Barrow continued, his voice, now more indomitable. "We ask this court to rule on the side of an attitude adjustment, an end to transaction manipulation, and compensation for those so injured. Thanks you, Your Honor"

This time, Judge Shilling shook her head indicating a liking for what she heard. A check of the audience showed many heads bobbling in agreement also.

****$$****

When the defense team returned with their final argument, I was in a daydream and missed what they had to say, but my carelessness didn't seemed as if it impacted a difference for them. Grace said they were weak and boring, anyways.

The significant thing, however, was the court came down with a scolding of the bank and its culture.

****$$****

Today, when I looked back at that day, it remember Judge taking the case very seriously. To me, her ruling and conclusion came across that way.

She said the bank was engaged in a scheme that was "siphoning your customers' money for un-explainable purposes," and she warned other banks to stop the practice.

She continued. "You, betted on catching your customers unguarded, so they would yield."

I glanced at Corporate and his possy as Judge Shilling spoke, and to me they appeared as tattered, worn and dirty—like men emerging from a month of the worse kind of mining work.

Temporarily, the judge took a special angry look at Corporate. "You can't be having a big appetite in the middle-class' refrigerator," she said to him.

He dropped his head.

Attorney Vargas leaned over to Attorney Barrow but both kept their eyes on the judge.

"She could be like reading tea leaves," Attorney Barrow whispered to his partner.

Judge shilling continued unremittingly. "What you have done is clearly abuse."

I looked at Grace, but before I could get to Newgrandma, the judge had stated her court's findings.

"The court rules on behalf of the middle-class," Judge Shilling announced, her face very telling of her discontent with Corporate and his system. Her voice was firm as her gavel came crushing to her desk.

Newgrandma looked at her two primary attorneys. She didn't know what to think.

"We won," Attorney Barrow said.

Newgrandma shouted. "We won!"

Attorney Barrow leaned over to Attorney Vargas. He whispered.

"I always felt it was in her DNA, her reflex, you know. From day one!"

Simultaneously, Attorney Sheniqua repeated something Judge Shilling had mentioned at a break earlier. "$2.1 billion," she said.

Newgrandma shouted again. "The middle-class won!"

She momentarily placed her fingers together and brought them to her lips. She kissed them and threw the kiss and her fingers towards Attorney Barrow. "This should help cripple the bastards," she said.

He shook his head.

Corporate was shaking his head too. He drag his eyes across my face and then to Grandma's. He pointed his finger at her. "You got me," he said.

****$$****

When Grace and I have the time these day to talk, whether on the phone, chat on the Internet, or even face to face, we never part without putting in a word or two about our times with Grandma Muley. It was probably the most important period in our young lives.

Grace remembers her as a "tough cookie." She was accustomed to telling us that if something's not fair we were supposed to stand up and be counted. She did that time and time again.

"Don't be beaten down by wrongdoers," Grace honed in on Grandma's words recently.

"And when her day came, she stood up like a mighty queen," I provided.

Grace summed it up that Grandma stood up for what she thought was right to the very end. She, with the help of Billy won the case in court.

****$$****

It then turned out that Grace and I could no longer stay at Grandma's in Miami after all that had happened. Things had begun to steam up with Billy and the lady I had known as Grandma.

Grace and I, in spite of getting to like it more at Jack Street had to go back with Mom and Dad. I recall that day quite colorfully. Grace and I were sitting in the Library with Newgrandma having some Haagan Daz when Billy came and gave her a French kiss. I knew what that meant, because by then I will giving out a few of those of my own. He pressed his body into hers. Grace looked at me and I at her. Our eyes fell to the floor. I was looking at Grace's feet and she at mine. We knew that things had come to an end. We would no longer qualify as "the old lady's companions."

I looked up and Mom and Dad were standing at the doorway, practically looking like Newgrandma's mother and father. They gestured at us to come towards them.

I remember how miserable I was. We got our things, and soon, Billy and Newgrandma were waving goodbyes to us. From our vantage point I could see the Purvis Young picture in the entrance of Grandma's house. I heard the sounds of Benny Goodman.

"Love you Granny," Grace forced out.

"Love you Grandma," I followed♦

## Author's Notes

This is a self-published book. It is experimental in that it was written, edited, designed and proofread by only one person, the author. It was written and produced between 2009 and 2012 during the most recent global economic downturn.

www.ingramcontent.com/pod-product-compliance
Lightning Source LLC
Chambersburg PA
CBHW031204020726
47499CB00002B/485
*9780615698427*